ONE HUNDRED YEARS

YEARS

OF

Betty

Debra Oswald is a playwright, screenwriter and novelist. She is a two-time winner of the NSW Premier's Literary Award and author of the novels *Useful* (2015), *The Whole Bright Year* (2018) and *The Family Doctor* (2021). She was creator/head writer of the first five seasons of the successful TV series *Offspring*.

Her stage plays have been performed around the world and published by Currency Press. *Gary's House*, *Sweet Road* and *The Peach Season* were all shortlisted for the NSW Premier's Literary Award. Debra has also written four plays for young audiences—*Dags*, *Skate*, *Stories in the Dark* and *House on Fire*. She has written three Aussie Bites books and six children's novels, including *The Redback Leftovers*.

Her television credits include award-winning episodes of *Police Rescue*, *Palace of Dreams*, *The Secret Life of Us*, *Sweet and Sour* and *Bananas in Pyjamas*.

Debra performed her one-woman show *Is There Something Wrong With That Lady?* at the Griffin Theatre in 2021 and a month-long season at the Ensemble in 2023.

ONE HUNDRED YEARS

YEARS

DEBRA OSWALD

ALLEN&UNWIN
SYDNEY•MELBOURNE•AUCKLAND•LONDON

First published in 2025

Allen & Unwin
Cammeraygal Country
83 Alexander Street
Crows Nest NSW 2065
Australia
Phone: (61 2) 8425 0100
Email: info@allenandunwin.com
Web: www.allenandunwin.com

Allen & Unwin acknowledges the Traditional Owners of the Country on which we live and work. We pay our respects to all Aboriginal and Torres Strait Islander Elders, past and present.

A catalogue record for this book is available from the National Library of Australia

ISBN 978 1 76147 061 5

Typeset in 12/17 pt Minion Pro by Bookhouse, Sydney
Printed and bound in Australia by the Opus Group

10 9 8 7 6 5 4 3 2 1

The paper in this book is FSC® certified. FSC® promotes environmentally responsible, socially beneficial and economically viable management of the world's forests.

FOR JUDITH WHELAN

ONE

12 April 1928.

I was born on the kitchen table of the Deptford house, whooshing out at speed and so slick with waxy vernix, that I shot off the edge of the table into the precarious air.

Clearly I survived because I'm telling this story now as I approach my one hundredth birthday. Trauma to my soft infant skull was avoided because I was caught, according to family folklore, by my second-eldest brother Michael.

Then again, when our father was sozzled in his more nostalgic mode of sozzlement, he would retell the story with my older sister Margaret cast as the slippery baby, or even Michael as the newborn who was caught, not the one who did the catching. We were ten kids in the end, so it was easy to mix us up.

I was number seven which would explain why my arrival was swift. Our poor mother's birth canal barely had a chance to contract between babies. (Am I being too vulgar and anatomical too soon in this story?)

They christened me Elizabeth, inspired by the princess born two years earlier, but no one in south London ever called me anything but Betty.

1931. I recall being hunched underneath the kitchen table. Three years old, head tipped way back, holding a tin can up to my mouth to receive the last dribble of condensed milk. Our Kenneth and our Bernard, the twins, had stolen that tin from the shop three streets away. Condensed milk—glossy, creamy, intensely sweet—was a revelation. I think I shuddered, a full body tremor, when my mouth filled with the taste. It would be some years until I experienced an orgasm—many, many years; so many I'm too embarrassed to divulge that yet—but the condensed milk was my first food orgasm.

1933. Our mother unfurled a bolt of cheap cotton cloth, printed with scrunched-up yellow flowers against an insipid green background, and spread it out on that same kitchen table. She had managed to pay off the fabric week by week at the draper's shop. (This must have been during an uncharacteristically stable period of employment for our father.)

Mum was making little happy noises in her throat, fizzy with optimism as she smoothed the shop-bought material. New dresses for her girls would be a huge step up from neighbourhood hand-me-downs. The first flourish in our new life of prosperity.

In turn, eleven-year-old Margaret, five-year-old me and three-year-old Josie lay flat on our backs on the fabric spread across the table. Mum cut around each of us in the rough shape of a dress, then used a borrowed sewing machine to join the pieces. Whatever ill-fitting garment a reader might now be imagining—well, it was worse than that. The yellow dresses were humiliating and a week later the vision of prosperity crumbled when our dad lost his job. Not *because* of the yellow dresses, obviously.

Let me interrupt myself at this point. Hanging memories off the kitchen table feels a bit laboured. And the truth is, I can't guarantee accurate recollections from my earliest years.

The neuroscience suggests our early, pre-language experiences shape who we are. That makes sense to me, to think how formed a child is by the time she's two years old. So, the experiences that matter most are inaccessible. I could try to rely on family stories about what happened when I was eighteen months old to decipher why my brain works the way it does, but such accounts are too dodgy to trust.

Some of the early childhood picture can be sketched from verifiable details—family income (in our case, pitiful and erratic), number of people in the house (too bloody many), or from guessable factors like my father's blood alcohol levels (ranging between 0.1 and whatever number is just short of lethal). Palaeontologists use fossil traces to understand the past, examining the gaps in rock layers where a creature, long ago dissolved, once lived. I've attempted to look at my own fossil record: measuring emotional gaps in my adult self to decipher the shape of the pre-memory moment that created such a hole—for example, the persistent doubt about whether I'm a lovable person, doubt about whether I'm worth a pinch of shit.

But I'm getting ahead of myself.

As a child, I was wildly curious about the world but not yet curious about myself. Not in the way so many people are now. Curiosity about myself came later, identifying patterns and motivations that, in retrospect, are embarrassingly obvious. But at the time, I blundered about, driven by unexamined impulses from inside my brain and body.

The memory business is untrustworthy, even with a robust attempt at candour, but I will do my best to be honest. I'll try not to distort the story to justify my own poor behaviour or to milk inappropriate pity. Mind you, feeling pity for each other and pity for our earlier selves is often the kindest response any of us can offer.

Let me jump straight to seven-year-old me, sitting at a wooden desk at the Clyde Road School.

'Betty Rankin, please wipe that look off your face,' said Miss Greene, our teacher.

I was never a cute child. This is not a coy self-deprecating statement. I've seen the hard evidence in the tiny square photos of myself. Not ugly but definitely not cute. Even when I was a toddler, no one could drink in the innocence of my baby-marsupial eyes or exult in the purity of my golden curls because I didn't have either. I could only offer deep-set brown eyes, a pronounced adult-sized nose and frizzy brown hair chopped short for parental convenience. Inside, my toddler self must have been as innocent and sweet as the big-eyed, button-nosed kids, but my face didn't have the infant proportions that release care-giving hormones in grown-up humans. And by the time I was seven, I resembled a small adult in a way which must've been off-putting.

Miss Greene's expression would soften when her gaze drifted over the pretty poppet girls in our class. She was also a pushover for the cheeky chappy boys, crinkling her nose indulgently, even as she shook her head about their naughtiness. But my face seemed to stir up insecurities inside Miss Greene, whichever way I set my features.

The randomness of physiognomy is not considered as much as it should be in how lives play out. Who knows how differently I would've been treated as a child had I looked endearing and how that might've changed the adult I became. I'm not saying it was a tragedy—possibly it's an advantage not to be cooed over and indulged.

If people were wary of me as a child, imagining I was thinking judgemental adult thoughts behind my adult-looking face, at least that gave me the chance to observe the world undisturbed by that 'isn't she adorable' fuss.

Whatever suspicions Miss Greene held about the content of my soul, she hadn't managed to catch me out and punish me during the school year so far. I did well at my work—quick with sums, reading fluently, including big words, and mad keen for any sort of writing task. Well behaved enough that I was instructed to sit next to Gregory Almond to help him moderate his naughty behaviour, not least the habit of picking at the many warts on his hands.

Miss Greene's chance to punish me came when the health inspectors visited the school.

Three women in brisk white uniforms marched into the classroom in clacking hard-heeled shoes, carrying their scales, measuring calipers and ledgers. I wonder now if those women even had nursing qualifications.

'Stand up, children,' chirruped Miss Greene. 'The nurses are here for your health inspection!' Her sugary voice was trying to make 'health inspection' sound like a delightful treat.

Miss Greene helped the 'nurses' hustle us out of our outer garments and into rows between the desks, shivering in our singlets and pants.

All forty of us were weighed on scales set up by the blackboard, then our heights were measured against the wall. Finally, the nurse who seemed to be in charge gave each child the once-over.

With her mouth pursed into a constipated rosebud, that woman yanked my hair aside to check my scalp for lice, poked at the glands in my neck, pulled my jaw down to peer inside my mouth, then cast her eyes over my carcass. She didn't apologise or seek permission—as if we poor children of south London should expect to be prodded and examined like livestock at the saleyards.

While we put our clothes back on and resumed our seats, the health visitors conferred, scratching notes into their ledgers.

'Betty Rankin. Stand up,' said Miss Greene.

I stood up.

The head nurse beckoned me forward and announced, at an unnecessarily high volume, 'You're undernourished, dear.'

Her two henchwomen held out a measure of cod liver oil and a heaped spoonful of malt powder that I was required to swallow on the spot, in front of the class. As if one dose of each could inoculate a child against poverty. The stupidities of the past, especially the ways kids were treated, still astonish me.

Why was I obedient? Why did I take the supplements and gulp them down? It was shame, I believe. I was shamed into compliance.

There are people who say, 'Growing up, we were poor but happy! I didn't even realise we were poor!' Yeah, well, I realised. I knew we were poor; poor but not happy, living in a rented two-up two-down house in a row of mean terraces squeezed tightly together to fit along the street, all of them damp, cold and sooty from coal fires. Even in that skint, scratchy neighbourhood, we were considered one of the hard-up families. Our father was known for being a drunkard, quick to lose his temper and his job, slow to find the next job.

The dry malt powder and the cod liver oil mixed together in my mouth into a foul paste. I was curious to see which other children would be declared 'undernourished' and I ran through the likely candidates in my head. Once the other malnourished kids came up the front with me, my plan was to smile at them supportively, as if to say, 'Don't worry. I swallowed the stuff and survived.' My pals and I would rejoice in the camaraderie, like soldiers in the trenches together.

But no other names were called out. It was just me standing there.

There were plenty of scrawny kids in our class whose families were at least as poor as mine, so there was a stab of unfairness about my involuntary solo spectacle. But I said nothing, paralysed by the humiliation and effectively silenced by the mixture of cod liver oil and malt powder which had formed a gluey coating in my throat.

Then, before I could slink back to my desk, the head nurse leaned down to grip me firmly by the shoulder.

'Make sure your mother gives you more to eat, dear.'

As if our mother had magical powers to conjure up more food for us. As if a single child in that classroom had a scrap of control over any of the pressing factors in their lives.

Fury about the stupidity of that comment, fury about the injustice of this woman sinking her talons into my flesh burned through me like a fuel, scalded my face and accelerated my heart in a way that scared me. But at the same time, I relished the power surging along my limbs until it finally came out of my mouth.

'Don't dig your fingers into me, you fucking cow!'

The four adults and the thirty-nine children in the classroom gasped, then one boy sniggered (I believe it was Gregory Almond). I'd heard my father and other shouty men in the street say the f-word, but I had never uttered the word before. Never even imagined saying it. But in that moment, it felt necessary.

I was ordered to stand in the corner facing the wall while the health inspectors packed up their equipment and left.

I expected Miss Greene would send me to the school principal but instead she decided to give me ten cuts on the hand with a ruler, there and then.

Years later, I understood why Miss Greene kept the punishment in-house. I understood why she wielded that ruler with such ferocity, thwacking the sharp edge down on my palm. The viciousness sprang from her own sense of inadequacy. It reflected badly on her to have a foul-mouthed pupil in her class, and it was especially mortifying in front of the health inspectors. But at the time, that didn't occur to me and I let myself loathe Miss Greene with a satisfyingly simple hatred.

For the entirety of the punishment, I stared at her through my off-putting unchildlike face. I imagined the pain in my hand as a power source I could soak into my body and save to use later.

When I sat down again, I rested my throbbing palm against the cool surface of the desk and felt the eyes of the kids sneaking looks at me, like dozens of tiny darts flicking at my back. I soaked in the power of those darts too.

Only two days after the visit from the health inspectors, I arrived home from school to find my mother preparing Mock Brains for tea.

When there were high-living weeks in our house, Mum might cook brains in white sauce or tripe in white sauce made with skimmed milk. I found the two dishes indistinguishable—both offering vile chewy bits embedded in pale grey glue. My father was adamant that brains were superior, but if he was sufficiently stonkered by teatime, we could convince him tripe lumps were brains and avoid having him flare up into a filthy mood.

In leaner weeks, Mum would sometimes placate him with Mock Brains, a dish so low-grade that it attempted to mimic offal. Here's a surprising thing though: it was rather tasty. Mock Brains consisted of leftover cold porridge mixed with flour, onion, salt, dried thyme and egg, then formed into rissoles and fried in dripping or bacon fat. Readers may wish to try it for themselves.

That day, Mum had a plate of flour on the kitchen bench ready to dust the rissoles, but she'd been pulled away from this cordon bleu cookery by the demands of her offspring. There was often chaos in the Deptford house and always a lot of noise.

I found my brother Kenneth wailing at a phenomenal volume while Mum dabbed at his forehead with a cloth, trying to wipe the grit out of a meaty wound.

'Shoosh. Stay still, Kenneth,' she said over and over. 'The more you wriggle about, the more the cleaning up will hurt.'

Kenneth briefly stopped howling but then the sight of his own blood smeared across the floor set him off again.

'You pillock! You stupid whiny plonker!' offered my brother Bernard.

How Bernard was capable of abusing Kenneth was a mystery because Bernard himself was shallow-breathing, sweaty and pasty, in what I now understand was a state of clinical shock. He was holding his left arm flopped across his body at an odd angle, clearly broken in the fall from the rooftop vantage point he had used to launch his homemade spear at Kenneth's head.

For years Kenneth and Bernard had been doing their bit to reduce over-population in the inner city by engaging in life-threatening activities. The twins had plenty of free time to injure themselves in potentially lethal games because they didn't have much to do in the way of chores (bringing in a bucket of coal occasionally when Mum's hands were full was about it). My three eldest brothers—Eddie, Michael and George—weren't expected to do anything around the house other than eat and sleep, but our Margaret had a big load of duties: laundry, scrubbing and child-wrangling. As for me, even at the age of seven, I had the peeling of potatoes, the mangling of wet laundry and the washing of pots to fit into my schedule.

I don't blame our mother for the gender injustice. She didn't understand she was operating as a tool of the patriarchy. But what did sting me then—and now, still—was the evidence that she favoured male offspring when it came to her affection. When any of her sons bounced through the door, Mum's face brightened in a way it never did for Margaret or Josie or me. I suppose my mother just preferred boys and she couldn't hide that. No matter how exhausted she was, no matter how pregnancy-heavy, she would muster a smile and the beam of her attention would land on her boys in a way that seemed to light them up, and light her up too. I yearned to be the object of my mother's doting gaze but I don't recall I ever was. That left me vulnerable, as an adult, to any person who seemed to be offering me their loving beam of attention. This is a tendency readers may notice later in this story.

'Betty, can you get your sister cleaned up?' Mum pleaded.

Five-year-old Josie had taken advantage of the hullaballoo with the injured twins to hop on a stool to reach the plate of flour on the bench. She was busy sprinkling flour over toddler Pauline for reasons that remain unclear. Pauline played along until the inhalation of flour set her off in a coughing fit and Mum roused on Josie for making a mess. While I did my best to brush the flour off Pauline, Mum hoisted herself up and manoeuvred her huge pregnant belly over to the sink to rinse out the bloody cloth.

I wasn't looking forward to squeezing another baby into our two-bedroom house. I was already sharing a bed with Margaret and Josie. Even now, if I close my eyes, I can see Josie's toenails a few centimetres from my face.

Our Eddie often slept at the back of the foundry where he worked, but that still left Michael, George, Kenneth and Bernard sharing the other upstairs room. Pauline, still only two, slept in the front room with our parents. How were more children conceived when there was always one in the marital bed? I suppose our parents had an efficient line in swift rutting that meant sperm managed to meet one or two ova on a regular basis.

Mum was raised Roman Catholic. When she married our father— a Protestant and a godless one at that—her family turned their backs. Those mean-spirited buggers never relented, refusing to see her again, and never met any of her children. Mum remained RC enough to have us baptised and she attended Mass most Sundays, always alone, having failed to chivvy any of us to go with her. Our father refused to send us to parish schools, which meant I never acquired the picturesque baggage my properly Catholic friends talk about. Never belted by nuns or molested by priests.

The gift that religion gave our mother was ten kids, two still-born babies and at least three miscarriages. She'd hung on to the Catholics' daft, cruel anti-contraception doctrine but lost her grip on the family support that might've helped with the upbringing of ten offspring.

Anyway, there must have been a brief pause in the noise of Kenneth's yowling, Bernard's singsong ridicule, Josie's sobbing and Pauline's coughing, because the next sound was very clear: our mother's waters breaking. For those who've never heard the whoosh or felt the sensation in their own body of a sac full of amniotic fluid hitting a kitchen floor—well, it's remarkable, cartoonish, like a water balloon exploding on a hard surface.

'Betty,' said Mum, with a breathy groan, knowing what was coming next, 'Margaret's home soon. She can look after the little ones. I need you to run and fetch our Michael.' (Michael, then sixteen, was the most reliable of the boys.)

By the time I ran to the plumber's yard where Michael was working as an apprentice, and ran home again, things had progressed. The next-door neighbour had taken Bernard somewhere to have his broken arm seen to, Margaret was helping Mum clamber up onto the kitchen table between contractions and the midwife was on her way.

Michael made the tactical decision to hustle sobbing Josie and bleeding Kenneth out of the house, on an expedition to track down our father. But little Pauline stayed behind, standing in a corner of the kitchen, her eyes out on stalks as she watched our mother bellow and heave.

I steered Pauline out into the street. I was failing to think of games to distract her, until I noticed there was still a dusting of flour on her hair and eyelashes.

'Pauline, what's the white stuff in your hair? Is that fairy dust?' I asked, matter of fact.

She put her hand up to feel her head and then nodded earnestly. I suggested she should shake her hair over the neighbour's window box to sprinkle fairy dust on the plants. Pauline took to this task with enthusiasm.

One of the childhood memories I trust to be accurate is the sight of my tiny sister waggling her head over those petunias and giggling so exuberantly that she laughed on the inhalation of breath as well as the exhalation, like a monkey.

Baby Paul was born an hour later. A surprisingly robust newborn. But Mum's health was far from robust and she was installed in the front room to recuperate. She was too poorly to breastfeed the new baby, so Paul was wet-nursed by a neighbour. When that goodwill dried up, Margaret resorted to feeding him watered-down evaporated milk from a bottle.

Paul was one week old when our mother was taken to the South London Hospital for Women and Children. My best guess now is that she was suffering a post-partum infection, but we kids were never told and none of us visited her in the hospital. When she died some days later, I don't even recall being told the news, but someone must have mentioned it. Keeping children properly informed of events—for example, the death of their mother—was not considered necessary in those days.

It stuck in our father's gullet, as sharp and maddening as a sideways chicken bone, to arrange a Catholic funeral.

Our Lady of the Assumption, Deptford.

In Roman Catholicism, the 'Assumption' is the belief that the dead body of Jesus' mother Mary was 'assumed' into heaven to be reunited with her soul—unlike my mother's body, worn out by fifteen pregnancies, which would just be rotting in the ground.

On that cold raw day, the clothing I wore—an outfit 'for best', borrowed from neighbours—was not warm enough. The chill went through the thin fabric, through my skin and right into my innards. It would be histrionic to say there are pockets of cold inside me that have never properly warmed up again since that day, but sometimes that image does wander into my thoughts.

The funeral Mass was in Latin, of course, and because I'd only been to church a handful of times, the whole baroque business was unfamiliar. The incomprehensible droning of the priests was like a powerful spell that didn't feel altogether benign.

My father held himself together until the Mass was over and most of the mourners had left. Two priests, in their rococo outfits, were standing by the church doorway as I walked towards it, with Dad just ahead of me.

It was easy to guess we were related. I shared my father's dark colouring, the nose, the same deep-set eyes, except that one of his irises was milky, blinded by shrapnel at Verdun in 1916. He had sustained other painful war injuries but no one would guess from the way he threw his sinewy body into a physical task. He wasn't a tall man but he was strong, when sober anyway, and quite a handsome man, still only thirty-eight when my mother died. The booze may have been rotting him from the inside but there were no outward signs.

On his way out of the church, Dad had just moved past the two priests when he suddenly spun around to face me. He did that thing when someone pretends to be addressing you, but really it's a performance for a nearby third party.

'Betty, why do you think these dressed-up vultures are standing here?'

I shrugged, playing my part in the show. I didn't know what a vulture was but I understood the 'dressed-up' part. One priest was in a creamy chasuble with scarlet embellishments, the other sporting a gold-embroidered purple number.

'They're making sure nobody steals their precious silver candlesticks.' Dad stood still, glaring at the priests, so I felt obliged to stay there too.

'Feast your eyes on these tossers in their finery. Ridiculous. They look like pantomime costumes, wouldn't you say, Betty?'

I'd never been lucky enough to go to a pantomime but I'd seen pictures, so I nodded.

'Did you know these parasites eat off gold plates—gold fucking plates—while your poor dead mother went hungry? She went without so she could put coins—shillings sometimes!—into their greedy paws at Mass. So they could stuff their faces with dainty cakes served on gold plates. She believed everything they told her but really these snobs didn't give a tinker's cuss about her miserable fucking life.'

Dad didn't mention his own not inconsiderable contribution to his wife's misery and poverty, but maybe this wasn't the occasion for that insight to be presented. And whichever way blame should be assigned, it was reasonable to lay a chunk of it at the feet of the church, represented by these two robed gentlemen.

My father's rage flared up even hotter and he addressed the two priests directly. 'Tell my daughter Betty the truth on this day we're burying her poor Catholic mother. Tell her that it's all a lie and that you two—with your fancy clothes and your Latin gibberish and your snouts in the trough—you know it's a lie. Your religion is a pack of fairy stories to bamboozle poor people and keep us in line. Tell her.'

The priests did not seem likely to tell me anything so Dad turned to me with a fervent aside. 'It's all lies, Betty. Remember that.'

I felt like I'd been let in on a secret—at the age of seven, granted access to the truth prematurely, on account of the extremity of our mother dying.

In my life since then, I have encountered devout individuals, truly decent human beings who've done valuable work in the name of their faith. But nothing I've seen in the ninety-three years since that day has made religion enticing to me. And don't get me started on the pernicious effect most religions have on the lives of women across the globe.

As my father railed at them, the two clergymen offered a stoic silence, their heads tipped slightly downward.

'They won't even look us in the eye! Do you see that, Betty?'

The way the priests stood there in their storybook costumes, ignoring a man's angry spit hitting the steps near their shoes, struck me as funny. I sputtered out a giggle but then suppressed the next one. It was wrong to laugh in church, especially at your mother's funeral.

Dad must've seen me fight the smile off my face. He suddenly barked a laugh.

'You're right, Betty. These people are a joke. We're wasting our breath on these limp-dicked fools.'

He scooped my hand into his—my hand cold as a fish, his warm from the rage circulating through his body. He swept me down the steps and away from Our Lady of the Assumption. That moment was the closest I ever felt to him.

I would like to be able to report that my father was jolted into sobriety and good parenting habits. But after Mum died, Dad slipped further into boozery and he seemed to give up on the idea of employment altogether.

He ended up sleeping so often among the kegs in the Chichester Arms that Margaret eventually commandeered the tiny front parlour that had served as our parents' bedroom, claiming it for herself and baby Paul.

I must confess I was resentful at the time—one more grievance to pile onto all the ways my big sister annoyed me. Margaret always seemed to be in a stinking mood, growling orders at me, slamming pots around the kitchen to express her bad temper. She was a cranky, humourless cow and I hated her for it.

My judgement of Margaret back then—harsh, ignorant, lacking imagination—that's one of the things of which I'm ashamed. She was only thirteen when our mother died, forced to leave school and take on the care of the newborn plonked into her arms, as well as doing her best to cook and keep house for the rest of us. Thirteen years old. No wonder she neglected to crack many jokes.

As for me, motherless and functionally fatherless, I still enjoyed learning whatever there was to learn in the classroom at the Clyde Road School. I still roamed the streets of Deptford with my neighbourhood pals, playing chaseys and rounders.

Sometimes, half a Sunday would go by and the thought, *My mum's dead*, would not have entered my head. But perhaps it would've been better if it had. There were times I would scoot into the house, my throat still buzzing from laughing and roaring out in games, and I would be struck, freshly, by the fact that she was gone. I had forgotten to keep myself ready, failed to keep my stomach clenched to withstand the sucker punch of it.

It was one of those Sunday afternoons when my brother Michael found me sitting there with the stuffing knocked out of me.

He walked slowly around me for a moment, muttering, 'Mm,

yes, mm,' in a silly posh voice. Then he made a show of being an old fusspot doctor, peering into my eyes, taking my pulse.

'Well, I've examined the patient and I believe there's only one treatment: the pictures.'

My brothers often took girls to the cinema on dates, but up until then, I had never been.

Top Hat with Fred Astaire and Ginger Rogers was the movie we saw at the Odeon Cinema. I gulped a big breath in with the first lush sweep of strings in the overture and I have no memory of breathing out until the film was over. I loved every tiny thing about it. Even Fred Astaire's odd pixie face, like a cheerful frog. Or maybe it was easier to love *because* Fred's elfin look was sexless, unthreatening to a pre-pubescent girl. And when Ginger gave him sass, then fell into step with him with such swagger, before the two of them swirled across the shiny dancefloor like exquisite birds—well, it was intoxicating. I didn't want the film to end, so we stayed in our seats, floating through the lovely syrupy score, until the very final credits.

'You know what I think about sometimes, Betty?' Michael whispered. 'You and I just watched the very same picture as the richest people in the world. The toffs. Even kings and queens. Our eyeballs and their eyeballs—all looking at the same picture.'

The weather turned icy on the walk home from the cinema and Michael must have noticed me shivering. He flicked his head, indicating that we should make a quick left turn down a street with a bakery. My brother showed me a trick he used when he was out and about for work in the cold weather. We ducked down a laneway on the side of the bakery and leaned our backs against the wall. The heat from the ovens, even this late in the day, kept the bricks warm and it was a special, delicious kind of warmth that soaked right into you. My brother and I leaned against the bakery wall for ages, talking about *Top Hat*.

When we got home, he grabbed one end of our kitchen table.

'Help me shift this,' he said.

We moved the table as far over against the sink as possible, leaving a patch of clear space.

'It's time you learned to dance, Betty.'

He held out his arms and made a froggy face like Fred Astaire. That made me laugh enough that I forgot to be embarrassed about looking foolish and threw myself into my first dance lesson.

Michael—he would've been seventeen years old then—had started frequenting dance halls around town and was never short of dance partners. He was popular with girls because he knew how to talk.

There were many Sunday afternoons, often after we'd seen a matinee session at the pictures, when we would push the kitchen table aside to dance. By the time I was ten, I was a tidy little dancer.

At that same time, I came across an intriguing piece of information about the world.

It was the end of a day at the Clyde Road School when an older girl appeared in the corridor outside our classroom, waiting to collect her little brother. It was hard to fathom that Roger Purley, a ferrety, flatulent, pustular boy, could be related to this poised young woman.

Roger began loudly skiting. 'My sister goes to the girls' grammar school.'

Dorothy Purley looked so swish and so confident in her uniform: a navy velour Panama hat with a green band, a crisp white blouse under a navy tunic, an emerald tie and a navy blazer with insignia embroidered on the pocket.

Dorothy saw me squinting at the unfamiliar words curving under the pocket crest.

'That's Latin,' she explained. '"Honesta Obtinete" which means "Hold Fast to What Is Good".'

I rolled the words around in my head. They sounded like a powerful incantation.

'We learn Latin at my school,' Dorothy explained. 'As well as French, history, mathematics—well, lots of subjects!'

Her voice didn't come out with the posh edge I'd expected. She sounded polite, clear, but still with the same accent as Roger, as me, as other common-as-muck south London types.

Several kids in the corridor were eyeing Dorothy's fancy uniform and the impressive satchel of books. We all knew the Purleys couldn't afford that kind of clobber.

Roger couldn't pass up another bragging opportunity. 'My sister got a scholarship to pay for the uniform and everything. After she finishes at the grammar school, our Dorothy's going to university.'

Dorothy discreetly scowled and shooshed her brother, then hustled him out into the schoolyard. She was too gracious for this kind of skiting. Which made her an even more impressive figure.

So, aged ten, I had my plan for the future: I would continue to work on becoming the best dancer in London—that went without saying—but I would also sit the test for entry to the grammar school, and after that, go on to university, even though at the time I had no clue what a university was. It was all set.

TWO

In 1939, two things happened: Hitler invaded Poland and I did not receive a letter to say I had secured a place at the grammar school.

On the first of September 1939, I was holding a scuffed cardboard suitcase, standing on the doorstep of the Deptford house alongside my three younger siblings—nine-year-old Josie, six-year-old Pauline and four-year-old Paul.

Bombs were expected to land on London any day and the call had gone out to whisk vulnerable persons out of the city to safety in the countryside. That morning, a stream of mothers and children was flowing past our front door to catch the bus to Paddington station.

We four Rankin kids carried gasmasks and were kitted out with the gear required for evacuees: strong boots, a decent warm coat each, plus pyjamas and a change of clothes for the journey. Josie was also carrying a small suitcase, while Paul's and Pauline's things were packed into a sturdy paper sack that Pauline cradled against her tummy like a baby.

Labels had been tied to our coat buttons, as if we were parcels to be delivered. I tried to jam my label (*Rankin, Elizabeth, 11 years*) under the lapel of my coat, in a small bid for dignity.

I'm still not sure why the twins, Kenneth and Bernard, weren't to be evacuated too—there were plenty of thirteen-year-olds who went on those first trains. Did the having of testicles create a forcefield that would protect my brothers from shrapnel and firestorms? I never knew how the decision was made to send the four of us away and no one ever consulted us.

'Betty, can we take Scruffy to the country?' Pauline had whispered to me the night before, as if proposing a smuggling operation.

Scruffy was her toy dog, which a charitable person might say looked like a Scottish terrier. There were patches where Scruffy's fur had been cuddled right down to the hessian backing, and so much of his stuffing had come out over the years that his abdomen was flaccid, like a human with loose skin after major weight loss. Now, balding, slack-bellied Scruffy was in my suitcase, ready to be evacuated to the countryside.

The little ones were well keyed up about this adventure, thrilled by their new boots and coats, and by the drama of a gasmask. But as we stood there waiting, their buoyant spirits began to sag.

Margaret had an early shift that day, so she'd tied the labels on our coats the night before, leaving it to our father to take us to the railway station in the morning. The trouble was, there was still no sign of him.

Dad must've slept the night at the Chichester Arms and not managed to make it home yet. He'd been sinking into a deeper sulk as our Edward, our Michael and our George were already away on military training, but Dad's milky eye meant he would never be able to enlist, however thoroughly he sobered up. This situation left him feeling unmanned and morose. Apparently, taking decent care of his children would not define his manhood as satisfyingly as trooping off to kill other men.

Eventually, Mrs Huntley, the last of the mothers rushing down our street, clocked the four pitiable Rankin children stranded on their doorstep.

'You lot can come with me,' she called out. 'But we need to get a wriggle on.'

Pauline hooked her hand into mine, trusting me to decide, but as we headed down the steps to join Mrs Huntley, Josie began to yowl behind us.

'I don't want to go! I never wanted to go!'

She launched into one of her award-worthy performances, dropping to her knees and sobbing. That set the little ones off and a moment later, the three of them ran back inside the house.

Mrs Huntley made an exasperated sound. 'Will they come or not?'

I shook my head. 'But I'll come,' I said.

The flock of mothers and children inside Paddington railway station was heaving in that mysterious, organic way crowds move, noisy with babbling voices, stinky with the combination of damp woollen coats, the fatty odour of the sandwiches some of the women had packed for the train, plus a hint of urine from the nervous little ones who had wet their pants.

We shuffled closer to the spot where children would leave their mothers to go past the barriers and onto the train. Some kids were laughing, eager like puppies, but others were hiccupping for breath in between sobs and pleas to stay home. Many of the mothers bunged on bright voices to present the evacuation as a marvellous lark, a day out. But I could see other women openly crying. Beside me, one lady squatted down to clutch her two kids tightly against herself, as if she could press them into her body.

In the years since, I've replayed that railway platform scene in my head. All those mothers, torn up inside, forced to choose: keep their children home and risk Hitler's bombs or, for safety's sake, send them away to live with strangers. I think about my own children and try to imagine what choice I would've made. And then my thoughts might stretch out further to the mothers in all the wars since then; wars started by self-important, blustering men; wars that meant mothers had to make such terrible calculations. Flee your village in Somalia, walk away from your home in Syria, scrabble to survive in a refugee camp to keep your children safe. (I realise it may come across as a maudlin cliché to talk about mothers in wartime but that doesn't make it any less potent.)

In September 1939, I didn't have any such expansive humane thoughts. My mind was too small, too busy frothing with anxiety and excitement, to imagine what other people might be feeling.

I let the press of bodies push me forward along the platform and then onto the train. Having lost sight of Mrs Huntley, I was suddenly conscious that I was alone, with no clue where I was going. My throat tight with panic, I made an effort to remind myself that evacuation couldn't be worse than my life in the Deptford house. Dad forever drunk, absent or foul-tempered. Our Margaret was so busy with work that the provision of meals had disintegrated. (My younger siblings had perfected the art of the big-eyed doleful expression that would get them invited to stay for supper at the neighbours.) And my brother Michael would soon be sent away to fight, which would mean there'd be no one in that house who gave a tinker's cuss about me.

I also felt a buzz of curiosity. I wanted to find out what might happen next.

When the train pulled away from the platform, I kept my head down so I wouldn't see other children's mothers running alongside the train to blow them kisses. Once we were out of the station, I avoided looking at my fellow passengers—many of whom were weeping—and anchored my gaze on the view through the window, staving off the urge to cry by using the method of being *interested* in things. I don't mean to sound glib about that idea. There have been bouts of fear or suffering in my life when taking an intense interest in what was happening, around me and inside me, has maintained my sanity, more or less. I do recommend 'being interested' as a method to endure difficult episodes.

While city buildings rattled past the train, a debate with myself was underway: when to scoff the cold sausage sandwich I'd packed that morning. The sandwich got me thinking about Josie, Pauline and Paul who were probably at this moment sitting round our kitchen table chomping on the sausage butties I'd made for them to eat on the train. And then, picturing our Pauline, I remembered Scruffy was still in my suitcase, accidentally kidnapped.

Two notions bounced inside my skull—fear that it was a mistake to head off alone to God knows where, but at the same time, fear that it was a mistake to leave my siblings behind, abandoning them to German bombs. My curiosity about this adventure was starting to dim. And the bravado of how-much-worse-could-it-be-than-Deptford had deserted me entirely. My eyeballs burned in that way they can burn just before the tears come. I took hold of myself by scoffing half the sausage sandwich.

I didn't fall asleep, even though it was a long journey—eight hours, to the extent that I can trust my memory. I felt intoxicated rather than sleepy. Dizzy with the distance travelled. I'd never been anywhere, never ventured more than a few miles from home, let alone outside London. People like us didn't. We were a troop of primates loping around and foraging for food within a very small territory.

On that journey, I saw cows for the first time. I'd seen them in books, of course, but never real-life cows, standing in the fields along the trainline.

At Redruth station, Cornwall, we were funnelled onto different buses in a flurry of children and suitcases and big-voiced grown-ups wearing armbands.

Waiting at the door of one of the buses, I noticed the driver, a grey-haired nugget of a man, bob his head in greeting to each kid who climbed on ahead of me. When it was my turn to receive a nod from the driver, I nodded back. I don't mean to exaggerate this nod of greeting—the bus driver wasn't beaming a smile of welcome or showering us with words of reassurance—but at least that little head tip, one for each child, acknowledged us as individuals.

The bus pulled over on the edge of a village, St Agnes, and we all followed the driver, on foot, to a church hall.

Let me pause my story briefly to sit with a moment of astonishment. How extraordinary that in those first three days of September, 1.5 million people were evacuated from the cities. That number included some mothers who travelled with their kids, plus disabled people with their carers, but even so, 827,000 were children sent away without their parents, sent to live with strangers. There was no vetting of the host families and no system of welfare oversight once you were tucked inside another family's house. That kind of risk to children is unthinkable now. I'm not suggesting the evacuation was a mistake. Thousands of children were saved from dying in air raids, that's for certain. But still, an astounding project, to contemplate it now.

Inside the hall, we kids shuffled forward, one by one, to give our names and city addresses to a man at a trestle table, then we gathered into a clump, about thirty of us, suitcases at our feet and labels pinned to our chests. Local ladies handed around sandwiches and mugs of very sweet tea, smiling at us ardently, as if that could plaster over the strangeness of the situation.

Billeting parents came into the hall to choose one child or several, depending on the size of their house. Older boys were the first chosen, plucked out by farmers looking for workers, and sometimes that meant they declined to take little sisters and brothers. I witnessed several sets of siblings being separated, weeping and bewildered. This was another moment when I felt relieved our Pauline hadn't come. Then again, if I'd been standing there as part of a package deal with my bewitchingly lovely sister, I might have been chosen sooner. On my own, I was an unappealing prospect. I'd set my face with fierce pride to endure the selection process so I must've come across as a flinty little creature.

In the end, I was the last child standing in the billeting hall, unpicked. Many years later, I came across interviews with evacuees and it seems pretty much every person claims they were the last to be picked. Of course that can't be possible, but we all enjoy being the object of Dickensian pity sometimes, especially via an image as blameless and abject as a lone child in wartime in a draughty public building. Maybe we all felt so unwanted and powerless in that moment, that's how we remember it in our guts.

In my case, it is a fact that I was last to be picked. The billeting officer was collecting his paperwork to go home, and kept darting his gaze to the door, hoping one more local couple would walk in to solve the problem of *Rankin, Elizabeth, 11 years*.

Finally, the bus driver, who'd been waiting to help tidy up the hall, took pity on me. He ducked around the trestle table to find my name on the list and exchanged a look with the billeting officer. Then he picked up my suitcase and gave me a small nod—not effusive, but kind, respectful, just the way he'd greeted every one of us at the railway station.

Mr Nancarrow drove the bus, with me as the only passenger, the two miles out of the village and along a curve in the road to a spot where the fields folded in around a cottage as if it were nestled in a plush green cushion. It was getting late by now and the velvety twilight made that slightly wonky stone house and its front garden full of flowers appear even more like a place in a picture book.

Mr Nancarrow parked the bus at the side of the house, alongside a shed full of tools and half-assembled vehicles. By this point, his wife had come out the front door of the cottage. She was in her mid-fifties, wearing a floral print dress. A short woman with a huge, almost perpendicular shelf of bosom, she resembled a flowery square with a head on top and stumpy legs sticking out the bottom.

Mr Nancarrow trotted ahead to explain the situation, pointing to me, while I hung back, embarrassed.

In the years after the evacuation, stories emerged of children being exploited or cruelly treated by their host families. A reader might be expecting this account to turn dark in just such a way, waiting for the sinister twist, maybe even hoping for an episode of florid trauma. I can't offer that here.

At the Nancarrows, I was never treated like a nuisance, as many evacuees were. They weren't hosting me for the sake of the ten shillings allowance or as cheap labour. I wasn't subjected to physical or sexual abuse in their house, as some children were.

That first evening, on the doorstep, Mrs Nancarrow looked down at the slip of paper her husband had handed her.

'Elizabeth,' she read aloud. 'Tell me, my lovely, do you like to be called Elizabeth or something else?'

I had no idea how to respond. I'd never imagined there was any choice in the matter of what people called me. I stood silent for several seconds (which is a very long time in any human interaction) until Mrs Nancarrow smiled and wiggled her shoulders, as if this were a delightful game.

'Shall I try to guess?' she asked. 'Do you prefer Betty? Or Betsy?'

I was thrilled at the idea of having the opportunity to 'prefer' anything but I was still unable to summon a preference, let alone say it aloud.

'Is it Lizzie? Or do you like to be called Beth?'

The name 'Beth' sounded good coming out of this lady's mouth. The strong plosive 'B' to launch and the soft landing of the lispy 'th'. The timbre of her voice saying that word sent tingles down my scalp and neck. I wanted very much to continue hearing this lady say 'Beth', so I nodded.

'Ah.' She laughed. 'Now that I look at you, it's obvious you're a Beth.'

At the time, this seemed a magical process: the revelation of my true name. Looking back, I realise she was just seeking a way to distract and calm this anxious eleven-year-old. I shouldn't say 'just'. An act of kindness from this good-hearted woman—that was no small thing.

'Well, Beth, I'm guessing you're hungry as a bear after that long train journey.'

I had just sat down at the round table in their kitchen, and was considering I could possibly relax a smidgin, when Mr Nancarrow opened the back door and a dog barged through to launch itself at me. I was dead scared of dogs so I yelped and scrambled to my feet, but my evasive manoeuvre made the springer spaniel even more excited about jumping up at my legs.

'Sadie! Settle down!' Mrs Nancarrow said to the dog and then turned to me. 'I'm sorry, Beth. She's still a puppy and she can be too friendly sometimes.'

'Shall I park Sadie in the back room for now, Rose?' suggested Mr Nancarrow.

'Good idea, Walter. Sadie and Beth can get to know each other tomorrow.'

Always, by my observation, these two people spoke to each other with respect and implicit affection, sorting out the small and large items of life's business without anyone resorting to foul words or slamming things on a table or taking offence to the point of a tantrum. That alone—their way of being with each other—was a revelation to me.

Mr Nancarrow hustled the dog out of the kitchen and Mrs Nancarrow busied herself with food preparation, keeping up a stream of chatter for my sake. (She must've been wondering at this point if she'd opened her home to a quivering mute.)

'I think Sadie's excited that you're here with us,' she murmured to me, as if confiding a secret. 'I must say I'm excited to have you here too. We didn't think any of the London children would want to come to our house. It's a two-mile walk to the school, you see. And my two are grown up and moved away so there are no other children here to play with. I hope it won't be too boring for you, Beth.'

What this lady didn't understand was that compared to the over-populated Deptford house, a residence with no other kids inside it was a luxury beyond all expression.

The three of us ate shepherd's pie with green beans and carrots cut into matchsticks. For afters, there was peach cobbler and custard made with eggs from the Nancarrows' own chickens. I was astonished to be offered second helpings of everything.

Eventually I found my voice. 'This is delicious. Thank you, Mrs Nancarrow.'

'You're very welcome, my lovely.' She did that happy wiggle of her shoulders again. 'Ooh, if you're going to live here with us for a good while, we can't be "mister" and "missus". What do you think, Walter? Should Beth call us "auntie" and "uncle", do you think?'

Walter Nancarrow did one of his nods and Rose Nancarrow patted my hand.

My suitcase was already sitting on the bed in the room that had belonged to the Nancarrows' daughter. She was now living far away in Hebden Bridge with her husband and babies. I'd clocked the photos of the daughter and the grandchildren around the house, alongside snaps of the Nancarrows' son, both as a boy and as a soldier in uniform. He was away doing military training and I wondered if he had met any of my brothers. The family photos sat in fancy frames, some made of silver or silver-plate at least—the only posh possessions in this modest home.

Mrs Nancarrow pointed out the row of books on her daughter's dressing table. 'Our June would be very happy if you borrowed any of her old books. This was her favourite.'

She selected a chunky book with ornate golden lettering, *A Treasury of Stories*, and put it directly into my hands. 'I'm off to bed now. But if you feel worried in the night—worried about any little thing—you come into our room and wake me up, yes? We can make hot milk and have a natter. Good night, Beth.'

I would be lying if I denied there was a pang of homesickness that first night. Well, not so much homesickness as wondering how everyone was back in Deptford. Mostly I missed our Pauline and worried how she would get to sleep now that I'd accidentally stolen Scruffy. But at the same time, I relished stretching out like a starfish with an entire single bed to myself. I sank into the luxurious quietness, without my siblings' snuffles and farts and bickering voices interfering with the meandering thread of my thoughts.

Mr Nancarrow dropped me off in the bus for my first day at the school in St Agnes. There were sixty pupils in one classroom, the local kids plus the influx of Londoners, so the place was hectic and noisy, not exactly conducive to learning. Eventually, a shift system was instituted, with half the cohort attending classes in the mornings, the other half in the afternoons.

At the end of my first Cornwall school day, Mrs Nancarrow was waiting for me at the gate.

'I asked Walter to spruce up June's old bike, so you can ride to and from school,' she said, presenting a bicycle to me with a little flourish.

'Oh. Thank you,' I murmured, but made no move to take hold of the handlebars.

Seeing my arms hanging limply and my pinched face, Mrs Nancarrow twigged that I had no idea how to ride a bike. Not wanting to embarrass me—there were other children in earshot—she deftly changed tack.

'But you know what?' she said. 'On the way here, I noticed the chain is too loose. What do you say we wheel it back for today and get that fixed?'

Over the next three evenings, Mrs Nancarrow taught me to ride a bike.

Mr Nancarrow was often away from the house working as a bus driver or he would be busy in his shed, tinkering with vehicles. He was a decent man who was kind to children and loved his wife, but he wasn't the central character for me. I was besotted with Mrs Nancarrow, as one sort of mother a person could have. Keep in mind that I was assessing her off a low base in terms of parental care. And I concede there's a chance my image of her is blurred and romanticised, but in terms of my own personal mythology, it doesn't really matter.

As well as learning to ride a bike, I learned to appreciate dogs. Once I put aside my terror and Sadie dialled down her boisterous response, we became devoted chums. These days, there is data on the role of companion animals in promoting human wellbeing, lowering our blood pressure and such. It may not work that way for everyone but my wellbeing, then and later, has been robustly promoted by dogs.

Rambles with Sadie were the best, the two of us scooting across the fields, then jumping between rocks and onto the beaches strung between the headlands on that stretch of coast. It was cold on the beaches and we were pummelled by strong winds most of the time, but that was fine by me. I loved the salt spray on my face, loved seeing our footprints, dog and human, crunched into the fresh expanse of sand.

When summer came, I swam in the sea for the first time. With the jolt of the cold water, my lungs momentarily tightened, paralysed almost, and the meat of my thighs congealed into a solid icy block, but then came the tingling euphoria.

A love of swimming has stayed with me. Surf beaches in Australia, the clear water around Greece, the soft, limestone-filtered cenotes in Mexico. Even today, if there's a chance to haul my ancient bones across sand or rocks or a jetty and into the water, I'm in.

In my letters home, I was dead keen to include drawings of the beach and the Nancarrows' garden for our Pauline, to sell her on the charms of the place. This was part of my secret plan for my littlest sister to come and live with Auntie Rose and Uncle Walter too. I cunningly included Scruffy in the drawings, placing Pauline's bald, flaccid toy dog in delightful horticultural settings. The problem, though, was I had no talent for drawing. 'Scruffy Among the Hydrangeas' looked more like 'Smudged Rat Among Pile of Pastel Rubbish'.

'This is the worst drawing ever done by any person ever,' I moaned. I was working at the kitchen table while Mrs Nancarrow was topping and tailing beans by the sink.

'I'm sure it's not that bad, Beth. Shall we work out how you can fix it up?'

But when she looked at the drawing, her face seized up—the kind of clenched expression people do when they don't trust their facial muscles not to reveal their true response.

'You don't have to pretend,' I said, 'I know it's terrible.'

We exchanged a look, direct and open, and then both spluttered into laughter.

'Does your Pauline like stories?' asked Mrs Nancarrow. I'd been chattering about Pauline for weeks, to convince her that my sister was a delightful little girl. 'Instead of drawings, would Pauline like to read a story about Scruffy?'

When a person—for example, me—has the particular kind of arrogance to think others might wish to read their stories, it doesn't take much encouragement to set them going. Auntie Rose's suggestion launched me into writing a series of tales about Scruffy's adventures in Cornwall. They ranged from slice-of-life naturalism describing his countryside rambles, to nuanced relationship drama between him and Sadie, to hearty adventure stories wherein Scruffy rescued children from tin mines, to wilder fantasies involving pixies and talking horses.

I would ask Mrs Nancarrow to check the spelling before I posted a batch of stories to Deptford. My spelling didn't need checking but I was hungry for an immediate audience, and yes, okay, hungry for praise. Auntie Rose was the best reader—smiling and gasping in just the ways I'd hoped, as well as offering an intoxicating amount of praise.

'Oh, Beth, this is a marvellous story! I think it's your best one yet.'

I celebrated my twelfth birthday with the Nancarrows. I was included in their family Christmas. Sometimes, I allowed myself the fantasy that I was really their child.

Even as a twelve-year-old, I had an inkling my time there would be important. Admittedly, there's no way of measuring who I would've become without it. There are no controlled experiments about how lives turn out. But I can say that for years afterwards, when circumstances pulled me into dark corners, I could remember how things were in St Agnes. If I felt wretched and worthless, I understood it was possible to feel differently. I knew, in my body, what it's like to be valued and cared for, how joy sits in my belly, how bold I can be to try something when I feel cherished.

I'd been living with the Nancarrows for a year when a telegram arrived from their daughter June. She and the children had contracted scarlet fever, which meant Mrs Nancarrow would have to rush to Hebden Bridge to nurse them and I would have to return to my real family. There'd been no bombing in London—the evacuation palaver had been a false alarm—and many children had already gone home to the city. Now it was my turn.

Redruth station, 6 September 1940.

Mrs Nancarrow looked strained as we stood on the railway platform, but I figured she was worried about her grandchildren rather than sad about my leaving.

'Let's see how we go, eh, Beth. I promise I'll write to you in London. And if you have time to write back, could I read some more of your stories?'

I shrugged, determinedly not meeting her gaze.

She opened her arms to hug me but I twisted my neck so it would seem I hadn't noticed. I stepped up onto the train abruptly, as if I could tear the connection between us into painless shreds as long as I did it in a swift and unsentimental way. I offered no affectionate moment or thanks for everything she'd done for me.

I don't know if she understood the reason for my coldness that day. (This is something I still think about.) I hope Rose Nancarrow realised that my behaviour, graceless and hurtful, was a measure of how much I hated to leave. I was angry with myself for having loved something so much, and I needed to cauterise the wound as quickly as I could.

'Betty! Here! Betty!'

I stepped off the train at Paddington to see my sister Margaret waving. Being addressed as 'Betty' again, I was aware of my posture shifting, shoulders slightly hunched, prickly, ready to be disappointed. Then again, it was an agreeable surprise to be met at the station and our Margaret was looking mighty impressive in her new Wren uniform. There was also the welcome news that the house would be less crowded, with the older boys away serving and Margaret bunking in the Women's Royal Navy training barracks at Mill Hill.

My first night back in the Deptford house, I could hear the slightly wheezy breathing of my little brother Paul, sleeping across the corridor in the bedroom he shared with Kenneth and Bernard. Josie, ever the princess, had claimed the front parlour as her exclusive boudoir and my father was now on a cot in the kitchen, snoring like a walrus. He'd been employed for the last six months, a steady job, and drinking less, according to Margaret. I was sharing a bed with

Pauline, who made only the softest and sweetest of sleeping noises. Under our bed was a Trafalgar Square biscuit tin in which Pauline kept all the 'Scruffy in Cornwall' stories I'd sent her.

Here's an odd thing: even though I desperately missed living with the Nancarrows, I was also relieved to be home with my family. That must count as a strange reaction given how much worse, in every measurable way, my life in the Deptford house would be compared to the St Agnes cottage, and given how annoying I found most members of our household. But the animal impulse to be with your own family, however objectively shithouse they are, is strong.

The next day, 7 September, was a Saturday so no school for me. It was an unusually hot day, a beautiful day, which probably helped me feel better about landing back in Deptford. In the late afternoon, I was in the kitchen making an apple cobbler with a bag of Keswick Codlin apples Mrs Nancarrow had picked for me to bring home.

As I peeled and chopped, I was concocting a story in my head, spinning future events the way I wished they would go, but careful to keep my storyline plausible so I could take genuine, realistic comfort from it. (I'm sure I'm not the only person who does this.) In my imagined future, I would receive a letter from Mrs Nancarrow to say June and her kids had recovered quickly. I'd be invited to return to St Agnes, with the suggestion that Paul and Pauline come too. In my more generous-spirited moments, the fantasy would stretch to take Josie back to Cornwall with me as well.

Air-raid sirens went off at about quarter to five.

'What's that mean?' I called out to anyone who might be within earshot.

'Nothing!' Bernard yelled from the upstairs bedroom, where he was busy throwing our Kenneth's barley sugar sweets out the window to torment him. After months of the bombers targeting the airfields, not the city, people in Deptford had grown used to the sirens and now ignored them.

I heard some shouting in the street but I was too busy with apples to pay attention. A second later the impact of the bomb threw me backwards against the pantry cupboard.

I won't attempt to generate suspense about my own survival, given I'm writing this account now. I was bruised and winded, but suffered no major injury. After the monumental blast of sound, I was sunk into deafness so dense I couldn't hear anything, and with the smoke and dust, I could hardly find my way through my own small house.

There are those moments when the eyes see something unfamiliar, and the brain takes a few beats to process the information into a coherent image. I saw shoes and then a patch of skin where a shirt had been rucked up. The fragments made no sense until I realised that it was my little brother Paul and the reason I couldn't see more of him was because he was buried under rubble from the shoulders up. As the realisation came—*Paul is dead*—a hunk of timber from the collapsing staircase thumped into the side of my head and I dropped into total darkness.

When I came to, there was blistering pain across my skull and a clumsy bandage wrapped around my head where the timber had broken the skin and left my hair sticky with blood. In later years, that mark was hidden under my hair (except during the months I was chemo-bald) but I've always been able to feel the ridge of the scar with my fingers.

I woke up in the shelter underneath Burtons' clothing store in the Deptford high street. Neighbours had carried Josie and me there as a place of safety. The bombers had apparently stopped for a couple of hours but then started up again, so we stayed underground.

My memories of that night are unreliable, if only because I was concussed and temporarily deaf. I do recall that our father found us in the Burtons' shelter and delivered the news that Bernard had been killed in the blast, along with Paul. Dad had searched the wreckage of our house and found Kenneth, injured but alive, but there was no sign of Pauline.

When the all-clear came the next morning, Margaret wanted me to go with her to visit Kenneth in hospital, but I insisted on helping Dad look for our Pauline.

Most likely, some neighbours had taken my little sister in, so we headed straight to our street. The house next door had taken the direct hit—it was flattened and all seven members of the Buxton family had perished. The force of the explosion had blasted off the front half of our place so it now resembled an open-fronted doll's house. Clothes, saucepans, bedsheets, broken remains of furniture— everything was on display, like showing your tatty underwear.

Dad took Josie to doorknock through the neighbourhood for word of Pauline, but I was too restless for that. People at Burtons' reckoned there were more temporary shelters, so I rushed off to check other places Pauline might have been taken.

The ornate façade of the Odeon Cinema was covered in a layer of sooty muck but otherwise untouched by the bombing. Once inside, I realised my mistake: the cinema wasn't being used as a shelter but as a makeshift morgue.

Maybe it was my prematurely adult face that meant no one questioned a twelve-year-old walking into the foyer where about twenty bodies were laid out in rows—neat rows, as if neatness could help make sense of this. My eye was immediately caught by a blue cardigan I knew well. It was Pauline.

I've asked myself why Paul, Bernard and Pauline died in that air raid and not me. Logically, I know it was random, but the mind is always trying to push the random into meaningful shapes and often those shapes are self-lacerating: the guilt, the pressure to make your life count for something and the shame when it doesn't.

At my age, I've seen so many people clobbered by loss. Something unendurable happens, after which it is impossible to go on, and then people go on. Well, most do. When one of us shatters into a thousand pieces, that seems the natural response to tragedy. But usually, even then, we eventually gather up our pieces and the possibility of joy and silliness and excitement is, almost inconceivably, there again.

THREE

20 October 1943.

My limbs felt loose, muscles liquified by a long hot bath, body wrapped in a quilted bathrobe, legs flopped happily over the spongey side of the armchair.

It wasn't my favourite armchair in the Mayfair residence—the brocade fabric could be a bit scratchy—but I preferred this level of the Upper Grosvenor Street house. The second-storey windows were six-foot high ovals which framed the sky and the treetops in a very elegant way. I usually brought books up from the reception rooms on the ground floor to sit in this front bedroom with its ovoid windows.

I had not been adopted by wealthy folk nor discovered I was secretly a duchess all along. This isn't that kind of story.

During the war, many grand buildings were requisitioned for use as hospitals and military facilities. I had unofficially claimed this posh Mayfair property for my own personal day usage. Among its many luxuries was an Ascot gas water heater mounted above the bathtub.

After our Deptford house was bombed, we retrieved a few belongings from the ruins before the structure was demolished.

For a time afterwards, whenever I looked at any building, I would see a flash of it as a pile of bricks and broken timbers and shards of glass. But I couldn't let myself entertain such images for long. To function in the world, an individual needs to operate on the assumption that their home will remain standing and people they love will come safely back down the stairs.

The one thing of monetary value salvaged from the house was a necklace my mother must've kept hidden away during various penniless crises in the past. Dad sold the necklace to pay for a special keepsake: three ornamental mirrors engraved with photographs of Bernard, Paul and Pauline. It was unnerving to see a combination of your own reflection and the face of a dead sibling emerging from a gilt frame. I understand the impulse of grief behind our father's choice, however tacky the result, but generally, I don't hold with spending limited funds on symbolic gestures when there are urgent practical needs.

For the last months of 1940, we camped out in south London houses that had been damaged enough to be abandoned but not enough to fall down. By 'we', I mean Dad, Josie and me. Once our Kenneth recovered from his injuries, he was sent to live in Kent, where extra workers were needed on hop farms. There was never any talk of Josie and me being evacuated.

Josie and I were kinder to each other for a while, because, I suppose, we were each other's only sibling on hand. The first time we went back to our bombed-out house, Josie was shaky, and I figured her insides were stewing up the same mix of sadness and ghoulish imaginings as mine. I set myself the goal of making my sister laugh.

As we approached what remained of our front steps, I bunged on a toffy voice, as if I were a butler ushering her inside a grand house.

'Let me show you into the parlour, madame,' I said, sweeping my hands where the door used to be. And as we picked our way around the rubble of what had been our front room, I made a goofy show of tidying up and fussing about. 'Oh dear. Please excuse the mess, milady. It must be the maid's day off.'

Josie giggled. She was never a big laugher—not like our Pauline—so there was a special sense of achievement in squeezing a laugh out of her. As Josie and I moved through the wreckage of our house, we kept that silliness going for a good few minutes before it suddenly felt too sad.

Whenever we moved to a new damaged house to set up camp, I identified the closest underground shelter. With air-raid sirens yowling, I would hurry to the shelter along with all the other people, but I always felt oddly calm. To my young mind, once my siblings had been killed, the worst had already happened. That sense of safety was ridiculous of course—no one was immune from further bomb hits—but it was a helpful delusion. A kind of consoling magic spell.

Our camping-out period ended on the night Dad woke up to take a piss and discovered two dogs humping enthusiastically right next to where we were sleeping. The house lacked a full complement of walls, so there was no way to keep local dogs from sauntering inside to engage in sexual liaisons.

'That's enough!' our father roared and, even though it was the middle of the night, immersed in the stodgy darkness of the Blitz blackout, he immediately started fumbling around to pack up our belongings.

Before I was born, there had been a vicious falling-out between Dad and his sister Eileen, but after the Night of The Rutting Dogs, he forced himself to make peace with her so we would have somewhere to live with intact walls and closable doors. I must acknowledge now that there was a certain amount of nobility in my father swallowing his pride and sucking up to Eileen. Even more so when I take into account what a vinegary, spiteful woman she was.

Aunt Eileen lived with her husband Gilbert in a house in Islington which had bedrooms spare now their two sons were away in the navy. The house may have been cramped and shabby but to move north of the Thames, far away from Deptford, was a relief, with fewer distressing reminders and no neighbours to spray pitying looks in our direction.

Uncle Gil was a creepy mouth-breather who always seemed to have a mysterious white scum settled in the corners of his mouth. It was easy to avoid him, though, because he worked nights and slept during the day. We were expected to be quiet around the house and not disturb his sleep.

Everyone in the Islington household was on a different schedule, so it was like living in a boarding house with shared kitchen facilities. I produced the best food I could for Josie and me out of whatever was left of the ration supplies. Mock Brains made an appearance more than once.

A local primary school was found for Josie but no one seemed fussed about any further education for me. With no school, I spent the first chunk of each morning queuing for rations, then the rest of the day was my own. I would wander for hours within the walkable radius of Islington, which included the well-to-do residential streets of Mayfair.

After a few days of surveillance, it wasn't hard to work out which houses were unoccupied, the owners having decamped to the safety of their country homes. It was also not hard to break into some of those places with their clunky old brass locks. No alarm systems or security cameras back then.

The Upper Grosvenor Street house with its oval windows became my favourite. I would spend entire afternoons there, sinking into the fantasy that it was where I lived.

I kept my thieving to a minimum, scooping up just enough stray coins to pay for a ticket to the pictures once in a while. I found a pen that sat so sweetly in my hand, it was asking to be pocketed. That one pen was nothing compared to what I could've stolen. I always remained on the comfortable side of a self-determined moral line.

With no schooling for my brain to soak up, I helped myself to the bounteous library of the Upper Grosvenor Street house then found a comfy spot in one of the upstairs bedrooms to read: *Encyclopaedia Britannica*, leather-bound sets of Dickens and other classic fiction, lusciously illustrated books on plants and birds, and a whopping dictionary to look up any words I didn't know. It was clear from the crackle of the pages that many of the books had rarely or never been opened—they just sat on the elegant shelves for show. I hummed with the satisfaction of stealing knowledge out of the books owned by posh tossers who didn't deserve them.

I've often thought about the role those two years played in my education. I ended up with a hodgepodge of knowledge, based on my whims in choosing books. I managed a reasonable grounding in traditional English literature and devoured particular chunks of history (for example, Ancient Greece and Rome, the French Revolution, the Aztecs) but with cavernous holes about other places and eras. I loved the giant atlas which I would open out on a French-polished table, in order to locate cities and rivers and mountains I was reading about or to trace my own fantasy voyages.

I confess there was laziness on my part about the sciences, apart from books about animals and about the human body. I spent many hours absorbed in anatomy books with the coloured plates showing different body parts. Sometimes, when I look at a person even now, I picture the cross-section of their skull, their coiling pink innards, and the map of blood vessels and nerve pathways through their spinal column and limbs.

I'd been competent at arithmetic in primary school but I missed out on advanced mathematics, which left me with a pathetic reverence towards people who possess mathematical skills—it seems like a form of wizardry to me.

Lack of formal secondary education also left me with a general anxiety—never being quite sure what is considered common knowledge and what I might be misunderstanding, feeling the gaps inside my head like cavities in the anatomy illustrations. Years later, I came to understand how inadequate and culturally distorted any individual's schooling can be, however erudite they seem. Even so, I can still tune into the ever-present hum of my education insecurity, like low-level tinnitus.

Without doubt, I lacked the social connections a school offers. I really did miss having chums. Still, the isolation gave me stamina for solitude and that has been a precious resource at times.

21 October 1943.

During the war, lads were employed by the post office to deliver War Office telegrams. Everybody knew the sound of the small motorcycles used by the telegram boys and every front curtain would twitch sideways, waiting to see which house they would visit. In stories, the messengers of death are usually glossy black ravens or the like, but in Islington in 1943, they were awkward seventeen-year-old boys, like pale-faced sheep, carrying out this terrible task.

That day, I willed the motorcycle to pass by Auntie Eileen's front door and visit another house. When the motorcycle engine puttered to a stop outside the house, I admit that I compiled a list of preferences. If someone in our family had to be dead, I would prefer it to be one of Eileen's sons. If it had to be one of my brothers, then let it be George or Eddie. Not Michael. I'm not proud of that selfish mental list but I'm endeavouring to be honest here. The list was not only shameful but also absurd; to imagine I, or anyone in that war, anyone in human existence, can submit preferences on such things.

Auntie Eileen opened the envelope and read out the name, like drawing a horrible raffle. I don't remember hearing my brother Michael's name—killed in action—but I do recall pacing through the house, unable to decide which room, which space, to put my body. I thought losing Pauline had used up all my capacity for anguish but it turns out there's a bottomless supply. I hyperventilated, over-breathing until I was gulping for air, all my limbs tingling, and so dizzy I stumbled over a chair and onto the floor.

Later, I sobbed in a more regular way, weeping for so long my eyelids were swollen almost shut, my throat excoriated and tight, until I slumped into exhausted sleep.

I woke up in the dimness of the late afternoon to feel the mattress bounce slightly underneath me. Uncle Gil was sitting on the side of the bed, stroking my thigh, rucking my skirt up further each time.

'Poor Betty. You must be very sad. Very sad,' he muttered over and over.

I pushed the hair out of my eyes, still groggy with sleep, and he leaned forward as if about to smooth down my mussed hair. Instead, he put his lips against mine—his lips crusted with white scum, breath sour from cigarettes—and his wet tongue pushed inside my mouth like a slug. I froze, the way so many victims of sexual assault do. (It is heartening that most people now accept the reality of this kind of paralysis of the vulnerable.) The next thing I felt was Uncle Gil's dry, raspy hand pushing aside the gusset of my underpants and pushing a finger inside my vagina.

So, here is the childhood sexual assault a reader may have expected earlier in this story. I apologise for the predictability of it, but the truth is this was an experience for so many kids in my generation (and generations before and after, too).

I like to think that my fury about Michael's death did one good thing: it gave me the energy to barge my way past the paralysis. I believe I let out a grunt of anger in the moment. What I certainly did was shove both my hands against Gil's chest. Because he was sitting on the side of the bed at an awkward angle, he toppled back onto the floor.

I ran out the front door and around the corner to a small park two streets away. I sat on a bench in that always damp, sunless spot until Uncle Gil would have left for the night shift.

My father finally came home in the evening, well drunk and shaky with grief about our Michael. I didn't want to allow Dad's boozy gusts of emotion to cheapen my feelings about the loss of my brother, so I chose a different topic of conversation.

'Uncle Gil is a revolting pig. He touched me downstairs,' I announced.

Dad rattled his head, as if trying to rearrange my words inside his skull into a comprehensible order. 'What? Down here?'

He ran his gaze around the room, as if I was referring to the downstairs part of the house. The misunderstanding would've been worth a laugh if the context had not been so disgusting.

'Uncle Gil touched me down there.'

Dad was scowling now, still confused but with an inkling this was something ugly. 'Beg yours? What rubbish are you . . . What?'

For the sake of clarity, I shouted my reply, complete with clear gesticulation to my groin. 'He touched me between my legs.'

My father's arm flew out so fast, I didn't register anything until the blow of his fist hit my left ear. A stream of words followed—I was a 'stupid girl', 'a liar', 'a slag' and the like. Why had a big-mouth liar like me survived when the precious children he loved best had been killed? His voice was soggy with booze, words crumbling like wet cake, and I was momentarily quite deaf from the whack to my ear, but I heard enough.

I recall packing a bag with a few clothes and walking out the door within two minutes. Even allowing for the heightened drama of memory, my exit was decisive and rapid. That was the last time I saw my father.

8 May 1945. VE Day.

Bells were bonging nonstop in every village. Added to that were car horns, yahooing, radios cranked up loud and the swooping voices of kids at street parties, eating treats conjured out of whatever rations their mothers could scrounge. At 3 p.m., all that happily raucous noise was clamped down into silence so everyone could hear Churchill's speech on radios or loudspeakers.

The exhilaration we felt on that day was intoxicating. Almost six years of fear and grief and dislocation—all those accumulated feelings had suddenly been transformed into euphoric brain chemicals by a powerful catalytic process.

Unlike moments of private joy, such as the birth of a baby, this was a public euphoria, sweeping us along on a gust of shared feeling that gathered even more air as people grinned at each other and hugged strangers in the street.

It was growing dark by the time my pals and I grabbed a lift into town, all four of us clinging to the running boards of a lorry, blowing kisses to folks as we trundled through villages. I felt a surge of delight to see lights everywhere—streetlamps, porchlights, strings of party lights—after years of blackout nights. We were headed to the Victory Gala at the Locarno Ballroom in Liverpool with the intention of dancing until our feet swelled up like turnips.

For eighteen months, I'd been working at ROF Kirkby, a munitions factory ten miles north of Liverpool—almost twenty thousand of us working in that Royal Ordnance Factory, almost all women. Like many of the single girls, I lived in the YWCA dormitory on site, eating meals in the canteen.

The work was a hard slog in grating, thudding, clanking noise, with three shifts a day so there could be continuous operation on the floor, producing detonators and filling shells. All of us understood the danger: the risk of explosions and the toxicity of the materials we were handling. During my time there, accidents killed sixteen people and many more were injured.

I realise it seems strange to say that I loved it. It was partly the sense of purpose: producing munitions to protect our brothers and husbands and sweethearts. (We never allowed ourselves to imagine the shells we made would likely kill someone else's brother, let alone children in a town somewhere in Germany.) But mainly what I loved was being folded into the camaraderie with those women— mostly working class, mostly Scousers, many of them boisterous and hilarious. I'd never been part of a gang of women before.

On my first day, moving into the dormitory, as anxious as you might expect a fifteen-year-old to be, alone in an unfamiliar place, I went to the communal washroom to splash my face with water. I was just turning on the tap, when I heard a young woman's voice behind me.

'Watch how you go with them taps. Look what happened to me.'

The woman held up her left hand, wiggling her thumb and two fingers to show off the stump of her third finger and the pinky missing altogether.

I jerked with surprise and yanked the tap round too far, sending a blast of water into the sink that bounced up to spray my face.

'Ooh, sorry, love! Didn't mean to scare ya!'

She laughed and bounded forward to offer me her bath towel.

That bold, kind young woman was Brenda Goodbody, an eighteen-year-old from Birkenhead, who became my best friend at Kirkby. Brenda Goodbody and I both had boozy dads. We both liked to joke about. We both loved to dance.

Most weekends, there would be a dance on someplace that Brenda and I could reach on foot, on borrowed bicycles or by cadging lifts. Dances full of local girls, British servicemen and the Americans. Brenda had impressive make-do sewing skills and, thanks to her, our gang of Kirkby girls would show up at those dances in snazzy dresses.

By the age of fifteen, I'd finally grown into my adult facial features, so I didn't unnerve people in the way I had as a child. Still, I was never one of the pretty girls. A charitable person might've described me as 'handsome'.

But I was a good dancer, so I could make an attractive impression on the dancefloor. Once a young man had asked me to dance and we were close enough to talk, I could often make him laugh. I told myself it was a good system: if a fellow made an advance to me, it proved he wasn't superficial enough to be dazzled by pretty, and then if he stayed around, it meant he was interesting enough to fancy a girl who talked and talked funny. So I was filtering out the shallow nincompoops.

Hang on, I need to be more honest here. There is some truth in the above paragraph but an honest account must also include how much I *yearned* to be pretty and any contortion of thought I applied to my situation was poor consolation for not being.

The first time I saw American GIs doing the new dances—the jitterbug and the Lindy Hop—I was busting to have a proper go. One night at the Grafton Ballroom in Liverpool, I scanned the dancefloor to identify a guy who clearly knew how to swing a partner through those nimble moves. I then steered my galumphing English partner across the floor to put myself into Jitterbug Guy's field of vision so he might notice I was a reasonable dancer.

When the band played the intro to the next number, Jitterbug Guy came over to me. 'Would you like to dance, miss?' Polite, the way the Americans usually were.

He was encouraging, a natural teacher, guiding me through the basic steps, then perfectly judging the moment to add a new move. By the third number we danced together, I was confident enough to let him swing me up and round and along the floor. Let me tell you, my ancient limbs can feel the thrill of those moves even now.

'Thank you! That was so wonderful!' I said, my words punctuated by gulps of air, breathless from the exertion of the dancing. 'Thank you so much.'

'Oh no, thank *you*, miss,' he replied. 'I gotta say, you're a quick study.'

If anyone is hoping this is the opening beat, the meet-cute, of a romantic story, I will have to disappoint. I never saw Jitterbug Guy again after that dance at the Grafton. He must've been shipped to fight in Europe or the Pacific. The reader might join me in hoping that sweet man survived the war and went on to have a happy life.

There were other dances and other GIs with whom I could Lindy Hop and jive. I suppose there was a sexual charge while dancing with American soldiers, but not always. Sometimes it was just about the kinetic thrill of swooping and bopping around the dancefloor with a skilful partner. Those young men were being constantly hurled into danger, death close enough to breathe on their faces, we girls were handling explosives every day and we had all absorbed the loss of people dear to us, so it's not surprising that we grabbed on to the life force of dancing together.

I won't be coy here. The 'life forces' pumping through those dance halls were not only of the chaste variety. Lust was present and powerful.

Lying on her bed in our dormitory room, Brenda could rabbit on for hours about the various GIs she imagined snogging. While she cooed about their eyes, their forearms, their lips, she would squeeze a pillow between her legs.

My friend's lust inspired me to try some pillow-squeezing and solo exploration of my own. The bathroom was the best opportunity—being one of the few places in dormitory life with any privacy. I found I could generate pleasurable sensations in my undercarriage but I had no idea how to direct those sensations towards anything like a climax. Years later, once I'd experienced an actual orgasm, it was a matter of 'oh, I see'. But back then, it was like wandering through a shop, searching for an item you couldn't describe to the retail assistant or even picture for yourself. It turned out I had been in the right shop but still clueless.

Some people may be discomforted or even disgusted by a woman approaching her hundredth birthday writing about her orgasms—or, as things stood in 1945, the lack thereof. But sexual pleasure is one of life's marvellous consolations and warrants a place in this story.

I pursued my libidinous explorations with human partners, not just pillows—sometimes with Americans, sometimes local lads—in laneways beside dance venues, on top of canvas bags of clean laundry in the back of a lorry, on gym mats in the storage area under a stage. I loved the kissing and the petting. Blessedly, Uncle Gil's groping had not ruined that for me. And a few times, when things went further with the young men, it was thrilling. The trouble was, before I had a chance to push those welcome sensations towards a climax, the men would push ahead on a different timetable.

I'll leave orgasms there for now and get back to VE Day.

That night, laughing with my friends in the Locarno, no one would have guessed, to see my exultant face, that there was a rumble of apprehension underneath my joy. Now the war was over, the Kirkby job, the purposeful structure of it, the sisterhood of it, would be over. I had no idea what my life would be after the war and that made me anxious.

There were too many revellers crammed into the ballroom, bodies pressed together, the lungs of all the people dancing and laughing were sucking up too much of the oxygen. I suddenly felt suffocated, woozy, and a gritty charcoal film spread across my eyeballs.

I heard Brenda's voice slice through the music. 'You orright, Betty?'

She managed to catch me just before my head hit the floor.

9 May 1945.

Thanks to the fainting spell in the Locarno, I found myself, the next day, in a doctor's consulting room in one of the posher towns somewhere east of Kirkby. I believe the appointment had been arranged by a nurse from our factory's infirmary.

Dr Prowse was in his sixties, wearing a suit made of tweed fabric so coarse and bristled you could've grated carrots with it. His hands felt rough too, as he dug two fingers into my vagina while his other hand pushed down on my belly. He pointedly avoided eye contact with me and his lips were pursed so tightly, they'd gone bloodlessly white.

'You're four months along,' he pronounced. 'So if you were planning on taking yourself to some backstreet woman to have this pregnancy taken care of, you've left it too late, missy.'

Having had no clue I was up the duff, I hadn't exactly been shopping for abortion providers. Brenda had advised me to insist the lads use rubber johnnies or pull out. I'd done my best to hold to that policy, but I suppose most men can maintain a better control of rhythm on the dancefloor than they can when approaching the climax of a knee-trembler with a girl in a furtive location.

My mind scrambled through the last four months. If I'd felt weary or a little nauseous, I had assumed that was the strain of shiftwork. My monthlies had been late—nothing unusual about that for me—and then I'd had a heavy, crampy period. It was only years later, with some reproductive education, I realised that I might have miscarried the twin of the baby that the doctor had now found in my uterus. I couldn't be sure who the father was—either an Englishman called Fred or Ted (the dance hall was noisy) or an American GI (Jim?). Either way, he was a good dancer.

'Get dressed,' Dr Prowse said sharply, disgusted, as if I was at that moment cavorting naked in his surgery with the loose morals that had landed me here.

When I reprocess the scene now—a frightened, anaemic seventeen-year-old subjected to an unnecessarily harsh pelvic exam by a censorious bastard—well, let's just say if it were my own daughter, I'd barge into that room, insert a speculum in that doctor's mouth, crank it open and shove his tweedy jacket down his pitiless, nasty, misogynist throat.

Apologies if that was a bit much. Satisfying to write it down though.

'Do you have family you can go to?' asked Dr Prowse.

I shook my head. What remained of my family wasn't a solution to this problem.

'No,' he grunted, as if the family situation was also my fault. 'The only thing to be done is to make sure this poor baby goes to a good family that can look after it, hmm?'

He snatched up an old-fashioned pen to write a note. Each scratch of the steel nib on the paper made me flinch. I was unprotected, skinless, vulnerable to each abrasive sound hitting my flesh.

There has been much written in recent decades about our capacity to block certain memories. The process makes sense to me at an intellectual level, but it remains hard to accept there are blanks in my own mental files. Here is the little I recall of the next four months.

Dr Prowse arranged for me to see out the rest of my pregnancy in Medford, a village in Cheshire. I was given board and lodging in exchange for housework and kitchen duties in a modest, freestanding brick house with a small garden.

The household was briskly run by a woman, Gertrude, and one of my duties was to cook a defined list of meals for her, her dozy elderly father and twenty-something son, Edgar. Edgar had been damaged in the war in some unspecified fashion and rarely came out of his room. Gertrude spent most of her days at Medford Hall, the stately home at the top of the hill overlooking the village, where she was employed in an administrative role.

Days would go by when I didn't address a word to another human being. I cooked and cleaned, slept a great deal and filled my limited leisure time reading the one small shelf of books in that house. During my time in Medford, it stands to reason that I would have felt the baby move inside me—those nudging, rolling sensations I treasured in my later pregnancies—but I don't recall registering any movements.

One afternoon, in my eighth month, I was standing sideways at the stove to accommodate my huge, taut belly.

Gertrude appeared in the kitchen doorway to announce, 'You're a lucky girl. They're arranging for you to have this baby up at the big house with the doctor who does the painless deliveries.'

I had no idea who 'they' were, nor did I feel especially lucky, but painless sounded like a good option.

There is an almost impenetrable blur covering the labour and birth, but it's not just a self-protective memory block. The mental fog was made denser by a chemically induced amnesia. 'Painless' or 'twilight' birthing was a fashion among some wealthy women at the time. That was why Gertrude was keen to point out that an unmarried working-class slag like me was lucky to have access to this privilege. For a twilight birth, women were given a combination of morphine, to dull pain, and scopolamine, an amnesiac drug derived from nightshade plants.

I have only a handful of fuzzy images—a woman in a white nurse's uniform steering me into one of the stately bedrooms at Medford Hall; heavy blue velvet curtains drawn so it was dark; a fair-haired woman coming into the room and saying hello to me in a peculiar, posh voice; a male doctor announcing to whomever else was in the room that the newborn was a girl.

My memory only properly rebooted two days later, back in the tiny bedroom in the Medford village house. I was woolly-headed, my belly loose and spongey, with a thudding ache in my breasts which were bound tightly with sheeting to discourage milk production. There were mysterious welt marks on my upper arms that didn't tally with delivering a baby. Years later, my research into twilight birth explained the welts: labouring women, in drugged confusion, would sometimes thrash about and injure themselves. Soft ties—scarves or towels—were used to restrain their limbs. Only wealthy women could afford this 'treatment'.

I never gave informed consent to that drug cocktail, but I suspect I would have signed anything put in front of me. I never signed adoption papers either. Even with my limited knowledge of the world, I understood that an unofficial adoption practice was happening. Some upper-class woman could pass my baby off as her biological child, with a fake birth certificate issued by the doctor, and no record of a relinquishing mother.

Once, for one brief moment during that pregnancy, I had fantasised about presenting my swollen self on the doorstep of the

Nancarrows' house. Rose Nancarrow would embrace me, cook me custard, deliver the baby, then help me give my infant a sublime Cornish childhood. But I shut down that fantasy quickly. I didn't have the practical means nor the sense of entitlement to attempt anything like that, so it was self-flagellating even to picture it.

Why didn't I ask where my baby would go to live? Why didn't I ask anything at all? We're back to shame. That's the only explanation I can offer.

A week after the baby was born, I was given a lift to the railway station in Chester. The pregnancy, the birth—it all seemed unreal, with recollections blurred by drugs and no external threads connecting me to any of it. It was as if it had never happened. But as we now know, the body carries memories the mind cannot always access.

FOUR

Thursday, 22 May 1947.

The SS *Asturias* pulled away from the wharf in Southampton, bound for a port ten thousand miles away, with me on board.

Don't picture a luxury ocean liner. The ships that ferried us all from Europe to the Antipodes were former troopships or merchant navy vessels that had been adapted for war, not for passenger comfort. Conditions were cramped and basic but we migrants—all of us displaced or hopeful or broken or adventurous or some combination of the above—we weren't complaining.

I shared a poky cabin with three other single women. There was a pair of friends, girls from Crawley who'd scraped together just enough courage between the two of them to make this journey.

'Hiya!' I said, as I swung my suitcase through the door. 'I'm Betty. Is this bunk free?'

The instant those two girls heard my working-class accent—it would only have taken two or three syllables—they calculated I was beneath them.

The slightly bolder one rolled her eyes and spoke to her friend as if I weren't right there, inches from them. 'Well, there you are, Eunice. The steward did say they'd have to mix all types together in the cabins.' Then she turned to me with undisguised contempt. 'I suppose if you've been put in here with us, you can take that bunk. I should say, we're hoping to keep our cabin nice and tidy.'

And then she sighed to express her lack of optimism that a low-class individual (me) could manage tidiness. I was tempted to give her a mouthful of filthy language so untidy it would make her hair curl, but I restrained myself, given we'd be sharing these close quarters for the next five weeks.

Please note: those girls were hardly posh types themselves, but as self-defined upper-lower-middle-class misses, the Crawley Two were confident they sat several rungs up from me.

Apart from the sunshine and open space, one of the reported main attractions of Australia was the lack of a class system, but it seemed these two had decided to smuggle snobbery on board, like an invasive pest they were importing to a new country. I pictured the bright Australian sun beaming down so hot and strong that it would dry up such fetid class sludge and leave a clean, sun-bleached, even platform for everyone.

When Pearl, our fourth cabin-mate, arrived and opened her mouth—"Ow do!"—she was also swiftly categorised and dismissed with a twist on the faces of the Crawley girls.

Pearl Jowett was a working-class Yorkshire lass who'd signed up for the journey on impulse after being jilted by her fiancé. She was extraordinarily pretty—the prettiest human I'd ever seen. Huge cornflower-blue eyes, cute nose, lushly curled lips, milky skin, all her features positioned perfectly on a heart-shaped face, framed by strawberry-blonde curls. I'd never thought of a person's ears as a body part that could be notably pretty, but Pearl's ears were. She was very short but very shapely and even the angle at which her breasts nestled on her chest was lovely.

In the presence of such a beautiful woman, I felt my internal organs clench into a defensive knot, as if her beauty were an assault on me. I'm not proud of this reaction, from a feminist perspective especially, but I'm trying to be honest about how my sense of inadequacy functioned.

Pearl Jowett was such a genuinely innocent soul, she didn't realise I had thrown up my guard against her. And I'm not sure she even registered the scorn radiating at her from the Crawley girls; she remained sweetly friendly to that sour pair for the whole voyage. Then again, Pearl had an instinct, like a small stray animal, to seek out a gentle touch, and the first day in our cabin, that instinct directed her to me.

She spun around to offer me a big-eyed smile. 'The boat is a whopper, isn't it! Do you want to come and have a stickybeak with me, Betty?'

Pearl was so unguarded, childlike in the best way, it would've been mean-spirited to resist. So I headed out into the corridor with her to explore the decks and dining saloons and recreation areas of SS *Asturias*. Pearl gasped with delight at everything we saw—it was all 'champion!'.

She was effusively impressed that I'd researched a few basic facts about Australia (population seven and a half million, Ben Chifley was Prime Minister, wombats and kangaroos have pouches but the platypus lays eggs) and she peppered me with breathless questions.

About fifteen minutes into our self-guided tour of the ship, Pearl clasped my hand in hers and said, 'I like you so much, Betty! I hope we can be friends!'

Her declaration was so disarming, so winning. Pearl Jowett and I were friends from that moment on.

Later that evening, after our dinner-sitting, Pearl and I returned to the cabin to find one of the Crawley girls (Eunice) sobbing on her bunk.

'Have we made a mistake?' she bleated. 'What if Australia is—oh dear . . . was it a mistake to leave?'

The other Crawley girl patted her back, but with brisk, firm strokes that landed somewhere between a comforting pat and a slap of rebuke. 'Come on now, Eunice,' she kept saying. 'Stop this crying. Those other two are back now.'

Pearl and I folded ourselves away in our bunks as discreetly as possible in that tiny shared space, and lying there, I interrogated my own feelings. I was apprehensive about jumping into the hot, marsupial-filled unknown but I did not regret leaving England for a new life in Australia.

Let me scoot back for a moment to the day I decided to emigrate.

Some months after my time in Medford, I found myself living in a two-up two-down in Streatham. The place was rented by my sister Margaret and her husband Duncan, with our Josie and me sharing the small back bedroom.

Our communal living situation was not about loving family togetherness. It was down to the housing shortage in post-war London, but it was also thanks to my sister Margaret's sense of responsibility to provide a bed for her younger siblings, however ungrateful we were about it.

Duncan was the most boring man on earth (although it must be said, I've met a number of strong contenders for that title). He had insisted that Margaret give up work after their wedding, even though she enjoyed her job and they could have done with the extra money. He saw it as a sign of upward social mobility that, even as a tenant in this mean little house, he could support his wife. It must have been brain-witheringly dull for Margaret to faff around that house all day, waiting to fall pregnant.

I stayed out of the house as much as possible, at my various workplaces or sitting in warm cafes with a book.

Josie's princess tendencies had taken an underworld turn during the time I'd been away. Still only sixteen, she peroxided her hair a brittle white blonde and plastered her face with makeup, including a slash of red lipstick the colour of dried blood. There were various boyfriends who all appeared to be low-grade criminals and Josie would often bring home items (watches, whiskey, parcels of meat, once an electric toaster) that were clearly stolen goods. Her employment status was sketchy but she somehow always had cash to pay rent to Duncan and purchase hair bleach. She was frequently drunk, her moods lurching between brassy vivacity and weeping jags with incoherent ranting about our father's failings.

I should explain that our dad had died by this point. A month after VE Day he disappeared, his body found three days later in the water near Camden Lock, wedged under a barge. Margaret had tried to send word of his death to me at ROF Kirkby, but by then I was ensconced in my shameful pregnant seclusion. When I eventually heard the news, I don't recall crying. But as many of us know, such losses can sit like unexploded ordnance in the body, to be detonated by some later trigger.

Back in London, I'd bounced between dull jobs, and by the beginning of 1947, I was working in a commercial laundry. Let me assure the reader that I have never been too stuck-up for manual employment—evidenced by the fact that I'd loved the factory work at Kirkby. But the only jobs I could find in London offered none of that purpose or a skerrick of the fun I'd had with the Kirkby girls. As the weeks unspooled, I could feel my innards shrivelling. And when I went out for the occasional night of dancing, looking across the dance hall at the sort of man I would most likely marry and envisaging the life I would most likely have with that man, my innards withered even further. The trouble is, an inertia can set in, making it seem impossible to determine your own future.

One evening I was sitting in the Streatham kitchen, and while Margaret was preparing some bland stew for dinner, I picked at the crumbly cuticles on my hands which were a lovely shade of Dermatitis Red thanks to the laundry job.

'Did you know,' I said to Margaret with a tart little laugh, 'when I was a kid, I really believed I would pass the exam to get into the grammar school and then I'd go to university? You all must've thought it was a sad joke, me thinking I was clever enough for that.'

'Oh,' said Margaret.

I looked up to see she had frozen, hands in mid-air above the gristly meat she was dicing.

'What? What kind of "Oh" is that?' I asked.

'I'd better—I don't . . . Wait here,' she said and ran upstairs.

Margaret brought down a carton with the papers our father had rescued from the bombed house. She flipped through the contents, then slid an envelope across the table to me.

It was the official letter to say I'd been offered a place in the grammar school. My eyes shot up to the date—June 1939.

Unnerved by my silence, Margaret voiced what she imagined my thoughts were. 'Dad should've shown you the letter back then. He should've let you go to the grammar school.'

My brain lurched around to calculate the life I could have had, but I couldn't picture anything, my vision blinded by rage. I'd been robbed. That booze-sodden man whose only real contribution to my life had been the sperm that had infiltrated my mother's exhausted uterus to produce me—that bastard had robbed me. (In the moment, I didn't take any comfort that I had passed the exam and so perhaps was not as stupid as I feared.)

Margaret prattled on nervously. 'You know our dad reckoned a grammar school education was a waste of time for a girl. And he got it in his head you'd be unhappy there, so he thought he was doing the right thing by you. Not that I think—I mean, he was wrong not to show you, Betty, but Dad just . . . Then, when the war started, he said you probably couldn't have gone to the grammar school anyway.'

'Hold on.' I aimed my attention fiercely at Margaret. 'When did you know about this letter?'

'Oh. Well . . . while you were living with the family in Cornwall, Dad showed me.'

'You never said.'

'It was too late by then anyway,' Margaret said in a small voice.

That was the moment I started shouting at her. I can't remember or maybe prefer not to remember my exact words, but it was something like, 'You should've told me, you stupid dozy cow!'

It was unfair to offload my anger on blameless Margaret but I kept shouting at her anyway. 'What am I supposed to do about this fucking letter now?'

Margaret's breathing was shuddery with tears. 'I thought you should know you passed the exam.'

'Well, it's too late now, isn't it, you daft cow! You let me down. You let me down and now—'

Josie's astringent voice cut through my rant. 'That's a bit rich coming from you, Betty.'

I hadn't noticed my younger sister had come in, leaning against the kitchen doorframe, with her peroxided hair like a stiff helmet and her lipstick-caked mouth stretched into a harsh smile.

'Don't you dare feel sorry for yourself,' snapped Josie. 'How about the way you let me down?'

'What? How did I—'

'You scarpered and left me with Uncle Gil. You knew he was a molester.'

'Oh—uh, I didn't exactly—I mean, he groped me one time but I didn't know—'

'Bollocks. Tell yourself that if it makes you feel better. But you knew.'

She was right. I must've known, but I'd been too consumed with my own predicament to think through what would happen to her once I left.

Josie was trying to sound hard-boiled, but I noticed her shoulder slip against the doorframe and heard the clack of her high heels on the floor as she lost her balance. She was already somewhere along the way to drunk and her tough performance quickly crumbled into shrill ranting and tears.

'I kept thinking, *My sister Betty will come back and rescue me.*' Josie fired the words at me with flecks of spittle. 'She'll punch Uncle Gil in the goolies and rescue me. But you never came. Two years I had him all over me and in me. You knew and you left anyway. It was your stinking fault.'

I can't blame Josie for tearing into me. Everyone left thirteen-year-old Josie at the mercy of that man. By 'everyone', I include our dad, Auntie Eileen, any adults in the vicinity who had eyes in their heads, and myself. I may have been a teenager with limited power, but I should have stayed, made more noise, protected my younger sister. That's one of the failings in my life I will always regret.

Margaret attempted to be a peacemaker. 'Come on now, Josie. No point churning up things we can't do anything about now.'

That was like hurling kerosene on a fire and Josie flared up, barking through a list of the ways Margaret had let her down too.

I walked out the front door, leaving my sisters shouting at each other, weeping. Our inadequate parents, poverty, a war—the saddest part of that legacy was that we siblings couldn't support each other. We were damaged in such a way that all we could do was add to the damage.

I figured there was nothing for me in England, other than dead people and corrosive feelings I could not manage. The next morning,

I caught the Tube to Australia House in The Strand and put in my application to migrate under the 'Ten Pound Pom' scheme.

On our second day at sea, the crew closed the portholes on the lower decks because the ship was moving into the rougher open waters of the Atlantic, passing the Bay of Biscay. To escape the over-breathed air of the shared cabin, I went up to walk on the deck and suck in lungfuls of oxygen.

The ocean swell was pitching the SS *Asturias* around and many of the passengers were feeling seasick, bellies roiling. Me, I have iron guts, so I felt fine to keep walking.

I turned a corner, past a huge metal funnel and saw a young man sitting on a deck chair, apparently as iron-gutted as myself. I noticed he was reading a book so I sidled around to get a squiz at the cover.

When the young man looked up, I quickly twisted my neck away so abruptly the movement was akin to a chiropractic adjustment of my cervical vertebrae. I stared out at the ocean until I figured it was safe to sneak another look at the reading man.

His eyes were still lifted from the page, gazing out at the same patch of ocean as I was. He was tall, lean but not scrawny, with strong-looking hands and forearms, shirtsleeves rolled back. There was a loveliness to his face, his neck, his jawline, that struck me as a physical pang. Grey-green eyes, luscious dark wavy hair and skin so pale that even though he was clean shaven, his facial hair created a five o'clock shadow that was pretty much round the clock. I've always found that an attractive feature.

Possibly my portrayal of this man is coming across as too superficial, but the truth is that his physical appeal, combined with the fact that he was reading a book, commanded my attention in a way I'd never experienced before.

Burmese Days by George Orwell. That was the book he was reading. I wanted to strike up conversation with something insouciant like, 'Oh, I've been meaning to read that book. Is it good?' But the truth is, I was too insecure to try any sort of conversational gambit.

Then—a miracle—the man offered me a cautious smile, an invitation to speak. All he received back from me was a gormless stare. He would have every reason to assume my demeanour was unsociable, possibly disapproving, certainly frosty. His smile duly froze on his face and crumbled away.

This self-sabotaging behaviour was typical of me. Often, the more I've liked someone, the more clumsily I handled myself—to the point of giving the exact opposite impression of my desires.

I strode quickly away along the deck, as if I had some urgent place to be, to remove my awkward self from the presence of this interesting young man who would not be interested in someone like me and who would surely be embarrassed and/or annoyed to have me hang around him. But a second later, I was forced to an abrupt halt when a spray of vomit flew across my path. A family of four had burst out of their cabin, with the goal of spewing their guts over the side into the ocean. Unfortunately, they didn't quite make it and the decking around my feet was very quickly slick with vomit. (The more squeamish reader may wish to skip over this section, but it is essential to explain an important encounter in my story.) Within seconds, more passengers came staggering out onto the deck to puke.

The reading man and I headed back to our respective cabins, but when the ship lurched sideways, both of us lost our footing on the slippery deck. I felt myself slide, off balance, about to fall onto that unpleasant surface, as was he. At just that moment, we were close enough to reach out and grab each other's hand to steady ourselves.

'Whoo!' I laughed and our eyes locked as he laughed too.

We held hands, two strangers, so we could pick our way to the other side of the slippery puddles, like beginner skaters stepping across an ice rink. We only released our grip once we were safely on a dry section of decking.

He introduced himself with a little formal bow. 'Leo Newman.' There was a slight accent I couldn't identify, or rather I could hear the precision of speech of someone for whom English was not their first language.

'Betty Rankin.' I did a mock curtsy, lifting my skirt clear of the vomit, and Leo Newman laughed.

''Scuse us, folks!' a crew member sang out, waving us aside so he could sluice the deck with buckets of water. Leo and I were required to hurry in opposite directions to shift out of the way.

Lying on my bunk that night, my brain chewed over which novel I should carry with me in the hope of running into Leo Newman on the deck. I had packed a few books to read on the journey, but most were old classics picked up cheap at second-hand stores—George Eliot and Dickens and such—and perhaps not modern enough to impress a man who read Orwell.

Leo had obviously been thinking about book choice too because the next day, there he was in the same chair. He nodded hello to me and then smiled as he lifted up the volume he was reading: *Nausea* by Jean-Paul Sartre.

We both grinned and with that, we were straight back to the level of surprising, sudden connection you can have with another individual when you have saved each other from slipping over in other people's vomit.

'What are you reading?' he asked.

I showed him the book I was nonchalantly carrying: *I, Claudius.* I figured the Robert Graves was the most impressive of the titles I could flash at him.

He nodded. 'Ah. I hear it's wonderful.'

'You can borrow it,' I offered.

'Thank you. I would very much like that. And you must also borrow any of the books I have.'

In the course of the voyage, I lent him *For Whom the Bell Tolls*, *Persuasion* and *The Getting of Wisdom*, an Australian novel by a female writer I was hoping would give me some insight into the country we were sailing towards. From Leo, I borrowed *Brave New World*, then Céline's *Journey to the End of the Night* and other European books I might never have found on my own.

By the fourth day at sea, the *Asturias* was sailing through the much kinder waters of the Mediterranean. Leo and I would meet up on the deck and take turns to look through his field glasses to pick out landmarks along the coastlines.

'The Atlas Mountains!' I squawked, excited to see the solid form of places I'd gazed at as coloured shapes on maps.

I pointed out Gibraltar to our left, the coast of Algeria to our right. I gauged the place beyond our view where Sicily would be. We convinced ourselves we spotted the island of Gozo where Calypso's cave from the *Odyssey* is supposedly located. We certainly scored a decent view of Valletta, capital of Malta, with its spires and domes and high wall.

There was a moment when I panicked that, in my excitement, I might seem to be skiting. I worried that Leo, like a lot of men I knew, would get a snout on about a girl making a show of her knowledge, but he wasn't the tiniest bit snouty. In fact, he smiled and declared me to be his 'valuable guide to the Mediterranean'.

Whether Leo and I were talking about Malta or books or the previous night's dinner, I had to control my tendency to chatter too rapidly, piling words into overstuffed sentences that tumbled out of my mouth. I so very much wanted this man to like me.

In instalments through the next days, we exchanged the stories of our lives so far—my nineteen years and his twenty-two. I did my best to leaven my tales with humour and emphasis on brighter notes (Cornwall, my brother Michael, jitterbugging). I had planned to tone down the portrayal of my father's drunkenness and other sources of family shame. But in the end there was something about this man that prompted me to be more candid than I'd intended. However, I did not mention having given birth.

Leo told me his history in layers, offering the basic timeline, events and locations but without digging down into the flesh of it at first. Leo Newman always avoided any utterances that might seem like an appeal for pity, but I subjected him to a barrage of questions and uncensored exclamations—'How did you feel then?', 'That's awful!', 'You must have been so afraid!'

He was born Leopold Neumann, in a Jewish family, in Leipzig, Germany, with two much older sisters. As the Nazis squeezed tighter, Leo's parents were forced to give up their jobs as teachers and get by working as cleaners. In May 1939, when Leo was fourteen, he was put on a ship sailing from Hamburg to Southampton, one of the Kindertransports, ferrying Jewish children away from danger. His parents promised they would follow as soon as they obtained the necessary papers. Leo never knew if his parents sincerely believed they would be able to join him in England.

He was billeted with a family in Manchester but once he turned sixteen, he was arrested as an enemy alien. One of the few times I ever saw Leo's face twist with bitterness was when he described the humiliation of being marched like a criminal through the streets of Manchester, to be locked up in Warth Mills, an old textile factory repurposed as an internment prison. He was eventually moved to a detention camp on the Isle of Man. Despite the barbed-wire fence, Leo spoke about the joy of being able to swim in the sea there and about the rich, if incomplete, education he gained from the classes offered by his fellow internees, many of them artists, musicians, academics.

He was eventually released from custody, allowed to work in a hotel kitchen, and later as an interpreter, thanks to his strong English.

When the war ended, Leo searched for information about his family. I don't know if it was preferable or much crueller that the news came to him so rapidly, within a few months. His parents, his aunts and uncles, his sisters and their families had all perished.

'I have no wish to go back to Germany. That's not my country anymore,' Leo explained, his voice even and measured, careful not to press into the intense feeling that lay underneath. 'The British sent me to prison for being German, so I don't consider England my country either. I thought, *Where in the world should I live?* I like to swim and they say Australia is a place with beautiful beaches, so here I am.' He punctuated that with a radiant smile, as if the prospect of swimming on an Australian beach could counterbalance all the rest.

The families with children travelling on the *Asturias* tended to stick together, colonising certain areas of the ship. That left the solo passengers, like Pearl and me, to form our own little on-board community with the other singles.

At our allocated times in the dining saloon, I noticed one woman always eating alone, always sitting very straight-backed. She had long dark hair, tied back with a blue scarf, resolute brown eyes and strong eyebrows. I'd never seen eyebrows that seemed to have their own defiant authority in the world. The expression on this woman's face was so grave, it was difficult to imagine her ever smiling.

My new pal Pearl was an enthusiastic collector of gossip. (Please note: there is no judgement in me saying that. I'd argue that a little gossip of the kind-hearted sort is better than a lack of curiosity about our fellow humans.) Pearl had collected some intelligence on the Dark-Browed Serious Woman: she was Greek, didn't speak much

English and was travelling to Sydney to marry a man she knew only from a photograph.

During dinner on the first two nights, the Greek woman was virtually trapped at the table with the Crawley girls who kept their nasty little backs curled away from her, whispering to each other with blatant contempt.

It's arguable that my main motivation was annoyance at the rudeness of the Crawley two, possibly it was sheer nosiness—me being curious to know what it would feel like to travel across the globe to marry a stranger—but I'd like to think it was at least partly kindness that prompted me to make one of the best decisions I ever made in my life: at the next dinner, I sat down at the table opposite the Greek woman and said, 'Hello. My name's Betty.'

She jerked her torso slightly back, wary to have someone bowl up to her like this, then she replied in a formal tone, 'I'm Athena.'

With no proper polite filter, I blurted at her, 'Crikey! You're a goddess!'

Athena laughed and a smile transformed her face into a luminous thing, with those fabulous eyebrows adding their own emphatically joyful brushstroke. (Excuse me going on about Athena's eyebrows to an extent that verges on comical. The point is, they were a notable feature of a woman I cherished; a woman I still miss very much.)

It was one of those accidents of physiognomy—Athena's face often looked so impenetrably solemn that when she did smile in such a transformative way, it seemed like an achievement to have elicited the smile. It certainly felt like a special gift to be on the receiving end of it.

Pearl zipped across to join our table with friendly exuberance, and Athena responded warmly. She conversed in tentative English at first, but as Pearl's chatter reached hummingbird speed, Athena struggled to follow, seeking extra clues by watching Pearl's mouth form words.

When Pearl excused herself to dart away, Athena exhaled, glad of a respite from the effort of deciphering another language. I made a show of eating my dinner to let the respite last a little longer.

Eventually, Athena said, 'I like your friend. But she speaks so fast.'

I nodded and laughed. 'I sometimes don't understand half of what she says.'

Athena smiled back, but also tipped her head slightly, wanting me to know she knew I was fibbing to be kind, wanting me to understand she was a woman of dignity and perception. I realise that's a lot of meaning to extract from one smile but I believe my interpretation was correct.

When I had signed up for this voyage, there was some courage required, I suppose, to travel to the other side of the planet, to a country where I didn't know a soul. But I was a native English speaker emigrating to an anglophone country. For Athena, the leap demanded a much larger amount of courage.

Suddenly buzzing with that realisation, I blurted, 'How about I give you some English lessons!'

I immediately regretted making such a blunt suggestion, which might sound patronising towards a woman who was clearly self-reliant and proud.

But then she replied, 'I will be glad. But for you, this is—'

When she paused to search for a word, I was able to reassure her. 'It'll be fun. We have a lot of days on this ship to fill up. You would be doing me a favour.'

So Athena Koutsis and I met up every morning for an hour of language learning. I would cook up useful scenarios that Athena would be likely to encounter once she was in Australia. I would act out the role of a butcher, say, while she ordered sausage mince. I incorporated phrases like 'g'day' and 'cobber' and our weather vocabulary focused on words like 'scorching', 'muggy'. Sometimes my butcher character would get carried away with chitchat about pet kangaroos and wombats, sending the two of us into fits of giggles.

It soon became clear that Athena's knowledge of English was already substantial, but she was tentative, wary of sounding stupid by speaking imperfectly. This was a blockage I experienced myself later in my life, learning Spanish: fluency is bound up with bold acceptance of the risk of sounding wonky. Anyway, I did my best to bolster her confidence with praise and Athena would tip her head down, awkward but delighted. In those moments this stoic grown-up woman looked like a vulnerable girl. I fell in love with her, in that way we can fall in love with a friend, platonic but thrilling to the soul.

Athena grew up on Kastellorizo, a small triangular island in the Dodecanese, a mile off the coast of Turkey. Snatched back and forth by Neapolitan kings, sultans, Venetians and others for centuries, Kastellorizo was now part of Greece. By the turn of the century, there was little on the island to keep people there and a huge percentage of the population just up and left, ten thousand inhabitants eventually dwindling to a few hundred. Athena's widowed mother still lived on the island with one of her sons.

In 1939, Athena had travelled to London to look after another brother's children. Stranded in England by the war, she helped out in the family's vegetable wholesaling business, picking up English and learning to do the book-keeping.

By 1947, Athena was considered cumbersomely old, at twenty-one, to be unmarried. She hated the idea of being a leftover, a problem to be solved, and she dreaded the prospect of life as one of the spinsters rattling around on Kastellorizo. As a last resort, her brother sent her photo to a friend in Sydney who showed it to Nick Samios, a builder, part of the Kastellorizian diaspora. After a few letters back and forth, Athena accepted Nick's proposal.

'He seems like a kind man. I believe we can make a life together,' she said. Whenever she spoke about entering into this marriage, she sounded unsentimental but at the same time hopeful and committed.

I confided in Athena about pretty much my whole life, except the baby and the fact that I was smitten with Leo Newman, the young man who joined our little gang of single travellers for evening strolls around the ship. Athena felt comfortable with Leo right from the start. I could hear the way he adjusted his English for her benefit, separating the words slightly and keeping the consonants crisp to ease comprehension. More evidence of the unobtrusive kindness of this man.

On 3 June, the *Asturias* docked at Port Said, the small Egyptian city at the entrance to the Suez Canal, and passengers were allowed ashore for four hours. Pearl had been keen to join our single travellers shore party, but after breakfast, she disappeared with some new friend. That left a trio of us to go exploring—Leo, Athena and me—until, at the last minute, Athena claimed she was feeling unwell.

'You two go. If I feel better, I will come later,' she said and darted a smile at me that expressed as clearly as a neon sign that she'd guessed I was keen on Leo, so she was scheming to send us off alone together.

Walking down the gangway alongside Leo Newman, my belly contracted in anxiety. If he suspected that I regarded this shore expedition as a date, he might feel snookered and be obliged to rebuff me. Which would be too embarrassing to endure. So I kept my jaw clenched to avoid any stray hopeful expression making its way onto my face.

'Are you feeling all right, Betty?' asked Leo, noticing my oddly tight facial muscles. 'We don't have to go ashore if you don't—'

'No, let's go.' I strode ahead of him. My plan was to be nonchalant, even taciturn.

Any restraint I was attempting failed me within moments of stepping into Port Said, hit by the intensity of the first properly foreign place I'd ever been. In the eight decades since, I've travelled to much more exotic places than Port Said, which is hardly a destination high on anyone's list. It did offer the grand Suez Canal Authority building with green domes and white colonnades stretched along the seafront, but much of the city had the charmless scrappiness of a town that had been assembled for the sake of the canal construction project. Nineteen-year-old me had no other exotic locations to compare it to, so I was intrigued. The air was thick with unfamiliar smells and everything about the place—the vehicles, the shop signs and food on display, the grabs of music through doorways, the way people carried their bodies, the vocal melody of the shopkeepers as they called to us in English and then to each other in Arabic—everything was different and so fascinating that I forgot to be taciturn and started exclaiming about it all to Leo.

We spent three hours wandering through the town together, swapping our observations and questions to decipher some of what we were gawping at. Back near the Canal Authority building, Leo and I found information posters in English mounted in a glass case and we stood side by side for a long time to read about the history of the canal.

'I can't believe it!' I said. 'The idea that someone looked at a map and said, "Hey, how about we dig out a waterway so a ship can slide in from the Mediterranean and pop out into the Red Sea. Come on, let's burrow through a continent." It's like a made-up thing in a book.'

I blathered on like that for some time, until I felt Leo staring at me, pressing his lips together as if trying not to laugh.

'You think I sound daft,' I said.

'No, not at all. It is absolutely like a made-up thing in a book.'

Making our way back to the ship, we bought snacks from a stall—delicious pockets of bread filled with spiced vegetables and crunchy nuggets of a nutty substance that I now realise must've been falafel.

I looked up at the huge metal bulk of the *Asturias* that had brought us here. 'It feels like we're very far from home now,' I murmured.

'Which is good,' Leo responded. 'To be far from there is good.'

'Will you miss anyone?'

He nodded. 'But only people who are already dead. So it doesn't matter which country I live in. I can miss them in Australia just as easily as I can miss them in Britain.'

Back on board, we noticed dozens of small hawker boats paddling around the *Asturias*. Some of our fellow passengers—the ones who had been wary of going ashore in a foreign place—were buying trinkets, hauling the purchased items up on ropes to the deck, then throwing the money down to the people in the little boats.

Other passengers were chucking pennies directly into the water for the nasty sport of sniggering at the Egyptian boys who would swim to grab the coins. Like tossing scraps of bread to ducks. Well, worse than that—these people would never have taunted ducks the way they treated those boys.

'Throw one there!' yelled one geezer to his mate. 'See how that one swims around like a brown frog!'

Much uglier words were hurled down at those Port Said boys. I'm sure a reader can imagine the sort of language I mean. It seemed many of my fellow Britons were brazenly, enthusiastically racist.

I don't want to claim some saintly prescience, implying that I held, in 1947, the sort of evolved beliefs that we would expect any informed and decent person to hold now. But I think it's accurate and not too self-satisfied to say that I never shared such contempt for people of colour. I didn't have the education to think in terms of racial equality, but at some gut level, I recoiled at the nasty slurs. Those local boys in the water were human beings doing their best to get by and it didn't sit well with me for any person to be spoken about that way.

On from Port Said, the *Asturias* made its way down the narrow channel of the Suez Canal, through the Red Sea, stopped briefly in Aden and then sailed south into the expanse of the Indian Ocean.

After two weeks at sea, my fervent friendship with Leo Newman had not erupted into a proper romance—many hours of enthusiastic talk, laughter and sometimes deep confidences, but neither of us had yet made an unambiguously flirtatious gesture, let alone a physical move.

On 7 June, the day after the ship crossed the Equator, passengers were treated to a program of celebrations, with crew members dressed up as King Neptune, mermaids and such, special games for the children with sweets flying about generously. Most of the kids and some of the adults donned fancy dress, including individuals in blackface—so shocking to our eyes now.

For the gala dance that night, I wore the most glamorous ensemble I could rustle up, borrowing a clingy pale blue blouse from Pearl. Pearl insisted on doing my makeup and somehow, by some sorcery, pin-curled my frizzy wad of hair into shiny, glamorous movie star waves. When I peeked in the tiny cabin mirror, I had to concede she'd made me look better.

Athena, who planned to enjoy the event from the sidelines, just wore her usual no-nonsense clothes. Pearl's party outfit, on the other hand, was full of nonsense. She borrowed an evening gown from one of the posher passengers in exchange for whipping up a hairdo for the lady. The iridescent turquoise fabric shimmered over Pearl's body, making her look even more luscious than usual. Through her rose-gold hair, she threaded chains with a dozen tiny starfish trinkets bought from the Port Said hawkers and she wore a necklace of caramel-coloured seashells like a saucy mermaid. Even the sulky Crawley girls were enjoying dressing up and Pearl was so fizzy with excitement—lordy, did that woman love a party—she took several swigs of rum to 'calm my nerves'.

I'd never been much of a one for alcohol but that night I grabbed two of the Tropical Delight cocktails the stewards were serving and drank the syrupy concoction so quickly that I was tipsy within a minute of arriving at King Neptune's Crossing the Equator Ball.

I was sitting with Athena at one of the tables when Leo came over, wearing a charcoal suit that made him look even more beautiful to my eyes.

'You look lovely, Betty.'

This comment sent me into a spasm of speculation about what he really meant: a) routine politeness; b) the non-specific lust of a heterosexual male towards pretty much any female; c) an expression of unending love; or d) a pitying insinuation that I had tried too hard.

I was rescued from my awkwardness by a commotion on the dancefloor—whooping shrieks of laughter and a clatter of high heels. Pearl, already well lubricated thanks to the swigs of rum and several cocktails, had lost her balance and barged into other dancing couples.

'Ooh! Sorry! I'm a right lummox! The floor must be slippery!'

Pearl's foxtrot partner, a bony young man, helped her off the slippery floor to the safety of the carpeted area.

'Do you think that dancefloor is dangerously slippery?' Leo asked me with a small smile.

'Could be,' I said with mock concern.

'Should we risk it anyway?'

I nodded. 'We've shown bravery in the past.'

Leo Newman wasn't an accomplished dancer, but he had a careful way of moving so there was no galumphing or toe-squelching. There being a scarcity of male dancers that night, Leo graciously danced with other partners, and I partnered some of the women who were happy for me to be the 'man'.

When the band played the intro to a sultry tune, perfect for slow-dancing, I gulped down another cocktail and smiled at Leo as boldly as I dared. He pretended to slide across the 'slippery' dancefloor and skid to a halt right in front of me.

With the slower tempo of the music, Leo was a more confident dancer, with an attentive, intuitive way of moving with a partner. (Yes, I realise that sounds like an annoyingly earnest sex manual.)

Speaking of sex, I was used to being grabbed by the insistent hands of American GIs and south London lads. There'd been no mistaking their libidinous intentions. But on the *Asturias* dancefloor, Leo never touched me like that, even when our bodies were pressed close, swaying together to the lush music. My churning thoughts were solidifying into a likely conclusion: Leo just liked me as someone to talk to. He enjoyed my company—I was confident of that. He was interested in my views, tolerated, even relished, my sometimes motor-mouth talk, and he appreciated my humour. But when it came to romance, he was after a different kind of woman. Or maybe he was the kind of fellow who was keen on other fellows.

But I was definitely feeling *something* as we danced close. The tingling heat of our hands touching, the delicious pressure of his hand on my waist, our faces only an inch apart so I was breathing against his neck and felt his breath, light but warm, across my temple. I was surely detecting an electric charge between us.

But the 'charge' could well have been static electricity sparking off the synthetic fabric of the blouse I'd borrowed from Pearl. Or maybe it was just the alcohol buzzing through my body. Or it was merely my own lust agitating the molecules in the air between us, so it seemed like a mutual sensation but was in fact a hum of desire moving in only one direction, not answered by matching desire. In those moments, a person can never be sure if she is pumping out hormones to manufacture the frisson unilaterally, and meanwhile the object of her lust just sees himself as dancing with a friend who is acting a bit oddly.

After three slow dances, I was exhausted from the hoping and the doubting and the effort to interpret every detail of Leo's behaviour.

'I'm tired,' I said. 'And the Tropical Delights have gone to my head. I might go to bed now.'

'Oh. Thank you for the dancing,' he said in his politely unreadable way. 'Sleep well, Betty.'

He didn't beg me to stay for one more dance. He didn't ask to escort me back to my cabin. I received the message with a slicing clarity.

Athena had already retired for the night and Pearl was at the far end of the room, in a clinch with a chap, so I was able to slip out of the event and back to the cabin without fuss.

I flopped on my bunk and listened to the Crawley two snoring, well drunk on sugary cocktails. After half an hour, the muffled *thoomp-thoomp* of the band stopped—King Neptune's Ball was clearly winding up. Through the door, I heard squawks of laughter as the last guests stumbled back to their cabins.

I dug the knuckles of my balled fists into my thighs, furious with myself for my cowardice. I'd survived a bombing, I'd manufactured hand grenades, I'd given birth to a baby, I was now sailing across the world to a country where I knew no one, and yet I was too piss-weak to ask a man I liked if he might possibly like me back.

Our ship had just crossed the Equator, the imaginary line slicing the globe into halves, and the symbolism suddenly felt urgent. Sailing into a new hemisphere was a time for daring, not timidity.

I checked my appearance in the cabin mirror—some eye makeup was smudged and my hairdo was breaking free of the smooth curls Pearl had created, the frizz reasserting itself, but I was still presentable.

I took my shoes off so I wouldn't disturb sleeping passengers with clippity heels, and padded along our deck, rehearsing the dialogue I would say when Leo opened his door. It would need to be something from which we could both step back without excruciating embarrassment. Something along the lines of: 'I just want to be clear about the nature of our friendship.' I imagined a variety of responses he might have and what my next line should then be. It was like the little one-act plays I had written for Athena's English lessons, the conversational scenarios with greengrocers and butchers. But this was a real-life scenario in which my heart would be vulnerable, raw. I pictured a butcher slapping my raw heart onto a wooden slab and I laughed at the gruesomeness of the image, even while I skated along on stockinged feet, through the passageways of the SS *Asturias*, to risk my dignity in front of a young man I desired with every part of my body.

I was emerging from a corridor near his cabin when I heard a murmur of voices around the corner. I hung back, not wanting anyone to see me knocking on Leo's door late at night. I recognised the cadence of one of the voices and peeked out to see Pearl, draping herself against a man whose arm was encircling her waist. I then realised it was Leo's arm, holding Pearl close while he fished his key out of his jacket pocket. When his hand slipped a little on the slick fabric of her dress, he pulled her body tighter against his. He was whispering something I couldn't make out but I could hear Pearl cooing, 'Lovely Leo. You're so lovely.'

Then they disappeared together into his cabin.

It can be surprisingly easy, even on a finite piece of geography like a ship at sea, to avoid someone. I would poke my head out to check that a deck was clear of Leo Newman before stepping onto it and I timed visits to the dining hall to prevent any crossover with him. The one time he knocked on my cabin door—'Betty? Are you there? Are you feeling all right?'—I stayed silent until he left. I wasn't angry with him. It was understandable that he would be attracted to gorgeous Pearl. But I didn't want to hear lies out of his mouth or, even worse, declarations of fond friendship. That would've been too humiliating.

I didn't have to try hard to avoid Pearl, despite our sharing a cabin. She took to staying asleep in her bunk in the mornings, missing breakfast, while I would be up early to meet Athena for English lessons. If I did run into Pearl on board, she always seemed distracted or quickly turned the other way, avoiding me, given the awkwardness of the situation.

Every night, just after midnight, Pearl would slide down off the bunk above mine and sneak out of our cabin for a rendezvous with Leo. Hearing the door click as she slipped out, I would lie in bed and conjure up the scene, in piercing detail, of Leo kissing her passionately. I will admit to the reader that I even imagined the two of them having sex. And I will further admit that I found the fantasy arousing—to picture the man I lusted after kissing and caressing and having sex with a woman, even if the woman wasn't me. The images were arousing but at the same time tormenting. The human brain can be a very stupid, self-persecuting organ.

Leo asked Athena about me several times, worried that I was unwell. She assured him I was fine, with perhaps a stomach upset from the heaving waves in the southern Indian Ocean.

Athena was aware something had changed after the ball. Sometimes, during our English conversation sessions, I would feel my friend scrutinising me, but I didn't volunteer any confidences and Athena Koutsis was never a woman who pried.

On 20 June 1947, the *Asturias* docked in Melbourne and many passengers disembarked there. Through the bustle of people hauling luggage along the walkways, sobbing their goodbyes with on-board

friends, squealing greetings from the deck to relatives waiting at the quayside, Athena managed to track me down.

'Leo looks for you,' she said. 'He will leave the ship here. He wants to see you.'

I did not wish to be seen, so I successfully dodged him until the *Asturias* pulled away from the Melbourne dock. Once we were safely sailing again, I sloped back to my cabin, planning to indulge in a cathartic weep, but someone had beaten me to it. Pearl was flaked out on the now-empty bunk of one of the Crawley girls, crying with heaving snotty sobs.

'He's gone,' she wailed.

'Mm, he disembarked in Melbourne.'

'You knew about me and him?'

'Well, I saw you together,' I said with as much dignity as I could dredge up.

'I never said nothing to you about him because you'd think I was a right slag.'

'Oh, Pearl, I don't think that,' I said and sincerely so.

'But he's married! With two little boys! So I *am* a slag!' Pearl crumpled into such tearful self-reproach that I wasn't understanding many of the words. But I did understand that I had misunderstood.

Once Pearl had calmed down a little, I asked, 'So the man was not Leo?'

'Leo? Why would you—? I always thought Leo was sweet on *you*, Betty.'

Pearl told me the story in pieces between shuddery intakes of breath. Since Port Said, she had been engaged in flirting/snogging with Keith, an accountant travelling with his wife and two sons. On the night of King Neptune's Ball, she had been seriously plastered, and a spat with Keith left her wretched, fending off several opportunistic men who kept pawing at her. Leo could see how vulnerable she was and offered to escort her back to our cabin. Pearl was worried Keith would come looking for her and worried she would be unable to resist sexual temptation if he did, so she begged Leo to let her hide out in his room for the night. That was the snippet I had witnessed. As it happened, Pearl enthusiastically gave in to temptation the very next night, sneaking out of our cabin to have sex with Keith behind a bulkhead.

'Leo was so kind on the night of the ball, Betty. He never touched me or nothing like that. Except took my shoes off and put a blanket on me. Brought me a cup of tea in the morning. He was just a lovely gent.'

I agreed with Pearl that Leo was a lovely gent, but two seconds later, any attempt to speak coherently was beyond me. I plonked onto the bunk and wept like an injured child. I'd liked Leo Newman so very much. But the moment we ended up dancing cheek-to-cheek, I had left abruptly and then went to some effort to avoid him for the rest of the voyage. The poor man must've assumed I had no romantic interest in him.

The rejection I'd imagined had not been real, but somehow, that realisation didn't lessen the fear that I would always be unlovable. And now, on top of that, there was despair about my own foolishness and self-sabotage. Pearl didn't understand that incongruous mix of emotions, but she didn't need to. She saw me—a nineteen-year-old girl weeping, her heart cracked. My lovely friend handed me a clean hankie and stroked my back.

I realise this story could appear quite sweet—an honourable young man loses his chance with the woman he desires because he does the right thing by another damsel. But let's not be sooky about what is really a tale of stupidity (mine) and damaged people with low self-esteem (both of us). Neither Leo Newman nor I felt worthy of being loved. We each needed the other person to pick us unmistakably, because we were both too insecure to risk being the picker.

As a young woman, I didn't believe in the idea of The One, one true love—I still don't—but maybe he was one of my potential Ones and I had mucked it. I offer the tale here in case a reader might join me in wondering how my story could have gone differently if I had managed things better back then, if Leo Newman and I had begun our life together in Australia as a couple.

Mind you, it was a shipboard infatuation and intense feelings are always harder to measure in the liminal space of travel, so no sense piling too much emphasis onto it.

The *Asturias* reached Sydney at 10 p.m. on Sunday, 22 June, and at seven the next morning, sailed through the heads of Sydney Harbour and under the magnificent arch of the bridge.

It was winter but still warmer and fresher and brighter than the best day Deptford had ever offered me. And good lord, Sydney was glorious to my eyes, with its old sandstone structures buttery like shortbread, the crisp new city buildings, and beyond that, where the fingers of the harbour pushed inland, there was a glimpse of red-tiled roofs surrounded by trees and so much clear sky.

I stood on the deck, opened the neck of my blouse and tipped my head back so the sun could hit my throat. I chose to imagine that the southern hemisphere solar energy would recharge me for the start of my new life.

FIVE

February 1948, Earlwood, Sydney.

Sweat was running down my spine and neck, pooling between my breasts. It wasn't a long walk from the train station to Nick and Athena's place, but this Saturday was humid and hot. I always loved the heat in Sydney, knowing that I could go to the beach and let the surf blast the sticky coating of perspiration off my skin.

In the late forties and fifties, Australian newspapers used to publish house plans for their readers. This was a country where regular people built their own homes from scratch. Athena's husband Nick Samios was using a blueprint out of *The Sunday Telegraph*, working every weekend and in between his paid jobs as a builder. In the meantime, he and Athena were living with his parents until the house was finished.

Walking up to their block it was clear he had made a mighty effort with the construction. The honey-coloured brick walls and some of the roof timbers were in place, so you could see the shape of the house—a generous bungalow with large windows, including a huge picture window where the living room jutted out towards the street.

When they spotted me, Athena and Nick both waved and grinned. If a reader was wondering how this arranged marriage had worked out, the answer is pretty bloody well.

The photo Athena had shown me on the ship was a fair likeness for Nick: short, well muscled from building, deeply tanned from outdoor work, a dapper dresser in his leisure time, always with a sharp haircut, and a man who rarely went more than a few minutes without a toothy smile.

I warmed to Nick from the start because he treated my friend Athena with respect and kindness, but I would have liked him anyway. Nick Samios considered himself to be lucky in life, which is an endearing mindset. He loved his parents, his siblings, his nieces and nephews. He loved the beach and playing cards and doing a swooping dance around his parents' courtyard after a couple of brandies. He loved his job, which earned him enough money to buy this block of land and build a house on it. When he looked at Athena, Nick considered himself even luckier—the luckiest man alive. I would often catch him gazing at her, smiling as if he'd just won the lottery.

Nick Samios was predisposed to think favourably of me because Athena had laid it on thick about our English lessons on the *Asturias*. He mentioned it repeatedly.

'I was born in Australia but Athena speaks better English than I do. That's thanks to you, Betty.' His tone was reverential, as if I had been part of the support team that had delivered Athena to him, a precious prize.

On the *Asturias* I hadn't appreciated the load of anxiety Athena had been carrying until I saw how she was now, once it had been lifted. She was simultaneously lighter and more solidly on the ground. She was married to a man who adored her. Her in-laws approved of her and were too busy with their crop of grandchildren to be meddlesome. An unexpected bonus for Athena was that she had the chance to use her brain, helping Nick in his building business, handling the accounts, preparing quotes, pricing materials. It turned out Nick was a man who didn't mind having a smart wife. And now, to add to her store of happiness, she was six months pregnant, standing with her pelvis tilted forward to show me the glorious curve of her abdomen.

As I walked up their muddy front yard, Nick called out, 'Betty! Hello! It's a scorcher! Let's have a beer.'

He cracked the top off a big bottle of Resch's Dinner Ale and poured some into enamel mugs for the three of us. (Beer was considered nutritious for pregnant women back then.) I sipped the froth, then took a big gulp of the beer, with its refreshing Australian fizz, still cold from being wrapped in wet newspaper and packed next to a block of ice in Nick's toolbox.

Enamel mugs in hand, Nick and I toured the house, stepping over floor joists, and moving between the almost-rooms, while he proudly explained the layout of bedrooms and the kitchen units he planned to build.

Meanwhile Athena found a shady spot to set up a rug and was busy chopping up the fruit I'd brought as my contribution to our building-site picnic. She laid out platters with Greek dishes, some cooked by her, some by her mother-in-law, all delicious.

As soon as he'd finished eating, Nick jumped to his feet. 'I better get back to work. But you two ladies should keep chatting. Athena misses you when we don't see you enough, Betty.'

Nick went back to hammering roof trusses together, which would be hauled into place later when he had his brothers around to help. While Athena and I nibbled on pieces of pineapple, she was describing her interactions with Australian butchers and greengrocers, laughing about the gap between the scenarios we had rehearsed on the ship and the reality. I told her about my latest adventures in the workforce, manufacturing men's underpants at the Stirling Henry factory.

When it was time to go, Nick grinned and blew me a kiss but kept on with his hammering.

'See those?' Athena tipped her head to point out four hurricane lamps sitting on a brick footing. 'The lamps are for tonight. Nick keeps working when it's dark. So he can get the house finished for us soon.'

From Athena and Nick's place, I took a train and a bus to Coogee beach, ran straight onto the sand, wriggled into my swimming costume and waded out until the waves broke against my belly.

I never regretted my decision to come to Australia.

At the start, most Australian people were so friendly it made me wary. I thought they were taking the piss out of me, but no, they really were just chatty, smiling out of their big tanned faces. Australians also went in for teasing—a bit like English teasing but more boisterous. Growing up in our mouthy family, working with the munitions girls and then in commercial laundries, I was hardly a delicate flower, so I relished the no-bullshit, don't-be-too-up-yourself directness of Australians.

It wasn't perfect, my new home. I would never say that. But I don't want to badmouth the country that gave me a great number of very good things. I might just mention one troubling matter from the early days.

My first week in Sydney, I was walking around the city with half an hour to kill before my next job interview. The wintry afternoon wind whooshed up the channel between the office buildings and it was chilly enough to sting. Passing a pub, I did what I would have done on a cold day in London—I ducked inside to sit somewhere warm with a lemon squash.

The place stank of beer—stale beer soaked into the wooden floor and fresh beer in the schooner glasses of the men at the bar who all stared at me, turning in unison like cows at a fence. These were not the friendly faces I'd encountered in Australia so far. Every gent appeared confused or worried or annoyed.

I froze, two steps inside the door. Had I done something wrong?

The barman could see I was bewildered. 'This is the public bar, love.'

Was that like 'public schools' in the UK and therefore posh? I glanced down at my clothes, wondering if I was dressed inappropriately.

The barman spoke more loudly. 'You can't be in here. It's men only.'

So the problem was not my clothing but what was inside my clothes. I had the wrong genitals.

'You go back out into the street, then round the side to the left.' The barman sounded weary, sick of redirecting clueless Pommy women to where they belonged. 'Find the door to the ladies' lounge.'

Off an alley that ran down the side of the pub, a narrow door had 'Ladies' Lounge' etched into the frosted glass panel. I pushed it open to see a small windowless room painted a mucosal green, with three round tables, half a dozen battered chairs, and a little hatch for serving drinks. The only patron in there was a fifty-something woman, her head drooped over the table where an empty schooner of beer had sat long enough to leave a lacework of dried froth up the sides of the glass. The woman must've been asleep because she didn't turn when I opened the door and she was still slumped there as I left.

That arrangement—the blokey public bar, hostile to women, with a miserable ladies' lounge out the back—was repeated in pretty much all Australian pubs of the time. Later, some fabulous dames would challenge this practice, chaining themselves to the metal rail of a public bar.

That February, after my Coogee swim, I went back to the squishy one-bedroom flat in Surry Hills I was sharing with Pearl.

Pearl Jowett would've located the fun anywhere she landed and since we'd docked in Sydney, she'd been gasping about the cracking weather, the cheeky people, the abundant supplies of lush food and dishy men. This evening, Pearl was out, as she almost always was.

I flopped on the bed, conscious of a lump of sadness that was often lodged under my ribs. I didn't blame Australia for my sadness. (If you're going to be sad, it might as well be in the sunshine.) Some of it was plain old loneliness. Athena was busy with Nick, and Pearl was always off somewhere with a new beau.

The risk, in moments when I wasn't busy, was that prickly thoughts could find their way up from the archives and infiltrate my conscious mind until it was awash with gloomy imaginings. I would rouse myself from those morose spells with *plans*.

The bookmark in the novel I was reading was a newspaper clipping, an advertisement for the shorthand and typing course offered by the International Correspondence School. My plan was to save up the fee to enrol and improve my options.

There have been periods in my life when I've been buffeted by external forces and, to avoid feeling powerless, I have used the making of plans to give me a sense of control. I was the one selecting door number one over door number two, even if the choice was as humble as enrolling in a secretarial course.

But then there were episodes when something unexpected whooshed in, so fast and so exciting it was difficult to know if I was making a genuine choice.

20 March 1948. The Trocadero.

Stepping into the Trocadero dance hall was like walking onto a movie set. The marble foyer swept guests from George Street through to the fabulous art deco ballroom and its most thrilling feature: the polished dancefloor with a shell-shaped stage for the band.

That afternoon, I didn't enter the Trocadero through the glossy marble foyer. I ducked in round the back, via the staff entrance. I changed into my waitress uniform and cap, then headed out into the main auditorium to see there were now hundreds of silver stars hanging from the ceiling, making the Troc look more dreamlike than ever.

The Trocadero was a glamorous venue every night, but the Silver Stars Ball was the highlight of the year, attended by the social elite of Sydney, covered by the newspapers in the fantasy-for-the-common-folk way the Oscars red carpet and celebrity shenanigans would be today.

With a couple of the other waitresses, I hopped to, setting the tables and tying silver fabric bows around each chairback.

I heard a doorway behind me flung open with a confident sweep. An expensive fragrance entered the room a second before the individual exuding it—a tall woman in her late forties, wearing a lilac shot silk suit with a full skirt and peplum jacket, a string of pearls with matching earrings, navy gloves, navy pumps with a lilac bow, coiffed hair and full makeup. The Trocadero manager barrelled out from the back office to welcome the lilac woman. 'Mrs Shaw-Preston!'

Mrs Shaw-Preston moved through the auditorium like a fragrant commanding officer, consulting the obsequious manager about the arrangements for the ball and giving instructions to three posh ladies—members of the Silver Committee who were fussing over the table centrepieces and name cards.

The posh ladies referred to each other by pet names: Pooky, Squidgy and Doody. I later came to understand that such names—infantile nicknames with a strange hint of the scatological—were quite common among eastern suburbs socialites. Pooky, Squidgy and Doody kept bickering, flustered, displaying none of Mrs Shaw-Preston's poise. A few minutes later, they rushed off, in a flap about having enough time to dress for the event.

Mrs Shaw-Preston didn't seem too sorry to see them go. I saw her discreetly swap a few of the name cards and she made an irritated 'oof' sound at the state of the centrepieces.

'Hello.'

I was startled to realise she was talking to me and jerked a smile in reply.

'You seem like a sensible young woman,' she said. 'Do you think between us, we could do a better job with these centrepieces?'

Not wanting this upper-crust lady to look down on me, I bunged on a genteel accent. 'Well, everything else looks wonderful but, I must admit, the centrepieces are a little—'

She jumped in to finish my sentence. 'The centrepieces are a little sad, aren't they.'

The assemblage of red roses and dyed-silver feathers was inelegantly done, with the feathers drooping, flaccid.

'Let's sort them out, shall we?' she suggested.

Then she lunged gracefully forward to offer me a handshake. 'I'm Helena Shaw-Preston. But you must call me Bunny.'

'Lovely to meet you, Bunny.' (And yes, the first time addressing a grown-up woman as 'Bunny' does feel ridiculous.) 'I'm Elizabeth Rankin.'

I presented myself as 'Elizabeth' because it was the matching accessory for the toney accent I was using.

'From your accent—you're English?' asked Bunny.

'I am,' I said, not technically lying, even if I wasn't the kind of 'English' she meant.

Bunny herself spoke with the plum-in-the-mouth, quasi-British pronunciation that upper-class Australians used in those days.

Bunny Shaw-Preston and I moved from table to table, rearranging the centrepieces, with me holding the roses in place, while she positioned the silver feathers so they sprang from the flowers at a jaunty angle.

'Thank you for your help,' she said, before striding out to get herself gussied up for the ball.

Guests began arriving at seven that evening, walking from George Street to the doors of the Trocadero on a royal blue carpet with silver stars strewn all over it.

The dress code required black tie and evening gowns with a 'soupçon of silver'. There was considerable cachet in using a French word when an English one would've done the job. Many of the gowns were voluminous creations, extravagant with fabric now the post-war restrictions were easing. Some were lovely but others were ludicrously unflattering, with odd protuberances of stiff taffeta that looked like worrying growths on the body of the wearer. Even so, the eastern suburbs ladies were busy offering each other admiring comments, in that flattery transaction expected of women.

Bunny made an impressive entrance in a Christian Dior off-the-shoulder gown, with folds of silver silk draped around one shoulder, swooping into a narrow waist and then falling perfectly into the full skirt. She came in on the arm of her husband, an unsmiling gentleman in his sixties, one of those men with a blockish body and a neck as wide as his head, so the tuxedo collar seemed to be throttling him. Mr Shaw-Preston spent the whole evening at the head table, conducting what appeared to be serious business-talk.

Meanwhile, Bunny was working the room, commanding the space like a cross between a queen and a headmistress. The Silver Stars Ball, raising funds for children's charities, was her creation—a product of her flair, managerial talent and social pulling power.

The mass of air in the Troc auditorium was pulsating with the nervy energy of three hundred people judging each other and being judged, singing out hello-darlings, air-kissing, their heads darting around like birds to ensure they didn't miss anything.

The band, Frank Ruby and His Musical Gems, was playing at a low volume underneath the burble of talk, which was punctuated by the occasional hoot of female laughter and a few of those self-assured male basso voices that cut through and swamp other speakers.

Some of the gentlemen at the ball were proper handsome, even adjusting for the extra quotient of handsomeness that black tie confers on a man. My eye fell on one man—maybe because of his attractive sandy-haired looks or maybe because he was surveying the room with curiosity, slightly to one side, rather than in any of the chattering clumps of people.

After the dinner was served, Bunny Shaw-Preston appeared on stage to give a perfectly judged speech of thankyous. In her elegantly bossy way, she announced that everyone must give it a go on the dancefloor.

'By way of inspiration,' Bunny said, 'Trocadero staff members have kindly agreed to give us a demonstration of the jitterbug.'

As one of those kind staff members, I now stood at the side of the polished floor with my dance partner (a chef from the Troc kitchen), along with two other couples who'd volunteered to do this for a small supplement to our wages. For the little demo, we were expected to change out of our uniforms and into something that fitted with the Silver Stars theme. I'd borrowed a dress from

Pearl—a midnight-blue number with silver beads sewn in contour lines down the bodice and skirt giving the dress that little bit of weight so it skimmed the body in an alluring but not sluttish way.

Frank Ruby led the band into a medley of swing numbers as my partner and I stepped to the centre of the floor with the other two couples. During our meal-breaks, the chef and I had worked out a few moves but on the night we winged it, both of us decent enough dancers to put on a good show for an audience that didn't expect championship stuff. And even if we were far from professional standard, anyone watching could see we were having a blast, grinning as we spun and bopped across the floor to that top-class band. I caught the odd glimpse of the room full of toffs watching us and that added to the thrill. When the chef swung me up and round in a move I wasn't expecting, I let rip with a burst of surprised laughter. In that moment, I caught the eye of the handsome sandy-haired gentleman.

As soon as the demonstration number was over, we'd been instructed to leave the floor to the guests who would supposedly be inspired to jitterbug themselves. But before I could scurry off, Bunny Shaw-Preston beckoned me over.

She was chatting with a group of guests, all seriously old, three with walking sticks, two with tremors and one with chalky staring eyes. One younger person was unaccountably sitting at this elderly table: the sandy-haired man.

'That was marvellous,' declared Bunny.

The man nodded his agreement emphatically.

I was so puffed out and revved up from the dancing, I had to remind myself to maintain the fake posh accent Bunny had heard me use earlier. 'Thank you. Mr Ruby's band is wonderful.'

Bunny swept her hand through the air drawing a line between me and the gentleman. 'Donald Burnley, meet—?'

'Elizabeth Rankin. Hello.'

'Hello.'

Bunny pointed an elegant finger at Pearl's dress. 'This is very chic.'

'Oh. Thank you.' Then I laughed. 'In this dress, I'm—well—'

Donald jumped in, fervent. 'In that dress, you look very nice.'

I guffawed—in fact I very nearly snorted like a pig. 'Uh—well— thank you . . . I wasn't fishing for a compliment.'

Donald winced. 'I'm sorry. I didn't mean to make you uncomfortable.'

His awkwardness was so disarmingly sweet, I forgot to stay politely restrained and I blurted at him, 'Oh no, you didn't make me— well, a bit. But that's my fault—I'm so bad at taking compliments. And don't worry—it was a good compliment. The thing I was *going* to say about this dress—the silver beads are so *spiky*, I was worried my dance partner would scratch up his hands when we were dancing. This dress turns me into a human pot-scourer.'

Donald laughed—surprised laughter like a kid, vulnerable and charming.

At that moment, the supervisor flicked his head, indicating it was time for me to change back into my uniform. Cinderella may have danced at the ball but she was still required to clear the tables.

The following Tuesday evening, I had just started my shift at the Trocadero when I noticed the sandy-haired man (Donald Burnley) hovering around in the foyer. He looked lost so I bowled up to him, remembering to use the posh accent he'd heard come out of my mouth at the ball. Once I'd started speaking that way, I couldn't suddenly drop it.

'Hello. I'm Elizabeth. I don't know if you remember—I was the one wearing a pot-scourer dress at the Silver Stars Ball.'

'I remember—uh . . . Hello,' he said.

'Are you waiting for someone?'

'Oh, no, no, I'm not going inside. I'm on my way to a dinner near here. I was actually hoping to . . .' And the next words crumbled in his mouth as courage failed him.

He fidgeted with the buttons on his suit jacket, and it was suddenly clear that he was there hoping to see me. I wasn't much of a one for arrogant assumptions like that, but it was pretty obvious even to a woman of my low self-esteem. As a nineteen-year-old, my social poise was minimal but Donald Burnley was so endearingly uneasy, I felt obliged to rustle up some interpersonal skills for both our sakes.

'Well, Donald, what a lucky coincidence that you're going to dinner near here because it's very nice to see you again.'

He smiled, with a little intake of breath, then quickly blurted, 'Do you work most evenings of the week?'

'It varies. But I'm often free in the daytime.' I waited for him to take the hint, but it became clear I would have to do the running on this, so I went on, 'I'm free tomorrow. Perhaps we could meet for a walk in the Botanic Garden.'

Donald was waiting at the Botanic Garden gate nearest to the harbour and when he saw me, he looked pleased but very self-conscious. To fill the uncomfortable silence, I launched straight into some chat.

After a minute of my babbling about the strange conductor on my bus, Donald suddenly dropped his head. I was afraid I'd bored the poor man into a state of despair, but when he raised his head, there was an earnest expression on his face.

'During the war, I didn't serve in the armed forces.'

'Oh,' I said, not sure what response was required to this non sequitur.

'I had rheumatic fever as a child so they wouldn't let me enlist. But I was keen to make a contribution. I worked as a defence department clerk.'

It was clearly important to Donald that he jump in ahead of any recrimination and explain himself. I met his gaze directly and nodded, but he still appeared stricken.

Trying to ease his discomfort, I grinned and said, 'I didn't serve in the army either, on account of being eleven when the war started.'

Donald smiled at my silly comment, relieved I wasn't judging him.

We walked through the gardens, along the edge of the water, with Donald pointing out landmarks around the harbour and answering my many questions. This seemed to put him at ease and from there, we fell into delightful conversation about the differences between Australia, England and the United States, where he had recently been travelling.

Our stroll in the Botanic Garden went well, quickly followed by a lunch and an evening at the cinema.

Donald (full name MacDonald) Burnley was thirty years old. Both of his parents had died recently—his mother of cancer, his father of a heart attack three months later. As their only child, it had fallen to Donald to take on the running of the family companies, including a shoe factory, commercial real estate and an importing business.

Apart from adopting a refined accent and the posher 'Elizabeth' version of my name, I was as honest about myself with Donald as I was with anyone in those years. (Even Athena still knew nothing about the baby I'd relinquished.) He switched between admiring my resilience—surviving a poor family, evacuation, the bombing—and being full of rather sentimental pity for me. The first time he insisted on walking me home to the Surry Hills flat, I thought the shabbiness of the area might put him off. But it added to the allure—in his mind, I was more down-to-earth than the young upper-crust women he was used to dating. On my Surry Hills doorstep, there was a chaste kiss but no more.

'Bunny Shaw-Preston is having a small garden party on Saturday afternoon. Will you go with me?' asked Donald.

My pals at the Trocadero warned me that Point Piper was an upper-class suburb, but nothing prepared me for the money-bags harbourside splendour of it. Mind you, Donald drove me from my scungy little flat to the garden party in the family Jaguar, so I suppose the journey there was some preparation for visiting the universe of the wealthy.

The Shaw-Prestons' home, 'Vue de Mer', was a Spanish mission-style mansion—creamy stucco walls, arched windows, long colonnades, terracotta roofing, little turrets, all sheltered from the street by high walls draped in bougainvillea. The front door was opened by a housekeeper in a gunmetal grey uniform—the servants' livery of this quasi-aristocratic household.

Donald and I were ushered through a grand entrance hall and several living rooms. Once inside, I could appreciate how truly massive the place was, spreading far out on each side, then spilling down the slope to a terrace, tiered gardens, a huge swimming pool and finally a boatshed with a jetty jutting out into a crescent of bright blue water. Beyond that, the spectacular harbour, bridge and city buildings were laid out as if they had been positioned for the benefit of this particular house. I guess I'd never thought about the fact that there were obscenely rich people in Australia too.

It would be naïve to deny the existence of a class system in Australia. Money, family connections and private school networks mattered then and still do now, but it was nothing like the pernicious snobbery and class restrictions of England. The idea that I could be a guest at a house like this, socialising with these people, was astonishing. It's true I was using a posh accent to make myself acceptable, but I had not actually lied. And, anyway, who was to say my new way of speaking was fake? We're all constantly adjusting and presenting ourselves to the world. It seemed to be one of the glorious opportunities of migrating to a new country that I could reinvent myself, a little at least.

On the main lawn of the Shaw-Preston mansion, fifty people were chattering in small groups, sipping on Pimm's or champagne and being served fancy canapes. I was busy gazing at the view (or should I say 'vue'), when a white-coated waiter offered me a coupe of champagne and a little crab doodad.

Bunny Shaw-Preston swept past in a flummery of a dress whipped out of pale lemon chiffon. 'So lovely you could both come,' she said. If Bunny was surprised to see a waitress show up as a guest in her house she didn't let on.

It then struck me that everyone at this event was wearing white or a pastel. Even the gents were wearing cream or biscuit-coloured suits, including Donald. My dress, another one borrowed from Pearl, was an intense bright green.

I whispered to Donald, 'Everyone here is wearing dairy colours, like scoops of ice cream—vanilla and lemon and caramel.'

Donald did his spluttery little-kid laugh again. It felt good to make him laugh.

I indicated my bright green dress with exaggerated dismay. 'I don't exactly fit in.'

'You look like a beautiful jungle plant,' he said and slipped his arm through mine. 'I never manage very well at this kind of do, but if you're with me, I know it will be much better.'

And so Donald and I kept each other afloat through the sea of chitchat. A couple of times people laughed—or more accurately 'tittered'—at some quip of mine and, in my peripheral vision, I could see Donald gazing at me with pride.

An hour or so into the event, I excused myself to visit the bathroom. When I emerged from the loo, Bunny beckoned me into an alcove.

'It's lovely to see how much Donald enjoys your company.'

'Oh, well, I enjoy—'

'You enjoy his company. Which is even lovelier.'

Bunny politely quizzed me about my life and I gave her a more or less honest account, just editing out the problematic details (molesting uncle, teen pregnancy) and turning up the volume on descriptions of my virtuous attempts at self-education through reading.

'Good for you, Elizabeth.' Bunny chose to regard me as a paragon of self-improvement, a plucky young woman from a poor background, who had worked hard to better herself.

Bunny scrutinised me. 'How old are you?'

'Nineteen.'

'Young. But, no, no, yes—a robust, practical young woman could be good for Donald.'

When I told Pearl that Donald was taking me to dinner at Romano's, she hyperventilated with excitement. Romano's restaurant was certainly the most glamorous joint I'd ever been in my life, with its own orchestra playing while we diners, all of us in evening dress, were mesmerised by the choice of the three hundred and seventy dishes on the menu.

I looked at Donald Burnley across the table as we ate our Paupiettes de Veau Brillat-Savarin. This man was handsome, gentle, drank only a moderate amount of alcohol, was (astonishingly) besotted with me and carried a vague sadness that made me feel tender towards him.

I was certainly drawn to his orphan status—either out of fellow-feeling or because it felt safer to be with someone who had no family to judge me as inadequate.

After dinner, Donald decided I should see his family home and drove us to Woollahra in the Jaguar.

'The Gables' was a big mock-Tudor residence set in a large garden. I like to think I wasn't primarily attracted to MacDonald Burnley's wealth, but it was hard to ignore. He parked the Jag outside the garage, in which two more cars were apparently housed, and ducked around to open the passenger door for me.

The interior of The Gables was huge but somehow managed to be claustrophobic with its restricted leadlight windows, sombre drapes and carpeting. Even when Donald turned on lamps and chandeliers, it was as if the house soaked up any light, leaving the place still sunk in gloom.

The rooms were laden with heavy brown furniture, including Tudor reproduction pieces. Chunky, unlovely silver jugs and platters covered many surfaces. The paintings were of the murky Scottish landscape variety, hanging in bulky gilt frames.

The place was ugly but there was something about the solidity of the house and its contents that appealed to me: the weight of it planted sturdily on the ground. Whatever life threw at you, you could cling onto that mahogany sideboard and hold yourself safely in place.

'It's like somewhere Cardinal Wolsey would live,' I said. 'It's very impressive.'

'I hate it,' Donald said. 'I'm going to remodel and refurnish. See these?' He pointed out two long slim pieces of silverware on a sideboard. 'Do you know what they're for?'

I shook my head. He lit a candle perched in a silver candelabra on the dining table, then reached over with one of the slim silver gadgets to snuff out the flame.

I laughed. 'Aha! I suppose everyone needs a candle snuffer!'

'That's probably the first time it's ever been used,' he said. 'My parents had all this *stuff* for entertaining . . .' He flung open the doors on sideboards to show me the vast collection of fine bone china with gold trim, matching soup tureens, gravy boats, and such. 'But they never invited people to the house.'

Donald prowled the dining room. 'This house is a dead thing and it makes everything inside it—ugh . . . But you're a—you have such life force, Elizabeth, you bring life back into it! Let me show you upstairs.'

I followed him up the hulking staircase and stood on the landing, trying to decipher one of the muddy family portraits, wondering if I'd been dropped into a Daphne du Maurier novel. That was the moment Donald pulled me close and kissed me with real passion for the first time. Lips still locked, we crab-walked our way inside one of the bedrooms and tumbled onto a four-poster bed draped in tartan fabric.

The foreplay was more a process of fumbling than sensual rapture but it was exciting that Donald was clearly so hungry for me. Being desired has its own compelling quality.

Then, suddenly, Donald lurched back from me and hunched himself up the end of the bed. I worried I'd been too responsive with the petting, too up for it, revealing a lewd tendency.

After several excruciating seconds, he murmured, face still turned away, 'I have to tell you. I had sex—quite a few times—when I was in the United States.'

'Oh,' I said. I did not volunteer that I'd had quite a bit of sex in the United Kingdom and had conceived a baby in the process. 'I don't mind. I mean, that's fine.'

Donald was so relieved not to be condemned, he threw himself back into our lovemaking with even more fervour. Then and there, on that tartan-draped bed, we had sex for the first time. As he was about to come, Donald pulled out and ejaculated into his hand. He then held his hand away from my bare hip to avoid getting any on me. I took this to be an act of gallantry.

When he returned from the bathroom, he looked at me lying on the bed and made a whimpering sound. 'You're so lovely. Would you marry me, Elizabeth?'

I was momentarily silent, shocked, and Donald winced. 'Is it too soon? Am I being foolish? I am. I'm being—'

'No, no, you're not foolish. And yes, yes, I'll marry you.'

The swiftness of it felt exciting, as if our courtship were a natural phenomenon, with its own unstoppable momentum.

Bunny regarded our engagement as her personal achievement.

'What we must do—since Donald has no family to speak of and you have no mother to help you—I will organise your wedding.'

'Oh, I can't ask you to—'

'Can't ask me to do that? You're not asking, I'm insisting. And, yes, we must hold the reception at Vue de Mer.'

Bunny cast herself as matron of honour and, after inspecting Pearl, authorised my friend to be the maid of honour. Pearl was so pretty that her lack of poshness could be overlooked for the sake of her ornamental quality. Bunny felt two bridesmaids were enough—more would be ostentatious, given the lack of family on either side—so there would be no role for Athena in the bridal party.

Athena was gracious about that and was mostly interested in knowing about the sort of man Donald was. 'Is he kind to you, Betty?'

I assured her my fiancé was a kind and honourable man. Athena could hardly be a stickler for a long courtship given she and Nick had married on the basis of grainy photos.

Bunny Shaw-Preston obviously felt some obligation to look after motherless Donald but I still didn't understand why she went to such trouble to help me. In retrospect, I believe she was hungry for novelty—well, peckish for novelty at least. And I, as 'Elizabeth Rankin', self-educated orphan washed ashore in the Antipodes, who had won the heart of a well-off but lonely man, could make for a diverting project.

If I think back to my wedding day, it plays like a movie in which I'm cast in the role of the bride. That's partly because Bunny had chosen my dress, my hairdo, the flowers, catering, music, everything, and partly because I was using a fake accent and name, so there was always a performative whiff about the day.

Because Donald was notionally Church of England, the ceremony was at All Saints in Woollahra, with the reception, as promised, at Vue de Mer. Two dazzling white marquees were erected on the lawn—one for the seated dinner, the other for a band and dancefloor. Bunny made all the arrangements and Donald paid for them.

Apart from Pearl, Athena and Nick, plus two girls I'd befriended working at the Trocadero, all the other guests were individuals I knew barely or not at all. There were quite a few older people, including the decrepit gang I'd seen with Donald at the Silver Stars Ball, all friends of his parents and grandparents, who were attending his wedding for the sake of Burnley dynastic honour. There were a dozen men who'd been in Donald's cohort at Scots College. Of those, he claimed to like his two groomsmen only moderately and to actively dislike the rest. The Scots old boys were all married to the kind of elegant St Catherine's educated women that Donald would've been expected to choose. During the reception, the wives were syrupy sweet to my face, but they made little effort to conceal their suspicions about me as a gold-digger.

After the dinner, I stepped away from the bridal table, hungry for fresh air. I noticed Athena and Nick get up from their seats at a table in the far corner of the marquee, pausing while Nick helped Athena arrange a shawl around her shoulders against the evening chill. I realised two of the Scots old boys and their wives were nearby, whispering about my friends.

One of the old boys, Charles Irwin-Bond, made a show of reaching across to run his hand over the chairs Athena and Nick had just been sitting on. He did an elaborate mime about the layer of grease they'd supposedly left, a disgusting oily deposit he was now forced to wipe off on his trousers.

Charles's three cronies were so busy cackling that it took them a moment to register that Athena and Nick were also watching this fellow's performance. One woman nudged her friend and eventually they were all sneaking looks at Athena and Nick. But instead of apologising or appearing in any way ashamed, the Scots crew sniggered together, which emboldened them to be more overtly offensive.

'You'll have to excuse us.' Charles smirked at Nick. 'We're not used to mixing with greasy wogs at social events.'

This sparked another flurry of laughter and I could clearly hear their unabashed discussion about 'dagos' and other obnoxious bigotry.

Nick stepped towards the ringleader, ready to verbally defend his honour. Athena tugged at her husband's arm to leave it alone, but she dropped her handbag in the process, spilling the contents onto the wooden flooring in the marquee. Nick squatted down to gather up her things, which left Athena stranded there, exposed, forced to listen to the sneery whispers.

That was the moment she looked over and realised I was witnessing this scene. She knew I had heard every slur, every bigoted word, every nasty cackle from these people who were guests at my wedding.

Athena pinned me with her gaze. She was trembling a little, clearly distressed, but still holding herself so proudly. She didn't need to speak. The challenge—that I should defend her—crackled through the air from her body to mine.

Even when Nick pressed her handbag into her arms and suggested they leave, Athena held her position for one defiant moment longer, giving me one more chance to offer a show of proper friendship—of proper human decency.

I stood there frozen. It was clear I wasn't going to intervene. I wasn't going to confront these vile people. I wasn't even going to step forward and acknowledge Athena as my valued friend. She frowned at me briefly but ferociously, then strode out of the marquee.

A second later, Bunny tapped my shoulder. 'Elizabeth, we need you and Donald for the bridal waltz.'

I would like to imagine that, had I not been whisked into the other marquee, I would have chased after Athena. I might even have torn strips off those racist toads attending my wedding. But I fear I wouldn't have. I had just watched my friends be insulted and I had stood there, paralysed by my own insecurity and the pathetic desire to protect the new life in which I'd landed. It's unlikely I would have suddenly found the necessary courage. If a reader judges me harshly for my failing that day, I can only say I share that judgement.

A few minutes later, waltzing on the dancefloor, Donald noticed my eyes were wet with tears.

'I feel the same way,' he said. 'It's overwhelming.'

He'd misread why I was upset and I couldn't explain. I just nodded and let his misunderstanding give me the cover to pull myself back from sobbing in the middle of the bridal waltz. My new husband smiled at me—kindly, but with no clue what was in my head.

When the other couples joined us on the dancefloor, Donald craned forward to whisper in my ear, 'The first minute I saw you at the Silver Stars Ball, I thought, *That's the girl for me.*'

A visceral relief flooded my body. This man had chosen me. And clutching on to that knowledge, I was able to steady myself, regain my composure and even feel a sense of joy about this day. I comforted myself with a plan: after my honeymoon, I would apologise and make it up to Athena. I was going to be the mistress of my own house and could invite over whomever I pleased.

As the band segued into a more up-tempo number, Donald did a jokey uh-oh face, worried about his lack of dancing prowess. I kissed him and squeezed his hand reassuringly.

MacDonald Burnley and I knew each other so little. We'd each taken a few observations of the other and spun those into a character who fitted the script we wanted to write for our futures. The character sketches were clumsy and stereotyped like the ones bashed out by scriptwriters for formulaic television drama series. (I'll get to that part of my life later.) For Donald I was 'vibrant no-nonsense young woman' who would bring a revitalising injection of life force into his world. Meanwhile, I had cast Donald as 'gentle man, honourable but emotionally wounded', whom I would heal by finding the key to unlock the rusty door to his heart. Many marriages are founded on that sort of romantic delusion and, with goodwill on both sides and some luck, it can work.

This man had picked me and I would make him happy. We were both orphans who hadn't been properly loved as children, but together we would build a life as solid as the heavy wooden furniture in his house and we would make our own family.

SIX

July 1948.

A fortnight after the wedding, when Donald was away on business, I caught the train to Earlwood on a mission to restore my connection with Athena. From our honeymoon, I had sent her a postcard, perky and affectionate.

Athena and Nick's house was built by then, with a few raw unfinished corners, but still a glorious thing. Nick was out on a job but Athena was home, tackling the huge task of clearing building debris from the muddy backyard, ready to turn it into vegetable patches and pergolas. Baby Sofia, then only three months old, was asleep in a bassinet in the shade of the one tree that had survived the construction.

'Hello,' I said.

Athena nodded, stiff, formal. If she was surprised to see me, she was too controlled to let on.

I peeked into the bassinet to see the baby, a perfect tiny creature with lavish dark hair. 'My goodness, she's so beautiful. I brought her a present, if that's okay.'

'Oh. Thank you.'

Athena took the parcel from me but made no move to open it, which was disappointing. I'd bought a playsuit with little boats on it, in the hope the gift might generate some nostalgic chat about our time on the *Asturias*.

'How are you?' I asked.

'I'm well,' she replied. Unyielding.

She did not invite me inside or offer me refreshments, which for a woman like Athena was a big deal.

Okay, obviously there wasn't going to be any chitchat. Straight to it then.

'Athena,' I said, 'I'm so sorry about the things those people said to you at the wedding. That was horrible and I'm—well, I'm . . .'

Athena let me squirm for a moment, then spoke very calmly. 'I can put up with it when people call me "wog". That's how things are. And these are just words.'

'Well, I see what you mean, but it's still awful—'

'I don't care about those rude people at your wedding. I care if my friend will stand up for me or not.'

My eyes burned with tears. I shook my head and kept shaking my head until I could finally get some words out. 'I know. I'm sorry. That was my fault. It was just—that day—everything was overwhelming and I was—'

Athena fixed me with those fierce eyes to shut me up. Excuses were not welcome. And fair enough.

'I'm sorry.' That was the best I could do in that moment. 'Please know I'm sorry.'

Athena nodded her acknowledgement of my apology, but she still held herself distant from me.

'I should go now,' I said and she made no effort to stop me. 'I'll invite you and Nick around to our place soon.'

Athena nodded again. She had good reason not to forgive me easily—and I respected that—but I was hopeful. It would be okay in the end.

Let me assure the reader that I truly had intended to invite Athena and Nick to dinner. But it turned out I'd fallen pregnant on the honeymoon. For the rest of my first trimester, I vomited up my guts so many times per day, I was unfit to leave the house, let alone play hostess. Athena would understand, I was confident, especially because Pearl had passed on the news of my pregnancy to her.

Halfway through my second trimester, when I was finally well enough to organise a baby shower, I posted Athena an invitation. A week later, that invitation came back, with 'return to sender' written in Athena's handwriting on the envelope. Seeing the decisive line she had drawn under the words, the pen pressed down hard enough to perforate the paper, was like a slap across my face.

After that, Pearl would tell me news about Athena, including the arrival of a second daughter, Thea, but there was no contact between us.

Once the morning sickness was over, I loved being pregnant. Astonishingly, I never made any conscious connection with my first pregnancy. It was as if that experience had never happened. My brain's mechanism for suppressing inconvenient memories was clearly in robust working order.

In the February of 1949, the days were sweltering hot, and for me, almost eight months along by then, it was a relief to immerse my enlarged body in water. I took to going to Nielsen Park, a harbour beach with flat water.

On one of those flotation days, I arranged to meet Pearl there. She kissed me hello on my sweaty, puffy cheek, then slipped out of her adorable summer frock to reveal a clingy red Jantzen 'Nylastic' swimsuit and tugged on a pink-petalled bathing cap. Pearl always seemed to have fashionable new outfits, despite her lowly paid retail jobs. She spent every spare dollar of her income on clothes but I imagine there was subsidy from her male admirers. Not that her beauty depended on trimmings—she was naturally gorgeous and vivacious. And she was still without a judgemental or conceited bone in her lovely body. Still a sweet friend to me.

I hauled off my maternity smock, a voluminous blue-and-white striped garment in which I resembled a marquee on legs. My maternity swimming outfit wasn't exactly elegant either—an abomination of flowery print and ruching—but I didn't care as long as I could slide myself into the water.

I waded out a few metres, then squatted down, water up to my chin, relieved to have Sydney Harbour take the weight of me, and swayed from side to side, a contented sea mammal. Pearl popped up from under the water like a water nymph.

'What's it feel like?' she asked, pointing at my belly.

'Strange,' I said. 'But wonderful.'

'I can't wait. I'd be chuffed to have a bun in my oven right now!'

Pearl had high hopes that her then-boyfriend Rodney might propose.

'Oof, the baby's doing tumbles,' I said. 'It's weird to think there's another creature with its own arms and legs swimming around inside me while I'm swimming.'

But Pearl hadn't heard me. She was distracted by a man walking down from the grass and she waved to attract his attention. I assumed it was Rodney or another one of her gentleman friends. But as the fellow scanned the beach, I recognised the shape of him. The glare of the sun off the water made it hard to see precisely but I recognised his gait.

'Leo! Here we are!' Pearl called out, then swished around in the water to grin at me. 'Leo's just moved to Sydney. He said he was dead keen to see you so I told him we'd be here today.'

His eyes locked on to mine. It was more than eighteen months since I'd last seen him. His hair was barbered more sternly, his face was more tanned, but it was the beautiful face I remembered, smiling at me so intensely, it generated tingles down my scalp and neck and spine.

When I stood up, the water level only came to my upper thighs. The size of my belly, plastered with clinging wet fabric, was impossible to ignore.

Leo's eyeline dropped to take in my pregnant body. He opened his mouth to suck in a breath and the smile was gone.

Pearl giggled. 'It's Betty, silly!' She assumed his stunned mullet expression was because he didn't recognise me. She then added, in her strangled version of a toffy accent, 'Well, beg your pardon—we call her "Elizabeth" now.'

Leo and I must have mumbled hello but I have no memory of it.

I had no idea that he and Pearl had stayed in contact for some months after the *Asturias*, sending each other the occasional brief letter. Apparently, Leo had asked after me and Pearl had relayed some of my doings to him, including dancing at the Silver Stars Ball. But Pearl Jowett was an erratic correspondent and in a long recent gap between letters, there'd been no chance to mention my marriage and pregnancy.

That day, on the sand at Nielsen Park, she filled in the biographical gaps with enthusiastic chatter.

'Oh, Leo, didn't I tell you Elizabeth was up the duff? I must have told you. Anyhow, Donald—that's her husband—oh my stars, he's handsome. And very rich! Ooh, except Elizabeth gets mardy if I talk about him being rich. She's all embarrassed about having that big fancy house. But if you ask me, it's just stonking good luck that she married someone good-looking *and* rich!'

Pearl prattled on, oblivious to the flow of feeling going on in front of her, even though she was receiving only vague murmurs and grunts from Leo and me.

She swung her attention to him. 'Leo's as handsome as ever, isn't he, Elizabeth!'

I made an affirmative noise, unable to look directly at him. Instead, I made my lumbering way up from the beach to reach my pile of clothes. The other two walked beside me, Pearl yabbering on.

'Leo's going to love living in Sydney, don't you think, Elizabeth? Mind you, Rodney says it's more classy down in Melbourne. Ha— Melbourne's prob'ly too classy for a scrubber like me. Anyhow, Sydney's champion.'

'Uh, yes, I'm sure I'll love it,' said Leo.

'Me and Elizabeth will have to show you around town!'

'Well, I think Elizabeth will be too busy for showing anyone around the town,' said Leo with a small smile.

The way he pronounced 'Elizabeth' was so lovely, the name sounding right in my ears for the first time since I'd adopted it. I managed a smile in reply, but as I pulled my maternity smock over my wet swimsuit, I felt light-headed.

Pearl was too busy chattering about places a Sydney newcomer must visit, but Leo noticed I was wobbly.

'Are you feeling unwell, Elizabeth?'

'I'm okay. Maybe a bit dizzy. I should go home.'

When I leaned down to tug my shoes onto my swollen feet, I lost my balance. Leo reached out to catch me and held my arm until I could yank the shoe on and stand firmly again. The touch of his hand on my arm, the sensation of his warm skin on my damp, slightly salty skin—it was too much and it was nowhere near enough.

I pulled away as soon as I was steady enough, using the excuse of gathering up my things. I shook off Pearl's and Leo's offers to see me home, insisting I would be fine, and managed to leave the park without making eye contact with him again.

During my first labour as a seventeen-year-old, I'd been drugged into an incoherent state. When my son Mac was delivered I was at least aware a baby was coming out of me. The birth was typical of the dreadful circus women in Australia had to endure back then— lady-bits shaved, enema shoved up the bum, kept immobile, feet in stirrups, barked at like a dim-witted child. Donald wasn't allowed in the labour ward, but when he eventually came to see me and our tiny boy, he wept, then grinned, then wept more.

'Look at him,' he said, the words exhaled more than spoken. 'He's perfect. Thank you, Elizabeth. I do adore you.'

Our child was christened 'MacDonald', in accordance with Burnley family tradition, but I always called him Mac.

Bunny Shaw-Preston sent a huge gift basket which included a toy horse.

'Congratulations on the arrival of your baby colt! Do I deserve a bit of the credit? Cheers, Bunny.'

In Bunny's mind, Donald and I were a breeding pair, the dam and sire she had approved to produce MacDonald Burnley Junior.

I was one of those lucky women who adored the early months of motherhood. Since I was without a mother or mother-in-law to observe me, I could make it up as I went along, unencumbered by nonsensical rules about proper infant behaviour, free to dote on Baby Mac without limits. I suspect there were pockets of love for my first, lost child that were still stored somewhere in my body, so Mac got that additional love as well.

I enjoyed breastfeeding, the satisfaction of nourishing another creature, the primal nature of it. Just by gazing at my baby or hearing him snuffle, I would feel the tingle of the milk let-down in my breasts, reminding me that I was an animal.

It's possible for a person to have compartments in their life— happy mothering in one section, even while there is desiccating boredom or wet misery in other compartments.

April 1952, Woollahra.

I listened for the shift in the rhythm of my son's breathing, the sign that he had drifted into secure sleep. Mac had turned three a few weeks before and his toddler face was morphing into what would become his boy face. But for now, hearing the tiny pants of air through his strawberry mouth, I could still picture him as a newborn.

Padding out of Mac's bedroom, I left the door open. His occasional nightmares were easier to settle if I heard him in time to gallop upstairs before he became too distressed.

Donald always worked in his study from the time he came home until he was ready for dinner. The workload of the various Burnley family businesses was onerous. Seeing the study door still closed, I crossed the vestibule, went through the dining room and into the kitchen.

We hadn't yet got around to remodelling The Gables. It was an airless house, always dark, but every surface was dust-free, glistening with polish. Donald had insisted we retain the housekeeper who came three times a week. For me, a common-as-muck person deep in my tissues, this arrangement felt uncomfortably close to having a servant. I did my best to pack away the jumble of Mac's toys and always laundered my personal things, not wanting Maureen (a lovely woman) to have to deal with my smalls. While Maureen cleaned the already-clean rooms, I would take Mac to the park. I didn't want my son to regard having domestic staff as a normal part of life.

This was the first time I had ever lived with money and, after almost four years of marriage, I still wasn't used to it. My 'well-off' status felt provisional, as if there'd been a clerical error that would soon be corrected. And in a way, the family wealth was a notional thing, given I had no knowledge of the household finances or access to the bank accounts.

Even though I was living in a huge house full of valuable paintings and silverware, I mostly experienced my affluence as an absence—the absence of worry about money and the constant mental arithmetic to make it through a week. Only people who have never known the marrow-deep anxiety about having enough cash to buy food would ever make light of the difference between poverty and the most basic financial security.

We lived in a big house cleaned by an employee, but when it came to preparing meals, I took on that mission myself. Mind you, it would not do to serve up Mock Brains on a Woollahra dinner table, so I had to lift my game.

I became a diligent follower of *The Australian Women's Weekly*. My childhood had given me bugger all in the way of training to be a middle-class housewife, so the good ladies of the *Weekly* were my guides, not just in cooking but in all matters related to etiquette, marriage and fashion.

Even with the generous budget I had to spend on ingredients, the cuisine of that time—the Anglo food anyway—was obstinately bland, either boiled into grey submission, gummed together with white sauce, given a laughably pretentious name or all three of the above. Donald never complained about the dinners I produced. I came to understand that he was a man with limited sense of smell (sinus issues) and who possessed only one, maybe two, tastebuds. If I'd served him Mock Brains and called it 'Faux Cerveaux', there would've been no problem. For my own sake, I did find ways to sneak a modicum of flavour into some dishes without jarring Donald's tastebud(s).

I also worked on the culinary skills I'd require for the dinner parties Donald planned to host. Judging by the magazines, for a dish to be impressive enough for a special occasion, the food had to be formed into some shape other than itself—rolled into a cylinder and pinned with toothpicks, entombed in savoury jelly (which was as disgusting as it sounds) or extruded into a cartoonish version of its original self (for example, salmon mousse in a fish mould).

While I practised for the time when we would actually have dinner guests, I tried to impress Donald with Beef Wellington and Bombe Alaska, which carried high risk of failure but were worth it for the impressiveness potential. Even if those meals were wasted on a man of limited gustatory appreciation, perfecting them gave me a project to stave off boredom.

According to the *Weekly*, a husband and wife sharing an evening meal free of interruption from children was important, nay essential. Looking like a 'frump' for your husband was unforgivable, so I made some effort every night to tame my hair, put on a crisp dress and a bright dash of lipstick.

The tricky part was estimating when Donald might emerge from his study and be ready to dine. The advice of the magazines was clear: I should not impose my housewifely timetable on him. It was best to maintain an agile approach to the timing of any meal. That night, I'd made coq au vin, kept warm on the stove until Donald was done with his work.

In the meantime, I could whip the cream for dessert. When I opened the fridge, the door nudged against my pregnant belly. I was eight months along with what would be my third baby (but officially only my second).

I'd made a potato galette to serve with the coq au vin. With Donald taking so long to leave his study, I checked the galette wasn't drying out too much in the oven warmer drawer, then I ducked into the vestibule to listen for clues about what time I should expect to serve the meal. Because I could hear papers being moved around, I knew he was still working, but I could never know the mood Donald would be in.

We had never entertained at The Gables. We'd been waiting for the moment when Donald felt the timing and the potential guest list would be right. That moment hadn't come so far. However, there had been some social invitations.

Back when Mac had just turned one, Bunny Shaw-Preston invited us to a cocktail party at Vue de Mer. I found a babysitter and dressed up, chuffed to go out and talk to adult human beings.

Driving us to Point Piper, Donald glanced across from the driver's seat to see me smiling. He exhaled briskly. 'Don't get yourself too excited. We're not staying at this thing for long. I'm tired.'

Donald worked six and sometimes seven days a week, leaving the house at seven, never returning before five, then working in his study before and after dinner. He never discussed the business with me, except to complain about the pressure on him.

Once, I'd suggested, 'Could you employ someone else to help?'

'Are you saying I can't manage it?' he snapped. 'Are you saying I need help to run the business properly?'

Donald could extract harsh judgement out of anything I said, receiving everything as an attack. There were an increasing number of landmine words, including any word associated with business or any mention of his father.

Before I had learned to be more cautious, I asked, 'Did your father ever explain his plan for the company to you?'

Donald made a sour hissing noise. 'My father didn't trust me to piss into the toilet bowl properly.'

If I were to pursue a comment like that, hoping it was a chance to connect with him, it never went well.

'It sounds like your father left things in a bit of a mess.'

'You have no idea what you're blabbing about! My father built the business that paid for the house you're living in, Elizabeth. I don't want to hear another word out of your ignorant mouth about my father.'

Eventually, the most anodyne question could detonate something in him.

'How are you, Donald?'

'What? Do you think I look like I'm—don't look at me with that *face*.'

'I'm sorry. I'm just—I'm not looking at you like—'

'Don't try to butter me up. I know what you think. I can hear it in your voice. I can hear it. I'll be in the study. I don't want any dinner.'

Even a talkative person like me can eventually learn not to speak very often.

That was the time when I started to wake up from my happy, milky stupor to realise our marriage was strained and joyless. I was quick to assume the marital deficiency was my fault. Having no decent model from my own family, I clearly didn't know how to love someone, how to be a wife. On one occasion, I patted Donald's hand supportively at the dinner table the way I'd seen Rose Nancarrow do with her husband. It didn't go well. Donald snatched his hand away as if I'd burned the skin and he scrunched his eyes, assuming I was ridiculing him.

So that was how things were on that evening in 1950, when we arrived at Vue de Mer. Bunny air-pecked me in greeting and the glow of her attention sparked a smidgin of optimism in me. A party would buoy Donald's spirits, give us a moment of shared fun we could use to reconnect.

'Now, I won't have married couples glued to each other at my parties,' Bunny said with mock bossiness. Maybe not so mock, maybe plain bossy. 'You and Donald must separate and *mingle*.'

Thirty people were already settled in conversational groups in the grand living room. I was anxious, never having felt welcome in Bunny's upper-crust crowd. I sometimes respond to nerves by being overly chatty and jokey (even now, as a phenomenally old lady). Luckily that evening I found a group of young mothers who seemed to enjoy my anecdotes about Mac, including an impersonation of the wildly happy noise he made the first time he tasted chocolate.

I sipped cautiously on one gin and tonic, not trusting my tipsy self (she might blurt out something gauche), but across the room, I could see Donald waving his glass to be filled by the waiter several times.

I focused my attention on the two young mothers I was talking to (Flopsy and Wiz, if memory serves), asking them questions about their children, their houses, their holidays. As a stickybeak, I'm always happy to ask other people a stream of questions and let them talk about themselves. And I've found people will often come away from a social encounter saying, 'She was very nice', for no reason other than I'd listened.

The next time I glanced over at Donald, he was wedged in a corner of the room in intense conversation with Charles Irwin-Bond, the Scots old boy who'd insulted my friends at the wedding. I couldn't hear the words Charles was saying but the smug singsong of his voice was audible. Donald guzzled another scotch and said little, but I could see the sinews in his neck were taut. He shifted his weight slightly and lost his balance, reaching out to grab a table, then angled his body to make the gesture appear deliberate, in that obvious way drunk people try to hide their drunken state. Only petite hors d'oeuvres had been served, so there were few carbohydrates to soak up the booze my husband was pouring down his gullet.

Donald's upper back and shoulders were hunched, curling up against Charles's many opinions. Suddenly all those muscles uncoiled and Donald started barking at the other man.

'Shut up, Charlie! You know bugger all about my business. But that never stopped you flapping your mouth because you're a prize bloody wanker.'

Charles tried to placate him but did so with a smirk on his face, which only served to wind Donald up into further belligerence.

'I told you to shut up! I said shut your mouth!'

Everyone in the room was gawping at Donald, and a second later, I registered a gust of perfumed air behind me and there was Bunny at my elbow.

'I think you'd better take Donald home.'

I flashed an apologetic smile to Flopsy and Wiz, then headed towards Donald. I stepped across the room as gracefully as a dancefloor move, bunging on a smile as a shield against the uncharitable stares from that pack of toffs.

'I'm not feeling well,' I whispered to Donald. 'Can we go home now?'

He nodded, so drunk that even the act of nodding threw him off balance. I looped my arm through his to steady him and steer him towards the door.

In the excruciating seconds we had to stand there waiting for the staff to bring our coats, Bunny came over to make an elegant show of saying goodbye so as not to ruin the vibe of her party. She squeezed my upper arm, letting her lacquered nails dig into my flesh ever so slightly.

'Elizabeth, you need to sort your husband out, don't you think?'

As we walked out to the car, I was mortified, but at the same time I had a flicker of hope: Donald and I could reconnect through our shared dislike of the odious Charles.

'You know, Donald, I think that man Charles is—'

He slammed his hand in the air just in front of my face. 'Don't you flap your bloody mouth either. You were too loud at that party, Elizabeth. Laughing like a fishwife.'

Snapping at me used up the last of his booze-sodden brain cells. He stumbled and sank down onto the gutter near our car, dropping the keys, not fit to drive. I considered going inside to call for a taxi but I was too ashamed to face those people again.

I picked up the car keys. 'Should I drive?'

To my surprise, Donald just nodded, sloppy with scotch and self-pity, and once I opened the door, he hauled himself onto the passenger seat and fell asleep.

Luckily we hadn't come in the old Jag. We were in the new Rover he'd bought a month before, which would be much easier for me to handle.

I confess that I did not have a driver's licence or any instruction, apart from a few lessons in a truck around the ROF Kirkby yard, taught by a young soldier who was motivated by a desire to get into my knickers. I had loved that first experience behind the wheel and I'd always watched Donald carefully when he was driving, picturing myself at the controls. But a couple of lust-inspired lessons and some imaginary driving weren't proper preparation for me to drive the Rover, a manual with the heavy steering of a 1950s car.

It was not an elegant motoring display. There was a huge amount of stalling, bunny-hopping, near misses with parked cars and grinding gears so loudly that people looked over in alarm. But I did get us home that night and, arguably, I had taught myself to drive, more or less, by the time I pulled into the driveway of The Gables.

After the party at Bunny's, Donald's drinking ratcheted up, or maybe I just woke up to the fact that my husband was often inebriated and there was always a bottle of Scotch on the go in his study. I was too afraid to let him drive pissed with Mac in the car, so I took lessons and secured my driver's licence.

When Donald bought himself a silver XK120 Jaguar Roadster, I didn't think of it as a pathetic bid for manhood. I just hoped his flashy new sports car might cheer him up. And I was glad the sturdy Rover was available for me to drive around.

After the Vue de Mer evening, we stopped accepting social invitations, which were not frequent anyway. Word had spread not only about Donald's altercation with Charles but also his generally morose demeanour. In my observation, people tend to sidle away from unhappy individuals, as if misery might be contagious.

Pearl Jowett remained my good friend and we were able to see each other more often once I had the use of the Rover. I would sit Mac on the back seat and drive to meet Pearl at a beach or park. She would make a glorious fuss of my little boy and Mac was as enchanted by her lovely nature as everyone else. The three of us would picnic, swim, play silly games and doze on the rug. Those were by far my happiest days during that period.

For Mac's second birthday, Pearl bought him a sailor suit and a toy boat. That day, on Bronte Beach, she told me she was moving to Melbourne where her latest beau, Victor, another married man, was setting her up in an apartment. Pearl believed this was a step towards Victor leaving his wife to marry her and give her the baby she yearned for.

I didn't say much in response to this news. I was walloped with self-pity about her leaving, but I didn't want to deflate Pearl's effervescent mood.

Once Pearl Jowett left Sydney, I was even more isolated. The pals I'd made working at the Trocadero were distant now—me marrying into the upper crust created a separation from the young women who were still serving wealthy people at functions.

My husband rarely spoke to me beyond terse comments regarding practical arrangements and the sex had only ever been serviceable at best. During my pregnancy with Mac, Donald had felt odd about having intercourse, for fear of harming the baby. Afterwards he found the idea that I was lactating a turn-off, and he took to sleeping in the back bedroom, to avoid being disturbed when I attended to Mac during the night. The baby in my uterus in April 1952 had been conceived on a night when Donald was in a foul mood for reasons he never told me. That night was less like lovemaking and more like being used as an anger-management prop, pounded into for release of tension. I've always chosen to believe that it did not affect the child conceived in the process.

The coq au vin was starting to form a gloopy skin on the top so I stirred it and turned the gas on again for a moment. Donald was staying in his study later than usual on this night and I was hungry, so I hooked out a drumstick to keep me going.

The longer my husband lurked in the study, the worse his mood was likely to be. Donald had always been secretive and withdrawn but lately more so, often going days without addressing a word to me. I've never been a fan of screaming rows and the throwing of missiles at loved ones, but hostile silence can eat away at your innards like a corrosive substance.

All of this I might have endured, assuming this was just how things went—or at least how they went for a person who had been found out as being unworthy of love (me)—but there was no doubt Mac was worthy of love, so I struggled to make sense of Donald's antipathy to our child.

Donald could be annoyed by any minor disturbance made by his son, barking at him to be quiet. Mac, unsurprisingly, began to shrink from his father, which Donald took as a personal slight. He would peer at Mac suspiciously as if a three-year-old might be laughing at him as part of a conspiracy with nasty judgemental people like Charles Irwin-Bond.

My solution was to keep Mac away from his father for most of the day and pick the moments when both were likely to be agreeable—when Mac was post-nap, full-bellied, and if I'd heard Donald speaking in a positive tone of voice on the phone. Then there might be a brief benign moment between them—like a testy monarch granting an audience to one of his children who'd been dressed and prepped for the occasion.

Now that Mac was growing from a toddler into a little boy, it was trickier. When the two of them had a play sword fight one Sunday afternoon, I was desperately pleased, but then Donald stumbled, landing in an undignified way, and bellowed at Mac. Donald Burnley still felt ashamed about not being able to enlist during the war and he could feel unmanned even by his three-year-old son.

'You love that child more than you love me!' he snapped at me once. Donald was one of those men who felt jealous of his own child, as if any love the baby received was pinched from the store of love owed to him.

I would not have used the term 'verbal abuse' back then, but much of the time Donald spoke to me in a lacerating, belittling way. The things about me that he'd found attractive now revolted him. If I displayed any liveliness, he felt that as a reproach, an irritant. If I was subdued, he took that as silent judgement of him.

I mentioned earlier that Donald and I didn't know each other very well when we married and that remained true. So it was by blind chance or destructive instinct that he managed to find the spots where a skewer could jam right inside my innards.

'You're a common little slut not fit to live in a house like this.'

'Stop opening your stupid mouth and showing the whole world how ignorant you are.'

'You're so fucking annoying, Elizabeth, I don't believe any sane person could love you.'

He would almost always mutter apologies the next day and I made allowances for the role alcohol played in his nasty rants. But there was a misery inside Donald Burnley that fermented to create its own noxious mind-altering brew.

In one recent argument, I'd suggested we take a family holiday.

'A holiday? I'm a busy man!' he shouted. 'I'm not some lazy dago who lies around on the beach. I'm not like your wog friends.'

I must make clear here that MacDonald Burnley was not an especially bigoted man by the standards of the day. He had just trawled around for something hurtful to say to me.

Seeing that he'd stung me with mention of Athena and Nick, Donald went on. 'That Greek woman—uh . . .'

'Athena.'

'Yes. Her. She showed up here. Ages back. Before MacDonald was born. She seemed to know you were expecting.'

Athena knew because Pearl had told her I'd fallen pregnant.

'Well, why didn't . . . Where was I?' I asked.

'You were upstairs vomiting. I told her you were out. She tried to leave some dago present for the baby but I said we didn't want it. And we didn't want her coming here.'

That was why Athena had sent back the invitation to the baby shower. Once I knew that, knew that she'd come to see me and been turned away so horribly, I should have reached into Donald's trousers and torn his balls off his miserable fucking groin. Then I should have driven round to Athena's house. But I didn't do either.

I was too diminished a version of myself at that point. I'd bought into Donald's 'you are unlovable' narrative and the flares of anger that had fuelled me in the past and had sometimes stood me in good stead—well, there wasn't enough of me left to generate a feeling as strong as anger.

Donald Burnley would have been outraged if anyone suggested he hit his wife. It's true he never struck me but there was shoving and gripping of my arms hard enough to leave handprints. More than once, he slammed my shoulder against the heavy mahogany wardrobe. I can still feel a crunchy twinge in that shoulder almost seventy-seven years later. It was violence, even though I didn't use that word then. Me now would like to peel the slate roof off that fake Tudor monstrosity of a house, reach my arms inside and pluck my young self out.

I was giving the coq au vin another delicate stir when I heard Mac cry out 'Mummy' at the top of the stairs, his voice pitched high from the terror of a nightmare. I bolted out of the kitchen, hoping to whisk him back to his room before he bothered Donald.

I was too late. Mac was already at the bottom of the stairs, bleating 'Mummy' over and over, and Donald had barged out of his study.

'What is that appalling noise?' he demanded. 'We do not bellow around this house like hooligans!'

He grabbed Mac's shoulders and squatted down so his head was at the same level as the boy's. Then he barked directly at Mac, his big angry adult face an inch away from the child's face. 'You do not run through this house bellowing for your mother! Do you understand me?'

Too afraid to respond, Mac twisted his face into what could appear to be a lop-sided smile but was in fact his self-conscious grimace of anxiety. I would see my beautiful son do that lop-sided smile many times in his life.

'Don't you dare smirk at me!' Donald shook the boy's small body back and forth as if he could shake the smirk off his face.

Mac's face stayed twisted, even as he started to cry, and that enraged Donald even further.

'Don't you even think about crying! And don't you laugh at your father! You are a naughty, dreadful, disgusting boy!'

Donald kept one hand gripping Mac's shoulder as he drew back the other to whack him on the side of the head. Mac went sprawling onto the bottom stair, far enough away from his father that I could throw my body in between to protect him.

I did not shout at Donald, but my voice was firm, moving from each word to the next with deliberate, steel-capped steps. 'Don't you ever hit him again.'

As I carried Mac upstairs, I heard Donald stomp back into his study and wallop the door shut. I let my little boy cry the tension out of his body, smoothing back the hair from his forehead over and over in a soothing rhythm.

When Mac drifted back to sleep, his rib cage shuddering with each breath, I packed a few clothes and toys into an overnight bag. I wrote a note and left it on the console table where Donald would be sure to see it. The note read: 'Popping over to Bunny's. Will probably sleep there tonight. Dinner on the stove.' Notice the perky tone (popping over!). At this stage, I just needed to get out of that house and think clearly. Since I had no viable plan, I couldn't risk the note being inflammatory or impossible to retreat from.

I bundled my sleeping child in his favourite paisley quilt, carried him to the garage and lay him on the back seat of the Rover.

The housekeeper in her grey uniform opened the front door of Vue de Mer to see me standing there with a sleeping child wrapped in a quilt. She looked confused and then embarrassed on my behalf.

From inside the house, I could hear a Tony Bennett record playing and the voices of Bunny's dinner guests.

When Bunny came to the door, she sussed out the situation with the sharpness I'd come to expect from her.

'Elizabeth. Oh dear.'

'Bunny, I'm sorry to show up like this. I was hoping—'

Bunny scrubbed her hand through the air as if she was wiping away any trace of my presence. 'No. Better you don't say anything to me. This is not the way, dear. You drive home right now and sort this out with your husband.'

I couldn't speak for a moment and Bunny chose to regard that as assent to her advice. She shut the door.

I drove around for some time so the motion of the car would keep Mac sleeping while I thought of where else I could go. Eventually, at about 10 p.m., I parked the Rover beside Steyne Park in Double Bay. There was enough street-lighting not to feel too scared, but it was not so busy a spot that passers-by would gawp at us.

I climbed into the back seat and lay down, finding a position in which Mac's little body and my eight-month-pregnant belly were curled together like jigsaw pieces. Blessedly Mac slept through all of this, only half waking briefly to wonder where he was.

Before dawn, I had decided I would have to go back to Donald. This may be a shocking decision to a reader but the options for someone in my situation at that time were—well, there were very few options. I had no family support or access to money, and there was no single parent benefit. Any court of the time would grant Donald custody of the children. And I couldn't live in the car with my son, and soon a newborn.

By the time I pulled the car into the garage of The Gables, it was 6.30 a.m. I could hear the sound of papers being moved around the study so I knew Donald was awake and still in there. I encouraged Mac to run up to his bedroom to play while I went into the kitchen to fetch breakfast for him. There were large, congealed puddles of coq au vin sauce on the bench and the remains of the potato galette, ragged as if an animal had gnawed at it.

I grabbed some fruit and buttered bread to take upstairs—quietly, not wanting an encounter with my husband. Meanwhile, my brain was whirring with plans, strategies to keep Mac protected from his father while still ensuring we had a house to live in. I mapped out a daily routine with limited contact between them, so fewer opportunities to shout and hit. When the new baby arrived, I would ask Maureen, the three-day-a-week housekeeper, to move into The Gables full-time for a month to take care of Mac while I recovered from the birth. I would devise ways to keep my children as safe and happy as all children should be. There was a hardness inside me now—not strength exactly, but a hardness that could buttress any self-doubt or anxiety.

I watched Mac playing on the bedroom carpet, feeding pieces of fruit to his wooden zoo animals, making the chewing noises for them. Then I heard the front door slam and a few moments later, the sound of Donald driving the Jaguar Roadster out of the garage and down the driveway. Hearing him go, I exhaled, not realising how tight my chest muscles had been until the moment I unknotted them.

An hour later, Mac was playing in the backyard while I stretched my swollen body out on a garden bench, hoping to soak sunlight through my skin. I pictured myself refuelling via photosynthesis, the way the plants in the garden drew energy from the sun, and that idea made me smile.

Hearing the doorbell ring, I wondered, for one naïve moment, if it was Bunny come to offer support. I opened the door to see two men in grey suits and hats, and behind them a workman in coveralls was parking a van. Mac ran up the hallway and wrapped himself around my legs.

'Good morning. Can I help you?' I asked the men.

The more senior of the two suited gents replied. 'Morning. Is Mr Burnley at home?'

I shook my head.

'Are you Mrs Burnley?'

'It might be best if you come back when my husband is—'

The man held up a document. 'By law, we can enter the premises and take the property without Mr Burnley being present.'

I peered at the document. Most of it was a blur of legal blah-blah in small type but I gleaned enough to understand these men were bailiffs, here to seize valuable items from the house. As a child, I had witnessed this scene played out on the front porches of our debt-swamped neighbours in Deptford. It was not something I expected to see in Woollahra.

A wave of wooziness hit me and I grabbed onto the doorframe to steady myself. The bailiff glanced at my pregnant belly, at the child, and he winced apologetically.

'I know this must be upsetting, Mrs Burnley. We'll be taking the paintings but very little of the furniture this morning, so you and your son should feel free to stay for now.'

I coaxed Mac back towards the garden, but he wanted to stay inside, curious about what was happening. I tried to turn it into a light-hearted educational activity. 'How about we watch these men do their special job! You know the painting with the ship in the dining room—the one you and I think is the ugliest one? Do you think the men will take that one first?'

Mac was entertained for fifteen minutes watching the removal of the gilt-framed artworks that weighed so heavily on every room of The Gables. He was intrigued by the rectangular marks left on the walls, the ghosting effect from damp, sooty air collecting around the frames over decades.

As we watched two men cart a large, dismal landscape to the van out the front, the senior bailiff touched my arm for a quiet word.

'Mrs Burnley, you do realise the house has been seized also?'

'Sorry?'

'Did your husband tell you about—' The bailiff twigged that my husband had told me nothing. 'Look, I shouldn't really say this . . .' His gaze flicked down, as if my eight-month-gone belly could grant permission to bend the rules. 'If you want to take clothes and a few things for the children today, we won't stop you.'

'Oh. Yes, I could—uh—'

'Any items you really need, you should grab them today.'

'Could I put things in the car?' I asked. 'I can drive.'

'Well, the cars are on the list of forfeited property. But if you want to transport some things today to wherever you'll be staying, we can turn a blind eye.'

'Thank you.' My throat was tight from trying not to cry. 'You're very kind.'

I did my best to turn the packing into a game for Mac. We laid out several suitcases in the upstairs rooms and I let him have the final say on which toys and baby clothes should go in them. He was so busy with his decision-making he didn't fret about why we were packing up. I suppose it was the same for me: the practical tasks soaked up my energy that might otherwise have gone into panicking. As I carried suitcases down to the Rover in the garage, Mac marched behind me, earnestly conveying baby paraphernalia in his arms as if he were in a royal procession.

I admit that I did exploit the kindness of the bailiff just a little. On my trips back and forth to the car, I ducked into the dining room, which had already been stripped of its artworks. I took six items of silverware from inside the buffet, plus the two silver candle snuffers, wrapping them in quilts and bundles of clothes so I could smuggle them into the boot of the Rover.

I drove half a mile down the street and parked where there was less chance of nosy neighbours seeing our Carload of Shame. I figured

Donald had a plan for where we would be living now and the pile of stuff I'd rescued could stay in the car until we moved there.

It was a slow walk back to The Gables, given I was puffy-ankled in my third trimester and accompanied by a three-year-old who had an urgent need to inspect fence palings and chat to ants on the footpath. I didn't mind that the walk took a fair time, hoping the men would be finished this stage of their removal work by the time we returned. There had been some satisfaction to observe those hideous paintings being removed but now it felt too sad to stand there watching the house be stripped around us.

We walked up our driveway to find a police car parked next to the van. I used to see police backing up bailiffs in the streets of Deptford when they expected trouble, but Donald and I were hardly an aggro pair.

Then I saw the bailiff point me out to the police officer and the look on the copper's face was enough to know something bad had happened.

Donald was dead. He'd been found in the Roadster a few hours before, smashed into a tree on the side of the road, a half-drunk bottle of scotch on the seat beside him, killed in what would be termed 'a single vehicle accident' these days.

Within seconds, grief overtook my body, involuntary and not fully conscious, like the onset of an epileptic seizure. I let go of Mac's hand and dropped down on all fours, moaning and gulping for breath. I wonder now if the cop and the bailiff thought I'd gone into labour.

I was utterly confused about my own reaction—about how I could be this distraught over Donald, a man I did not love, possibly hated; a man I wanted to escape. I'm sure some of it came from reservoirs of grief about Michael and Pauline that had been released by the news of Donald's death. But now I understand that the intensity also came from the detonation of emotions about my father—a broken, angry man who, like Donald, may or may not have killed himself.

The policeman and the bailiffs who watched me weep frantically on the front porch must have assumed I'd truly loved my husband. Probably just as well that was how it appeared. The policing of women's emotions, the prescription of appropriate responses, was a thing then as it is today.

What I do regret was that three-year-old Mac had to stand there holding the hand of the bailiff, watching his mother wail and pant like a wounded creature who was not in control of herself enough to see him safely through the world.

That afternoon, I wedged my pregnant body behind the wheel of the Rover, with Mac in the front passenger seat and the boot and body of the car packed so full I couldn't see out the rear window. We drove to Earlwood and I pulled up outside Athena and Nick's house.

By the time I'd hauled myself out of the driver's seat, Athena had come out onto her front verandah. She saw my face, bloated and blotchy from crying, saw the car full of possessions, and she understood the desperate nature of our predicament.

She called back through her front door. 'Nick! We need a hand!' Then she trotted across the lawn towards the passenger side of the car. 'Hello. I'm Athena. You must be Mac. It's very nice to meet you. Run inside and find my girls. They would love to play with you.'

She looked up at me. She didn't smile—thank Christ—I would have shattered into tiny pieces if she had smiled. But my friend's gaze was unguarded and loving, her forgiveness not needing to be spoken. That woman was a goddess.

Nick ran outside, paused to tie up his shoelaces, then the three of us carried the bags and bundles from the car into their house.

The funeral was held at All Saints. Pearl and Athena were there to support me, while Nick stayed home to babysit Mac. Word had spread in eastern suburbs circles about Donald's debts and business disasters, so attendance at his service was very small. A few of the ancient folk I'd first seen at the Silver Stars Ball—the trembling pair and the chalky-eyed fellow—showed up.

Over the next two weeks, I made several visits to the law firm that had handled the Burnley family's affairs for decades. It emerged the business had been in trouble long before Donald took over. His father had mishandled things, plastering over the oozing losses of one business by using equity from another, accruing more debt, not paying taxes. Donald should have cut away the dead tissue and consolidated into one viable business, but instead he had taken on more debt, until the house and every skerrick of property was on the line. The lawyer explained all of this to me in a censorious tone, as if it were somehow my fault.

It was not difficult for someone to make me feel guilty about my dead husband. I had never found a way to save Donald Burnley. By marrying him in such a rushed, foolish way I had probably made things worse. Alongside guilt, there was plenty of anger. Rage about the unhappiness Donald had transferred from his own wretchedness onto me and our child. And rage about the mess he'd now left for me to manage.

Around this time, I thought a great deal about my father. I tried to calculate how much I should forgive him for the misery he'd visited on his wife and children, taking into account the misery I knew had been inflicted on him as a child. Sometimes I could make the sums come out so I was less angry towards my dad. At other times, I feared that if I were to let go of the anger, I would be relinquishing my self-worth, my right to be treated decently. The resentment I harboured towards people who'd hurt me was my way to hang onto a little wad of pride.

On my most expansive days, I am able to pity my father, an abused little boy whose own kids deserved to be treated better. Most of us can't help but pass some of the damage done to us on to those we're supposed to love. If I see a person being obnoxious in the supermarket I can think, *What happened to you when you were little that makes you act like this?* I try to show myself similar kindness and dial back the self-blame. But I also believe I should hold myself responsible for my choices and behave as if I hold the agency in my free clean hands.

The Rover had been repossessed the day before the funeral, so after one of my meetings with the lawyer in the city, I travelled back to Earlwood on the train. Nick was always offering to drive me places but he and Athena were already doing so much for me, I didn't want to drag him away from his work.

My back was aching on the walk from the railway station and I had to stop several times to breathe through a cramp. By the time I reached Athena and Nick's street, I couldn't ignore the fact that I was in labour.

I dropped onto all fours on their front lawn and called out in the brief gap between contractions. When Athena ran outside and saw what was happening, she went straight into practical mode, delegating her daughter Sofia to go next door and ask Mr Andrianakis for a lift to the hospital.

This was my third delivery and the labour progressed rapidly. Athena tried to help me to my feet but I refused to budge. I stayed on my hands and knees, undergarments yanked down and skirt hoisted up, bellowing like a sea lion, putting on a show for any Earlwood residents who cared to flick their curtains aside.

When Athena saw the baby crowning, she bolted inside to get some clean bedding to put under me and two minutes later, she delivered my daughter.

Athena always liked to remind people that she met Rose Athena Burnley before anyone else and I must say that my friend and my younger daughter had an especially powerful bond from that moment onwards.

We lived at Athena and Nick's house for three months after Rose was born. I sold some of the silverware I'd smuggled out of The Gables and used the proceeds to pay my friends for our board. (I put Athena into a wrestle hold to force her to accept anything.)

With the rest of the silverware money, I estimated I had enough cash to pay rent for a few weeks while I found a job and the childminding I would need. That was the plan.

It turned out that in 1952, for a 24-year-old widow with two small children, renting a house was not an easy thing. After several failed attempts to convince landlords I would be a reliable tenant, Nick agreed to pose as my husband. I finally took possession of the keys to a stupendously shabby semi in Marrickville, with a lease signed by my pretend husband, Nick Samios.

Before I moved the children to that house, I took round cleaning gear to give the place a good scrub. While I worked, I kept the front door open, to let fresh air in and to sweep the dead cockroaches out. When I looked up at one point, there was a dog staring at me through the doorway.

'Hello. Where do you belong?'

The dog, a red and tan kelpie, decided she belonged in the house, marching straight inside and following me from room to room as I swept and scrubbed. Sadie II was about two years old when she showed up and she was with me for the next thirteen years.

The day we moved in, I put Baby Rose on the kitchen bench in the fancy bassinet the bailiff had allowed me to take. The house was echoey because we had so little furniture, other than a few items Nick had scrounged for us. Mac looked around at the tatty house with disappointment ready to slip into weepy dismay.

'We will get some more furniture,' I said. 'But you know what's good about the way it is right now? We've got room to dance, honeybunch!'

I switched on the radio and in one of those scraps of luck that can come when you need it, there was Rosemary Clooney singing 'Come On-A My House' with its irresistible beat and wonderfully silly, joyful lyrics. Mac could not stay glum with Rosemary singing that song to us and we danced between the bare rooms of our house, Sadie skittering around our feet, until we were both puffed out and giggling.

In the next part of this story, I will finally have my first orgasm. I realise it's been a long wait. I, more than anyone, regret how long it took.

SEVEN

Before we reach first orgasm, I should establish context. These things require some build-up and are better if not rushed.

March 1955.

I'd instituted a routine of setting my alarm clock for an hour before I would need to get the three of us (Mac, Rose, me) dressed, breakfasted and out the door to school, childminder and work. Sacrificing an hour of sleep was worth it to have that slice of time at our kitchen table in the Marrickville semi, with Sadie II sprawled at my feet, huffing and twitching in her dreams. There was a cushiony quiet in the house and the streets around us, apart from the occasional tradesman motoring past or the clinking bottles of the milkman.

I would sit in my nightie and bed socks, drinking tea and writing in an exercise book, channelling the thoughts of Mrs P. Marshall of Randwick, Mrs F. Jorgensen of Penshurst and other ladies.

I had discovered that *The Australian Women's Weekly* and other magazines offered money for stories ('Strange But True') and readers' letters—the amounts of cash not inconsiderable for someone wedged in my layer of the economic pyramid.

I'd started with a story about Brenda Goodbody, my eight-and-a-half-fingered friend from the munitions factory and the piece was published in the *Weekly*, scoring me two pounds. My next submission—about no one believing Mac when he saw (truly) an escaped circus elephant lope through our local park—had cracked the ten-pound 'story of the week'. I was on a roll, dredging up any life scraps that might be of inoffensive interest and spinning them into pleasing narrative morsels. The worry was that a barrage of anecdotes and letters from one source—Mrs E. Burnley of Marrickville—would end up being unwelcome, so my solution was to conjure up other fictional ladies who could write pieces, via postal addresses borrowed from my friends, thereby ramping up the production line of stories and maintaining the flow of cash.

This might be regarded as a form of cheating, but I would argue there were mitigating elements. I was a cash-strapped widow with little kids. The stories must have been passably entertaining for readers because my publication strike rate was strong. And I made a full imaginative investment in my characters, respecting the ways they saw the world differently, which enabled me to differentiate our personas and generate fresh material. The writing was always underpinned by affection for my made-up women.

I pictured 'Mrs F. Jorgensen' as a crusty dame who'd spent years on outback properties before retiring to the city, so 'Freda' was good for yarns about bushfires, stumbling over sleeping livestock in dark paddocks, and using undergarments for makeshift repairs to broken-down vehicles. 'Mrs P. Marshall' ('Phyllis') had a superstitious streak, handy for stories of ghosts who turned out to be dogs tangled in bed linen, odd-shaped pennies that would reappear in haunting fashion and other tales of mystery.

The money I earned from these stories went into the Biscuit Tin Fund, a stash I was accumulating to pay for piano lessons, ballet classes, art materials, encyclopaedias. I'd be buggered if my kids were going to miss out on the extra stuff that middle-class children with extant fathers would have. There were some occasions I had to raid the tin to cover our rent, but I generally managed to quarantine that money for educational purposes.

After some experimentation I found that early morning was best for this self-assigned freelance writing, better than last thing at night when tiredness would swamp my brain.

Occasionally during my writing hour, almost three-year-old Rose would weave out of the bedroom she shared with her brother, pad into the kitchen in her pyjamas, climb onto my lap and snooze against my belly. Her wilful dark hair (like mine, poor kid) was matted from a night of thrashing her head on the pillow until it formed a frizzy shrub in which scraps of food and toys could hide like small animals in a hedgerow. Her little body, straight from the snug bedclothes, radiated warmth into me like a hot water bottle, but left my hands free to keep scribbling during that hour before the obligations of the day crashed in.

I submitted some stories to the magazines in longhand, using different stationery that suited the personality of each of my characters. The pieces written under my own name were typed up on the second-hand Smith Corona typewriter I'd bought to practise my typing skills.

I'd completed a shorthand and typing course by correspondence, but it soon became clear that the rigid office hours of secretarial jobs didn't suit my situation as a single mother of two small children. Instead, I structured my workday so I did a daytime barmaid shift, scooting home in time to bathe the kids, cook dinner and read bedtime books. Then I would pay someone (for several years it was our lovely grandmotherly neighbour) to mind sleeping Mac and Rose while I went out again to clean those offices in which I was *not* working as a secretary despite my stenography certificate.

I managed to stagger through those years thanks to the network of favours between women, a system based on unspoken reciprocity—you would always say yes to a request to mind another mother's kids on any occasion you possibly could, trusting you would receive the same support when needed. I also had Athena as my safety net: if desperate, I could take Mac and Rose to Nick's building yard where Athena worked in the office five days a week, and I often collected Thea and Sofia from school if Athena was caught up.

So it was that in the February of 1955, I was doing early shifts behind the bar of The General Gordon, a pub in Sydenham—a quick gallop across the railway lines from Mac's primary school.

Cy was one of the regulars in the front bar of The General Gordon, always coming in alone around midday.

'G'day, Lizzie.'

I should explain that most people called me 'Lizzie' in those years, in the boldly friendly way Australians often do without consultation. I didn't mind. 'Elizabeth' carried unwelcome associations and a lot had happened since 'Betty'.

Cy always ordered a schooner, which he downed within seconds, then a nip of brandy, which he would make last for twenty minutes before heading off. He was in his mid-forties, not especially handsome, but with his tumble of black hair, chubby face, stocky body, brown eyes and extravagantly long lashes, I thought he resembled a pretty bear. He was always rumpled, as if someone had just pulled him out of a bag, but he washed himself and his clothes regularly, so he didn't pong. I'd heard Cy mention growing up rough in timber camps around Nowra and he still spoke rough, with sinewy vowels.

Not a bloke who came from money. A bloke who did not appear to be employed but still had some cash.

My curiosity, eventually, burst out of my mouth and I asked him, 'What do you do for a job that you can be in a pub in the daytime?'

'Ha!' He grinned, not offended by my potentially offensive question. 'I'm a painter.'

'Do you paint houses or art?'

'Art.' He offered this reply without any pomposity, as if he would've been just as proud to say he painted houses.

'Do you make a living out of your art?'

'More or less,' he said, pulling up his eyebrows as if he was as surprised as anyone about this.

What I didn't know at that stage was that Cyrus John O'Farrell was a legit Australian painter whose work hung in galleries, sold for serious sums and won prizes. He just didn't behave the way that I, in my ignorance, expected a proper artist would.

A week later, as I handed him his brandy, he made me an offer.

'So, Lizzie, I need a life model for some work I want to try. Would you be up for it? I mean, it'd be kit off.'

He squinted at me, checking to see if the 'kit off' requirement was a dealbreaker.

I confess I did blush. 'Oh . . . I wouldn't know what to do.'

'Nah, no prior training required. You just stand there—or sit or lie down, depending—in the nuddy.'

'But I'm not a proper model. I mean, I'm not . . .' I looked down at my nice-enough but not model-type body.

'You're perfect. You've got the shoulders I'm after. Look, no worries if you don't fancy it. It'd be two days a week, for three hours a go. I'd pay twice the hourly rate they pay here and you'd be done in time to pick your kids up from school.'

Two days later, I showed up at the address Cy had written on the back of a crumpled receipt. Halfway along a Marrickville street, crammed with foundries and industrial workshops, number 22 was a large disused garage, still stinking of motor oil, now a dumping ground for old car parts and junk. This was hardly a place an art-gallery-type artist would hang out, so I was doubtful as I called out into the dark windowless space.

'Hello? Excuse me?'

'That you, Lizzie?' It was Cy's voice funnelled down the narrow wooden staircase I could just make out at the far end of the garage. 'Come up!'

Towards the top, the stairs turned at a sharp angle and suddenly delivered me onto the second level which was saturated with yellow light, as if I'd ascended into a Golden Syrup heaven. Windows filled three of the four walls on this floor, from knee-height up to the tin roof. The glass was too dirty to see through but that film of grime acted as the perfect filter, transforming midday glare into this honeyed glow.

'Welcome to my painting cubby!'

Cy did a dancing spin around, his feet bare on the paint-spattered wooden floor. Everything in there was flecked or splodged with paint, including Cy's hair, baggy trousers and shirt. He had two easels on the go, next to a large table covered in a jumble of tubes, jars and rags.

Against the brick wall near the top of the stairs was the area that served as Cy's living quarters: a single bed, fruit boxes stacked on top of each other as shelving for clothes, groceries and books, next to a small table with a camping stove and an electric kettle. In the corner was an industrial sink, with hoses running from the taps into a huge clawfoot bathtub. Shirts and other laundry items were hanging up to dry on a rope strung between two windows.

'Thanks for showing up, Lizzie. If you're having second thoughts about the modelling, no worries at all.'

'No, no, I said I'd—I want to try.'

'Whacko. I'd offer you a brandy to relax but I can't have a bottle in the place.' Having one daily nip of spirits at The General Gordon was Cy's method to control drinking.

'That's okay. I'm not nervous at all!' I did a little pantomime about how nervous I was, and he laughed. Laughing together about my nerves made it our shared issue and much less nerve-racking.

Cy indicated that I should go behind a tapestry screen also spattered with paint. A peacock-blue silk robe was hanging there for me to change into. It felt safer to undress in privacy, even though seconds later, I would be entirely naked in front of an almost-stranger.

While I was behind the screen, Cy dragged an old sofa into a clear area and threw a sheet over it. When I emerged in the robe, he waved his hand at the sofa.

'I'm just after a few charcoal sketches today. If you get yourself into a comfortable pozzie, I'll sing out when I need you to shift around.'

I let the silk robe slide off my shoulders and draped it over the sofa. For those first few seconds, the air in the room stung every molecule of skin on my body. I quickly positioned myself on the sofa, feeling Cy's eyes on me. I was not used to being stared at naked—in fact, I was not used to being stared at so intently even when clothed. Until that point in my life, I'd manoeuvred to avoid such a moment—either by dancing around or running off at the mouth with chat, anything to avoid being scrutinised. This was based on the fear that if I were thoroughly seen, the viewer would realise the very essence of me was horrible.

I arranged my body in a pose so stilted it was as if I were a robot who didn't understand how human beings were meant to look.

'Thank you, Lizzie. That's great. That's the sort of thing I'm after. Just relax there, okay?'

I was so relieved I hadn't let Cy down that I did relax. It was astonishing how rapidly it felt comfortable and ordinary to be lying there in the nuddy being looked at, occasionally changing the angle of my torso, or draping a leg over the arm of the sofa or leaning my head differently, as requested by Cyrus.

My motives—need for rent money and curiosity—meant I'd submitted to an experience I would never have sought out, an experience that required me to dive into my self-consciousness, the body shame, and sit with it until it dissolved. It was a kind of desensitisation therapy which also happened to earn me cash. After the first hour, I began to enjoy being looked at—not in a conceited way, not as an object of desire or as a point of comparison with anyone else, but just as one example of a human figure, being appreciated as all humans should be. It was liberating.

When Cy called a tea break and filled the kettle, I put on the silk robe and padded around to look at the sketches. A few sweeps of charcoal had captured the contours of my body with particularity but transformed it into something beyond any particular body. A few sweeps of charcoal and suddenly on the inanimate flat surface there was flesh, vitality, yearning.

'How do you do that?' I asked. 'You must be a wizard.'

'Crikey Moses, I've been called a lot of shit but never that.'

Cy handed me an enamel mug of tea and we perched on camping stools, chatting about everyday stuff as if he hadn't just been looking at my breasts and thighs for two hours.

That was how it went every Tuesday and Thursday for the next month. I would disrobe and adopt whatever pose Cy required while he drew or painted. He was never sleazy towards me, never came on to me, always showed concern for my comfort.

During the tea break, me in the peacock-blue silk robe, we would talk, and our conversations would carry over to Mondays, Wednesdays and Fridays when I was working, fully clothed, at The General Gordon and Cy came in for his brandy.

I talked about my kids and Cyrus was genuinely interested in hearing stories about six-year-old Mac and three-year-old Rose, in part because he was nostalgic about the time when his two children were that little. Cy always sounded sad but resigned to the fact that his sons, teenagers by this point, wanted nothing to do with him. His wife had left him and taken the boys years before.

'She was dead right to leave me,' he said. 'I wasn't much use to her. I used to drink.'

I bombarded Cy with questions about his early life, wanting to understand how someone could grow up living in tents in the forest with a violent father, minimal schooling, no experience of the artistic world, and yet become this extraordinary artist. Cy had started doing little sketches and comic drawings as a seven-year-old to make up for the fact that he couldn't read or write properly. During one of his brief stints at a primary school, a teacher had lent him a book, *The Wonderful World of Art*. When his father moved them the next day, Cy had no chance to return the book, so it travelled with him from then on. He became obsessed with *The Wonderful World of Art*, copying styles and images, sketching and painting on whatever paper or fabric or bits of masonite he could get hold of. He could escape his father and the packs of drunkenly volatile men around him by slipping away to draw, whether it was in the forest or a wrecker's yard or the back of a pub. Once he was absorbed in the process of creating, he could block out whatever ugly scene was happening nearby, and feel his body shift into a different gear.

In his teens, every December, he would set himself up in the main street of Nowra, offering to do quick portraits from life or photos as Christmas gifts, earning the shillings to buy art supplies for preparation of his portfolio to apply to art school in Sydney.

Cyrus John O'Farrell won an important portrait prize early on but, since then, his work had mostly been a mixture of landscapes, exuberantly coloured female nudes and scenes with figures—workers in a timber mill or on a fishing boat, groups of people in a pub, a couple lying together in long grass. By 1955, he only ever painted portraits when he needed cash and there was a lucrative commission on offer.

At the back of the studio, I noticed the empty rectangles on the brick wall where previous paintings had been leaning before the edges were dry. I wondered if Cy ever saw his pictures again once they'd been sold. It's a peculiar thing about painting that the works are commodities which leave an artist's hands in a transaction that isn't the same for musicians or writers.

Over those first weeks I visited the studio, I observed his new works develop—simple life sketches transformed into richly coloured, tender, voluptuous oil paintings. In some of the canvases, I recognised body shapes I'd adopted as poses which had now been woven into group scenes of people on a beach.

In the decades afterwards, I would sometimes walk into the foyer of a city office tower and I'd be hit by the sight of a large Cyrus John O'Farrell painting on the wall. In 1987, I made it a project to track down as many of Cy's paintings as I could—the ones in galleries or places accessible to the public—and I would occasionally spot an O'Farrell in the living room of people wealthy enough to own one.

His work always moved me. Cyrus painted ordinary people doing ordinary things, depicting us as we are, no prettying-up, but still glorious, luminous, in an authentic no-bullshit way.

But let's get back to those Tuesdays and Thursdays in 1955. One week, I climbed the stairs into the studio to see the beach painting he'd just finished, the work full of vitality but also melancholy; earthy but also soulful. It felt as if a light inside the canvas were shining directly on me, sending an electric charge through my blood into every tiny cell of me.

A reader may have guessed by now that my response to this man's artworks seeped across into sexual attraction. I'd always found Cy the pub patron to be an enormously likeable fellow, but it never would have occurred to me to find that forty-something, shabby, thickset teddy-bear of a man attractive. But talent, especially the sort that grabs you in a visceral way, is an aphrodisiac. I have friends who respond that way to musicians. A guy may have an unfortunately shaped body, regrettable facial features and questionable hygiene, but if he is a thrilling guitarist, he can become knee-tremblingly sexy. I suppose it's a matter of admiration but also a desire to tap into the creative power they are generating.

One Thursday, Cy was by the sink, making tea, when I could no longer hide my lust. Walking over, barefoot, wrapped up in the robe, I was unsure how to do this, never having been a smooth operator in such matters. There was a specific weirdness about trying to be seductive a minute after someone has not only seen your bits but studiously looked at them. I probably should've created a distance, like an airlock, and maintained the distance long enough for the space between us to shiver a little bit with mystery, even if there could be no possible mystery about my body.

Despite my being clueless and unconfident, all doubts were pushed aside by an imperative: I was a 27-year-old libidinous woman and I wanted badly to have sex with this man. Keep in mind I'd had a short, mostly sexless marriage and in the three years since, had not felt a lover's hands on me at all.

When Cy sensed me close behind him, he turned with a questioning smile. I leaned forward to kiss his lovely smiling mouth and, in order to underline my intentions, I took his hand and slid it inside the silk robe.

He jerked back and looked at me. 'Don't feel you have to do this, Lizzie. I mean, I don't expect this.'

I dropped my head, mortified, assuming I had misjudged. But I didn't move away. (The need was great!) A moment later, Cy undid the sash on the robe with one hand and threaded his other hand through my hair.

We stood there kissing as Cy ran his hands down my back and the curve of my hips, gentle, but with the assurance you would expect from a man who could've drawn me blindfolded.

'The sheets are clean,' he said, indicating the single bed. 'But are you sure?'

I made an exaggerated show of throwing myself onto the bed to demonstrate my sureness and we both laughed, which helped ease the awkwardness of this shift in our relationship.

Cy looked at me stretched out there, naked, and made a half-sigh half-growl sound, then quickly stripped off his shirt and trousers as if the chance might evaporate. He wasn't svelte or sculpted by today's standards but his body was tanned and muscular, stronger than it appeared in his baggy clothes, with black hair (just the right amount) down his chest and belly.

I was waiting for him to climb on top of me but he crouched at the end of the bed, slid my legs apart and went down on me.

I'd heard about this sexual practice existing in the world—women talk—but I had never imagined being one of the lucky recipients. None of the gossipy talk had prepared me for how intensely pleasurable it was. I can state with authority now, having experienced oral sex with various other men in the years since 1955, that Cyrus John O'Farrell was especially gifted at it.

Feeling the powerful sensations building, I grabbed his head, wanting to control the rhythm and exact positioning, but most of all wanting him not to stop. Cy lifted his head briefly and smiled at me.

'I promise I'll keep going,' he said with a laugh. 'So you don't have to dig your fingernails into my scalp and draw blood.'

He followed through on his promise and I experienced—finally, gloriously—my first orgasm. He planted celebratory kisses on my feet and ankles, then grinned up at me, delighted with this accomplishment, mine and his.

When I reached to pull him up onto the bed, he again asked, 'Are you sure?' and waited for my enthusiastic 'yes' before we had intercourse, in a negotiation of consent that would pass muster even today.

Afterwards, Cy made the tea and we lay on the little bed for a while.

'Can we do that again sometime?' I asked.

'If you'd like to, that would be delightful.'

'Two conditions.'

'Oh, okay . . .' He grimaced, expecting disappointment.

'You get some rubber johnnies for next time.'

'I will do that,' he said.

'And I will arrive here half an hour earlier, so us doing this—' I waved my hand over our naked bodies on the bed. 'So this is separate from the time you pay me to model. I don't want to feel like I'm a prostitute.'

After that first time, we fell into a routine. Every Tuesday and Thursday, I would show up earlier than before and for the first couple of hours, I would pose and Cy would draw or paint. We would then have sex, followed by a cup of tea and a chat, lying on the bed. We would resume our model/painter roles for another hour before I walked round to pick up Mac from the Marrickville Primary School gate and collect Rose from the babysitter.

My time with Cy was separate from every other part of my life. I told no one, apart from Athena. She was simultaneously worried about me, keen for stickybeak detail and glad to see me enjoying myself.

My Tuesday and Thursday experiences inspired me to masturbate on the other days of the week, with reliably pleasing outcomes, a practice that enlivened my life for decades thereafter. It may seem shocking that it took a hairy-chested bear of a painter twenty years older than me to show me how to properly pleasure myself, finally, at the age of twenty-seven. It *is* shocking. Most of us had so little information back then—a lot of stabbing in the dark went on—and there was nothing like the robust info and joyous permission of later eras. It saddens me to think of the potential orgasms that were never enjoyed by many thousands of women.

In my life, I've had various lovers of differing skill and compatibility but because of my experiences with Cy, I've been able to take control of the management of my own enjoyment. I consider myself very fortunate in that regard.

Over the next year, I missed a few Tuesdays and Thursdays—when Mac had chicken pox and when I couldn't swing school holiday childcare. Apart from the income and the meeting of my sexual needs, it was fascinating to be around a creative person, hearing him talk about his anxieties, his moments of satisfaction. Sometimes as I lay in a long pose, I would stare at one of Cy's paintings and make up stories about the people in the picture, imagining their lives in the moments before and after the moment captured on the canvas.

Towards the end of that year, I became aware that Cy was sinking into a gloomy state. The easy chat between us dried up and I judged it was better to let him work in silence. He wasn't even in the mood for sex. Then came two weeks when the downstairs door to his defunct garage was locked, with no amount of knocking eliciting a response, and no sign of him at The General Gordon either. There was a chance he'd gone bush to paint without bothering to tell me. Even so, I was worried.

When I turned up at his studio on the Tuesday of the third week, I found the place still locked and a burnt smell coming from inside. I yelled his name and kicked uselessly at the door, eventually finding a piece of metal pipe on the ground to wrench and splinter open the lock.

There was no water in the clawfoot bath—just Cy lying naked in it, breathing but passed-out drunk, with the smell of urine and vomit fruity enough to make me gag. Half-a-dozen empty bottles of brandy, the nasty cheap stuff, lay on the floor and there were probably more bottles hidden in the rags, paint tubes, clothes, broken plates, rotting food, scrunched-up papers and other detritus he had tipped out of boxes or swept off surfaces in an intense emotional squall. A few of his paintings lay amid the mess but others were missing altogether. In the far corner, a forty-four-gallon drum was still faintly warm, stuffed with charred paper and canvas, having been used to incinerate many of the drawings and paintings that used to be in the studio.

As I stepped closer to Cy, figuring out how best to help him, I heard footsteps on the stairs, then a woman's voice calling up. 'Cy. It's me.'

The woman groaned when she reached the top, her eyes flicking round to analyse the scene rapidly.

'Are you the one who's been modelling for him?' she asked.

I nodded. 'I'm Lizzie.'

'Hi, Lizzie. I'm Evelyn. Ex-wife.' She pressed her mouth into a polite joyless smile.

Evelyn was forty years old, almost six feet tall, wearing bohemian loose pleated trousers and a white cotton shirt, with a pile of auburn hair swept into one of those messy chic twists I could never manage. She had a strong nose, elegant cheekbones, and hooded green eyes that still managed to be beautiful despite the pouchy tiredness in her face.

She moved close enough to peer at her ex-husband. 'He does this sometimes—stays in the bath when he's on a bender so he doesn't make a mess.' She then launched into a startlingly accurate imper-sonation of Cy, saying, 'Did you know, Evelyn, this is what Spencer Tracy does?' Then she switched back to her own voice to add, 'As if, because this is Spencer Tracy's party trick, it counts as a reasonable thing for a person to do.'

I puffed a little laugh. Evelyn looked at me and assessed that I was not overwhelmed by the scene.

'Can you help me clean him up?' Evelyn asked, throwing me one of Cy's paint-spattered shirts to put on over my clothes while she did the same. 'If you could operate the hose, I'll hold him up. I'm used to the weight of him.'

Evelyn got behind Cy and hoisted him up under the armpits. That woman was impressively strong. While she held him upright, I turned on the hose connected to the sink and used a spray of warm water to sluice him down, rinsing bits of vomit out of his hair and off his skin so it all ran down the plughole.

I realise it sounds harshly undignified—to hose down an unconscious man like washing an animal carcass—but it was done with tenderness by both of us. My gaze fell briefly on Cy's limp cock hanging below his black-furred belly before I looked away.

I dried him off with towels before Evelyn counted a one-two-three to coordinate our combined effort to heave him out of the bathtub and onto the bed.

'We've organised for him to get a travelling art grant,' Evelyn explained.

'Who is "we"?'

'His dealer, me, a couple of his friends who could see he was tipping into one of his spirals. We've got to get him on a ship to Italy tomorrow.'

Then she looked over at the forty-four-gallon drum. 'Jesus . . .'

Evelyn and I sorted through the mess, sweeping up the charred stuff and unearthing intact works from the debris in the studio.

'Why would he burn them?' I asked.

Even though we were strangers, Evelyn spoke to me with the kind of direct tone that becomes appropriate after you've hosed down a naked man together. 'He thinks he's no good. He's ashamed. Thinks he's putting ugly things into the world.'

I opened my mouth to argue his paintings were the opposite of ugly, but she waved her hand to indicate she believed the same. 'When we were together, if he went into this mood, I used to make him sit still and *look* at the work while I described how good it was, to make him *see* that it was. If that didn't work, I'd hide the paintings until the mood passed. These days, I just try to get the work out of here and sold before he can destroy it.'

Evelyn shot a look at me, keen to defend herself against any accusation of thievery. 'I give him the money from the sales.'

Together, we carried Cy's surviving artworks down to Evelyn's dented FX Holden parked outside. Some of the O'Farrell paintings you can now see in major galleries were rescued that day by his ex-wife and current model/lover (me).

At one point, I moved aside a stack of works to reveal a portrait I'd never seen before—oil on canvas, on a stretcher but unframed. The cheekbones, the nose, the hooded eyes—there was no mistaking the subject.

'It's you,' I said.

'Well, younger me.'

'It's wonderful. Did Cy paint this when you were—'

She jumped in. 'Uh, no. That's a self-portrait.'

I recalled that Cy had met his wife when they were both in art school. 'Evelyn was very good,' he had explained to me once. 'But she lost her confidence.'

She'd given up painting, and for some years had been doing admin work for galleries instead.

Evelyn glanced over at her painting, and I saw her flinch before she turned away completely. At the time, I did not understand that reaction, but now my guess would be that Evelyn O'Farrell flinched from the pain of being reminded of her artistic hopes.

'I know my opinion doesn't . . . I mean—I think—' I stammered. 'It's a wonderful painting.'

'If you like it, take it.'

'What? No!'

'Take it,' she insisted. 'Stop him from accidentally setting fire to it.'

'Can't you sell it along with Cy's stuff?'

'Lord, no. It's not worth anything. Please, take it.'

Evelyn refused to accept money for the painting but, eventually, to end my discomfort, she took the few shillings I happened to have in my purse that day.

'Sold! Thank you,' she said with an aching smile. Then, to shake off whatever painful slurry had been stirred up in her, she switched tone, speaking as the practical woman who spent her time managing the affairs of hopeless artists like her ex-husband. 'Speaking of money, Lizzie, what does Cy owe you?'

'Oh, don't worry.'

'No. Come on. You have children to feed. You showed up here these last weeks with the expectation of being paid. Which meant you missed the chance to earn money somewhere else. He owes you wages.'

Finding no cash in his wallet, Evelyn gathered up three of the undamaged charcoal sketches and offered them to me. 'Take these as payment. Unless you'd rather wait until they're sold and I could send you the money.'

I argued back for a while but when it was clear she wouldn't budge, I took the drawings gratefully.

In 1957, two years after that day, there was a news story: Cyrus John O'Farrell had died in a housefire in Puglia. It's fair to say O'Farrell is a well-regarded Australian painter today but not the major figure he would've been had he lived longer and done the work he was supposed to do.

I'm wary of romantic talk about damaged artists, the spinning of narratives about torment and creativity. I think it's true that damage is often bound into their talent—individuals who've been thrown off kilter in a way that can give them a deep empathy for human suffering and a perspective that can be skewed, ravishing, incisive, moving, transcendent. And I think it's true that childhood wounds can leave many of us, not just artists, with a vast psychic hole that needs to be filled with validation and the frantic creation of new things. But the creative work only gets done and done in the rigorous way it needs to be, if the artist can control their pain sufficiently, shove it to one side, muscle it into silence with one arm while they draw or write or compose with the other arm. If the pain thumps them to the ground or their body is flooded with self-loathing like a paralysing neurotoxin, then they stop producing work, or good work anyway. For me, as a listener, viewer, reader, I feel colossal gratitude that so many individuals wrestled with their damaged spirits to give us glorious works and I feel sadness that there are many glorious works we will never see because despair engulfed the person who might have given them to us.

At a juncture when I needed money, I sold two of Cy's drawings but I always held on to one. It's hanging in front of me now, across from the armchair/table/laptop set up for 99-year-old me to write. On the wall, charcoal on paper, is my 27-year-old body, my thighs and shoulders and breasts, caught in the gaze of an extraordinary artist.

There's no question in my mind that Cyrus was brilliant. His work still thrills me. But I'm reminded that we all missed out on seeing whatever thrilling art Evelyn O'Farrell may have produced if she hadn't had time and vitality sucked out of her by her voraciously self-absorbed husband (however adorable a vampire he was), if she hadn't had to look after the children he left with her and if the world had bolstered her confidence just a bit fucking more.

Next to Cy's charcoal is Evelyn's self-portrait. In 2015, I lent it to a major gallery to be part of a 'Neglected Women Artists' show, but she's back on my wall now, blazing at me with candour and strength and vulnerability—a woman I met once for little more than an hour, as we sluiced vomit off a man and swept up ash.

September 1958.

Our household budget did not allow me to use many of the culinary skills I'd taught myself during my marriage. No Beef Wellingtons or Trout Meuniere Amandine in our house. But on Sundays, I would often make a Navarin of Lamb, using cheap cuts of mutton to produce a dinner for the three of us that felt special and a bit luxurious.

Rose, six years old by then, was helping me top and tail green beans while nine-year-old Mac finished his homework on the raspberry-swirl Laminex kitchen table. When I heard him emit a small groan of frustration at himself, I sneaked a look. He was trying to complete the neat hand-in version of his composition about kookaburras, marred by a few minor handwriting mistakes.

'I think your composition is wonderful, sweetheart,' I said brightly, as if I hadn't noticed his handwriting struggle. 'I learned lots of stuff I didn't know but you also *wrote* it so well. So many good adjectives. I bet Mrs Shelby will especially love the part about the sound of kookaburras laughing. A few crossings-out won't matter.'

Mac didn't seem to hear a single positive word and scrubbed away with his rubber at small errors until he was wearing holes in the paper, his face pinched with anxiety.

I'm one of those parents—there are many of us—whose belly can still twist up with the guilty fear that I damaged my children. Even now, all these decades on

Mac was always a sweet boy, never showing one spike of my temper and none of his father's sulky belligerence, thank God. He was a clever lad too, but so afraid of making a mistake that he often held himself back, worried about what people thought of him, alert for criticism and always waiting for others to set the agenda. He hated being seen to be bad at something—drawing, swimming, piano, riding a bike—and he would find ways to practise skills in secret until he could do them properly in front of others. Even when he had mastered something, his anxiety would still be buzzing underneath. Seeing his fretful lop-sided smile made me want to bundle up my lovely boy and whisk him away from anything that could bring him pain.

And there you have it: did my fear that he was a vulnerable soul cause extra damage? I can never be sure if I imposed my own anxiety onto my son, interpreting every skerrick of his behaviour and demeanour as evidence that his father's bullying, then sudden death, my emotional turmoil, and other traumas of his early years had irreparably injured him. Mac had the same sandy hair, blue eyes and fine facial features as his father and maybe the resemblance set off a fear that he'd inherited depressive tendencies along with the physical traits. I didn't get Mac psychological help—that wasn't a thing then. I bumbled through, trying to coax my tender-hearted son to be as kind to himself as he was to other people.

Mac tore the page out of his workbook, screwed it up and started on a new sheet. But once he made his first mistake in that fresh copy, he sank into groans of self-reproach.

'Come on, my chicken,' I said. 'Don't get yourself into a tizz. Calm down.'

And as in almost every instance in the universe in which one person tells an agitated person to 'calm down', it only made Mac feel worse. Much less calm. And believing his feelings were being dismissed.

He swept the school workbook and pencil case up against his

chest, and retreated to his bedroom. When I wiped my palms on my apron, ready to go after him, Rose patted my hand.

'I'll talk to him,' she said in an unflappable therapeutic voice that sounded a bit spooky coming out of a six-year-old child. The truth was, Rose could handle Mac like no one else, including me. Even though she was three years younger, she was sensitive to her brother's anxieties, judging when to leave him be, when to come on a bit bossy, when to chivvy him back to his happier self. She also understood, even as a little girl, how to leave space for Mac to be the more knowledgeable sibling sometimes, how to let him take the role of the helpful, protective big brother. Maybe it was part of her essential self that had been born on Athena's front lawn, arriving with a canny assessment of how best to manage the world in which she'd landed.

Rose was a passionate child, tempestuous even, but there was a stable core inside her. She could perceive how other people regarded her without feeling totally at the mercy of their opinions, in the way Mac and I so desperately did. She was determined, pursuing her goals through tenacity more than tantrums. She'd badgered me to teach her to read when she was three because she hated the idea that there was information in books that was being kept from her. She'd begged me to send her to Big School when she was just four. I believe now that was a mistake, but in 1956 it had seemed like a top idea, easing my childcare problems and soaking up my daughter's busy mind.

Five minutes after Rose went to speak to her brother in their bedroom, she re-emerged.

'We can dish up the Fancy Lamb now. Mac's coming in a sec,' she said in a steady, gentle tone, as if she were handling me as well. Which I suppose she was.

When Mac appeared a minute later, he looked embarrassed about having made a scene.

Rose rescued her brother from his awkwardness by teasing him. 'So, me and Mac made a deal,' she said. 'He gets to play his "Alligator" record. Even though it's stupid and nowhere as good as Elvis.'

Mac grinned, delighted to be teased in just this way.

We had a gramophone at home by then and a small collection of 45s, some purchased, others borrowed from neighbours.

After we ate the Fancy Lamb followed by pineapple upside-down cake (a Sunday night special treat), Mac helped me shift the chairs against the wall so we could dance. First up was 'See You Later, Alligator' which was Mac's current favourite. Rose was scornful of 'Alligator' on account of her devotion to Elvis, whom she considered superior in every way and in need of her support. As if the fierce preferences of a six-year-old Australian girl would count in the cosmic tally for Elvis over Bill Haley. However, she abided by the deal and endured 'See You Later, Alligator', after which we played 'All Shook Up' to unanimous approval.

She insisted we then play the B side, 'That's When Your Heartaches Begin'. Mac was unimpressed by that mournful ballad, but he obliged his mother by waltzing around the room with me. When the track reached the section where Elvis speaks, ponderous and heartbroken, I grabbed three spoons from the kitchen. Mac, Rose and I lip-synced into our spoon microphones through the rest of that song and then a repeat spin of 'All Shook Up'.

Nine-year-old Mac Burnley doing the twist in our loungeroom, singing into a spoon, boisterous and gleeful—I hope that image can adjust the impression I may have given the reader earlier. Mac was a happy kid a lot of the time, alive to fun, able to appreciate a good joke even if he didn't tell many himself. Even as a young fellow, he was an excellent listener, fixing his gaze on someone and truly giving them his attention, so people would come away feeling they had been listened to. That's no small thing.

I don't want to boil up a toffee-sweet impression of family bliss. Nights dancing together happened regularly but such times were punctuated by moments of bad temper or sadness and, later, verbal volleys with intent to wound.

And if I focus too much on childhood moments in which Mac was anxious or suffering, that's my scrambling attempt to make sense of what happened later.

EIGHT

April 1959.

Pink and white balloons flapped around the front gate of Athena and Nick's house on the occasion of Thea's ninth birthday party.

Mac, Rose and I walked up from the bus stop, watching parents drop off the other guests—all girls, apart from Mac. Young boys would never have accepted an invitation to a girls' party in those days for fear that their tiny penises would fall off. Mac counted as Thea's de facto cousin, so his genitals were safe.

We'd already attended the gloriously noisy birthday celebration with the extended Samios family the week before, but for Thea's sake, Athena was determined to have a crack at an Aussie kid's party. She stood in the doorway to welcome party guests, offering refreshments for the parents if they wished to come inside too. None of them did. Parents guzzling wine and scoffing hommus at kids' birthday parties was not the custom then.

I noticed one of the mothers hesitate on the footpath, keeping one hand on her daughter's shoulder. This woman was scrutinising the exterior of the house, alert to the risk that leaving her child in the home of these 'wogs' could trigger some unwelcome wogification of little Susan.

Nine-year-old Susan was dolled up in a white party dress made of scratchy nylon lace with stiffened underskirts so it puffed out. The poor kid's hair had been tortured into long ringlets like a series of pale sausages hanging off her head, each sausage tied to the scalp with a small white ribbon. Susan's mother had her own bottle-blonde hair curled into a perm so tight that the chemicals must've permed her brain matter into bitter little twists as well.

Susan nodded dutifully as her mother whispered in her ear. I overheard the word 'dago' and I heard 'these people' but couldn't hear the detail. *Susan, if the dagos offer you dolmades, don't eat them.* Something along those lines is my guess.

Meanwhile Mac and Rose had galloped up the front path to give Athena a hug. Susan's mother watched my kids—horrified, disapproving, worried for their safety.

I made a show of politely waving Susan and her mother through the gate. 'After you,' I said with a high-wattage smile. 'I think this party will be oodles of fun!'

I've found that relentless cheeriness can be a good way to handle unpleasant individuals. It doesn't always work as a sweetener, but it can still be perversely amusing. If grumpy people are faced with unremitting volleys of smiles and friendly responses, they are often thrown so far off balance, it becomes a form of entertainment to watch them squirm. The mother frowned at me, shoved the wrapped gift into her daughter's hands, whispered a few final instructions and sent her inside to face the dagos.

Athena and Nick's backyard was huge, so that even with the vegetable beds and rows of productive trees—olive, apricot, almond, lemon, mandarin—there was still a large lawn ideal for party games.

Bunches of pink and white balloons were hanging all through the garden and the courtyard, along with skeins of pink streamers.

The paved courtyard was shaded by a trellis smothered in grapevines. Nick harvested the grapes to make his own wine. I loved Nick Samios like a brother, but it must be said that his wine could burn the lining off your oesophagus and eat away your stomach lining.

The long outdoor table used for regular family feasts was covered with a pink flowery tablecloth, set with red drink cups, and paper plates with a pink and white gingham pattern. There were butterfly cakes, chicken sandwiches, devilled eggs, fairy bread, chocolate crackles and 'frogs in ponds' (chocolate Freddo frogs set into cups of green jelly). It was only in the sausage rolls that Athena dared to add any Greek flavour, smuggling oregano and garlic into the filling. The girls wolfed down the delicious sausage rolls and it pleased me to imagine Susan trotting home with garlicky breath.

The girls' party dresses, lace-trimmed socks and shoes-for-best were not ideal attire for energetic fun, but the kids were soon skipping around the yard screeching party blowers in each other's faces and giggling their gorgeous heads off. Mac just stood there with his lop-sided anxiety smile.

Nick noticed his awkwardness. 'Mac, can you help me set up the record player?'

He appointed Mac as his sidekick to help with practical tasks and Mac was happy to trail around after Uncle Nick for the rest of the party. My son's father hunger was so obvious, almost heartbreaking to witness, but Nick Samios, lovely man that he was, didn't make a big deal of it.

Eleven-year-old Sofia Samios took charge of wrangling the kids through the various games. (Sofia was a kind-hearted girl, but she certainly did enjoy the rigorous application of rules.) Pin the tail on the donkey, musical chairs, snap apple, egg and spoon relay, duck

duck goose. Back then, nine-year-olds still seemed like little kids and it was glorious to watch them let rip. I could see the determined set to my Rose's face as she strove to keep up with the older girls.

Susan of the Ringlets was hesitant in the games at first, her mother's waspish warnings still buzzing in her head, but after an excited round of musical chairs, she got into it, the tight ringlets unravelling into a bundle of wonderfully symbolic messy curls.

'Congratulations,' I said to Athena as we both helped ourselves to a second sausage roll. 'I hereby declare you to be an Australian mother.'

Athena raised her eyebrows doubtfully, but then she looked over at Thea's shining face and laughed with relief.

Pearl showed up as she did to most events: late, wearing unsuitably glamorous clothes, bringing an inappropriate gift. The outfit consisted of a cerise satin dress with a halter-neck that left her beautiful shoulders and half her back bare, worn with high heels so spiky, she kept sinking into the lawn at a bizarre angle. The gift she brought was a makeup kit in a lurid pink travel case. There was no way Athena would've allowed Thea to use makeup at her age and that kit was destined to be the subject of tearful arguments in the Samios household.

Pearl threw herself into the festivities with childlike gusto, yanking off her unhelpful shoes and joining in a round of musical chairs. My children and Athena's were used to Auntie Pearl, but the other girls gawped at her, puzzled by a grown-up lady carrying on like a two-bob watch. But once the kids sussed out that Pearl was pure of heart, they let themselves enjoy her as a strange but fun playmate.

When it was time for the limbo competition, I was surprised to see Pearl wasn't lining up to have a go. Then I spotted a patch of cerise satin in the narrow garden up the side of the house and I found Pearl vomiting into a hydrangea bush.

She came up for air. 'I'm in the pudding club.'

'Oh, love.' I handed her a hankie to wipe her mouth. I was surprised there hadn't been more buns in Pearl's oven, given her eager participation in sexual activities. 'Whose is it? Ray's?'

She winced at the mention of her latest beau but then tried for a hopeful smile. 'He says he's going to leave his wife and marry me.'

'But if he doesn't, have you thought about what you'll do?'

We were both running through the shithouse list of options in our minds: abortion, adoption, unwed motherhood, hoping the embryo might fall out of its own accord. I considered telling her about the baby I gave up when I was seventeen, but then chickened out.

'If you decide to get rid of it,' I said, 'Ray should give you the money to go to a proper doctor.'

After another bout of retching, Pearl checked if Athena had noticed anything. 'Please don't tell Athena I'm up the duff. She'll get a face on.'

Which was probably true. Athena could be sternly disapproving about that sort of thing and I would not want to be the recipient of that face.

'You go back to the party,' Pearl urged me. 'I'll be right as rain in a minute.'

Later, I grabbed a moment with her as she sipped gingerly at a cup of cordial.

'Listen, Pearl, I really do think you need to—'

'Not to worry, Lizzie—it's going to be grand!' she said. 'I've been thinking I could just have this little baby and look after it myself— like you did with Mac and Rose.'

Pearl's bright eyes looked over at the cluster of girls, imagining her own child. Athena and I would be around to help her, sure, but I was in no way confident Pearl could manage on her own. I was forming a plan—that Pearl should drop round to my place that evening for a proper discussion—but then Mac tapped me on the arm.

'Mum, there's a man out the front to pick up Auntie Pearl.'

Pearl went skipping through the house and I followed.

In the street outside, Ray was leaning against his bomb of a car, sucking on a roll-up cigarette. Even by the standards of Pearl's dodgy men, Ray was a spectacular dud—rarely employed, no control over a taste for gambling, with two small children he'd fathered by some poor bloody woman. That afternoon, he was wearing only a blue singlet and shorts, so his many maritime-themed tattoos were on display—sailing ships, fish, coils of rope, mermaids. Ray was not, as a reader might imagine, a sailor. Not only had he never been to sea, I doubt Ray came into regular contact with water of any kind, judging by his body odour.

'You see, Lizzie, he does love me,' Pearl whispered to me before rushing towards him.

She threw herself into Ray's nautical arms and the two of them started pashing in that writhing-tongues fashion which can leave onlookers mesmerised or disgusted.

It was at this moment that Susan's mother came stalking up the street and was treated to the sight of Pearl in her shiny backless dress, the ankle straps of her stiletto shoes hanging from one hand, snogging a tattooed man against the front gate of the Samios house, only breaking the passionate clinch to vomit on the nature strip.

I did not share Pearl's confidence in Ray. The next day, I went to Surry Hills Public Library and found the corner where the phone books were kept. I looked up the medical practitioners' section and found small, pencilled asterisks next to a few names in the listing. These were the doctors who would perform abortions secretly but with the extra safety that came with medical qualifications. A dame I worked with had told me about this coded system by which pregnant women could share the precious intel.

That evening, I left my kids with a neighbour and raided the biscuit tin. The proper doctors cost way more than the backstreet operators and I doubted Ray would be able to give Pearl the cash she'd need. I made my way to Pearl's place in Chippendale, with a roll of banknotes and the doctors' addresses stashed in my purse, so my friend would at least have some options.

Pearl's bedsit was on the ground floor, so when she didn't answer the door, I was able to peer inside her room from the street. The place had been divided into bedsits using cheap materials and I managed to force the flimsy door open by slamming my shoulder against it.

In the airless room, the metallic smell of blood was like a blow to the face. On the floor were sanitary napkins and wadded up items of clothing Pearl had obviously used to staunch the bleeding. On those, the stains were the reddish-brown colour of old blood but where she lay on the bed in her nightie, there was a bloom of bright blood spreading out from between her legs. She was unconscious, pallid, her hand cold and papery, but I could feel a pulse.

I insisted on riding in the ambulance with Pearl, hating the idea that she would be alone for another minute. When we reached Royal Prince Alfred Hospital, though, she was whisked out of my sight into a treatment area.

I plonked down on a bench and it was only then, once my friend was being looked after, that fear flushed through my body and I had a bit of a cry. My sister Pauline came into my mind—the vision of her shaking the flour off her eyelashes onto the window box plants—and it struck me that Pearl was lodged in the same part of my brain as my little sister.

Eventually a granite-faced nurse in her forties came through a swing door. 'Are you the friend?'

I nodded.

'She went to some backyard butcher, did she.' The woman offered this more as a statement than a question.

'I don't know. I think so.'

After Thea's party, Pearl and Ray had tumbled from passionate kissing into a steaming row, during which he'd barked harsh things at her. 'Get rid of it' and the like. In a panic, Pearl had gone for the cheapest abortion practitioner she could find.

The nurse exhaled loudly. 'Always a blessed shame these girls don't ask for help when they start losing blood like that. They worry they'll go to gaol if they tell anyone what they've done.'

This lady wasn't exactly oozing compassion out of every pore but she was not pitiless. 'Anyway,' she said, 'you should go home. Your friend's going to the operating theatre now.'

'An operation? Will she be all right?'

'Well, lucky thing you found her when you did. They don't think she's going to die.'

The next afternoon, I was allowed to visit Pearl in the women's ward. I brought her favourite treat—Darrell Lea chocolate licorice bullets—and lay the packet on the bedside console. Pearl was lying on her side, feeble, bunched up with pain, but at least her face wasn't as horribly pale as when I'd found her. She had pinked up thanks to a blood transfusion.

'Hello, my lovely friend,' I said and squeezed her small limp hand.

I didn't expect any conversation. I'd been told what had happened. Pearl's uterus had been so badly perforated by the piece of wire or whatever implement had been used on her that a hysterectomy had been the only way to stop the bleeding and save her life.

With the thoughtless cruelty that was common in medical situations then, she'd been put in a ward with three women who had just given birth, so the room was alive with the mewling of newborns and the hearty voices of families congratulating new mothers. Pearl just lay there crying, and I sat on the side of the bed rubbing her back in rhythmic circles, the way I did when my kids were upset.

When I visited a day later, Pearl was sitting up in the bed, still wincing from the abdominal incision but smiling brightly. She'd got hold of some makeup, fixed up her hair and made the decision to be chirpy.

'You know what, Lizzie, I think it's all for the best. I would've been a flippin' terrible mother. And this way, there'll be no more messing about with rubber johnnies and whatnot. No more worries at all! Ooh, quick, have a few of those choccie bullets before I scoff the lot.'

While she dug out the Darrell Lea packet, I scrambled to get my head around the way my friend was choosing to process this. Pearl had yearned to have children of her own. Having her baby-making organs cut out must surely have felt like a catastrophe.

'Oh!' she gasped, flapping her hands to get the attention of the new mother in the opposite bed. 'Deirdre, remember I was telling you about my friend Lizzie?'

She had already befriended the three other women in her room and spent much of the day chatting to them, gushing over their babies, putting in her two bobs' worth about the names they should choose.

If it were me, I would've been ablaze with anger—anger at Ray, at the incompetent abortionist and the censorious doctors. I would've been resentful that the other women in the ward could have babies. I would've been furious that I'd ever been pushed into such a wretched choice. But all that seething would have done me no good.

I realise there's a valuable place for rage. A considerable amount of bullshit in the world has only been sorted out because a number of people became monumentally angry and forced changes. And at certain moments in my life, I had successfully used anger as a fuel to survive whatever the world had thrown at me, if only out of spite. But I would not promote this as a healthy way to operate and I would say that, in 1959, I had not yet found a useful way to channel my rage. The point is, I envied Pearl's Pollyanna approach—she was happier and she was certainly kinder to everyone around her. I was built differently. I could no more be like her than I could suddenly be six inches taller.

It must also be said that sitting alongside Pearl's cheerfulness, there was enormous pain. Over the years I saw my dear friend go through intense grief about her childlessness. Even so, Pearl Jowett's bright spirit was never phony. It was a marvel.

After Pearl was discharged, she came back to stay at ours to convalesce. I slept in a camp bed on the built-in verandah of the Marrickville semi, which meant she could have my room. Sadie the kelpie, having assessed that Pearl needed looking after, curled up next to her on the bed day and night.

Athena dropped food around to the house, insisting that Pearl eat the beef stifado and stewed okra to make her blood strong again. Athena guessed what had happened, but it wasn't a subject we discussed until some years later. Not that Athena withheld emotion about the loss our friend had suffered—the first time she'd visited Pearl in the hospital, she clasped her so firmly I was concerned she might burst open the surgical incision.

The first Monday of Pearl's recuperation period, I'd left instructions for Mac and Rose: when they arrived home from school they were to make Auntie Pearl a pot of tea, offer pieces of Athena's shortbread (properly, on a plate) and keep her company until I got back from work.

I walked in to see Mac, Rose and Pearl had our big atlas opened out on the kitchen table. A few steps further into the house, I realised there was someone else standing in my kitchen.

'Mum!' Mac called out. 'This man lives in Papua New Guinea!'

I was so overcome I had to force my lips to form words before my throat tightened up too much to speak.

'Hello, Leo. How wonderful to see you.'

We did that little dance people do when they aren't sure what level of greeting affection is appropriate: a half-step towards each other, right arm bent in case the other person might go for the handshake, but head jutted forward in case it will be a peck on the cheek. After some chicken-necked gestures, we settled on the peck with zero body contact.

'It's wonderful to see you—uh—Pearl tells me you go by Lizzie now?'

'Whatever. I mean, you can call me Lizzie or Betty or Elizabeth or—'

'Or Mum,' Rose offered helpfully.

Leo smiled and nodded at Rose, with chivalrous acknowledgement of her contribution.

In the ten years since I'd last seen Leo Newman, he had—and I report this in an entirely objective way—become even more handsome.

'I'm sorry for showing up at your house uninvited,' he said, in his unplaceable, elegant accent. 'I lost contact with Pearl—stupidly—so it took some detective work to find her.'

'Then when he found my flat, I wasn't there. Luckily my neighbour sent him to this address!' Pearl added, as if she'd won a prize.

'Mr Leo lives *here*,' Mac announced, twisting his finger on the page of the atlas to show me Port Moresby.

'That's fascinating,' I said. I couldn't believe I was capable of basic chitchat in this moment. 'How long have you been up there?'

'I moved to PNG in fifty-one.'

'Leo left Australia before he even heard about ... Well, he had no idea—not for ages—that Donald died,' said Pearl.

'I'm so sorry about your husband,' Leo said.

I tipped my head to thank him for the condolence.

'Did you make Mr Newman a cup of tea?' I asked the kids.

Leo jumped in. 'They did. They also served Pearl and me some delicious Greek shortbread. On a plate,' he added. 'By the way, I've asked Mac and Rose to call me "Leo".' (Generally, back then, children were required to 'mister' and 'missus' any adults they addressed.)

'Show Lizzie the photo!' sung out Pearl.

Leo produced a photograph from his wallet—a beautiful fair-haired baby sitting on a porch surrounded by lush foliage. 'This is my daughter Ava.'

Pearl launched into a run of breathless chatter. 'Leo met his wife Ellen when—oh no, hang on, not Ellen, it's *Helen*. Helen went to visit her brother who lives in Port Moresby and two months later Helen and Leo got married! Just two months! And then they had this little angel in hospital in Brisbane. But now they're all living in New Guinea together!'

'We're back here on leave,' Leo explained. 'My wife was keen to show Ava off to her family.'

'I bet. She's a doll, isn't she, Lizzie?'

I gathered myself to speak to Leo like a normal human and not a woman who had just had her hopes soar up into sparkly clouds and then crash into a cliff face in the space of thirty seconds. 'Yes, yes, congratulations, Leo. Ava's ridiculously gorgeous. How old is she?'

'Fourteen months.'

Pearl clapped her hands together. 'When do we get to meet them? Your wife and your baby?'

'Oh . . . They've gone up the coast, to Wyong, staying with her parents. Helen says she doesn't want me underfoot while she spends time with her family. I've got things to sort out in Sydney so . . .'

Leo's sentence trailed off, as if he could hear how lame this explanation sounded. Why didn't this Helen woman want him 'underfoot'? If you had a decent husband, why would you not want him around?

I wondered if this woman appreciated the man she'd married. Before I had a chance to indulge in more uncharitable thoughts about Helen Newman, Pearl was seized by an enthusiastic idea.

'Ooh, let's invite Leo to stay for dinner, Lizzie. The poor man's staying in a hotel all on his own.'

Luckily, I had one of Athena's pre-cooked meals in the fridge—lamb with tomato and orzo. I fussed with preparing the vegies to serve with it and sent Mac outside to grab a few passionfruit off the vine hanging over the fence from the house next door. We had enough eggs for me to make a Passionfruit Delicious for dessert. Thanks to the cooking tasks, I was able to avoid eye contact with Leo as I asked questions about his life working for the Australian civil service in Papua New Guinea.

The five of us squeezed around our kitchen table, which Rose had set using our best napkins and precise cutlery placement she deemed worthy of our special guest. Leo waxed lyrical about the food, about how long since he'd eaten such a wonderful meal.

Over dessert, Mac bombarded Leo with questions about jungles and volcanoes and cannibals, all of which he answered with care and no condescension. By this point, Pearl was sleepy, each blink of her eyes elongating until her eyelids closed for three long seconds before she jolted awake. She finally retired to bed, but not before extracting promises from Leo to visit her again.

I then hustled Mac and Rose through teeth-cleaning, pyjamas and into their beds. When I came back to the kitchen, Leo was at the sink, washing the dishes and pots.

'You shouldn't be doing that! You're a guest.'

'Please let me do it,' he said. 'In Moresby, everyone has house staff, so I never get the fun of doing domestic tasks.'

'Well, I wouldn't want to deny you that fun. I'm not a monster. Would you like tea?'

'That would be lovely.'

As I filled the kettle, standing near him, I realised the air in the kitchen had altered now that it was just the two of us.

I spun round to face him and blurted out, 'Look, I have to ask— what's the story with you and Pearl? Are you in love with her? I mean, she's in a fragile state at the moment and if you keep popping up in her life and you aren't—I'd just like to understand the nature of your feelings.'

'Oh . . .'

'I'm sorry if that sounds—'

'No, no, I understand. You're protective.'

He didn't say anything for a moment and my brain raced ahead, filling in the silence with tormenting thoughts.

Finally, he said, 'The thing is, in '47, when we were all on the ship, Pearl asked me to be her friend on the first day I met her.'

'Me too. It was startling. And irresistible.'

Leo smiled. 'It was. And in '47, I had plenty of vacancies for a new friend. Well, for a sister even. I would say I love her like a sister.'

'Right, yes. I see that. Sorry to put you on the spot. I shouldn't have pried or made you feel—'

'Pearl's a lovely person but not the kind of woman I could imagine falling in love with.'

I stared intently at the kettle as if it might explode the instant I took my eyes off it. I did not dare to breathe for several long seconds.

Leo huffed a laugh. 'Not that I have much talent for managing my love-life.'

I was about to joke along, but then he jumped in, 'Forgive me, Lizzie, I let you down back then. Not being brave enough.'

'Me too. I was a fool. I mucked it.'

'Oh no, well, I should've made it clear much sooner what I—'

'We both mucked it.'

And that seemed to crack things open for us to talk about our time on the *Asturias*, our failure-to-launch romance, why we'd both been afraid to declare ourselves.

I suppose it felt safe to be candid because we were enfolded in a chaste quarantine zone created by my children sleeping in the next room and the photo of Leo's daughter sitting in his wallet. Thus buffered, we could speak about our younger selves having fancied each other, without there being any dangerous sexual frisson now.

For the rest of that week, Leo visited every day. In the mornings, he had business to attend to—the life admin a person faces when back on leave from Papua New Guinea—but once he'd finished he would come to our house. He took Pearl on slow strolls through the park, longer distances every day, trying to build back her strength. By the time I arrived home from work, he was there, helping my children with homework, showing Mac an album of photographs of New Guinea, listening to Rose chatter about how the blood had oozed out of her grazed knee.

He would always come bearing treats—magazines and fancy soaps for Pearl, lollies for the children, flowers for me, a bottle of wine for us to share. He brought the Elvis single 'A Fool Such as I' for Rose once he understood her devotion to Mr Presley, and a small carved wooden crocodile from PNG for Mac. When I objected to so many gifts, he said, 'Please let me bring a few offerings to express my thanks. You're giving me a beautiful dinner every evening.'

I will admit to the reader that I pulled out all stops on those dinners, getting up at dawn to prepare, and obliterated our food budget for the month. I finally had a chance to serve coq au vin and other dishes I'd practised during my marriage, plus more adventurous foods I'd picked up from the Samios family. I made proper dessert every night. Yes, even Bombe Alaska.

I played it cool, as if these dishes were typical weeknight dinners for us, but my mouthy daughter would not let me get away with that.

'Mum, how come you're making fancy birthday dinner food even when it's nobody's birthday?'

I flicked Rose a look to shoosh her but I could see Leo glance at me with a faint smile.

'Because, Rose,' I said, 'I've been showing off to try to impress our guest.'

'And I have to tell you, Rose,' said Leo, 'it's working. I'm terribly impressed.'

Pearl always headed to bed not long after my kids, leaving Leo and me to talk in the kitchen alone for hours.

Most people would have experienced—at least I hope they have—that phenomenon when two individuals (friends, partners, whoever) can talk and talk, galloping from one topic to the next, lurching into excited detours then looping back, shifting from serious to silly with no awkward grinding of the gears. When two people have that conversational harmony and vigour, it feels as if a fabulous chemical reaction is underway.

Leo Newman and I discussed books, as we'd done when we met twelve years before. I described the foolish choices and misery of my marriage. He talked about baby Ava, how the strength of his love for this child had taken him by surprise. For Leo, having lost everyone in his family, there was unexpectedly deep satisfaction that Ava was related to him by blood.

He described his early days in PNG. Being thrown into that wildly different place had been exhilarating, visiting remote valleys, learning to speak Pidgin. He joked about the diligent efforts of various expat wives to match-make him with any single white female. The project to marry off lonely bachelor Leo went on for years until Helen landed in Moresby. Their marriage took place in an Anglican church up there, despite the groom being Jewish. For the sake of social ease, Leo had made a tactical decision to play down both his German background and his Jewishness. I gathered that in the years since we'd met on the *Asturias*, Leo rarely spoke to anyone about his early life.

He didn't offer up much detail about his wife and I noticed he rarely called her 'Helen'. Almost always 'my wife'. I did not know if that signified anything.

On the Sunday, Athena invited us all over for lunch so she could also spend time with our old friend from the *Asturias*. In the Samios courtyard, we feasted on wonderful food, the four kids romped around the yard together and, as I would have expected, Leo and Nick warmed to each other immediately. Pearl declared that this was a perfect day and that she had the most champion friends in the world.

Once Athena had a couple of glasses of wine in her, she asked Leo if she could have another look at the photo of Ava. Athena fussed over the loveliness of the baby and shot me a look. *He's married. He has a baby. Don't be hopeful.*

Leo's visits continued into the following week. Mac and Rose were both starstruck by him. When he bought them copies of *The Little Prince* and *The Secret Garden*, they insisted he read the books aloud to them at bedtime. Over the next run of evenings, I listened to his voice reading to my children while I folded laundry.

For those two weeks, Leo Newman and I were playing house.

In our after-dinner chats, we talked a great deal about our wish to be good parents, given the inadequate parenting we'd received ourselves. When I confided my worries about my anxious son, Leo was quick to reassure me that Mac was a terrific kid and that I was a wonderful mother. But alongside the reassurance, he also listened, respecting my instincts rather than dismissing my fears as foolishness.

When I told him about the fictional letters I'd written for women's magazines, Leo was quick to encourage me to take it further, to see myself as a writer. I had never admitted to a soul that I fantasised about writing longer stories than 'Strange But True' letters. I had not even allowed that aspiration to form into a sentence in my own mind for fear my brain would twist around on me and punish me for having tickets on myself. But one of those evenings in my kitchen in 1959 I admitted that fantasy to Leo Newman.

He dreamed of doing a law degree so he could put things right for people, even if that might seem naïve. But he couldn't study law while he was living in PNG.

The more he talked about his life in Port Moresby, the more dissatisfied he sounded. He felt increasingly distant from his fellow expats, who loved swanning about like ersatz aristocrats, dressing up for soirees in each other's homes and lording it over their native staff.

'I'm a bureaucrat in a peculiar colonial throwback, going to cocktail parties with an incestuous little club of white people, all of us being served by houseboys who live in huts in our back gardens. It's awful. This is not a life I want to be living.'

'Can't you leave? If you came back to Australia, you could do a law degree,' I argued.

Leo shrugged. 'My wife very much wants to stay in Moresby. Her brother and sister-in-law are there. And it's easier for her, with the baby, having the house staff. She enjoys the social life, the drinks parties and all that, even if I don't.'

That was the closest he came to badmouthing Helen to me. He would not wish to be disloyal. I respected that, however desperately I wanted him to badmouth her.

I did push him a little. 'Come on, Leo, you have choices. You talk as if you're trapped.'

He smiled wanly. 'Am I not trapped? I love my daughter. Even during this fortnight—which, by the way, has been the most happy time—I've missed Ava terribly. If we love our children, if we don't ever want to be separated from them, that's a kind of trap. Even if it's a lovely one.'

At the end of the second week, there was no avoiding the reality that Leo would soon have to catch a train to collect his wife and baby. Pearl was well enough to move back to her own place. In fact, I believe she had feigned being weaker than she was, just to extend Leo's visits.

Leo borrowed a colleague's car to drive Pearl and me back to her bedsit in Chippendale. When she opened the door, she was relieved to see her room had been cleaned up. Weeks before, I'd gone round to dispose of the bloody bedding and to talk the landlord into providing a decent second-hand mattress.

While Pearl unpacked the clothes from her suitcase, Leo arranged a bunch of flowers in a vase on the dresser and I fitted as much food as I could inside the small fridge. Then the three of us spread a rug on the threadbare carpet and shared a picnic lunch, as if we could exorcise any bad spirits from the room by filling the air with convivial chat. Even so, the stress of moving back there was draining for Pearl and not long after lunch, she flopped onto the new mattress to nap. Leo and I promised we would check on her in the morning.

It was 1 p.m. when the two of us stepped outside into the street.

'Let's walk for a while,' Leo suggested, and we headed down Shepherd Street, past where he'd parked the car. As we reached Broadway, walking towards Central, he reached out and took my hand. I felt exposed, as if all my clothing had fallen off me and onto the footpath. Without my children sleeping nearby, there was no protective forcefield preventing me from doing something I knew I shouldn't do.

Outside a Haymarket pub, The Great Southern Hotel, he asked, 'Shall we have a drink?'

I sat at a table in the saloon bar, watching Leo order beers for us at the counter. I found myself ogling him, imagining his naked body inside his clothes, in a way I had not allowed myself to do before.

We sipped on our beers—carefully, as if restrained sipping might hold us in a more cautious place. We chatted about the pub, the other people sitting around us, his impressions of the ways Sydney had changed. We didn't utter a word about my kids or his daughter or his wife, as if any of those words said aloud would set off strident alarms and trigger squads of disapproving people to burst into the bar and haul us apart.

Leo fell silent for a moment, and then asked, 'Should we see if they have a room available?'

I nodded.

In the main foyer there was a window, like a cinema ticket booth, for booking the accommodation upstairs. I hung back, leaning against the wall, while Leo went up to the sour-faced woman at the window. Leo Newman was the person handing over cash, signing the register ('Mr and Mrs Steinbeck') and taking the room key, but I was the one being given the hairy eyeball from the clerk for being a hussy.

I wanted to shout at that judgemental cow, 'This is not some tawdry affair between a married man and a besotted, desperate woman. This is a long-awaited fulfilment of a promised love, thwarted by misunderstanding and mistiming. Can't you see this is special and beautiful, lady?'

But he was married. I was besotted and desperate. It was tawdry if the hotel clerk wanted to regard it so.

When Leo swung open the door to the room—tea-coloured stains spreading across the flowered wallpaper, an ugly dark dresser, a sink attached to the wall, a high lumpy bed with a bilious green chenille bedspread—'tawdry' was one word that came to mind. Leo strode across the room and closed the curtains so at least, in the dim light, the place might appear less depressing.

Before we removed a single item of clothing, we kissed for a long time. There was a lot of catching up to do. The kissing was as wonderful as I had always imagined it would be.

I'm not going to attempt to describe the sex. Such scenes are almost always unintentionally comic when written down, and a description of the mechanics rarely captures how it feels for the individuals doing it.

I will say that once we dropped the clothes and hit the bed, there was an urgent bout of fucking which served to get the nerves out, burning off the fuel that had built up over the twelve years since we'd first started lusting after each other.

After that, we lay there for a good while, keeping our hands on each other's bodies.

'I've always prided myself on not being the kind of woman who would sleep with a married man,' I said.

'And I've always disapproved of men who cheat on their wives,' he replied. 'I'm sorry if I've lured you to shred your principles.'

'This'll teach us not to be too self-righteous.'

We kissed and talked and kissed some more, which then turned into another round of lovemaking, much slower this time, paying attention to every moment with an intensity that came from knowing this would be it forever. Not that we had those anguished looks on our faces that people often do in such scenes in movies. Leo and I were smiling and talking and laughing and gazing at each other in blissful pleasure.

I was glad that my experiences with Cy had given me confidence when it came to sex and Leo proved to be as considerate and passionate a lover as I had hoped. Even with the weight of expectation built up over twelve years, I was not disappointed. Let's just say that the afternoon exceeded all my expectations to a blazing, glorious extent and leave it at that.

We both dozed off briefly and when I opened my eyes, I could see from the gap around the curtains that it was almost dark outside. I jumped up and pulled on my clothes.

'I should get home,' I said.

Leo reached for his trousers. 'Let me drive you.'

But I was already in the doorway. 'I'll catch a bus. Thank you though.'

As I ducked into the corridor and closed the door behind me, I heard him say 'thank you' to me.

The next day, I watched Leo walk inside Pearl's place, to visit as promised. I waited outside in Shepherd Street, planning my next move.

I considered the direct approach: brazenly rushing up to him. 'Leave your wife and be with me.' Or maybe the more realistic: 'Move back to Australia and have an affair with me.'

The trouble was, during the previous sleepless night, my mind had begun imagining the steps ahead and the likely consequences of each choice. Leo could never be separated from his baby daughter and if he tried he would be wretched. I would think less of him and he would resent me. If we tried to have some kind of secret affair, we would both feel guilty. I could see no viable way to make the story work out happily.

There have been points in my life when I've been impulsive, diving in without doing any forward plotting, and there have been junctures like this one, when I mulled over all the likely repercussions of a choice and thought myself to a standstill.

An hour later, I watched Leo Newman come out and look along Shepherd Street for me. I kept myself hidden behind a van until he finally gave up and walked away.

Pearl greeted me at the door a few minutes later.

'What a shame! You just missed Leo.'

NINE

December 1963.

In the office workplaces of the 1960s, many secretaries developed tactics to avoid the groping of male bosses. A repertoire of manoeuvres like a secret martial art. There were agile swerving actions or the sudden jabbing back of an elbow when trapped at a desk by the boss leaning over you. There was the cheeky duck-and-twist to escape when you were pinned against a wall. Nearby objects could be commandeered when necessary—for example, upon seeing an especially handsy man approaching, the female office worker could grab a stack of files and hold it in front of her body as a shield. With her arms full, the woman might be vulnerable from the rear, in which case she could spin around and 'accidentally' gouge her assailant in his soft areas with the sharp metal bits on the corners of the files. All these moves were conducted in such a way that the groping men would remain unaware it was happening.

I was regarded by the blokes in the office as a dame not easily rattled, who didn't mind a blue joke. That was genuine, more or less, but it was also another survival strategy.

By 1963, my kids were old enough to walk home from school by themselves, so I had finally been able to make use of my stenography certificate and take a job as a secretary in a big insurance company in the city. I had good shorthand and typing speeds, but my real value lay in spelling and vocabulary skills. When one of the executives was dictating sentences full of grammatical errors and awkward wording, I could offer synonyms and suggestions—gently, of course, careful never to scuff any shine off the ego of the male in question.

My boss Geoffrey was tall and knitwear-model handsome, educated at a posh school where he'd excelled at sport. He had an affable confidence that came from having enjoyed a frictionless, lubricated run through life. No one ever questioned that he was the kind of man who should be at a senior level in the company. But I realised—to my astonishment—that Geoffrey was dim. I'm talking seriously thick. But because he exuded self-assurance, no one realised he was dead stupid, not even Geoffrey himself.

The ones we really had to watch out for were the cocky younger blokes, especially on days they came back to the office from a boozy lunch at the Angus Steak Cave. I would write a warning in shorthand on memo pads and distribute them to each woman's desk. None of the men could read Pitman's so it became our version of wartime coded messaging.

On those post-lunch afternoons, we were extra vigilant, making sure no office junior was stranded behind a closed door with a fellow who had a bellyful of Johnnie Walker Black Label. If that happened, one of us—'us' being the older women—would barge in and loudly give the young woman a task at the far end of the building.

I'm aware that a reader from a later generation might judge me harshly for my lack of direct action against these sleazebucket men. I could argue that it was a different time, we couldn't risk losing our jobs, blah blah blah. But I must also accept that our strategies—nifty tactics, coded notes, extracting vulnerable girls, joking along—were forms of collaboration, managing the bullshit instead of challenging it. To all the young women I failed to save from being pawed and ridiculed and assaulted, I offer my apologies.

A Wednesday evening in the run-up to Christmas, I left the office in Pitt Street at five thirty, then walked across Hyde Park and down behind the Australian Museum, attempting not to sweat too much on my Courtelle dress.

By the time I reached Beppi's restaurant in East Sydney, Pearl was hopping out of a taxi, waving to me. Our dinners at Beppi's happened every few weeks and they always had to be early: as soon as the place opened at six and out again by seven thirty. That suited me—I could get home to Mac and Rose before their bedtime—but the timing was really about Pearl's obligations.

For the past two years, Pearl had been the mistress of Gerry Stankovich, a fifty-something businessman who owned a couple of nightclubs, a construction company, illegal gambling joints and other dodgy operations. There was a Mrs Stankovich and grown-up Stankovich offspring, but all Gerry's previous lovers had been tolerated, as Pearl was now.

Stankovich had first spotted her out dancing with a bunch of her girlfriends. Gerry wooed her zealously, making her giddy with the intensity of his pursuit. When it came to romance, Pearl had always allowed the decibel level of the man's desire to drown out whatever she might or might not be feeling. She accepted the role as Gerry's mistress, ensconced in a petite but luxurious art deco apartment in Potts Point. To his credit, the arrangement was straightforward and transparent from the start. Pearl's discretion would be obligatory, her expenses would be covered, and the original Mrs Stankovich would never relinquish her position.

Pearl spent her days at the hairdresser, Madame Korner's beauty salon, the pictures, or lunching with whichever girlfriends were available to play. In the evenings, she was on call—dolled up and ready by 8 p.m. any night to accompany Gerry to a nightclub or to stay in the apartment with him, depending on his mood. On nights when Gerry didn't call, she would curl up on the sofa and watch TV.

Beppi's restaurant was a big deal, a place where famous people ate. Even though the sun was still bright outside at 6 p.m., once we walked into the dining area, it felt like night-time in the most elegant, velvety way. There were murals of Italian scenes between the brick arches, waiters with continental accents and leather-bound menus offering mussels, artichokes, fritto misto, zabaglione. It was fabulously cosmopolitan. Expensive too, but Pearl always insisted on paying.

'What's the point of me getting an allowance from Gerry if I can't use some of it to have fancy tea with my best friends. Ooh, what should we eat this time?' She pointed out an item on the menu. 'Does that word mean some sort of vegetable or a slimy creature from the sea? Mario! Mario, my love, can you help daft old me understand the menu?'

Pearl was on hugging and kissing terms with the waiters, flirting with them, asking after their families. I once came back to our table from the ladies to find she'd gone. I then spotted her in the kitchen, peering into pots on the stove, charming the bejesus out of the kitchen staff.

It was the same in her new neighbourhood too. You couldn't walk through Kings Cross and Potts Point without Pearl stopping constantly to chat with bouncers, shop-owners, drag queens, working girls, homeless men. People could tell she didn't have a single judgemental cell in her lovely body.

That night in Beppi's, I sat in my sweaty synthetic dress, my hair like a frizzy Russian fur hat thanks to the humidity, and looked across the table at Pearl. Every time we had dinner, she would be in a new fashionable outfit, with her hair teased, beehived or flipped into a different perfectly lacquered shape.

She still looked much younger than her thirty-five years, helped by hormone supplements (they existed, in rudimentary form, even back then) which compensated for the abrupt lurch into menopause brought on by the hysterectomy. She wore too much makeup—that lovely skin did not need a thick layer of foundation trowelled onto it and those eyes did not need so much tarry black eyeliner—but that was just my opinion.

Pearl always gushed about the food but rarely ate much of it. She would sometimes order half-a-dozen oysters, eat four of them, then claim to be full, having eaten a massive lunch. Other times she would admit to being on a 'desperation' diet, patting her flat belly that showed so little evidence of a bulge I would defy a geometrician to measure it. She would urge me to order three courses and wine, and I chose not to feel guilty about partaking of sustenance—especially when it was as delectable as the dishes at Beppi's. Pearl did have a childlike passion for sweet things and when she allowed herself a spoonful of my tiramisu, I could see the sugar hit her with a rush.

I only ever met Gerry Stankovich once, when he'd arrived early at the Potts Point apartment and Pearl insisted the three of us have a drink. I felt his eyes run over me, checking for signs I could be a problem—before he suggested we all have a Moscow Mule.

Stankovich was a step up from Pearl's previous boyfriends, as long as one overlooked his criminal activities, and I don't believe he ever hit or mistreated my friend. Still, watching that man slide his hand down Pearl's back from shoulder blade to hip, then hook her round the waist, securing his territory, gave me the heebie-jeebies.

'I'm happy, Lizzie,' Pearl would always reassure me. 'I'm not a prisoner. I like Gerry. I like sex.'

I was also a fan of having sex. Particularly if it could be good sex.

By 1961, Leo Newman was still living in Port Moresby with Mrs Newman, daughter Ava and, according to Pearl, a little boy now too. I had decided there was no point pining over him and I was too bloody young to give up hope of ever having another partner.

I made a list—typed up so it would feel more significant—of the reasons I should consider a new husband: 1) Regular sex with a teachable man; 2) companionship; 3) a father figure for my children; 4) someone to share the financial burdens of life.

If that list appears unromantic and cynical, it was me trying to be hard-boiled, to take the sting out of the vulnerability of my situation.

As is my way, I made *plans* for solving this problem. Two other single mothers and I ran a system of reciprocal babysitting so we could go on night-time dates. In those days, for a fellow to be single in his mid-thirties, he was likely divorced or living with his parents or in some other questionable situation. I was in no position to be picky, given I was hardly a bargain: a widow with two kids, no money, and a mouthful of opinions. Then again, I was a goer when it came to sex, which men found to be either terrifying or a heaven-sent bonus.

I would say the divorced guys were the worst, many of them still so volubly angry at their former wives, with the toxins leaking out onto all women. When they whined about how they'd been mistreated by their exes, I would find myself sympathising with the poor woman who had once been married to this bozo. One freshly divorced fellow was not so much angry as heartbroken. He spent the entirety of our dinner together weeping about missing his wife.

Sometimes, after a few dates, things would progress as far as sex, so I kept myself prepared, with a diaphragm in a pastel pink case in the zipped section of my handbag. I carried the diaphragm with me everywhere not just for contraceptive purposes but also to avoid Rose finding it again and flicking it across the room like a miniature frisbee.

I did have some fun in my occasional sexual encounters, but most often, I was treated to a whole new world of awkwardness and disappointment. Let's just say my breasts endured a lot of clumsy handling and my nether regions were pounded with limited finesse.

One of my sexual partners avoided eye contact and was utterly silent during the act, even breathing inaudibly, until he finally said in a flat, mechanical voice, 'I'm sticking it in you now.'

Another bloke was much more loquacious during our sexual encounter, barracking like a football coach, urging himself on as he thrust away. 'Go, Derek! Come on, mate! You can do this, Derek!'

I did not sign up for a rematch with Derek.

30 December 1963. Narrawallee, south coast of New South Wales.

Nick Samios and my son Mac trudged up the grassy slope from the inlet. Their pre-dawn fishing expeditions had become a beach holiday tradition and Mac loved grabbing some time on his own with Uncle Nick, the closest person to a proper father he'd ever had.

Athena and I were drinking tea on folding chairs on the front lawn and, even though there was only dim early morning light seeping through the trees, we could clearly see Nick's white teeth. He was grinning, holding up the ten bream they'd caught.

Back in 1959, Nick had decided that the building business was sturdy enough that he could afford to take a week off during the Christmas break. Athena found two holiday-let cottages side by side on a slope above Narrawallee Beach, several hours' drive south of Sydney. One house would be for Nick's family while his older brother Basil, sister-in-law Evi and their three teenagers took the one next door.

With their typical and constant kindness, Athena and Nick had invited me to join them that first summer. There were only two small bedrooms plus a double bunk on the built-in verandah of each cottage but the younger kids were keen to sleep in tents on the lawn, so the Samios family could always find room for Mac, Rose and me.

The fibro cottages were basic, with tank water, cold showers, shabby furniture and rudimentary kitchens. On hot nights, it could be so stifling in the bedrooms, even the grown-ups would drag mattresses outside to sleep in the open air. This was our fifth summer sharing those glorious beach holidays.

If there was a sameness to our days in Narrawallee that was part of the pleasure. We would spend the morning swimming and sunbaking on the beach then back to the cottage for lunch, followed by board games, reading and snoozes during the hottest part of the day. Our kelpie Sadie would come to the beach in the mornings, but she was an old dog by this time and usually dozed under the verandah from noon onwards.

For dinnertime, picnic tables and hurricane lamps were set up on the lawn between the cottages so both households could join together while the bedrooms hopefully cooled down enough to sleep that night.

On portable charcoal barbecues, Basil Samios cooked the fish Nick had caught, or lamb, or octopus from the Italian fishermen in nearby Ulladulla, with a huge array of vegetable dishes. There was always too much food.

Music would blare out of the tinny transistor radio and we made do with whatever songs were on the local station's playlist.

That year, the kids were thrilled if The Beatles came on ('I Want to Hold Your Hand' was huge), immediately jumping up to dance. Rose was delighted the DJ spun Elvis's latest single 'Return to

Sender' and when it was 'Summer Holiday' everyone belted out the chorus along with Cliff Richard and grinned like a bunch of happy fools as if the song were being played in our honour.

The moment a Nat King Cole ballad came on the radio, I closed my eyes to let his voice pour over me like liquid caramel. Then, over the top of Nat singing, I heard a squawk of protests from the teenagers. 'Dad!' 'You're so embarrassing!' I opened my eyes to see Nick was dancing with Athena, gazing into her eyes as he mimed along to 'Unforgettable', half-jokey, half-serious. Neither of them was a dancer really—they just turned a few circles and swayed to the lush strings—but it was lovely. The kids continued wailing in mock horror to see their father/uncle/de facto uncle romancing their mother/aunt/de facto aunt. Athena and Nick made a show of ignoring them. When the song ended, Nick was beaming with a mixture of love for his wife and enjoyment of the kids' carry-on.

On the morning of New Year's Eve, I drove Mac, Thea and Basil's son George into Ulladulla to buy supplies for our celebration that night, including fireworks. The agreement was that the kids could choose Roman candles, fountains, sparklers and such, but no bungers or screechy fireworks that would freak Sadie out.

In the afternoon, Athena left the beach early and headed back to the house to start cooking our New Year's Eve feast while I wrangled Rose, Thea and George to hop out of the water and scoot up the hill for showers. Walking along the track from the beach, I saw Nick twenty metres further ahead. He was nodding and listening to Mac who trotted beside him, his gangly teenage-boy shadow.

Nick suddenly stopped, then staggered back a step, as if he'd lost his balance. A second later he collapsed onto the sandy track. For a moment I wondered if he was clowning around.

I ran forward, just as Basil came belting up from the water and slid down next to his brother, shouting his name loudly. Nick was unresponsive. Not breathing. Basil had done some CPR training at his job and he threw himself into giving his brother the breath of life and then chest compressions. When I knelt down to help, Basil talked me through how to pinch Nick's nose and blow air from my lungs into his airway.

I've revisited this moment often. Mostly I would replay the version of the memory that I edited together urgently on the day. A close-up shot of Nick's chest rising as I blew in another lungful of air. Basil, breathless from exertion and panic, thumping at his brother's sternum. But sometimes I looked at mental footage from other camera angles—angles that took in the sight of Mac standing only a few feet away, all the light crushed out of his face, watching Nick die. One of my regrets is that in the immediate aftermath, I was so caught up—following Basil's instructions, asking George to hustle Thea and Rose away, calculating how long it would take me to run to the phone box to ring an ambulance—that I didn't pay enough attention to how this moment would fracture my boy.

Mac was tormented by the thought that, because he had been chatting to Nick a few seconds before, he had failed him by not noticing the problem. He only divulged that thought to me years later, so at the time, I didn't think to reassure my fourteen-year-old boy that he had not failed Nick.

I'm confident Basil did the best anyone could have done for his brother on that beach track. Nick Samios suffered a catastrophic blockage of the left anterior descending artery—a 'widow-maker' heart attack.

When Athena came running down from the house towards the body of her husband, she stumbled on the uneven surface of the sandy path. I reached out to steady her and she paused there for a moment, squeezing my hand.

I appreciated the structured rituals of the Kastellorizian community that swung into place after Nick's death. Before the funeral a wake was held in the house Nick had built with his own hands. The coffin sat right there in the living room, surrounded by candles. For the funeral service, the Greek Orthodox church was packed, standing room only, the way it is when a person dies so young and as beloved as Nick.

For a week after the funeral, Athena received a stream of visitors at the house, with her girls and various family members on hand to help serve brandy, coffee and small dry paximathia biscuits to the mourners. Rose, Mac and I dropped round a few times during that week and, even though the extended family always welcomed us, we felt a little separate from the process.

I noticed Thea was clingy and tearful, rarely leaving her mother's side, while Sofia had taken on the role of the responsible almost-adult. In that period, Sofia seemed to accelerate in maturity, while Thea regressed a little.

Rose had been sleeping in my bed every night since Nick's death and Mac would usually come in at some point in the early hours. Selfishly I was glad to have my children snuggled in beside me.

I was awake for long stretches of those nights, monitoring my heartbeat obsessively. At other times, I fixated on my breathing, listening for raspiness or other clues my bronchioles might be riddled with tumours. I'd never been a cigarette smoker but the majority of my friends and work colleagues smoked, exhaling several lung cancers' worth of smoke into the air I'd been breathing. I kept picturing the anatomy illustrations I'd studied as a kid and relating those diagrams to my own innards. There were so many organs and physiological systems that could go wrong in a lethal fashion. I started palpating my belly, prodding into my torso, feeling for lumps and abnormalities. I ended up with bruises on my body, and then I would fret that those self-inflicted marks were symptoms of leukaemia.

Even as these night anxieties took hold of me, I understood they were panic attacks—racing heart, clammy skin, tingling limbs—but the brain is a difficult organ to control. Eventually I would ease myself out of bed so I wouldn't wake the kids, pad into the kitchen, make hot milk, read a novel, anything to throw myself clear of the spinning blades in my head. Then, loaded on top of the health anxiety, there would come a generous layer of guilt. It was shameful that I was wasting energy on phantom illnesses when Athena and her children were dealing with the thumping reality of Nick's death.

One morning, after a night of panicky insomnia, Rose shook me awake to take a phone call from Sofia.

'Can you come over, Auntie Betty?' asked Sofia. 'Mum needs you.'

Once the structure of the formal mourning was over, Athena had crumbled, taken to her bed, refusing food, refusing to speak to anyone for three days. Sofia had been getting her little sister off to school every morning but staying home herself to look after her mother.

When I walked in the door and hugged Sofia, I was struggling not to weep and pour more tears into that sad house. 'Oh, sweetheart. What a wonderful girl you are. I wish you'd called me sooner.'

'Mum wouldn't let me.'

Athena had instructed Sofia to make excuses to anyone who called, telling me she was with the family, telling the family she was with me.

What had finally propelled Athena out of bed that morning was anger.

The one phone call she had chosen to take was from Theo, the eldest Samios brother, letting her know he was in the process of selling Nick's construction business—the business Athena had helped build. Theo never put serious weight on the fact that Athena had been handling the accounts, the quotes, dealing with sub-contractors and suppliers, and never contemplated the idea that she could go on running things. He didn't think she was up to such a job. Both Samios brothers believed they were doing Athena a favour, relieving her of a burden and providing her with whatever cash could be extracted from the business.

By the time I found Athena in her bedroom that morning, she was just out of the shower and getting dressed, defiantly yanking a bra round her torso with enough force to break a person's neck.

'I want to go to the yard right now,' she said. 'I must tell Theo he can't sell it.'

'I'll drive you,' I offered.

On the way to the building yard, I glanced at Athena in my passenger seat, with her back straight and strong enough to take on anything, the way I'd seen her sitting on the *Asturias* seventeen years before.

Her plan was to go into the office and argue her case, but when I pulled up outside the gate of 'Nick Samios Constructions', she didn't move for several moments. I said nothing, assuming she was pausing to draft a speech in her mind.

When she eventually spoke, her tone was not defiant, as I expected. She sounded resigned. 'The bank will not let me have overdrafts—not without Nick. A business like this, you need overdrafts to manage the cash flow.'

Without the backing of her brothers-in-law, there was no way any bank manager would offer the necessary line of credit to a woman in 1964.

'No point going in there and shouting,' she said. 'I won't win.'

The two of us sat in the car outside the building yard for some minutes.

Athena still smouldered with insulted pride, but she had switched into pragmatic mode. 'I'll use the money Theo gets out of this place to make sure my girls have a good education. I can get work with other builders—book-keeping, estimating.'

'Yes. When you feel up to it.'

'Can you teach me to drive, Betty?'

'Oh. Sure. We can certainly give it a burl.'

On the drive back to Earlwood, Athena stared out the window and I let the silence go.

Suddenly she said, 'Pull the car over. Pull over here.'

'Eh? I can't give you a driving lesson right this minute.'

Athena just kept gesturing for me to pull over, so I did.

She twisted her body round to face me square on and waited until I did the same.

'I need for you to make a promise to me,' she said.

'Of course.'

'I've been thinking, over and over. Nick is gone and if I die—'

'Why would you die? You won't—'

'I could die. An accident, an illness, whatever it could be.' She sounded irritated with me—this was no time for meaningless reassurance. 'If something happens to me, Nick's brothers would be around, yes, but that's not—Betty, I want you to promise you will look after my girls.'

'I would. I promise.'

Athena closed her eyes for a few beats, letting the reassurance settle in her body, and then she added, 'I would do the same. If something happens to you, I would look after Mac and Rose.'

'I know you would.'

We embraced for a long time, which gave me a chance to recover my composure sufficiently to drive us safely the rest of the way to Earlwood. The obsessive anxiety about my health stopped that day—like switching off an unhelpful circuit in my brain.

TEN

April 1969.

In 1965, once I'd purchased a TV set, I got stuck into various British offerings (*Morecambe and Wise*, *The Forsyte Saga*, *Softly, Softly*) and I enjoyed American shows like *Get Smart* and *Ben Casey*. Local dramas *Homicide* and *Bellbird* were favourites in our house too.

The television set was also a source of stress. News of assassinations in the US, earthquakes and fires, terrible murders, and distressing footage from the war in Vietnam. Sometimes I would feel myself too porous, too caught up in the suffering on the screen—suffering that I could do nothing about.

I was especially careful not to allow our home to be bombarded with news stories about nuclear weapons. The fear that we could all be vaporised—the low humming threat of Mutually Assured Destruction—was always there, and from a young age, my son Mac had often fretted about the arsenal of atomic bombs. When he was a teenager, I didn't find girlie magazines hidden under Mac's bed. Instead, I found an official government brochure, 'Survival from Nuclear Warfare'.

Anxieties had whirred inside my beautiful son's head all through high school. There were panic attacks about exams, periods when he couldn't face school and torment over friendships. Although he was a tall strapping teenager, Mac was never good at sport and never found his way in the blokey customs of young men. (The range of 'man' on offer to young males in 1960s Australia was neither broad nor subtle.) My son was desperate to fit in, but he was bullied and friendless for agonising stretches of time until he finally found a small cadre of unblokey boys he could hang with. Which was fine by me.

Girls liked him because he was kind and he was a listener, but lamentably, he fell hard in love with a lass who toyed with him before deciding she didn't love him back. The day Mac's seventeen-year-old heart was broken, I found him vomiting into the toilet bowl, next to a half-empty bottle of liquor. Putrid as he was feeling, he managed a self-mocking smile, and showed me the bottle of Southern Comfort.

'I picked it for the name,' he said. 'I thought there'd be comfort in it. There wasn't.'

The reader might imagine the relief I felt when Mac Burnley made it through to the end of high school, spent a year working as a builder's labourer to earn money, then enrolled in a teaching degree at Sydney University, doing building work on the side. I could picture Mac being a wonderful, thoughtful English and history teacher. I could imagine a good life for my son. By '69, with Mac in his second year at uni, I was worrying about him a little less.

Rose was the child I never had to worry about. Clever, diligent, with wisely chosen friendships and too much focus on books to go silly over boys. Because she'd started school early, she was sixteen and a half when she finished the Higher School Certificate, earning marks high enough for any tertiary course she fancied.

What came next was a surprise.

'Mum, I'm not going to university. Uni is what you want. It's not what I want.'

My daughter threw a series of statements at me, which hit like shrapnel tearing into flesh.

'No, Mum. I don't want to hear the story—again—about your grammar school letter. You would've given anything for an education, blah blah bloody blah.'

'Shut up, Mum. You don't get it. I don't want any of this. The whole system, the entire set-up of this society is phony and full of shit.'

Rose had been reading a lot of politics and philosophy books in her final school years. It had never occurred to me that my daughter's love of reading could incite her to throw away education. And I was surprised to hear her special scorn for Australia.

'I have to get out of this narrow-minded country. A stupid little country at the arse-end of the world. I mean, nobody *thinks* here. This place is a joke. Marcie and Jen and me are going travelling. There's a guy who'll give us a lift to Darwin.'

Rose, being under eighteen, needed my signature to obtain a passport. She held out a pen to me, defiant.

'You always told me to think for myself, so that's what I'm doing now. I don't need money from you. I don't need anything from you. Just your signature.'

I refused to sign the passport papers, hoping that if she had to wait until her eighteenth birthday, she might change her mind and go to university.

In her determination to wear me down, Rose turned a little cruel.

'You're pathetic, Mum. With you it's all—"Oh poor me, I didn't get an education." Well, I'm sorry your life is shit, but that doesn't mean you can make me live some life you missed out on.'

Then my daughter swivelled the big guns round to aim at me.

'You never even cared that much about me anyway. You've always been obsessed with Mac. So just sign the form. I'll fuck off and you'll have more time to worry about him.'

I argued back, swore that I adored her, tried to explain that Mac had needed me more, apologised if she'd ever felt neglected, and attempted to convey how much I admired her. I don't think any words I said penetrated her sixteen-year-old skull and, besides, by then the anger I'd seen in her eyes had shredded my resolve. After holding out for two weeks, I signed the passport papers.

Rose had been squirrelling away money from school holiday jobs and weekend shifts at a supermarket—enough cash, according to her, to travel to Southeast Asia, then overland on the hippie trail to Europe.

In the April of '69, my daughter, about to turn seventeen, had been gone three months. I'd received one postcard from her—not so much a message as a scrawled list of place names. I opened the atlas and traced the path she'd taken from Darwin to Timor to Lombok to Bali and now travelling east to west through Java. The postcard ended: 'Going to stay in Surabaya. Don't know how long.'

Hoping to reach her while she was still at the Surabaya address, I wrote back immediately, making a strategic choice to keep my letter full of questions about her travels and free of lecturing. I chose safe topics, including anecdotes about our dog Gidget. Sadie II had passed away in '65 and, not long after that, Rose had brought home a stray who was so winning there was no choice but to keep her. Gidget was by my reckoning a genetic combination of *every* terrier breed, with a wiry coat like an unravelling hessian mat.

Rose replied with a fuller account of her journey so far. Her friend Marcie had piked on the trip even before departure and Jen had flown home after breaking her leg on a motorbike in Bali, but Rose mentioned wonderful new travelling companions she'd found along the way. She wrote earnestly about 'the *community* of travellers, all of us supporting each other' and emphasised that 'the locals are so friendly and helpful'.

I wept when I read her letter—not that there was anything sooky in it, but because her eagerness to share her experiences with me felt like the beginning of détente.

That April, I came home from work to find Mac holding a letter. I knew he and Rose were maintaining their own separate correspondence, so I assumed it was a letter from his sister. That was why he had a strained expression on his face.

'Is that from Rose?' I asked. 'You don't have to read it to me. Just tell me if she's okay.'

'It's not from Rose.'

That was when I noticed the official-looking envelope on the table.

'My birthday came up in the ballot,' he said.

During this period, all Australian men turning twenty in a given year had to register for national service. If a young man's birthday was written on one of the little balls pulled out of a barrel, he was conscripted into the army and obliged to serve two years of national service, almost certainly in Vietnam.

I'd seen Mac's birthday come up in the lottery but I wasn't worried. As a university student, he could defer, and I believed the war would be over before Mac graduated. Nixon was already pulling US troops out of Vietnam.

'It's fine, sweetheart. You just apply to—'

Mac shook his head. 'I'm not enrolled at uni anymore.'

That was the moment I discovered that he'd dropped out of his course towards the end of '68, having found the whole thing too stressful. Since then he'd been taking on more labouring hours and filling up the rest of his time at the park or the library, so I wouldn't notice.

'I was worried you'd be disappointed,' he explained.

The day before Mac was due for his army medical, I was sitting at my desk in the insurance company conjuring up a plan, picturing each step as if it were the storyboard for a short film.

Open on a close-up shot of the bottle of liquid Phenergan in our bathroom. Mac had bought it for his hay fever but found that even a small amount of the antihistamine zonked him too much to stay awake. The first step of my plan was to lace his ginger beer with Phenergan and secrete more of the stuff into his favourite dishes, Navarin of Lamb and Rizogalo with baked peaches. Once Mac sank into a stupor at the dinner table, I would tie him to the chair with scarves.

I pictured myself taking off my beautiful son's shoes and resting his bare feet gently on a folded towel. Then I would fetch my new electric carving knife from the kitchen bench. I would never have the steely nerve of a surgeon to saw away at a body part, but an electric knife might make it doable. I would just cut off the little toe on his left foot. My supposition was that the loss of one toe would be sufficient for him to fail the army medical.

The reader should not be alarmed—that was a fantasy sequence, not something I would ever have done. In that make-believe trade, one small toe would be sacrificed to keep the rest of his precious body safe from bombs and landmines and bullets. Of course, the fantasy was nonsensical. Tyrannical too—my son was twenty, an adult with authority over his own body. I offer my imaginings here in the hope it can convey the level of desperation I felt.

If Mac had chosen to be a draft dodger or conscientious objector, I would have supported him with every ounce of my being, but he refused to listen to such talk, numbly resigned to being conscripted. I mentioned earlier that my son was a kid who let others set the agenda for him. Well, in 1969, he allowed a stupid government policy, dreamed up by desiccated old men, to direct his life.

Bear in mind that the shift in attitudes we think of as 'the sixties' didn't really happen, especially in Australia, until the seventies. Most folks were still very, very conservative. It's true that after distressing news footage of the Tet Offensive in '68, public opinion was starting to turn against involvement in Vietnam. But still, draft dodgers were considered by many to be nutjobs or cowards. A number of people said to me, 'Going to war will be the making of your son' and similar asinine comments. I controlled the urge to decapitate those people.

Mac did basic training at Kapooka and I drove down to the army base for his passing-out parade. With his lovely thick sandy hair chopped off, the military uniform made him look unnervingly like my brother Michael.

Mac joked, 'I was thinking, Mum—I've been a worry wart since I was a kid. Maybe all that worrying can count as useful practice now people are really going to be shooting at me.'

Not long after Mac finished his corps training at Enoggera and was shipped out to Vung Tau, I received a letter from Rose. A blistering letter, accusing me of failing Mac, of serving up her beautiful gentle brother to be sacrificed on the altar of an American imperialist war. According to Rose, if she had been in Australia, she would have persuaded him to defy the draft. But my 'blinkered obedience to the system' meant that I had acted like a 'pathetic sheep' who had allowed my son to be handed a gun to fight in a phony war. She then wrote a long screed about the moral abomination of the Vietnam War (all of it in line with my own views). My sense of failure was fresh enough that my daughter's words landed like punches into an existing bruise.

Any thread of rapprochement between us was severed. There was no word from her for many months. I kept writing though, addressing letters and small gift parcels to the poste restante in whichever town or city I estimated she would arrive in next. Rose was writing regularly to her brother and occasionally to Athena, so at least I knew she was alive.

Mac's letters from Vietnam were full of local cultural detail he thought might interest me and his tone was always doggedly cheerful. Soldiers were required to be cautious about operational detail in their correspondence, but even allowing for that, Mac offered me a version of his experience that was so filtered by the desire to reassure me, that there was little reassurance to be had.

And even when I received a letter from my son or second-hand news of my daughter, I still had no idea where either of them might be, moment by moment. Even though there was no way to protect them, I still focused all my attention on their safety.

At times, having Mac and Rose far away and out of contact created physical distress. I would lie on my bed overcome by the sensation that chunks of my body had been torn out.

No, it was worse than that, because those missing chunks were still somehow tied to my body by a fragile string of connective tissue stretching out, and then stretching even further to remain attached to my distant children.

8 May 1970.

The women in the Save Our Sons movement had been fighting conscription since '65. I'd seen them in the newspapers and on TV— respectable women, most wearing hats and gloves, with perms and going-to-church clothes, not at all like hippies or anti-war protestors. They would peacefully picket, support the young men taken to court for draft evading and stand in silent vigil outside government buildings, often with signs around their necks protesting the call-up.

Some were thrown in gaol for their non-violent protests. A little later in 1970, a group of SOS women from Wollongong chained themselves inside Parliament House in Canberra. Magnificent.

I had always quietly applauded those women, but what value were my unexpressed supportive thoughts? Zero value. Until my own son was sent to war, until I sought some way to channel my fear and anger, it had never occurred to me that it was my business to get involved.

I joined Save Our Sons in November 1969—leafletting and doing whatever tasks I could fit around my full-time job. I stood holding anti-war placards—'No Conscription', 'Say No to the Death Lottery'—outside the gates of the army depot in Marrickville where conscripts were processed.

My SOS sisters were a splendid bunch of dames—all different ages, lefties, housewives, church ladies. One of them, Nola, known for her fabulously raucous laugh, remained a good pal of mine for decades afterwards.

On 8 May 1970 the first of the Vietnam moratorium marches in Australia took place. Conservative scaremongering ahead of the day talked of 'communist anarchy' and 'blood in the streets'. Billy Snedden, a minister in the Liberal government, described the moratorium organisers as 'political bikies pack-raping democracy'. It is amusing to read such wrong-side-of-history nonsense now—lord knows, it makes me laugh—but it's worth reminding ourselves how hard some people with established power have fought against what now seem to us the most just and humane of changes. It is still so.

There was no blood in any street on 8 May despite the heaving numbers in those streets. I took my placard on the train to join our SOS group and the twenty thousand other people gathered at the Sydney Town Hall.

I could try being kind to myself about my lack of commitment to social causes until that point in my life. Here is the kind view: I knew the world was unjust but my response to that had always been to put my head down and struggle along whatever path I could bash through the crappy system for the sake of my kids and a few dear ones. It never seemed possible that someone like me could improve anything beyond my own small orbit.

I accept there was stonking selfishness in my attitude and a dose of self-pity (poor widowed me), but there was also a sense of powerlessness and a cavernous lack of confidence that an unqualified and imperfect woman had anything to offer.

At the age of forty-one, I finally understood: if the possibility was there for collective action to change some stupid, cruel, rusted-on part of the apparatus, then I had a duty to make whatever tiny contribution I could. At that first Moratorium rally, I chanted until my voice became raspy and then was entirely gone. I relished the notion of my one body contributing to that huge mass of other bodies, lost in the multitude and at the same time, I could soak in the power of the crowd around me like a fuel.

I walked into my house afterwards, still buzzing from the day, throat still raw. I was just pulling the shoes off my swollen feet when my neighbour appeared at the door with a telegram.

Mac had been wounded and they were sending him back.

For the first two weeks my son was home, I would wake up in the morning to examine the clues about how bad the night had been. There would be evidence of Mac's many sleepless hours—an ashtray full of cigarette butts, books, dirty glasses, little bits of paper torn into shreds.

Hearing him prowl the house at 2 a.m., I would come out and offer to make tea, but he would always urge me to go back to bed. My hovering irritated him.

At dawn, he would often still be on the couch, technically asleep but with his jaw clenched tight. He wore old school PE shorts to sleep and his bare leg often hung off the couch, so his injury was clearly visible. Two bullets had ripped into his calf, leaving ugly craters, the skin puckered around them.

Those first few weeks, when his school and university mates dropped round to visit, I offered food and drink to entice them to stay. But Mac made his old friends uncomfortable. He wasn't unfriendly so much as uncommunicative, leaving their good-natured questions unanswered as his gaze drifted away from people's faces.

Mac did come to Sunday lunches at Athena's place. He seemed to enjoy Sofia and Thea fussing and adoring him.

Sofia had qualified as an accountant, was already in a steady job and engaged to a young Greek-Australian lawyer. Athena wasn't thrilled about Sofia's plan to marry so young (twenty-two) nor about the choice of fiancé (Athena's magnificent eyebrows arched whenever the guy uttered a word), but her concern was focused more on Thea who hadn't yet found her way, having dropped out of both university and nursing training. It is a mark of the grace of my friend that she managed to confide her worries over her daughters without ever making me feel terrible about the fact that my own kids were both much more lost.

A few weeks after he came home, Mac pretty much stopped eating, claiming lack of appetite. He started going walking at night when sleep was impossible and then would spend all day in bed while I was at work. He claimed to be looking for employment but shook off Athena's attempts to line him up with building-site jobs. He spoke to me less and less and eventually not at all, dead-eyed, his manner lurching between agitated and drowsy. Some readers may be ahead of me here, but in fact, I wasn't too far behind.

One night I wore warm clothes to bed, lying quietly until I heard Mac go out our front door just after midnight. I yanked on sneakers and followed him. I would not claim to be a skilled surveillance operative but Mac was so focused on his destination, he didn't notice me a few metres behind. It would never have occurred to him that his crazy mother might be on his tail.

I followed him across Marrickville, then up the hill to Enmore Road, before dog-legging through the side streets. When he reached a terrace house with a rusted iron fence, crumbly façade and one window covered in plywood, he knocked on the door and went inside.

I was unsure what to do. Following him had made sense but I'd not thought beyond that. I stood on the opposite footpath for fifteen dithering minutes before turning to walk home, but I then abruptly swivelled back, marched across the road and knocked on the door.

The guy who opened it had pin-prick eyes and a huge cold sore like a crusty mouse on his upper lip. He grunted, not expecting to see a forty-something lady with a perm and a bobbly hand-knitted sweater standing on the doorstep. His surprise and general doziness gave me the chance to push past him and walk inside. Perhaps I should've been more afraid at this point, but I was compelled beyond any caution. And in fact, Cold Sore Guy was so scrawny, his bony shoulders no wider than a dinner plate, I reckon I could've wrestled him to the ground.

The smell inside the place was thick, as if I were wading through a soup of urine, dried sweat sourness and rotting food. I turned from the narrow hallway into the front room—frayed flowery carpet, an old sofa regurgitating its stuffing, an upturned milk crate with a table lamp draped in a piece of blue fabric, and in the dimmest far corner, a mattress on the floor.

Mac was sprawled on the mattress, torniquet loose on his upper arm. Ignorant as I was, I understood it was heroin paraphernalia on the carpet beside him. As mothers do with new babies, I nervously looked to check his chest was rising and falling. My boy was pale, out of it, but breathing.

'Do you have a telephone?' I asked Cold Sore Guy.

He nodded.

'Ring a taxi. Tell the operator this address.'

The guy's mouth opened and closed a few times like a fish close to death.

'Call a taxi. Do it now.'

Maybe I reminded him of his cranky mother who used to thrash obedience into him. Whatever the reason, he did what I asked.

I took the torniquet off Mac's arm, rolled his shirtsleeve down, put his shoes on and heaved his upper body up to lean against the wall so he was in a sort of sitting position. (I'm not sure what good I thought that would do.) Then I sat by him, smoothing the hair back from his forehead and murmured, 'It'll be all right. You'll be all right.' Cold Sore Guy hovered in the doorway, watching as if this were an intriguing wildlife documentary.

Hearing the toot of the taxi's horn outside, I recruited the guy to help me get my six-foot-two son out into the street. The cabbie would've seen two short individuals (me and the scrawny fellow) holding up a tall groggy man, stumbling their way out of a squalid house towards his vehicle, so it was no surprise the driver released his park brake, ready to drive off.

I lunged forward to the driver's window and smiled. 'Hello. Thanks for coming so quickly,' I said. 'My son is a war veteran and he's in a bit of pain.' (Not technically a lie.) 'If you could take us to RPA hospital, I'd really appreciate it.'

I had called a taxi rather than an ambulance because I wanted to avoid police involvement. For the same reason, I whisked my son out of the hospital quick smart once it was clear he was stable.

At home, I filled the boot of my '65 Chrysler Valiant with clothes, food, books, and plonked Gidget the terrier on the front seat. Mac was still drowsy, or at least pretending to be, so he was content to doze on the back seat while I drove.

There was no logical reason to dash out of Sydney before dawn but it felt fitting to do so. The sun came up just as we swept down from Bulli Pass towards Wollongong, and I inhaled symbolic encouragement from the signs of a day starting fresh.

In Nowra, I stopped at a phone box and rang in sick to work. In Ulladulla, I stopped by the real estate agent and picked up the key to the Narrawallee holiday cottage. It was July, a Tuesday in wintertime, so the place was not booked. Mac helped me carry groceries inside the cottage where we'd spent summer holidays with the Samios family. This was a risk, I suppose—to revisit the place where we'd lost Nick—but it was also a place of lovely, fortifying memories.

'We're going to stay here until you dry out—or whatever you're supposed to call it when it's drugs and not booze,' I said.

Mac said nothing, just nodded.

We took Gidget down to the beach, hearing our shoes squeak on the cold sand.

My son's compliant streak proved to be an advantage at this point. He could easily have taken the car keys and driven away. He could've hiked to the highway and hitched a lift back to Sydney. I'd like to think that he stayed there with me for the next two weeks not only out of inertia but also because the desire to stay alive was still inside him.

I understand now that Mac's heroin habit had not been massive by the point I found him, so although the physical withdrawal was bad, it wasn't as bad as it could've been. The second twenty-four-hour chunk was the hardest—fever, chills, headaches, aching muscles. He chain-smoked and prowled from room to room to burn away the agitation in his limbs.

I'd picked up packets of aspirin and bottles of Lucozade from a pharmacy, hoping they might be useful, and from home I brought the Valium I'd been prescribed for my 'nerves' when Mac was first shipped out. I didn't like the muffled sensation of benzodiazepine so had stopped taking them. I was wary about Mac taking those pills but I figured the occasional Valium was preferable to frantic sleeplessness that might spin him down a more dangerous path.

He had little appetite for the first four days, but on the fifth day, we did a shopping run together to buy fresh stuff. I cooked his favourite foods and he ate with a gusto that made me want to cry.

After dinner, we would read or listen to the radio next to the pot-bellied stove. During those evenings, and on morning beach walks, the two of us talked about Nick's death and Mac started telling me about his time in Vietnam.

He described the chest-crushing uncertainty, never knowing in which direction the danger might lie, the location of boobytraps, the spots where a sniper might be. The constant stress had combined with Mac's own anxious brain chemistry to create a toxic blend.

He talked about the day his platoon was trapped in a clearing, under fire from several sides. When one of his fellow infantrymen collapsed, wounded, Mac ran back through the gunfire to pick the man up in a fireman's carry, taking him across the clearing, then along a jungle path to the medics. He swore he did it without thinking about the danger.

'But you know, Mum, whenever I think about it now, it freaks me out.' He laughed. 'I reckon I used up every globule of bravery inside me in those two minutes, so I don't have any left.' For years afterwards, he used to joke about his 'depleted supplies' of courage.

An officer sussed out that Mac had an aptitude for languages and sent him for language training classes. Even the rudimentary Vietnamese he learned was enough to chat to locals and reinforce how much he liked the people.

Going into the villages on patrol, he enjoyed joking with the children using his limited Vietnamese phrases, laughing about his mistakes and bad accent. Days later, he might go back to that same village after a bombing strike and find the bodies of the children.

In his downtime, he'd started reading magazine articles condemning the involvement in Vietnam and the distorted political background to it. This fuelled his awareness that he was part of something futile, wrong, with no moral purpose, and intensified his distress about the suffering of the civilian population.

In Vung Tau, Mac avoided the boisterous beer-drinking Australian soldiers. Maybe it would've been better if he had chosen to hang out with the blokey Aussie blokes, because instead, he gravitated towards Americans, the chilled-out ones—GIs who were laid-back because they were off their faces much of the time on opiates. That was when Mac started to dabble.

He told me about the skirmish in which he was wounded, the fiery pain of the bullets tearing through his leg, then his head whirring into a morphine blur as he was loaded into a helicopter. Next to him in the chopper was a mate of his, Gary, who was much more lucid than Mac. The two of them joked about Mac being chock-a-block full of morphine but still bellyaching about his sore leg, while Gary was feeling tiptop. Just before the chopper landed, Gary fell silent and a few minutes later, died from internal injuries.

All of this was painful to hear, but I figured talking about it was preferable to bottled-up suffering. Then again, it was not cathartic in the restorative way I might've hoped. Movies have primed us to expect that once a character blurts out their traumatic memories, they are healed in a pretty much immediate and complete process.

It doesn't work that way in reality. Insight is helpful but not curative. Mac was in pain—physically from his bung leg, and psychologically—for many, many years.

And in a way, his confiding in me during our time down the coast created a vague distance between us for a long while. It was as if he'd deposited those awful memories with me and whenever he looked at me, he knew I knew.

In our second week at Narrawallee, we braved the wintry surf. After the chilly water in Cornwall, I didn't find it that bad, and when Mac submitted himself to the waves, he finally believed me about the euphoria of cold-water swimming. We swam every day, while Gidget sat on the beach, letting the wind ruffle her frayed hessian coat.

Once we were back in Sydney, Mac took labouring work on building sites, wearing himself out physically so he slept a little better. Even if he seemed stable, I wanted to be around to keep watch over him. I quit my secretarial job and found work typing up university theses so I could be at home more. I ended up an expert at deciphering scrawled handwriting and learned more than I ever expected to learn about the mating habits of the platypus, starch-degrading enzymes, and ideas of social justice in early Tudor England.

When Mac came home from a building site, I would be there at the kitchen table, typing, happy to go for a swim or not, ready to talk or not, as he needed. Possibly there were lapses with drugs during those months, but I was not aware of any.

I didn't raise the question of the future. There are periods when you just need to hold on, when the goal is simply to keep your child alive.

ELEVEN

January 1971.

'Welcome home.'

The immigration officer at Heathrow was stamping my British passport, so it was a reasonable thing for him to say. Still, it was a jolt to hear those words. My first time on a plane, for my first visit to the UK since 1947.

I climbed onto the bus that took passengers from the airport to West London Air Terminal. (This was before the Tube went as far as Heathrow.) The view out the window did my head in—there were stretches of the city that appeared unchanged to an unnerving degree, as if I'd never left, but then a moment later, a clump of ugly concrete buildings would erupt in a streetscape which was entirely alien to my eyes. I'd been away almost twenty-four years and I was too jet-lagged to handle the re-entry shock. I closed my eyes and tried to doze.

From the terminal in Kensington, I needed to find my way on a series of buses across the city, south of the Thames, to Denmark Hill. Each time I asked a passer-by for information, I found myself using a different accent. I started off speaking in the hybrid accent I'd ended up with in recent years: the rounded vowels and clear diction from my time as a Woollahra married lady, mixed with enough of an earthy twang that I could work in pubs without sounding like 'a posh wanker'. But when I approached people in Kensington who looked a bit snobby, I adopted a cut-glass aristocratic tone to ask directions. Later, as I continued moving through London streets, some kind of muscle memory was activated and I could hear my south London working-class pronunciation ooze up. Then, inexplicably, I said 'g'day' to one fellow—a greeting I never used in Australia—and heard my voice come out like a parody of an ocker tourist.

My anxiety about this trip had been numbed by the many hours of travel, but once I was inside King's College Hospital, the nerve fibres came throbbing back to life. I hurried to find the right eight-bed ward and it only took two seconds to locate Rose at the far end.

She was asleep, propped up on pillows, so I had the chance to soak in the sight of her for a few minutes. I had not seen my daughter for two years, apart from a hazy photograph she'd sent Mac, with her posing next to a dusty bus. Eighteen going on nineteen, her teenage plumpness was melting away to leave a more defined adult face. She resembled my younger self more than ever. Rose had let her hair grow into a frizzy mass tumbling past her shoulders, lightened from the months she'd been travelling in sunny countries. She was pale, with a drip in her arm and a metal cage under the blankets to keep them off her leg, but she didn't look as desperately ill as I'd feared.

Rose had made her way along the overland trail from Asia, through India, Pakistan, Afghanistan, Iran, Turkey, then meandering across Europe. For the last six months she'd been living in London working as a cleaner and a nanny, couch-surfing in houses with other 'travellers'.

She wound up in hospital after a small cut on her leg turned into a bout of cellulitis so serious she required intravenous antibiotics. The doctors contacted me, concerned sepsis might spread to a dangerous degree, and I immediately booked a flight to London. In the early seventies, the flight from Sydney to London was unimaginably long for any passenger, but I can assure the reader that there is no journey longer than when a parent is flying across the planet to a gravely ill child.

At the other end of the ward, a nurse dropped a metal dish and the clanging noise startled Rose awake.

'Mum.'

I rushed over to the bed and Rose allowed me to hug her. She let herself fall against me, weepy, like a little kid.

'My darling girl, it's wonderful to see you,' I said. 'I'm so sorry this happened to you.'

I felt her body tighten up and disconnect from mine.

'What's that supposed to mean?' she snapped. She flicked her hand to indicate her infected leg. 'This has nothing to do with my trip. I won't let you criticise—'

'What? That wasn't criticism, Rosie. I'm only—'

'The last couple of years have been amazing. Maybe the most incredible thing I'll ever do in my life. I don't want you to pour shit on—'

'No shit is being poured on anything. I'm dead keen to hear all about it.'

She squinted at me, trying to verify if I was genuinely curious about her travels. (I was.) But before I could convince her, a doctor came over to the bed.

'Mrs Burnley? Hello, I'm Doctor Fisher. Rose has been a silly sausage and a very sick girl indeed, but she's on the mend.' He poked his head forward in a patronising pose to address Rose, 'Your mum's come a very long way to rescue you!'

Rose sniffed, properly pissed off by that. And even if it were true that she needed her mother to fly across the world to look after her, Rose was embarrassed to be reminded of it.

Dr Fisher filled me in on her condition: she was responding well to the IV antibiotics and would be ready to be discharged in a day or two. He spoke about Rose as if she wasn't there, or worse, was a gormless child.

By the time he marched off to patronise some of the other silly sausages in his care, Rose was in a right foul mood. All my attempts at chat were met with bored grunts or were misconstrued as criticism. Not wanting relations to deteriorate any further, I played up my tiredness from the journey. I'd go to my hotel, sleep off the travel and be back the next day.

'These are for you,' I said, leaving a packet of Caramello Koalas on the bedside table.

I dropped my suitcase at the cheap hotel I'd booked near the hospital. It was still the middle of the night in Australia so I would have to wait a few hours to ring Mac with a report about his sister. I was ragged, with that jet-lag queasiness, but because I was too restless to lie down, I went walking.

I walked for an hour or so, through Peckham and New Cross, until I reached Deptford. Although the high street shops had new façades and signs, it didn't look so very different, but my childhood street and other spots I'd played in as a kid were unrecognisable. Bombed houses—many of them barely fit for human occupation even before they were bombed—had been torn down and forests of council flats had sprouted in their place.

In 1947, I'd written a letter to my elder sister Margaret to let her know I'd arrived safely in Australia. I'd sent her Christmas cards, news of my wedding, babies and such, to which she replied with similar letters on tissue-thin airmail paper. Our cordial but dull correspondence had petered out in the last ten years, so I had no idea if my sister still lived at the last address I had.

I employed my full-bore south London accent to ask directions from the locals and found Congers House on the Crossfields Estate, not far from our bombed house. Using the word 'estate' seemed like a patronising joke to me. 'Estate' conjured up the image of extensive landholdings surrounding a stately home—nothing like these ungainly groupings of lumpish council blocks. Five storeys high, with grimy brick façades, austere exterior walkways, they'd been built just after the war and were already shabby. Because it was January, the sky was low and grey, the few trees were bare and there was nothing to soften the bleakness of the place. Then again, the residents of those drab blocks had central heating, indoor bathrooms and other luxuries not available in our nasty little pre-war terraces.

I knocked on the door, with the slim hope that Margaret still lived in the flat she'd moved into fifteen years before. And there she was in the doorway, my 48-year-old big sister—stouter, greyer, her face puffier, but it was the kind, stoic face I remembered. She was just back from her job as a school dinner lady, still wearing the pale blue uniform and flowered apron.

'Any chance of a cuppa? I'm parched,' I said, trying to send up my surprise reappearance.

'Betty! You'll bring on a heart attack!'

She folded me into a hug, which felt strange, because we'd never been a family who went in for hugging. Not that it wasn't wonderful to be hugged by my sister.

Margaret quickly drew me inside her home as if I might suddenly try to escape. The flat was a boxy two-bedroom unit, closed up to keep in the heat and with no air flow to dissipate the smell of boiled vegetables and Cussons talcum powder. Margaret kept the place very neat, with antimacassars on the three-piece lounge suite, every surface adorned with ornaments and little vases of plastic flowers; modest but house-proud—in the way of a person who appreciates that it's a precious thing to have your own home.

While Margaret made tea and we both rattled through recent news, I checked out the framed photographs in the living room—a wartime snap of Margaret in uniform with her Wren pals, photos of her son at various ages and a formal portrait of our mother. Hanging on the wall above the television set were the three peculiar ornamental mirrors Dad had commissioned, etched with photos of our siblings killed by the bomb, Bernard, Pauline and Paul.

Margaret's husband Duncan had taken off with another woman in '62 and my sister was surprisingly candid about how miserable her marriage had been. She lit up whenever she talked about her son Paul, now twenty and away in the merchant navy.

Once we were sitting down with cups of tea and a plate of Jaffa Cakes, Margaret switched into a more sombre tone. She dutifully ran through Rankin family news—not so much news as a series of death notices. Our never-married brother George died of mesothelioma from sleeping under pipes lagged with asbestos in the navy. Our Eddie had been estranged from his wife and three kids for some years before he was killed when a work lorry rolled on him. Josie had the tormented, volatile life I would've predicted and died of cirrhosis of the liver in '67. Josie's one child, a son, was in gaol serving a long sentence for manslaughter after a knife fight. Our brother Kenneth had never reconnected with the family after his wartime evacuation to Kent and finally severed all contact.

The relaying of so much sadness sat heavily on my sister and I felt the weight of my poor treatment of her, my lack of appreciation, my neglect.

'Margaret, I should say—well, I'm sorry I stopped writing,' I said. 'But, more importantly, I'm so sorry for—'

When she put her hands up to stop me saying more, smiling calmly, it made me think of a saint dispensing blessings. I didn't know which of my failures she was pardoning but I was happy to soak up whatever forgiveness was on offer.

'You did the right thing emigrating, Betty. It was the best thing for you. Out of all of us, you were the one who would make something of it.'

I didn't consider I'd 'made something' of my life at this point. Both my children were unhappy and unmoored, I'd had a disastrous marriage, no career, just getting by as a typist, never having had a crack at things I fantasised about doing. Then again, sitting in that flat in the Crossfields Estate, I didn't regret leaving the life I would likely have had if I'd stayed.

Margaret sounded resigned to the run of miseries she'd copped: our early losses, her dismal marriage, absent son, even her bunions and aching varicose veins. But she hadn't simply accepted the disappointments. She nursed those miseries as if she were making a contribution to a cosmic balance sheet. It struck me that there was an unexamined mentality in our family, and many of the families I'd known in my childhood: the idea that the world contained a finite pie of happiness, so if a person were miserable, they left more of the happiness pie for others to enjoy, and if an individual were too happy, it raised the suspicion that they were taking more than their share. Remnants of that thinking were still embedded in my own brain and I resolved to be alert for them.

The morning Rose was due to be discharged, I walked up to the ward and heard the lovely sound of my daughter laughing. I hung back in the doorway and watched. She was sitting on the edge of the bed, wearing jeans and a sheepskin coat, her hair tied back, boots on, ready to leave. A little group was gathered around her—two student doctors and a couple of nurses. I couldn't hear what was being said but it was clear they were yabbering happily together.

The moment the young medical staff had gone and I walked up, Rose's face scrunched into a scowl of irritation.

'Ready to go?' I asked, gamely throwing a smile back at her ill temper.

She pointed at a large army disposal pack on the floor. The pack, containing all her possessions, emitted a smell of patchouli and marijuana.

'The doctor said you need to take it easy on your leg. So maybe I'd better carry that,' I said and hoisted the pack onto my shoulders.

After she'd signed the discharge forms and we walked out into the street, I asked, 'What do you want to do now?'

'Yeah, right, I knew you'd start interrogating me,' Rose snapped and then she did an accurate but uncharitable impersonation of me. 'What are your plans for the future, Rose? Do you have any plans?'

'I actually meant, "Do you want lunch now?".'

'Oh. Whatever.'

We wandered indecisively for a few blocks until the piercing January cold and my concern about Rose's leg forced us into the next available place—a Wimpy Bar. We ate an unappetising lunch in total silence. My provisional plan was that we'd stay a few nights at my hotel until Rose knew what she wanted to do. But sitting in that fluorescent-lit burger joint, looking out the big window at the crowded, polluted, grey city, I felt decisive.

'I reckon we should hire a car,' I said. 'There's a place I want to visit. And a road trip will get us out into the lovely English countryside.'

That same day, we motored out of London in a rented Ford Cortina, with me driving and Rose staring out the passenger window, radiating displeasure, music from the car radio covering the silence.

When 'The Wonder of You' came on, I turned to grin at Rose. 'It's Elvis.'

She immediately flicked the station to something else. 'I won't listen to Elvis anymore. Not after he met Richard Nixon at the White House. Anyway, I was a kid when I liked that music.'

I tried asking questions about Rose's travels, but she would deflect me.

'It was incredible. Too hard to explain.'

I avoided any talk of her future plans, but Rose claimed to divine what I was thinking anyway. 'I know you're busting to ask me, Mum. And the answer is no, I haven't decided what my plans are. Once my leg is better, I might go travelling, I might stay here, or I might go back to Oz.'

I continued driving, sifting through theories about why my daughter was so bad-tempered with me. She still blamed me for Mac going to Vietnam. Resented me, legitimately, for times I'd been inattentive to her, siphoning off too much of my energy for her brother. Perhaps Rose was feeling bad about hurtful things she'd written to me in letters, afraid I was angry with her, so choosing to be pre-emptively angry with me. Maybe she needed to establish a demarcation line, to tear away from the strong ties binding a single mother and a daughter. Maybe she was anxious about the future. The truth was floating around somewhere in that list, but there didn't seem to be much I could do about it.

We stayed a night just outside Exeter and were back on the road the following day. I kept trying to slather on the enthusiasm. 'Oh! We're officially in Cornwall now. We should find somewhere to have a Cornish cream tea!'

'Ugh, Mum, will you give the nostalgia bullshit a rest!' Again, my daughter did another uncomfortably precise impersonation of me. '"Oh, Rosie, isn't this teashop quaint! Don't you love the cosy village pubs? Look at that beautiful gothic church! And what about the thatched cottages!" Jesus, Mum, *you* didn't exactly grow up in a quaint thatched cottage. All this English romantic crap is phony stuff you swallowed from books while you were living in a slum. They fed you nicey-nice children's books. Enid fucking Blyton.'

There was truth in what she said, but her derision still stung me.

'Well, as it happens, Rose, we're heading for a place where I did experience some of that English romantic crap for real. For a little while anyway.'

She must have heard the injury in my voice because she didn't bite back.

It was a relief to discover Cornwall truly was spectacular, and not just a sentimental delusion from my childhood. The villages, beaches, coves and headlands all looked ravishing in the grey wintry weather—maybe better than in sunshine—and in my peripheral vision I could see that even Rose was taken with the place.

Driving into absurdly picturesque St Agnes, I located the church hall where we evacuees had been assembled for selection in 1939. It turned out my brain had stored a reasonably accurate mental map of the area.

Once I'd booked us into a B'n'B in the village, Rose wanted to lie down in the room, still not fully recovered from her illness. I left her to rest, relieved to explore on my own for an hour or so.

There was little reason to believe Rose and Walter Nancarrow would still be alive in their late eighties but I was hoping to see the house. I steered the Cortina along the route I used to ride my bike back from the school and as the road curled around, there was the house.

I saw a square-bodied fiftyish woman in the side yard, hanging up washing. Rose Nancarrow at the age I'd last seen her. I figured the intensity of my affection for the place had conjured up this hallucination. I'd happily take the mirage, if it meant spending a moment in that lovely woman's company.

But then the person turned and I realised who it must be: Rose's daughter June.

'Hello. Are you lost?' she asked.

'Not lost. Excuse me, are you June?'

She smiled and squinted at me.

'I'm Elizabeth Rankin. Beth. I had Christmas with you in 1939.'

'Yes! Beth! Wonderful to see you. Come in.'

The cottage had been modernised a little and handrails installed through the house. Rose Nancarrow had died in '59, and when Walter suffered a stroke, June and her husband had moved in to look after him until his death in '66.

Even with the Nancarrows gone, being in that house was peaceful, as if I could get direct access to how happy I'd felt there. June made a pot of tea and we chatted about our wartime memories along with recent biographical particulars.

Suddenly I blurted out, with too much intensity, 'Your parents were so kind to me. Your mother was a very important person in my life.'

June nodded, not at all thrown by my outburst. 'Mum loved having you here. They both did. They worried about you, wondered what happened to you. Ooh, wait, maybe I can . . . wait here a moment.'

She went into a bedroom and I heard her rifling through boxes. She returned with a wad of ten unopened envelopes, all addressed to 'Elizabeth Rankin' at our Deptford house, all stamped 'Return to Sender'.

'Mum did wonder if your house had been bombed. But she had no way to find you.'

I held the letters delicately, as if they might disintegrate in my hands. 'I should've written to them, explained what happened. I feel terrible.'

June smiled, as good-hearted as her mother, and said, 'Oh, Beth, you were just a kid. And you went through a lot, being bombed out and the like. No reason to feel terrible.'

I declined June's invitation to stay for dinner—in part because I needed to get back to my Rose and in part because I was too churned up to be socially competent.

After a largely silent dinner with my daughter, I waited until she fell asleep, then took the stack of envelopes out of my handbag. I didn't want any cynicism from Rose to sully the experience of reading them.

There was nothing in those letters of interest to anyone other than my twelve-year-old self—mostly cheerful news about Sadie the dog, the garden, a mighty storm and what had been washed up on the beach. In the early ones, Rose Nancarrow reported she was back home, inviting me to return and live with them if I wanted to. She always signed off with 'Hugs and kisses, Auntie Rose xxoo'. I've reread those 'Dear Beth' letters many times over the years, whenever their therapeutic effect is needed.

The visit to the Nancarrows' house had triggered an urge in me to connect with another person I'd disappeared on—my friend from the Kirkby munitions factory, Brenda Goodbody.

At breakfast, I announced to Rose, 'I'm driving to Birkenhead today.'

'What? Why? Where even is that?'

'Just south of Liverpool. I'd like you to come with me but if you'd rather go back to London on the train, we can sort that out.'

The Ford Cortina chewed up the miles on the new motorways north and I sucked in energy from the music on the radio cranked loud. I was surprised Rose had chosen to come with me. I could only imagine she still felt too physically fragile to be by herself.

In post office telephone directories, I looked up Birkenhead listings for 'Goodbody' and on the third try I landed on Brenda's mother.

It was 6 p.m. on a Saturday by the time we pulled up outside the address I had for Brenda Parry (nee Goodbody). I was barely out of the driver's seat when Brenda came roaring out of her house.

'Hiya! Betty!' (Imagine the word 'Betty' elongated to last several seconds.) 'When my mum said you were coming I was made up! You look exactly the same!'

Brenda hugged me, took a step back to gaze at me, then crushed me against her chest again. I hadn't seen the woman since 1945 but our connection was as intense as it had been back then.

'This is my daughter, Rose,' I said.

'Oh! Rose! What a gorgeous creature you are!'

Brenda flung her arms out, inviting but not insisting on a hug. Rose threw herself happily into the embrace, knowing, with the excellent judgement about people my daughter had (most of the time), that Brenda was a good one.

She wouldn't hear of us staying in a hotel—'Our Robbie can sleep on the couch'—so Brenda's lovely husband Reg put our bags in eighteen-year-old Robbie's room. Then we were whisked out the door to the Birkenhead Arms in Market Street where Brenda's nephew Kevin was playing in a band.

Waves of introductions, hugging and squealing continued over the next hour as each new lot of Parrys or Goodbodys arrived at the pub.

'This is my friend Betty. We made grenades together,' Brenda announced. 'Betty's come all the way from Australia to see our Kevin's band play!'

Rose was sucked out of my orbit by the Goodbody maelstrom in the pub. I worried she'd be overwhelmed, but when I looked over, she was already in the boisterous swing of it, tuning her ear to the chewy scouse accents, joining in the teasing and cheerful vulgarity.

Brenda leaned close to me and I got a whiff of the Babycham on her breath. 'She's sound, your Rose. She'd make a friend in an empty house, that one.'

Even though my daughter wasn't being very friendly to me at that time, I was relieved to see she'd grown up to be open and affectionate. Rose told me later that she felt way more at home in Birkenhead than she ever had in London.

When the band started playing, Brenda's son Robbie was keen for Rose to be impressed. 'Lots of boss bands round this area,' he explained. 'We made The Beatles up here, y'know, not down in London.'

I was enjoying the music, bopping around on my chair, when I noticed Brenda point me out to Rose.

'Have a look at your mum,' Brenda said. 'What a queen. I bet she's still a great dancer.'

Brenda was well tipsy by this point and began plying my poor daughter with stories about my dancing prowess in the forties, how clever I was, always reading books, always full of ideas.

After a Sunday morning sleep-in, Brenda and Reg took Rose and me to have a look at the Cammell Laird shipyards, where Reg had started as a welder during the war. He still worked there, along with his son Robbie and most of their male family members.

'We built the ships that helped win the war,' Reg said.

Rose asked a string of questions and Reg happily soaked up her curiosity and the respect she showed. He raved on to her proudly, until Brenda told him to 'give the poor girl's ears a break'.

It's grim to recall that within a decade of our 1971 visit, those shipyards and the bustle of activity around them would wind down and the whole Mersey area would be given a walloping in the Thatcher era. I know there were many hard years for the Goodbody-Parry clan.

The next day, all of Brenda's kids came round for Sunday roast lunch and Rose started telling stories about her travels. My daughter proved to be a terrific storyteller, especially with such a gasping, attentive audience as Brenda's lot. Rose hadn't told me any of these travel tales, and even now she resolutely avoided eye contact with me. At least I had the chance to observe her being fabulous for other people.

Brenda and I stayed up talking in her kitchen when everyone else had gone to bed. She finally had a chance to ask about my pregnancy back in '45 and what had become of the child. I told her the limited things I knew. It was the first time I'd acknowledged the baby's existence to another person. My friend was tender with me, but it still felt as if my chest had been suddenly hollowed out.

When it was time for us to leave, Brenda hugged Rose. 'Your mother's a queen. Don't forget that.' Then she embraced me. 'See you in another twenty-six years, you dirty stop-out.'

As we drove away from Birkenhead, Rose had slumped back into her sullen manner.

'Where are we going now?' she asked.

'A village called Medford. I want to check something out.'

Rose huffed out a breath.

What I should've said in response was nothing. But instead, foolishly, I asked, 'What happened to the smiling storytelling young woman from last night?'

'Hunh . . . Well, Brenda and her rels—they're a big happy family. That's not us, is it.'

I was offended enough to be sharp with her. 'We've made our own family.' And I reeled off the names of the friends we'd adopted as our loving, loyal family—Athena, Pearl, our wonderful neighbours, parents we'd befriended through the school, people who often ate at our house and danced around the living room after dinner.

But Rose didn't listen to any of that, choosing to attack from another flank. 'Last night I heard you telling Brenda about how much you hated my father, how miserable you were. You must've hated being pregnant with me. You never wanted me.'

'Not true,' I shot back. 'Not true at all. The opposite. You are the precious thing I salvaged from that marriage.'

The truth of that did not make it past Rose's outer ear. I do believe it filtered into her brain later, but in that moment in the Cortina, she was locked in wounded mode.

'You think I'm an idiot,' she said. 'You think I'm a fuckwit for not going to uni. You think the travelling—you think it's all stupid.'

'I don't. I wish I'd gone travelling like you've done. Stop imagining you know what I'm thinking, Rose.'

'Well, how about you stop imagining you know what's right for me!' she yelled, far too loud for the interior of a small car, then jerked her head to face the window, indicating that the discussion, such as it was, was over.

It was easy to find the house in Medford village where I'd spent the last months of my pregnancy, but it proved to be a dead-end, occupied by a couple who knew nothing of the people who'd lived there in 1945.

I was unsure of the location of the stately home where I'd been taken to labour, but some animal memory led me out of the village, past a run of newly built houses, through fields, then finally up to the ornamental lake and grand stone entrance of Medford Hall.

I sat behind the wheel, staring at the elegant façade. The place had been converted into a 'Fine Country House Hotel'.

'Why are we here?' Rose asked. 'Are we staying here tonight?'
'Yes, we are.'

I'm not sure if the decision to stay at Medford Hall was made out of curiosity or from a self-torturing impulse. It was probably a juicy combo: curiosity about how the self-torture would feel.

As we took our bags inside, I was acutely aware of Rose's army disposal pack and sheepskin coat looking out of place, especially when the hotel doorman appeared in white tie and tails like an Edwardian butler.

The curved central staircase and reception rooms had a kind of grandeur, with elaborately decorated ceilings, furniture upholstered with brocade, huge mirrors in heavy gilded frames. Brochures in the vestibule advertised Medford Hall as a wedding venue and I could see why. Up close, though, everything was shabby—the woodwork scratched, the velvet drapes balding, the enormous billiard table pocked with cigarette burns. But if an optimistic person were to squint, they could imagine they had arrived as an aristocratic guest at a country mansion.

I booked for dinner and one night. Because it was the off-season, a night in a twin room was stupidly expensive but not impossibly so.

Heading up the stairs, I clenched my stomach muscles. The ground floor hadn't stirred memories but I was expecting some detail on the first floor—the blue curtains or the ornate ceiling of the grand bedroom in which I gave birth—to trigger a collapse.

In fact, while the reception rooms had been kept in a shabby version of their original state, the upper floors had been transformed, with plasterboard walls dividing the space into mean little rooms. Nothing to trigger a memory.

The hotel rooms had obviously not been refurbished since they were first thrown together in the 1950s. Our bathroom was notably gross with chipped tiles and a whacking great dirty ring around the bathtub.

Behind the two single beds in the room, I noticed brownish crescents on the paintwork—oily stains left from the many guests who had sat on the beds and rested their greasy hair against the wall. I laughed out loud at that point—to think of patrons who'd forked out considerable money to pretend they were gentry for a weekend and then found themselves in this scruffy, grubby joint.

The dinner was thematically aligned with the whole establishment—that is, fake-posh, substandard, moderately disgusting. I was too jangled up, too afraid I would crack into a thousand pieces, that I couldn't manage any conversation while we ate the gluey, salty food.

'Wow, the silent treatment,' said Rose. 'You're so angry with me.'

'It's not always about you, Rose. I have my own fucking life to deal with sometimes.'

I snapped at her so harshly that she flinched and didn't say another word all night. Nor did I. I had no spare emotional energy to feel bad about hurting her feelings.

I lay sleepless on the bed that night. The hollowed-out feeling was still there, now with a cold wash of shame through my whole body. Staying a night in this place was a mistake.

Next morning, the breakfast buffet in 'The Conservatory' met the standards I'd come to expect from Medford Hall Fine Country House Hotel. There were recently thawed white bread rolls, served with sachets of margarine and cheap marmalade, orange cordial, a choice of teabags or instant coffee next to the lukewarm urn, while the array of silver chafing dishes offered tepid fried eggs floating in oil, suspiciously grey chipolatas and slimy bacon.

I'd already decided that I would give Rose the money for a flight home and we would go our separate ways. I had no more stamina for her resentment. I pushed the plate covered in congealing grease away from me, about to tell her my decision, when Rose leaned forward to whisper.

'Mum. That guy keeps staring at me—I mean, really giving me the hairy eyeball.'

I twisted to look at the staring man. He was about fifty, dressed in a morning suit in keeping with the Edwardian pantomime of the hotel, with a 'Manager' badge on the lapel. When I looked more intently, I saw through his ageing features and recognised Edgar, the son who'd lived in the Medford house during my pregnancy.

He recognised me, too, judging by the way he ducked out of the breakfast area. I pursued him until I cornered him in a panelled office.

'It's Edgar, right?'

He nodded, slightly breathless. 'I'm guessing that girl is your daughter. She looks so much like you did back then, it was a shock.'

'When you last saw me, I was only seventeen.'

He had the decency to wince, acknowledging that it had been a bad business.

'Is your mother still alive?'

He shook his head.

'Ah. Do you have any idea where my first daughter ended up?'

There was no reason to believe he would know and if the guy had been a competent liar, he could have easily fobbed me off. But when he splayed his hands out in a helpless gesture, his eyeballs flicked sideways and I knew he knew.

'You have to tell me.'

If only to stop me glaring at him ferociously, he snatched up a pad of Medford Hall notepaper and wrote down an address.

On the drive to Buckinghamshire, I was agitated, eyes fixed on the road like a crazy person, only speaking to Rose when I needed to check a turn on our route. She was navigating with an unwieldy foldout roadmap.

'Are you okay, Mum?' There was a smidgin of care in her voice but I couldn't absorb anything through the roar in my head.

On the outskirts of a Buckinghamshire village, the house was imposing enough to be easily spotted—a three-storey Georgian with extensive grounds. I parked the Cortina alongside the brick and wrought-iron front fence, a few metres away from the gates, out of sight.

'Stay in the car, please,' I said to Rose.

Through the front gate, a gravel driveway curled around a central fountain, with geometric topiary hedges punctuating the lawn and framing the façade of the house. Beyond that were wider lawns mowed into neat stripes and I could see a tennis court, garages and stables. There were two cars parked to one side of the gravelled area—a burgundy Bentley and the same car in light blue.

I walked straight up the front steps and hit the doorbell. I was expecting to be greeted by a butler but it was clearly the lady of the house who opened the door. A woman in her late fifties, watery pale blue eyes, hair in a French roll, wearing a blue tweed skirt and a beige cashmere sweater with a string of pearls—the full *Country Life* stereotype. I couldn't be sure this was the blonde woman who had come into the room just after my baby was delivered. Then again, this lady's hair was dyed the ashy colour favoured by posh dames who used to be blondes.

'Hello. Can I help you?' she asked. There wasn't just a plum in her voice. There were several plums.

'I hope so,' I said and sucked up a breath, determined not to cry on this woman's doorstep. 'Is there a young woman living here who was born at Medford Hall in 1945?'

The physical signs were unmistakable—a jerky inhalation of air, her hands bunched at the sides of her skirt, the muscles along her jaw pumping and tight. It was clear she saw the resemblance between me and the child she'd raised. The shock of that hit her hard. In any other circumstance, I would have felt compassion for this woman, facing the surprise and fear of such a moment, but I didn't have any compassion to spare at the time.

Mind you, she gathered herself pretty damn quickly, addressing me with that brittle assurance upper-class people can switch on when they need to.

'No. I'm sorry. You must have the wrong house. Or the wrong idea about something. If you'll excuse me, I'm rather busy. Have a good day.'

And the door was shut.

I could hear my shoes crunching on the gravel driveway in time with my thudding heart as I walked away. Outside the gates, I was burning. That woman had felt entitled to take a baby off a helpless teenager—maybe she'd been in a desperate state herself, maybe she thought it was the best thing for that kid, who knows—and she was still lying about it. I was too wild with anger to get back in the car.

'Mum, you're freaking me out.' Rose hopped out of the passenger side, watching her hyperventilating mother stamp back and forth on the roadway. 'Who lives in the house? Please tell me what's going on.'

'Give me a minute,' I said.

Rose fetched a can of lemonade from the car and I crouched on the roadside to guzzle that down. I stayed there for ten minutes, letting the sugary drink fizz through my system.

Rose had just walked up to the gates to have a stickybeak at the house, when she said, 'Oh, someone's coming out the door.'

I rushed over to see a woman in her mid-twenties walking from the front door to the blue Bentley. She was wearing jeans, knee-high boots and a camel overcoat, her curly dark hair held back with a plum velvet headband, revealing her dark eyes and strong nose. No DNA tests would be required to know that was my daughter.

She was loading something into the boot of the car when the pearl-wearing older woman came out onto the porch, called out

'Frances!' and trotted across the gravel with another bag for the car boot.

Hearing that woman say 'Frances', I was suddenly conscious that, in my head, I had named the child 'Pauline' after my little sister. I was hit by the sensation of the baby kicking and squirming inside me during our last months together. The surge of love was almost more than my system could take.

I walked through the gates towards Frances. I wanted to look at her up close. She'd obviously had a privileged life but I wanted to know if she'd had a happy life.

The adoptive mother spotted me approaching first and she let loose a panicky yelp. She hadn't expected me to hang around. There was a whispered exchange between the two of them before the daughter shepherded her distressed mother, tenderly, into the passenger seat of the Bentley.

Then she turned to address me. 'Look, whoever you are, please leave us alone.' Posh accent but the same vocal timbre as my Rose. 'Mother's not well and you're upsetting her. Please leave us alone.'

It might sound bizarre but I was relieved that this young woman was so self-possessed, so attentive to her mother, capable enough to take charge in a distressing scenario—even if that meant she was tearing my heart into pieces as she did so.

Frances got into the driver's seat, started the engine, drove carefully past where I was standing, then out the gates and away.

'Who was that person?' Rose asked. She'd scored a good look through the windscreen when Frances had paused to make the turn onto the roadway. 'Was that your sister?'

I was in no state to reply, breathless from great wrenching sobs—the anguished sounds that have overtaken me on a few occasions in my life. I apologise to the reader for the histrionic tenor of this episode but it's difficult to avoid the inherent melodrama of such a moment.

'Oh. Is she your child?' And as Rose said the words, she knew that was it.

My daughter took charge of the situation, much as Frances had done with her mother, and steered me over to the car. Rose, who'd barely driven in her life, drove the Cortina very gingerly along the road while I wept.

When I'd calmed down a little, Rose decided food and drink were needed, so drove to a pub twenty miles further on. In that pub, I told my younger daughter about the existence of my elder daughter.

Rose was magnificent. She hugged me repeatedly but still let me talk. She was angry on my behalf but mostly sad. She acknowledged she could never fully understand my experience but she made a full-hearted go at understanding.

Later that evening, after several glasses of wine, Rose reciprocated by spilling her guts about something that had happened to her. In India she'd become besotted with a young French traveller, and stayed in Goa with her new love for some months. It seemed fateful that they'd crossed paths, each travelling from the opposite direction on the overland route to arrive in Goa just in time to fall in love. When Rose discovered she was pregnant, my daughter—generally a logical person—figured the baby was fate at work too. She was excited to tell her boyfriend the news and plan their future together. But she never did tell him about her pregnancy, because the next day, the French boy returned from a hiking trip, announced he'd fallen for a Dutch girl, then left immediately.

A week after he'd gone, Rose miscarried, alone in a beach shack, flailing around with a mixture of sadness, relief, humiliation.

'I'm so embarrassed, Mum. I was scared you'd think I was a total idiot.'

I grabbed my Rose and embraced her tightly enough to squeeze any such mistaken thought out of her clever, beautiful head.

With all this crying and hugging, we had attracted the attention of other pub patrons—dour home counties types troubled by uninhibited emotion. We then found a way to annoy them even more: Rose spotted a jukebox in the corner of the bar. We were delighted to find a family favourite, Eartha Kitt's version of 'C'est Si Bon', and the two of us sang along to Eartha's purring voice with exaggerated French pronunciation to ridicule the Frenchman who'd broken Rose's heart. Then we danced to Nancy Sinatra's 'These Boots Are Made For Walking' in a thoroughly satisfying fashion.

Heading out to the carpark, Rose said, 'Hey. Let's go back to that house where your daughter lives.'

'I should leave her be for now.'

'Well, then let's go home.'

Home meant Sydney, and yes, I wanted to go home.

'But you should write her a letter,' Rose urged.

I wrote many drafts of that letter but I finally opted for something restrained, giving basic details about my life, with special mention of Mac and Rose. I briefly explained the circumstances in 1945 in which I had allowed her to be taken from me, but careful not to put blame on her adoptive family. I expressed my deep regret about giving her up but I tried not to pile emotional debt for my pain onto Frances herself. I said I would love her to contact me but would understand if she didn't. I wished her a good and happy life. It was a decent letter, to the extent that I could ever judge such a thing.

I don't want to set up any false hope for the reader or dangle any red herrings. Frances never made contact with me and I could imagine the reasons. Perhaps her mother found my letter and destroyed it. Perhaps Frances herself did not want the disruption in her life and resented me for abandoning her. I sent a few other letters over the years and always kept my contact details up to date with every family reunion service I could find. From a little bit of research, I discovered that the woman who adopted Frances was the niece of the family who had owned Medford Hall in the forties, but it was difficult to find out more. When Facebook came in, I searched but found no mention under the names I had.

It could have gone differently. If I had been honest with myself and the people who loved me much earlier, I might have handled it better. But I managed things clumsily, ambushing the poor young woman. There's no getting away from the regrettable truth of that. Still, I did see my first daughter as a grown-up that one time and could tell she was okay.

I could go on and on about the grief of a coerced adoption, but I will leave that part of my story there for now, sure the reader will understand that the grief stays in the belly like a great undigested lump of suffering.

Once I'd posted the letter, I felt a tiny bit freer. Rose and I decided that before we left the UK, we should take a few days to tour the countryside and gorge ourselves on London museums and galleries.

On the last day, I took Rose to meet her Aunt Margaret. My daughter was delightful with my sister—asking enthusiastic questions, admiring the photographs of her handsome cousin Paul, eager for stories about me as a kid.

Rose spoke to Margaret about her gratitude for the care she'd received in King's College Hospital. After the suffering she'd seen in many countries on her travels, she appreciated what it meant for people to have proper medical care. Margaret lapped up that NHS-positive talk. (You could easily flatter a British person by praising the NHS—in 1971 anyway.)

Rose had been so inspired by the doctors and nurses, she explained to Margaret, that she was determined to study medicine when she returned to Australia. It was the first I'd heard of the plan. While Rose told her aunt about this decision, my daughter avoided eye contact with me. I was careful not to make a big deal of it.

TWELVE

August 1972.

For some months, I'd been noticing the Women's Liberation posters glued onto telegraph poles—purple images of clenched fists on female symbols and the like. I'd been seeking out feminist books in shops, never buying them, just flicking through the pages, almost furtive, and the scraps I read became itchy spots under my skin.

One Wednesday evening, I caught a bus straight from my temp typing job in the city, but by the time I reached the Glebe address, the Women's Lib meeting was well underway. I've always hated being late for things, so I was off-balance before I even walked in.

The room was packed, with women on chairs, on cushions or the floor, and as I stood in the doorway, I looked out over a sea of orange and brown knitwear, tie-dyed garments, denim and cheesecloth. I could smell patchouli oil, apple shampoo and Caterer's Blend instant coffee served in lumpish hand-made pottery mugs. A few people shuffled their bums sideways to make room for me to sit on the floor with my knees hunched up.

A young woman wearing a purple T-shirt and jeans, her voluminous hair held off her face by an Indian scarf, was addressing the gathering, outlining the sexist practices at her university campus and weaving in bits of theoretical terminology with ease.

I glanced around the room, suddenly reminded that I was a 44-year-old typist and mother of two, wearing a polyester blouse, a navy gabardine skirt, pantyhose and the heeled court shoes expected of a lady office worker. This meeting seemed to be full of much younger women, many of them tertiary students or experienced campaigners or some other intellectually impressive type. Sitting there stirred up my deepest working-class-girl-with-no-education discomfort. The more the university activist spoke, so articulately, about legal statutes and government policy, the clearer it became that I wasn't the right sort of person to be here. I should leave.

I realised it would be tricky to sneak out of the room without clambering over people and drawing attention to myself. I had just spotted one possible path to the exit when the young woman's voice sliced across the self-absorbed burble in my head.

'Shut your mouth. You need to go home and shut up.'

Obviously, she wasn't speaking to me. She was sharing with the group the exact words a man had yelled at her during a demonstration the week before.

'You belong on your back, you ugly bitch.'

Fury burned through my body as if that man were right in front of me saying those words. Then around me, I heard murmurs of recognition and laughter—weary, angry laughter shared with every other woman in that room.

Not everyone at the meeting was so young, it turned out, and most were not intimidating. As the session went on, some of the women spoke about their struggles to find childcare, about male doctors treating them like naughty children, about their longing to be valued as more than just someone's wife or someone's mother.

One twenty-something student made me laugh when she joked, but in a fabulously angry fashion, about the degrading and exhausting demands of femininity, requiring us to rip body hair out by the roots, strap our bodies into absurd undergarments and footwear, plaster on makeup, keep our voices sweet and gestures demure. (Which had never been my strongest suit, it must be said.)

Every woman in that Glebe room understood that we'd been conned into thinking we were inadequate. Every single one of us knew about being groped and silenced and coerced and punched and bullied and ridiculed and shamed.

It's difficult for me to convey the potency of those other women's words landing in the head of someone who had never heard this kind of talk in quite this way. The discussion that went on would probably sound absurdly obvious today, but at that time, and for me, it was a revelation. It was liberating—I'm using that word with all its juice—to understand there was a systemic problem beyond any of our individual shortcomings. I could scoop in fistfuls of anger and frustration and shame from my life and gather them into a form I could then reconfigure and understand in a different way. It wasn't just about my own failings. It wasn't only me. It was all women. It was the whole damn thing. And it was liberating to envisage that things could be otherwise.

July 1975.

After that first meeting, I began devouring books (*The Female Eunuch*, *Sexual Politics*, *The Dialectic of Sex* and *Our Bodies, Ourselves*). I worked diligently to raise my consciousness. I marched for equal pay and abortion rights. I donated my typing skills as needed. I never had the confidence to put myself forward for political committees, so it took me a while to find a place in the movement where I felt properly useful. But the first time I showed up to do a volunteer shift at a women's refuge, I was in the right place.

I often signed on for overnight shifts at the refuge because my employment was flexible—typing work and temp jobs. Rose was living with me, waitressing to earn money, while she powered through a medical degree. Mac was working for builders, living in a share house, possibly using substances, but holding it together.

The refuge house wasn't always quiet on the overnight shift, the silence broken by a baby waking or a child upset by a nightmare. And our residents weren't at peace—their lives in the most horrible upheaval—but at least they could spend a night safe from immediate peril.

At 2 a.m. on one of the quieter nights, I was sitting in the kitchen when a twenty-something woman, who'd only just come to us that evening, wandered in wearing pyjama bottoms and a sweatshirt.

'Hi, Sandra,' I said. 'Do you need anything? Kids okay?'

'Yeah, nah, kids are fast asleep.'

Sandra scuffed around the lino floor, not sure how to absorb the stress hormones jangling through her body after the rush of fleeing with her two little boys.

'I might make myself a chamomile tea,' I said. 'As an experiment. Somebody told me it can make your wee smell funny.'

Sandra did a breathy giggle, sounding so young it almost broke my heart. 'Maybe I'll have one too,' she said. 'See what happens.'

We sat at the kitchen table with our tea. She talked about her kids—not about the trauma of them seeing their father slam their mum's head repeatedly into a door—but about small, delightful things. Her one-year-old, who'd previously only ever sat on the floor 'like a blob, like a melted candle' had just started crawling. As Sandra spoke about the kids, her body, which had been so tightly clenched against danger, loosened a little.

In the morning, the daytime volunteers could help Sandra apply for the single mother's benefit. After the '72 election, Gough Whitlam's government had blazed its way through some of the country's antiquated structures and sorted out a lot of overdue shit. No-fault divorce, ending conscription, a start on Indigenous land rights, universal health care, equal pay legislation.

It was a buoyant time we didn't know was about to end with the thud of an administrative coup, The Dismissal, in November '75. Don't get me started on the outrageous situation that a prime minister elected by the Australian people could be thrown out of office by some appointed bozo in a morning suit and a top hat, invoking the powers of the Queen of fucking England. Anyway, of all the Whitlam reforms, my personal favourite was the pension for single mothers. Before then, a woman (for example, me in 1952) might have no choice but to stay with an abusive man because if she left, she would have no way to house and feed her children. The new pension was far from lavish but it was powerful.

Of course, there were piles of patriarchal rubbish still to be dealt with. Until 1983, any married Australian woman needed her husband's permission to obtain a passport. A married woman had to wait until 1984 to have the right to open a bank account without her husband's signature. Rape within marriage was not a crime in New South Wales until 1981.

I'll control myself and leave it there—well, let me say one more thing: it is worth reminding ourselves how far we've come. Yes, we're all frustrated about how little progress has been made on many fronts. But there were meaningful improvements, achieved with hard work by fabulous women.

The above rave might give the reader an inkling of what a zealot I was during this period. I accept that my passion made me pretty annoying to some people.

Rose would interrupt me mid-sentence. 'Okay, Mum. I know all this stuff. And I'm also aware of the location of my clitoris so please don't go on about it.'

Whenever I launched into one of my women's lib raves to Pearl, she would close her mouth tightly and squint her eyes to stop my words entering her head. I guess if any skerrick of feminist thinking had penetrated her skull, it might've fried the brain circuitry she needed for her life to make sense. Pearl was still Gerry Stankovich's mistress, fourteen years on, living in the Potts Point apartment and receiving an allowance. It was surprising, and in a weird way laudable, that Stankovich had not chucked her aside for a younger floozie. In her late forties, Pearl Jowett was undoubtedly a beautiful woman, expensively dressed and groomed, filling many of her daytime hours with exercise to keep her body taut, and by 1975, she'd had the first of her face-lifts.

Pearl and I would meet for lunch at a cheap joint like Una's in Victoria Street where Pearl would watch me eat a schnitzel the size of a frisbee while she picked at a cabbage salad.

She never stopped coming to family events, birthday celebrations and such, but it's fair to say that my connection to Pearl was at its thinnest during these years, glued together by loyalty and old affection.

One of my last attempts to convert Pearl to women's liberation happened at Una's. I was excavating my way through a mountain of goulash with spaetzle when Pearl took advantage of a momentary chewing pause and interrupted my proselytising.

'Sorry, Lizzie, not being rude or anything . . . but I don't like it when you go on and on about—I mean, Gerry reckons the things you say are just a bunch of slogans.'

Pearl did an apologetic wince—to the extent that her surgically zipped face could manage any specific expression. She was nervous,

---

not wanting to lose my friendship, and I certainly didn't want her to feel bad.

'Yeah, fair enough,' I said. I hated the idea that I might have been mouthing empty slogans at people. But a moment later my head filled with images, running through memory-bank footage like a recap sequence for a TV drama—'previously on *Shit Women Have Endured*'. Pearl almost bleeding to death after an illegal abortion, Uncle Gil assaulting my teenaged sister Josie, underpaid secretaries dodging the groping hands and erect penises of their bosses, men talking and talking at women without listening, the frantic young mothers showing up at the refuge and on and on and on. Urgent stories that demanded attention. Never just slogans.

The women's movement did deliver me many new friends—most importantly, Patty Reynolds. One night I stepped into the narrow, concreted passage along the side of the refuge house to empty a bucket of dirty sudsy water down the outside drain. I was startled to see a tall woman leaning against the wall, rolling herself a cigarette before starting her volunteer shift. By way of greeting, I did a flamboyant flourish with the toilet brush I was holding in my spare hand and she hooted a laugh.

Patty was a striking 38-year-old woman—bony face, pale skin spattered with freckles, framed by crinkly auburn hair. She was six feet tall, with long limbs that she folded carefully to fit into chairs or car seats. She had developed the habit of stooping slightly so as not to tower over others, but when she did let herself stretch out and take up space, she was like a red-headed waterbird, gangly but magnificent.

Once we'd found each other, Patty Reynolds and I aligned our shifts at the refuge so we could spend time together whenever there was a break, and then we'd move on to the pub afterwards.

She'd grown up in Deniliquin, escaping her very conservative churchgoing family by marrying a man who turned out to be violent.

She escaped him by hitchhiking to Sydney, working in a factory filling shampoo bottles, living so frugally she saved up enough money to go backpacking around the world for two years. Since then, Patty had been making a living as a piano teacher at private schools around Sydney, while she threw herself into the women's movement and other adventures.

She was even more of a stickybeak than I was, always asking people questions about their histories, choices and opinions. Patty was curious about others because she was in a sort of research phase, on the lookout for ideas and options she might incorporate in her own life. If I happened to mention a book I'd read, a film I'd seen, an old song from my youth, an unusual dish I liked to eat, Patty would write it down in a small spiral notebook she carried. Sometime later, she would have read the book, watched the film, tracked down a recording of the song, sampled the dish, keen to discuss it with me and exchange thoughts.

Even her clothing was an assortment of other people's cast-offs, all purchased from op shops, including second-hand men's clothes since they were often the only garments long enough to fit her. Her eclectic wardrobe—mustard-coloured gents' flares, paisley silk tunics, a Chanel jacket, bib-and-brace overalls, Indian wrap skirts—always ended up looking as if it belonged on her.

Having torn up the template she'd been handed—destined to be an obedient churchy country-town wife and mother—Patty was experimenting and constructing what her life might look like from here on. There is something thrilling about being around a person who is in the throes of honest exploration.

The first time she invited me to meet up with her at a pub gig, I walked through the front bar, engulfed in the murk of cigarette smoke that filled all licensed premises then. In the back room, four musicians were playing on a small platform to a crowd of patrons who mostly looked to be in their twenties and thirties. As a 47-year-old mother of adult children, I felt excruciatingly out of place, about to scurry away when Patty waved me over to her table.

She pulled up an extra chair and introduced me to her friends, all of whom seemed to know the guitarist on stage. The band was terrific, playing a mixture of folk and blues. It wasn't music I was familiar with but I reckon good music can always grab you.

Towards the end of the gig, the guitarist signalled to Patty. 'Will you sing a couple of songs for us?' Then he made a show of adjusting the microphone stand to suit someone so tall. She grinned, jumped onto the stage and said, '"Diamonds and Rust" okay by you?'

The guitarist accompanied Patty as she sang the melancholy Joan Baez ballad. The first time I watched my friend sing, hearing that glorious voice come out of her body, was astonishing—like seeing someone I'd known as a regular mortal person suddenly sprout wings to soar into the air or shoot magic spider webs out of her hands.

I made a spectacle of myself applauding and whooping at the end of the song. Patty squirmed, awkward but pleased. I noticed her glance over at a woman at our table. Sal was in her late twenties, looking shyly out from behind her dark brown fringe. When she met Patty's gaze, there was a look between them which any person with eyeballs in their head would have identified as a flirtatious spark. Later in the night, I saw Patty and Sal pashing up against the cigarette machine in a dimly lit corner.

I went to a lot of music gigs with Patty. I was an enthusiastic convert to the thrill of performance—witnessing musicians making the music together, feeling the drums and bass thud through my body, allowing the vocals to connect with my emotions in a direct way that bypassed the tangle of regular thoughts. Glorious and good for the soul.

Sal dumped Patty within a few weeks of the cigarette-machine pash. I nursed Patty through that heartbreak and then the string of misguided romances which followed. I, as her unquestionably hetero friend, was a safe person to confide in. I did my best as a listener, but I was no expert in the subtleties of lesbian dating and my own romantic record was hardly sparkling.

Patty's love life was in an exploration phase like the rest of her life. She'd had the research breakthrough that she was attracted to women but still hadn't figured out what kind of woman was right for her. Research continued.

January 1976.

The bonnet of the Valiant appeared to be a liquid, simmering, almost at a rolling boil. I couldn't tell if the car had overheated to the point where the metal was melting, or if this was just an optical illusion caused by the intense heat coming off the road surface.

I'd driven over the Blue Mountains, beyond Dubbo and Nyngan, then stayed a night in Cobar, before driving further west where the trees petered out, until there were only low dry bushes and ground cover snaking along the roadside and growing in patches on the red oxide dirt. I'd read about the landscape out here, I'd seen pictures, but nothing prepared me for the visual wallop of it. So beautiful, but alien, unnerving. I'm ashamed to admit it was the first time in the almost thirty years I'd lived in Australia that I'd ventured so far inland.

When I pulled over to check the Valiant's radiator, the forty-degree heat outside hit me like a solid dry wall. If I stayed in the desiccating sun for more than a few minutes, it would surely suck all the juice out of my body. I glanced down at the silvery green plants that were managing to survive, trailing across the red soil, and I said 'Good on you' out loud.

When I reached the town nearest to my destination, it was late afternoon, but still so hot the wide main street was understandably deserted.

The Imperial Hotel was a single-storey, flat-faced brick building with heavy-duty blinds covering all the windows, so when I pushed through the central door, it took a moment for my eyes to adjust to the dim interior. There was a handful of blokes in the front saloon, and, on the other side of the bar, I could make out a hatch which served drinks to patrons in a back room.

The joint was dead quiet apart from a bit of phlegmy throat-clearing. I wasn't sure if the silence was because a stranger had walked in or if the repartee in The Imperial generally operated at this level of sparkling.

I nodded hello to the chunky man behind the bar.

'G'day,' I said.

'You want the other pub.'

'I'm just looking for a room for one night.'

'Not here,' he said. 'The other pub.'

I drove down the main street in the direction the guy had waved his meaty paw and booked myself into The Royal, one of those huge two-storey hotels with deep verandahs and wrought-iron balustrades. The room was basic—worn carpet, narrow bed, bare bulb hanging from a pressed metal ceiling, sink in the corner. It reminded me so much of the hotel in which I'd spent an afternoon with Leo Newman that I felt a physical pang, a stab of sexual desire. Sexual response is such an intriguingly odd thing sometimes—in this instance, attaching itself to the memory of a shabby pub room.

In The Royal's dining room, the table had a cloth covered in a transparent plastic overlay, tacky with grease, and the vinyl menu folder was equally sticky. Inside, one typed page was headlined 'Dulcie's Hot Suggestions'. I ate gristly lamb chops, served with stale white sliced bread and margarine, powdered mashed potato and greyish beans, once frozen, now lukewarm and soggy.

After I knocked back a second middie of beer, it was still only 7 p.m. I decided to go for a walk now the sting of heat had gone from the day.

I walked the length of the main street, past the bank, butcher, newsagent, Fay's Frock Shoppe, police station and post office, interspersed with many empty shops. I crossed the road to walk back on the other side, and from that angle, I could see down the street that ran alongside the other hotel, The Imperial. I realised the pub had a separate entrance into the back bar and there were only Aboriginal people using that entrance. So the area I'd glimpsed through the serving hatch in The Imperial was a segregated bar for Black patrons who would never be tolerated in the front bar, let alone 'the other pub'.

In my early days in Marrickville—this was in the mid-fifties—an Aboriginal family rented a house a few doors down and Mac used to play in the street with their little boy. I rarely saw the father but I had passing chats with the mother, a funny woman who reminded me of my old friend Brenda Goodbody. I remember hearing bigoted talk from some neighbours and I'm ashamed to say I didn't challenge that talk. Later, when the family was evicted, I didn't ask the questions I should have.

By 1976, we smugly thought we were so much more aware. I'd read about the 1965 Freedom Ride—Charlie Perkins taking a busload of students and Indigenous activists through a series of towns to bring attention to racist policies, discrimination and shithouse living conditions. I remember the shock of seeing footage of Indigenous kids being denied access to the Moree Council swimming pool. It was like something in the Deep South of America.

I'd cheered on the Aboriginal tent embassy camped outside parliament house and I'd applauded the attempts Whitlam had made to get cracking on land rights. Many of us naïvely assumed this was the beginning of a process that would rapidly improve things. But there I was in 1976, standing on a pavement in a New South Wales town looking at a racially segregated pub.

I watched a police vehicle turn into the street at the side of The Imperial. The cops were following a gloriously battered ute, side panel missing and its front grille tied on with rope. When the ute pulled up on the side street, the driver, his passenger and the two guys sitting in the back tray hopped out.

The police officers, a young chubby fellow and an older bloke, emerged from their vehicle and bailed up the four Aboriginal guys as they headed towards the entrance to the bar. I couldn't hear what was being said but I know bullying when I see it. The body language is loud when powerful individuals are treating less powerful people with no respect, as creatures of no value. And I reckon physical threat by a man in a uniform is unmistakable.

I stood watching until the older cop spotted me.

'You all right there?'

'I'm all right,' I said.

'Look, love, you don't want to hang around here.'

He didn't threaten me—I was a nice white lady—but he eyeballed me and made sweeping gestures with his hand until I finally turned and walked away.

I hurried back to my hotel room, feeling queasy that just by staying at The Royal, I was colluding with the racist demarcation of this two-pub town. Yes, I hear how that sounds—a white lady feeling queasy does not matter one tiny fucking jot. White guilt, awareness, outrage—these can be a useful spur, I suppose, but so inadequate.

There was nothing I saw in that town I didn't already know in theory but still, it was shocking. A reminder of shameful history, stolen land, stolen children. The moral wound deep in the flesh of the country I'd adopted as my home.

I was relieved to get out of town early the next morning.

The Valiant bounced along corrugated dirt roads until my teeth rattled in my skull. On the passenger seat was a map with a pencil mark showing The Community, the place my son was living.

Eighteen months before my outback trip, Mac had wandered into a Sydney cafe in search of a caffeinated beverage. The cafe was run by a Christian group, The New Brotherhood, Bible-based but rejecting existing church structures. Mac joked years later that it was the deliciousness of their baked goods that kept him going back every day, but he also admitted the serenity of people who worked there had intrigued him. The church members showered him with positive attention in a process we would now understand as 'love bombing'. They offered my anxious, aimless, fragmented son a cushioned structure to sink into.

After a year of cafe chats, the self-appointed leader of the group, Pastor Tim, invited Mac to visit their outback community. My son told me none of this before he left because he knew I would rail against religious fanaticism and he didn't want to have that voice in his head.

There was no phone line at The Community but Mac wrote impenetrably cheerful letters to me and to Rose. After several months, a letter came with a photograph enclosed—a wedding snap of my son, the woman he'd married, and her eleven-year-old son. Mac wanted me to visit, keen for me to meet Gail and the boy, Jacob.

I spotted a 'The Community' sign and turned off the dirt highway onto the rutted track to the settlement. There was a long grey cinder block building, and in the paddock around it, twenty dwellings—caravans and old construction-workers' huts—had been towed onto the site. Everything was coated with a layer of red dirt and the instant I opened the car door, my lungs were clogged with the dust my tyres had stirred up.

Mac and I had agreed on this date, via letter, so the minute my car appeared, he hurried over to meet me. He was leaner but not unhealthily so, very tanned, hair clippered short in a way that looked good on him. It was mighty good to hug him and there was nothing in the strength of his embrace to make me feel my son was lost to me.

'Thanks for coming, Mum. I know it's a long way. Thank you. It's great to see you.' Mac turned to one of the caravans and called out, 'Gail! Jacob! Come and meet my mum.'

Jacob, my son's new stepson, came out straight away. He was smiling, awkward in his skinny boy body with a tussle going on between his shyness and his curiosity.

'This is my mum—oh, what should he call you?'

'You can call me Lizzie. It's lovely to meet you, Jacob.'

Gail walked up to stand behind her son. She barely met my gaze as Mac introduced us. It was understandable that this woman would be feeling strange, meeting the mother of the man she'd married so abruptly.

Gail was three years older than Mac (who would be turning twenty-seven in the March) but she looked younger. She had green eyes and small sharp features like a pretty fox, so slightly built that her body disappeared inside the long skirt and loose shirt she was wearing. I should admit—spoiler alert—I only ever met Gail on that one day. My impression of her, augmented by things I learned later, was of an unhappy young woman, generating constant low-level vibrations of anger (possibly for good reasons I will never know).

'So, Mum, do you want the tour?' Mac asked.

'Yes, I very much want the tour,' I said. Rose and I had agreed that I should be positive and hearty during my visit.

Gail ran her small hand along Mac's sleeve. 'I might . . .' She gestured at the van.

'Oh, of course, honey. You lie down.' My son was tender with her, which I was pleased to see.

Gail jerked a wan smile at me and retreated to the caravan. I don't wish the reader to jump to the conclusion I did: that Gail was pregnant. She was not pregnant and—again, a spoiler—she and Mac never did have a baby together.

'Gail gets bad headaches,' Mac explained quietly, then spun round to grin at Jacob. 'Shall we start the tour for my mum?'

The central building contained a meeting/dining hall, a communal kitchen for the fifty residents and a classroom for the dozen kids of The Community. On the tin roof were two evaporative coolers— Mac called them 'our swampies'—so the building could be bearably cool. Tacked on the end was a corrugated iron shower block, with water pumped up from the creek. Generators provided power to the communal areas and most of the vans. Across a dusty bare stretch, a row of corrugated iron cubicles perched over the drop toilets.

Jacob was proud to show me the enormous vegetable garden he helped tend. I made suitably impressed noises and clucked approvingly at the chickens in the chook yard.

When Mac led the way to the creek behind the settlement, I could see him flicking looks at me, hoping I would be impressed. Rows of beautiful eucalypts arched over a wide gully that was filled with a surprisingly abundant stream of water across a stony creek bed, with banks of rust-coloured sand on each side.

'Oh, Mac, it's gorgeous. Good for the soul, I bet.'

'It is, yeah.'

During our tour, we met up with various members of The Community who all seemed wildly enthusiastic to meet Mac's mother.

I was on the receiving end of many beatific smiles. I'm a fan of smiling, but there was altogether too much smiling going on.

Like Gail, the women were all wearing long cotton skirts and tops that left very little skin exposed. They all had long hair in dowdy plaits.

For the first time, I dared to say something slightly cheeky to Mac. 'What's with the plaits and the clothes? Are you all Amish?'

'It's just practical, Mum. Loose clothes are cooler and it's good to keep the sun off.'

Many of the men seemed to be managing in the sun while wearing shorts and singlets, but I let that topic go and instead asked about The Community's finances. According to Mac, they all shared the income from members who did labouring work on surrounding properties, supplemented by welfare cheques—a temporary arrangement until they established a cafe in a nearby town.

'The thing is, we don't need much,' he said. 'We grow a lot of our own food and we live simply.'

Years later, my suspicions were confirmed: the long-term community members were largely funded by new recruits who were required to hand over their assets to the sect in a kind of spiritual Ponzi scheme.

When we returned to the central building, Jacob ran off to check on his mother and I went to my car to fetch a parcel.

'I brought a couple of books for Jacob,' I said. '*A Wrinkle in Time* and that lovely Nan Chauncy book, *They Found a Cave*. I hope I got the right sort of thing for him.'

When I offered Mac the parcel, he put his hands up as if I were threatening him with a poisonous item. 'Ah, no. Sorry, Mum. Nice of you to think of—but . . . sorry. We're pretty careful here about the materials the children read.'

Nan Chauncy dangerous to young minds? The idiocy of that made me cranky and loosened my self-restraint a little.

'Mac, I raised you to be a logical thinker. Are you telling me you believe all the stuff they preach here? You think Jesus wants you to live in a caravan in the desert and deny books to children?'

'I know what you—look, please trust that this is the right place for me.'

'You haven't exactly answered my question—'

'Brother Mac!' An American voice boomed across the red dirt. 'Is that your mother? Hello!'

Pastor Tim was mid-forties and charismatic, I suppose, in a domineering hippie style. He'd spent so much time in the sun he looked like a handsome barbecued chicken with electric blue eyes. The eyes must've been part of his pull with devotees. Human beings tend to ascribe more spiritual wisdom to beautiful people than to the plain or the ugly.

'Sorry I wasn't here to greet you,' he said. 'I was meditating. I bet you could do with a cold drink, Liz!'

'Oh. Yes, that would be lovely.'

After following Tim into the dining hall, I discovered that Mac was not joining us for the jug of homemade lemon barley cordial. The idea was for me to have one-on-one time with the pastor.

'I can see what you're thinking, Liz—"What nutjob outfit has my son got mixed up in?"'

'Oh, well, I'm—'

'We don't claim to know all the answers here, Liz. We're *seeking* the answers.' He was one of those people who uses your name repeatedly. An annoying tactic. 'Let me assure you, Liz, this is not one of those spiritual movements that insists our brethren cut themselves off from their families.'

'Bringing your followers to a desert campsite without a phone line is effectively cutting them off, isn't it?'

Tim dialled up a knowing smile, one of his avoidance manoeuvres.

'You and I are a similar age, aren't we, Liz? I bet you've seen how lost a lot of people are out there in the world. Your son's been lost, yes?'

Even though I was aware this was a destabilising ploy, it still bloody well worked, making my heart clench with worry and guilt about Mac. I wanted to punch the smirk off Pastor Tim's stupid overcooked face.

He did his spiel to me: how he'd been swept up in the hippie movement in 1960s America and seen how all that permissiveness and the denial of God had left a lot of people spinning, adrift, but not being served by standard religious structures anymore.

Tim arrived in Australia in 1972 peddling a grab bag of ideas—the standard Jesus-dying-for-our-sins palaver, but with a layer of Amish (long plaits, voluminous skirts, eschewing physical comforts), plus spoonsful of meditation, hippie aesthetic and communal principles. He advocated conservative controls on many fronts: no drugs or alcohol, no TV or radio, no sex outside marriage. Mac had not been permitted any kind of physical contact with Gail until after they were married. Which may have explained the brevity of the engagement.

According to Pastor Tim, all true things came from the Bible and any doubting thought was a message that the doubter needed to dig deeper into themselves. And so the belief system tucked back into itself, leaving no loose threads of scepticism that might unravel the certainty of the whole construction. Stray logical holes were filled with 'mystery'. As it happens, I reckon the universe is chockful of mysteries, but I don't trust the self-saucing mindset of religions which use mystery to stop people questioning. And I think doubt is a sign of intelligence, of the appropriately humble variety.

My plan, as soon as I had time alone with Mac, was to engage my son in discussion and appeal to his considerable intelligence.

If he had troubling doubts, I would offer to drive him, Gail and Jacob back to Sydney. The three of them could live with me while they set up their life together somewhere.

As I was rehearsing this in my head, Pastor Tim surprised me with a new angle.

'Mac tells me you're a women's libber, Liz. Let me assure you that I happen to appreciate the power of women.'

'Oh. Good to hear.'

'That's one of the reasons we encourage celibacy within our community. All that free love stuff I witnessed in California . . .' A sad smile. 'When men ejaculate, they give up some of their life essence. And women can absorb that fluid, draw power from it. That's why we believe marriage and the having of children is the way to maintain a balance.'

How bizarre that the pastor chose to tell me this particular tenet, assuming I would be impressed by it. He even flashed me a conspiratorial smile. 'We know what you powerful women can do.'

Leaving aside the physiological nonsense of this belief, the deep misogyny of it felt like an assault—the idea that women were temptresses who lured men to have intercourse in order to harvest their life fluids.

Before I had a chance to respond, a bell rang outside and there was a flurry of activity through the dining hall.

'Lunch!' said Tim. 'I hope you'll stay and share a meal with us before you go, Liz.' He then disappeared into the small office where he stayed when visiting The Community.

Within two minutes, Community members filled the hall and covered the tables with platters of food. It was healthy stuff—eggy vegetable pies, grainy salads, claggy nutmeat rissoles—all so bland I assumed the Lord was protecting his followers from the dangers of flavour.

Mac waved hello as he helped Jacob and Gail bring dishes through from the kitchen and the three of them came to sit at the table with me.

During the meal, I noticed a number of things. Gail's clenched miserable vibe eased a little when she was close to Mac. I also observed the camaraderie of the whole group, and how comfortable in his skin Mac seemed to be with these people—a rare thing for him. I saw how that support, coupled with the isolated location and the teetotal regime had created a safe place for my son. And I observed the bond between Mac and eleven-year-old Jacob, a lovable nervy kid. Mac had clearly given his heart and his loyalty to Gail's child.

By the end of the lunch, I reached a decision: I would not harass Mac with questions. Maybe his involvement with the sect would keep him alive, ensuring he had time away from the temptation to use substances, so he could get strong, eventually strong enough to break away from The Community.

Anyway, I had to accept this was Mac's choice. It was arrogant of me to think I knew better than him. That didn't mean I liked the situation. Indeed, it was so unbearable, I made an excuse to leave early.

'I should get on the road to Cobar soon. Don't want to be driving at dusk when I might hit a roo.'

'Oh. Okay.'

Mac walked me over to my car, promising he would keep writing letters.

'I love you very much,' I said and wrapped my arms around him.

'I love you too, Mum. And please don't worry. This is right for me.'

I understood that some of the elements that had thrown my son off course were out of my control. But in my most self-blaming moments—and yes, still, today—I stew on the idea that I must have failed to give Mac enough love, enough certainty, enough of some bloody thing he needed, and as a result my son was vulnerable to the appeal of something like The Community.

I can still recall the peculiar sound I made as I drove away—the jerky staccato noise of my crying while the car bounced along the corrugated dirt road.

On that long drive back to Sydney, with no reliable radio reception, there was a lot of time for rumination.

At this point in the story, while I'm stuck on that long drive, I will admit something I've been coy about: Leo Newman and I had been writing letters to each other since February 1975.

He started it. A parcel arrived at the house I was renting in Erskineville. Inside was a paperback novel, *Angle of Repose*, and a brief note from Leo. He apologised for bothering me (having asked Pearl for my new address), explaining that he'd recently read the novel by US author Wallace Stegner and was keen to exchange views with someone else who might like it. No obligation of course and all good wishes. The return address was a commercial law firm in Brisbane.

I read the book rapidly but waited another week to respond, so as not to appear too keen. I wrote a short letter offering my take (positive) on the novel and posted it to Brisbane along with a copy of *The Persian Boy* by Mary Renault which I was pretty confident Leo would enjoy.

More novels were posted in both directions—*The Edible Woman*, *Breakfast of Champions*, *India Song*, *The Lost Honour of Katharina Blum*, *A Pagan Place*, and others—the transactions of a book club with only two members, both of whom wanted to have sex with the other.

Our comments about the reading material grew longer. We initially used the novels as reference points to discuss matters in our own lives, but we soon gave up any literary pretext and just wrote long meandering letters.

Our correspondence, over the next months, was not the epistolatory version of sexting—there was no dirty talk, no mention of sex or romance whatsoever—but there's no denying Leo was being emotionally unfaithful to his wife when he wrote to me. The fact that I didn't discuss the letters with Athena was a clue that I knew my actions were questionable.

Leo had finally extricated himself from Papua New Guinea in 1964, moving to Brisbane where he'd completed a law degree part-time. For several years, he'd been working in a commercial law firm—not exactly the fighting-for-justice legal work he'd dreamed of, but well paid enough to send his two kids to private schools, buy a lovely house and afford the accoutrements of life in Australia that came close to the life of colonial gentility the family had had in Port Moresby. He didn't say that this way of living was to please his wife Helen but I assumed (correctly) that it was.

Leo's daughter Ava, now seventeen, was in her last year of high school, emotionally turbulent, in constant conflict with her mother. His fourteen-year-old son David was an earnest boy, desperate to placate his volatile mother and keep the peace at home.

Early on, I asked Leo why I was required to send letters to his office rather than his home address. I could guess the reason but I needed him to be honest about it. And he did reply candidly: his wife would be upset about him writing to a female friend.

Helen had had an affair when they'd first moved to Brisbane. Leo had secretly hoped she would leave him for the Brisbane fellow, but she'd ended the affair, weeping with remorse, begging to keep the family together for the sake of their children. Since then, she'd gone through phases of consuming jealousy, showing up at Leo's office to 'catch him out', snatching the phone receiver from his hand, checking his pockets, accusing him of flirting with women at social events. The truth was Leo had never been unfaithful, except for that one afternoon with me in 1959. Then again, Helen must have known, subconsciously at least, that Leo didn't truly love her, so her insecurity was understandable.

Leo began to write openly about the misery of his marriage, describing how he would stay late at the office in a bid to shorten the time between his arrival at home and a reasonable bedtime. That way, he reduced the risk that some random comment would detonate a weeping or shouting jag from Helen.

Part of me wanted to scream, 'Leave her! Be with me!' but I didn't want my romantic self-interest to distort things. But I also didn't want to censor myself, so I offered the comments any decent friend would make in this scenario. Don't stay in a marriage if it's making both people wretched, especially now your kids are older. Don't be a coward, emotionally absenting yourself from the relationship, hoping she'll have an affair so you can extract yourself without feeling like a bad guy.

More and more I found myself feeling sympathy for Helen, even though I'm pretty sure I would have disliked the woman if I'd met her. She was a snobby, narcissistic person who had managed to alienate her own parents, siblings and every friend she'd ever had. But that poor woman was married to a man who was carting a truckload of damage from his childhood which he refused to examine, a man who felt stuck in a life he didn't want and which he blamed, partly, on her, even if it was never said aloud. Leo was staying with her out of some misguided charitable impulse and as a buffer to protect the children from her emotional storms. Every person deserves the chance to be properly loved and Leo had never properly loved his wife. Poor Helen.

A year before our letters started, Leo had suggested a trial separation to Helen and moved into a hotel. She became very distressed and, being friendless by this point in her life, the burden of her distress had fallen on Ava and David. Three days later, Leo returned to the family home.

Leo felt obliged to please people, never putting his happiness ahead of what he saw as his responsibilities. The trouble was, that sometimes increased the misery for other people, however decent his intentions. He was not a stupid man and he understood that his choices had not helped. I believe he was using our letters and my comments as a way to grant himself moral permission to leave his marriage.

On Boxing Day 1975, ten months after Leo posted me the first book, he told Helen he was moving out again. He had already rented a small apartment in the city, with a spare room so Ava and David could stay if they wished.

On 27 December, he phoned me from his new flat. This was the first time we'd spoken in sixteen years and I heard his beautiful voice in every cell of my body. I could also hear the echoey sound of his new, unfurnished living room and I laughed.

'It's marvellous to hear you laugh,' he said.

We agreed on a plan: I would visit Mac at The Community, then drive north to Brisbane for a few days. Beyond that, Leo and I made no firm decisions about the future. We would see where things were between us.

But my mind had galloped ahead, conjuring up the life we would build together. I accepted that he needed to stay in Brisbane to be near his teenaged children for the next few years. If I were to move up there, it need not be a story of me trailing after a man. I could use the move as a chance to reboot, maybe enrol in university or push myself into a professional life that used my brain more.

On 10 January, the night before I'd left Sydney to visit Mac, Leo had phoned me again, this time from a phone box round the corner from his family home. It only took a few syllables for me to hear the shift in his voice. Helen was in a bad way. The kids couldn't cope. He'd already moved back to the family home.

I couldn't bear to listen to explanations or apologies or promises. Very quickly, I put down the receiver, then let the phone ring unanswered.

I suppose I could've kept waiting, hanging on for him to visit Sydney on 'business trips' so we could conduct an affair for however many years it would take for his children to be sufficiently grown up. But I didn't want Leo to line me up as a lifeboat to jump into, with the chance his guilt could send him scrambling back to his family at any moment. That was too risky for me. And it shook me to realise how much I'd been keeping my life on hold for the last year, waiting for him.

If a reader had been hoping for a big romantic turn here, I'm sorry to disappoint. People do royally stuff up their love-lives sometimes, and that was what Leo Newman and I had managed to do repeatedly. But I believe I made a wise, self-protective choice at that point.

I stayed up on the night of the 10 January phone call, writing drafts of a letter to post to his Brisbane office. I kept a carbon copy of the final version and, reading it now, I do flinch at the harshness of my tone.

One section of the letter read: 'You hate your marriage, your job, you even despise great chunks of the content of your own mind but you don't seem able to change anything. I hope you can get some therapy or whatever might help you. But I can't fix you and I don't think we're very good for each other. Maybe we're too caught up in nostalgia about what might have happened, based on the infatuated notions of the barely adult people we were in 1947. Our brief time together in 1959 was blissful but that was a long time ago and probably a bit of a fantasy anyway. And in the present, we can't make this work. It's painful for me and not helpful to you or your family. Please don't contact me again.'

The next morning, I'd headed west to visit Mac and now I was driving back to Sydney.

It struck me, on that long drive, that there was a debt built up inside me, a debt from all the times I hadn't been loved enough, and it was unfair to expect any one man to pay that off. Not even Leo; not even if he'd left his wife that very day, flown to Sydney and run towards me in a train station or airport or some other major transport hub, as in a romcom finale. The coda scene in that romantic movie might be a sequence in which Leo and I are painting his Brisbane apartment, sipping wine from paint-spattered coffee mugs, laughing and kissing. That's an appealing scene, but not plausible. If I'd moved to Brisbane in 1976, there was little guarantee it would turn out well and a huge likelihood of misery for me.

I'd been on my own—in a romantic sense—for most of my life and I was okay. I had wonderful friends and my precious children. I could always find some man to have sex with when I really wanted to, and there was still a chance I would find a life partner who could properly commit to me. I would be okay.

And if I'd accused Leo Newman of being stuck and making excuses for not doing things, the same was true of me. My friend Patty had been urging me to head off on an adventure. By the time I was driving into the outskirts of Sydney, I had decided this was a good time to follow her advice.

THIRTEEN

October 1976.

My 48-year-old body floated in water as clear as vodka, clear enough to see fish and little turtles swimming through the pockets of sunlight. Overhead, the vaulted limestone roof was decorated with luxurious ferns, bright moss and vines which hung down into the pool.

The cenotes of the Yucatan peninsula in Mexico are natural swimming holes formed when limestone has collapsed, offering humans a way into the system of underground rivers. The Mayan people, quite reasonably in my view, considered cenotes to be sacred.

I was so captivated by my first swim in one, it had become the inspiration for my travel itinerary in recent days: to check out a variety of cenotes, riding on local buses from Cuzama just south of Merida, through Valladolid, then on to the Caribbean coast. Some of the waterholes were huge, saturated with sun, set up with boardwalks and swimming pontoons. Some offered their own waterfalls and glamorous rock formations; others were the entry point for long subterranean waterways. A few times I was lucky enough to find small cenotes, ones which had narrow openings on the surface and wobbly wooden stairs leading down to hidden rock shelves and deep pools of water, with only delicate strands of light making it through from the world above.

When I'd made the decision to travel, I sold two of the charcoal drawings Cyrus had done of me in 1955. In the unpredictable way the art market can suddenly declare an artist to be valuable, work by Cyrus John O'Farrell was fetching high prices in early 1976, so I was able to realise a decent pot of cash. From then on, every time I paid for a plane ticket, a cheap hotel room, a theatre ticket or a proper meal in some foreign city, I imagined I was spending the proceeds from the sale of first my left thigh, then my right, then my left buttock, and so forth. It amused me to picture my younger body being consumed piece by piece while my older body was exploring the world.

I'd set off in March, initially using tips from my daughter Rose to travel through Indonesia, Malaysia, Thailand and Burma. In Singapore Airport, I spotted a cheap standby flight to Tokyo, so I let that decide the next leg of my journey. From Japan, I flew to San Francisco, then roamed the US, using novels I'd read or recommendations from people to steer my travels. I felt wonderfully dizzy to have no plans beyond the next day and there was a pleasing lightness about moving through places where nobody knew me, with no connections to past events to define me.

In Tokyo I had a delightful week-long affair with a surprisingly hirsute businessman from Madrid with whom I'd got chatting in a rooftop bar, and I had a most entertaining fling with a lovely Irish guy in New York.

By October of '76, I'd been in Mexico for six weeks and the country had turned out to be my favourite by far. Certain places grab you through some combination of the people, the landscape, the history, food, music, art. If that combination lands at just the right point in your own storyline, the place can hook you forever. I wanted to stay longer, but after seven months of travel, however frugal I'd been, my funds were almost gone. I had to be realistic.

Even so, back in Mexico City, whenever I looked into flights to Sydney, I would stall, too itchy in my own skin to return to my life yet. I can see now that this hesitation was to avoid the difficult business of working out what to do with myself next.

Then I spotted an advertisement for teachers of English as a foreign language.

The Condesa district of Mexico City was still upper-middle class in the 1970s, full of beautiful art deco houses along its leafy streets, arranged around graceful parks and fountains. Many of those homes would end up badly damaged by the 1985 earthquake and the tone of the area shifted as a less wealthy, more bohemian lot moved in. Then, in the way these cycles go, that bohemian edge, coupled with the original elegant town-planning, made Colonia Condesa desirable again and the gentrification process kicked in.

But back in 1977 someone like me couldn't afford to live in Condesa, even though it was the location of the language school in which I'd been working for the last year. I was renting a tiny studio flat in Zona Rosa, with my one window overlooking a tight alleyway filled with rubbish bins. The flat suited my needs—cheap, clean, quiet enough to sleep—and I spent most of my waking hours outside the building in cafes, teaching or wandering around.

The 'English Now' language school occupied the ground floor of a picturesque building—the façade painted terracotta, with ornamental turrets sprouting from its upper levels and ornate stonework around the windows and doors. The communal kitchen was enlivened by the presence of Juana and Alejandra, the two chatty Mexican women who ran the 'Spanish Now' school on the floor above.

For the last ten months, I'd been teaching a class of eight students from 9 a.m. to 1 p.m., Monday to Saturday, and I took on as many additional one-on-one lessons as I could get. English Now clients were the kinds of individuals who could afford the courses: businessmen, affluent women planning to travel or young adults from well-off families.

My first day in front of a class had been a terrifying exercise in faking it. Poorly. At the point I was about to declare myself unfit to teach, there came the intoxicating moment when I saw in a student's face that I'd helped her understand a component of English in a useful way.

In those early weeks, I was only ever two pages ahead of the class in the textbook, scrambling to get a handle on grammatical terms and the linguistic structures native speakers use without awareness of what's coming out of our mouths. Countable and uncountable nouns, transitive and intransitive verbs, possessive adjectives and possessive pronouns.

I came to love grammar, picturing it as the beautiful connective tissue of a language which enables us to organise thought. Not that I support pedantry around grammar. Obsession with correctness is rarely about communication and is usually wielded as a pompous weapon to whack less educated people over the head.

In the classroom, I kept the lessons lively, carrying on like a fool, doing woeful drawings on the blackboard and getting everyone on their feet to act out conversational scenarios. But I would also try to detect the moments in the day when we all needed a spell of quiet consolidation work. My other educational tenet was to be generous with praise, a principle based on my experience teaching Athena on the SS *Asturias*, my experience as a mother and, well, my experience as a human being in the world.

Meanwhile, to help me lift my Spanish a few notches, Juana and Alejandra, were kind enough to let me sit in on their classes whenever I could manage it.

Locals in my neighbourhood—shopkeepers, cafe staff, the postman—were encouraging and entertained by my clumsy efforts to converse. Guadalupe, the woman who ran a tiny, over-stuffed grocery store in my street, was especially keen to motivate my language acquisition. She made it a game: with a mock-stern expression on her face, she would refuse to sell me an item unless I correctly said the word in Spanish without consulting my pocket dictionary. The result was a thorough grocery vocabulary as well as a solid friendship with Lupe.

In the afternoons, her eight-year-old granddaughter Jimena would usually be in the shop doing her homework. Lupe was keen for me to teach the girl a few words of English, which seemed like a fair trade. Jimena was a clever kid and she quickly learned enough to tease both me and her grandmother.

At a certain point every weekday, Lupe would leave Jimena to mind the shop while she ducked to a cramped storage area where she kept a television set to watch her current favourite telenovela, *Mañana Ser Otro Día* (*Tomorrow Is Another Day*). Unlike English-language soap operas, Latin American telenovelas are voluminous but have a limited story arc, like a long florid novel, played out in more than a hundred episodes broadcast over several months.

The first time I overheard telenovela dialogue coming from the back of Lupe's shop, my ears grabbed hold of it. The actors tended to speak more slowly and distinctly than regular folk in the street, and the scenes often involved repetition of words, which made comprehension easier. Quick example—Shocked woman: '*Cómo? María es prostituta?*' Disapproving woman: '*Sí. Es prostituta!*'

Lupe was happy to scooch her bum sideways on the boxes of tinned vegetables so there was room for me to sit and watch telenovelas with her whenever I had the time. If I missed a crucial episode, she would kindly fill me in on the plot as best she could, given my limited comprehension. The shows she was watching in 1977 involved a lot of missing children, orphans and similar anguished story material, and the emotional pull of it snuck up on me. In one mother and lost child reunion scene, I crumpled into unexpected tears and Lupe clutched my hand until the episode was over.

Over the months, in my halting Spanish, I told Lupe about my dead sisters and brothers, my relinquished baby, my troubled son, my thwarted romance. Lupe told me about the true love she hadn't been allowed to marry, her baby son who died, her worry about her elder daughter who was living in Veracruz, married to a violent man. A lot of crying and hugging went on in the back of that shop.

By October '77, I had a settled life in Mexico City, with a postal address, which made it easier to maintain a proper correspondence with my dear ones in Australia.

Rose was flat out with her studies, an almost-doctor now, so she only had time to scrawl brief letters.

In my letters to Mac, I made a point of describing things I observed on my travels and I controlled the urge to badger him about his choices. Mac responded with thoughtful follow-up questions about Kyoto or New Orleans or Oaxaca and wrote about construction projects he was working on for The Community and his pride in Jacob's vegetable-growing achievements.

My pal Patty Reynolds didn't write letters in the usual sense. An envelope would arrive with a few pages torn out of her spiral notebook with lists of books, movies and songs, along with half-a-dozen newspaper clippings about matters seizing her attention. She scrawled comments up the white margins of the clippings with her thoughts about the article or with snippets of personal news about gigs she'd performed or a new woman she had a crush on. Those envelopes were like delightful capsules that landed in my letterbox straight from Patty's curious mind.

My time overseas rescued my bond with Pearl and I discovered that my old friend occupied a significant place in my brain. In moments I was frazzled by the aggravations of travelling on the cheap, I might chance upon a beautiful sight and then I'd hear Pearl's voice—'that's champion'—and I'd pull my whingey self together. Wandering through a market in some foreign city, my eye would fall on a colourful doodad and I could picture Pearl gasping over it. I began to send her trinkets, exotic paper items from Japan, bright woven goods and the like, with notes explaining where they came from and why I thought she'd appreciate them. As I hoped, Pearl interpreted those parcels as reassurance that my affection for her had not been obliterated by our current differences.

The arrival of a neatly typed letter from Athena would be the highlight of my week, with news about her grandkids and her job as a project manager at a construction company. In one letter, she described the night she was roped in as an emergency Greek interpreter at the women's refuge, and since that night, she had thrown herself into a migrant women's support organisation. I could tell she was charged up by this new mission.

In letters home, I sometimes attempted to share my impressions of Mexico. If I were to describe the chaos of the city, so many buildings crumbling and tacked together, how any encounter with the bureaucracy was tortuous, how the streets were noisy, choked with diesel fumes, sometimes bristling with armed police and the occasional truckload of soldiers, it would not convey how this was all astonishingly functional and cheerful (most of the time) and how everything was invigorated by the warmest people I'd encountered in my travels. Then again, to blather on about friendly people and festive moments and life force and delectable street food could smack of that kind of folkloric poverty-exotica in travel impressions that I find troubling. Not to mention having an unsavoury whiff of the 'poor but happy' romanticised bullshit I cannot abide. A visitor would have to be blind not to see the neediness and inequalities in the place. As a temporary resident, my understanding of the country was gauze thin and I had no right to offer an opinion beyond a basic belief that people should be fed, housed, and treated with dignity. My point is, I could barely formulate my own thoughts about Mexico so it was difficult to write letters back to Australia explaining why I loved being there.

On an afternoon in October 1977, I was heading home from English Now, wondering whether to order the tacos with seared tuna from my favourite *taquería*.

Turning into Avenida Amsterdam, I saw the grand peach-coloured house on the corner was being used as a filming location, the street crowded with equipment trucks. Inside the wrought-iron fence, the garden and front porch were full of crew members, generators, reflectors like silver sails, huge lights on scaffolds and other paraphernalia. I picked a spot to stand so I could watch without being in the way.

'*Silencio, por favor!*' called out some guy I couldn't see. The front door of the house opened and a woman wearing an electric-blue tailored suit stepped out into the pool of artificially bright light. It was Ana Teresa Villanueva, the glamorous star of *El Precio del Deseo* (*The Price of Desire*), one of the telenovelas I'd been watching with Lupe.

A yelping sound escaped from my throat when I first saw Villanueva only a few feet away. A man swung his head round to look at me and I flinched, thinking my yelp had been loud enough to disturb the shoot. But then the guy smiled and whispered '*Sí.* Ana Teresa Villanueva.'

I assumed the smiling man was a stickybeak like me, but a moment later, he hurried through the front gate and joined a huddle of people standing around the actress.

While the crew were setting up to do another shot, he came back out and stood next to me, with a smile that I took as an invitation to chat. I introduced myself in clunky Spanish and he replied in excellent English.

'Lovely to meet you, Liz. I'm Diego. You know Ana Teresa Villanueva?'

'Just from the TV. I love the way she plays a ball-tearer. Takes no shit from anyone,' I said, over-excited, then immediately regretted using a swear word.

But Diego did not seem bothered. 'She's like this in life also. Excuse me, what's your accent? I can't pick.'

'Oh. A weird mixture. English, then a spoonful of Australian, then English-teacher plain vanilla spread on top.'

He laughed. 'I like your weird mix with the vanilla icing. Easier for me to understand.'

Diego was working as an assistant to Fernanda Elezondo, the woman who steered the writing of many telenovelas, including this one being filmed in Avenida Amsterdam.

'Dona Villanueva has many opinions,' Diego explained, 'so Fernanda sends me here to talk to our star when she is unhappy about the scripts. It seems she likes me. For the moment, at least.' He pulled a nervous face that made me laugh.

For the next three days, I stopped by Avenida Amsterdam to watch the filming. Diego was always there and when he wasn't required to negotiate lines of dialogue with Ana Teresa Villanueva, he would come over to chat with me.

'Villanueva has always been a diva,' he said, 'but because she's good, everyone—what's the expression? Ah . . .'

'Everybody puts up with it? Works around her moods?'

'Exactly. But now there's a new problem.'

During the filming hiatus, Villanueva, a beautiful woman in her early sixties, had gone to Brazil or Colombia—no one knew for sure—and there, she had ordered the full menu of cosmetic surgery, so on her return, she suddenly appeared twenty years younger.

'Now she looks younger than the actors who play her adult children. My boss tried to get her to wear a grey wig.'

I laughed. 'Oh no.'

'Yes. You understand the problem.'

Diego and I exchanged a grimace of jokey despair, then he added, 'Probably I should not tell you about Villanueva's surgeries.'

'Don't worry. I'm good at keeping secrets.'

Diego looked at me intently, as if assessing my self-assessment.

'And don't worry about Villanueva's new face,' I added. 'She's so fabulous, she will make it work.'

'I hope so. Thank you for the positive spirit.'

The fifth day, I rounded the corner into Amsterdam to see the peach-coloured house but no trucks and no sign that a film crew had ever been there. It was disappointing to miss out on the novelty, the gossip and the company of the interesting man.

This was one of those moments when the loneliness of my life made itself felt in the form of a hollow sick feeling. I had my connection with Lupe and some friendships at the language school. Even so, and as much as I loved living in Mexico City, I was often lonely.

To cheer myself up, I walked straight from there to my favourite cafe and ordered a phenomenally rich hot chocolate. I was draining the delicious cocoa sludge from the bottom of the cup when Diego appeared by my table.

'Hello,' he said. 'You mentioned you come to this cafe. I hope you don't think I'm—uh . . .'

'Stalking me?'

'I can go away if you—'

'No, please sit. I'm very happy to see you.'

He sat down and signalled to the waiter for a coffee. 'I like talking with you to practise my English. But I also like talking with you.'

'Your English is already so good.'

'Thank you but I don't agree. I'm going to work in the US very soon, so I want to be as fluent as possible.'

Before I had a chance to ask about his US job, Diego started asking me dozens of questions about my life, listening, making thoughtful comments and laughing (at the appropriate points). In my experience, the only men who ask women a lot of questions about themselves are either gay, conmen or writers trawling for story material. It turned out Diego Fonseca Torres was the latter—an aspiring screenwriter who was as nosy about people as I was.

And so our friendship began.

Diego and I would meet up at that cafe, talk our heads off, then go walking around the city.

Even though he was only thirty-six, Diego had one vivid streak of silver through his dark hair, sweeping back from his left temple, the result of a childhood injury. 'My skunk hair,' he called it. He wasn't drop-dead handsome but with strong cheekbones and golden syrup eyes, I assumed he would be considered attractive by the women of Mexico City. Because he'd been chubby in his teens and twenties, he had little confidence about his attractiveness and had developed self-mocking face-pulling quirks. That made him even more likeable to me.

Diego grew up in a middle-class family in Condesa—father a lawyer, mother a teacher. He'd always been obsessed with movies but his father pushed him onto a more reliable path: a business degree at university, then a job with a mining corporation. When his father died in '68, Diego felt free to ditch the job he hated and go travelling. He came back to study film at university in Mexico City, falling in with a group of friends, all fired up to make movies together, and falling in love with a journalist, Julieta.

Then Diego's mother died from a stroke, Julieta dumped him, and he became disheartened about his career prospects, hammered by the reality of trying to make movies in Mexico in the mid-1970s.

'There's nothing for me in this country,' he said to me more than once.

He'd fixed on the idea that he must move to the US to be a film-maker. To get the necessary money together, he was working on telenovelas and writing TV commercials, with the intention of flying north very soon.

It took a few weeks for Diego to let me see where he lived, because he was uncomfortable about staying in his parents' bourgeois house in Condesa. Mind you, the place didn't radiate privilege, given its crumbly state, with a large 'En Venta' (For Sale) sign on the flaky front fence. Diego was desperate to sell the place and pay off the family debts. Trouble was, his sister refused to allow the sale, so the En Venta sign was a source of sibling conflict.

I could see what an elegant house it had once been, with high ceilings, tall arched windows, stone fireplaces and an art deco wrought-iron balustrade on the stairs. But the interior was now gloomy, with broken windowpanes covered by wooden boards, damp seeping up walls, electrical wiring hanging loose, paint bubbling off surfaces. Diego had made a nest for himself in the living room, with just a bed, an old desk and a few suitcases of belongings.

'You're not really living in this house,' I said. 'You're camping inside it.'

'This is true. But no point fixing anything because I'll be gone soon.'

Diego made us a pot of tea in the dilapidated kitchen, while raving about why he couldn't stay in Mexico.

'People here chatter and sigh about the Golden Age of Mexican Cinema. Great! But that's all finished since 1956, '57. For us here now, it's shit. It's the Rust Age of Mexican Cinema.'

I laughed and Diego spun to look at me. 'Did I say the wrong word? Is "rust" not right?'

'No, Rust Age is funny, in the way you meant it to be funny.'

'Truly? I trust you to tell me when I sound like an idiot asshole.'

'I will always tell you if you sound like an idiot asshole.'

'Good. I need good English. I'm so itchy to leave this place. I've got to get out of here. To live in a corrupt country like Mexico, it's . . . It drives me crazy.' Then he laughed. 'Maybe the truth is, what I really want is to be a famous movie director in the US and everything else I say is bullshit.'

We took our tea to the living room and sat on the floor.

'And I must get out of this house so I can start my life,' he said. 'I wasted too many years living the wrong life because my father was in my head. I have to be bold. This is why I admire your boldness.'

'Me?' I'd never thought of myself as a bold person.

'You ran away from home when you were fifteen. You got on a boat—nineteen years old—and went to a new country. You raised your children alone. You were a model for a brilliant artist. You rescued your son from an overdose. You found your child who was stolen from you.'

As he went on, detailing my 'bold moves', I laughed. In a Mexican accent, my life sounded like a telenovela plotline.

'Then you came here where you didn't speak the language.'

'But this isn't my real life,' I said. 'And I don't want to hang around like some sad, irrelevant expat. I have to go back.'

Diego grinned at me. 'And then you will make your next bold move.'

I was glad he felt so confident about that. I was unconvinced.

I would sometimes tag along on nights out with Diego's film school and journalist friends. A dozen of us would move from bar to bar, stopping to fill up on food from fluoro-bright *taquerías*, then ending up in some tiny dark joint with a live band.

Because Diego had come to film-making late, many of his friends were ten years younger. And that meant many were the age of my children. I tried not to dwell on that and just enjoy their company.

Two tequilas in, my inhibitions were lowered enough that I became more confident to speak Spanish and they all did their best to speak slowly to me, with Diego translating when we hit a pothole. But as the night went on, Diego's friends would be so fired up about politics and cinema that the conversation accelerated beyond my comprehension. I was happy to unplug myself from the effort of understanding and just watch the floorshow of these young people talking with such passion, punctuated by bursts of laughter. And if the band was playing danceable music, I would find a spot to bop around. Dancing was a pleasure that had been mostly absent from my life in recent years, and it felt mighty good to move, even as an ancient 49-year-old woman.

One night in December, in the small space that counted as a dancefloor in the back corner of a Zona Rosa bar, several of Diego's friends jumped up to dance too. Right next to me, Javier and Luisa started kissing passionately. I glanced over to where the others were sitting and wondered which of the three remaining young women at the table might be keen on Diego. (My bet was on Valeria.)

It was only a short walk—well, more of a pleasantly intoxicated stagger—from that bar back to my flat. Diego kindly walked me home and I figured he was even drunker than I was, because when he leaned in to give me a peck on the cheek goodnight, he got the angle wrong and kissed me on the mouth. But then he kissed me again and it was clear this was not a clumsy mistake. It was a good kiss. So good it took me a few moments to wrench myself clear and take a step back.

'I'm forty-nine years old.'

He pulled a face—*who cares.*

'Come on. I'm so much older than you. Thirteen years older.'

He shrugged. 'I don't care about maths. If you ask my parents—well, you can't ask them because they're dead—but if you could ask them, they would say, "Diego is thirty-six years old, unmarried with no children—he's already an old man." So, there's no problem about age. But if you want me to go, I will just say goodnight and—'

I was suddenly aware that I didn't want him to go. I lunged forward to kiss him back as unmistakably as possible, and we went upstairs to my flat.

Diego hadn't had sex with anyone since Julieta broke his heart. The last year had been celibate for me, so a combination of bottled-up lust and both of us being drunk meant I didn't have a chance to be self-conscious about my body with a younger lover. And then I was having such a good time, I didn't care.

12 April 1978.

I turned fifty.

The multicoloured mountains of the Quebrada de Humahuaca in the north-west of Argentina were preposterously beautiful—vast dry hillsides with coloured rock in layers of purple, orange, cream, rust, chocolate, mauve—swooping down into creek-bed valleys with strips of green and villages with adobe houses, and a little further off, blinding white salt plains stretched to the Bolivian border.

It felt good to put something so startling in front of my now fifty-year-old eyeballs. In honour of this significant birthday, Diego and I had carved out time for a trip—a weekend in Buenos Aires, then a flight to Salta where we hired a car to drive north to Jujuy. A few days exploring, then back to Mexico City.

We were both supposed to have left Mexico for good by now. I was still expecting to return to Sydney soon and Diego spoke, often, about his imminent move to Los Angeles. Our relationship over the last four months had been intense but in a provisional way that attached no expectation and required no analysis. We were just having a good time together while we were both still around.

For the sake of record, let me say the sex was very pleasing. It was the first time my adult self had the chance to develop a lovemaking repertoire with someone over a decent amount of time. Fumbles in my teens with GIs didn't count, Donald had been a miserable business, the affair with Cyrus was wonderful but unequal, and my liaisons since then had been too short-lived to develop the sexual rapport with a partner where things get really interesting.

My friendship with Diego had been fuelled by a mutual love of talking and that carried over into our sex life—we kept on talking in the bedroom too. And afterwards, we would lie in bed, raving about stories, discussing people we'd observed in the street that day and what we would eat for dinner.

In a letter to Athena, I mentioned I was having a 'fling' (leaving out the age difference) and she was happy to hear I was having fun. Pearl was positively in a lather about my 'Latin lover'.

The Christmas before I turned fifty, I had moved into the Condesa house to save paying rent. Diego and I acquired more furniture so we could use one of the bedrooms, but we still lived like squatters occupying the house rather than respectable residents of Colonia Condesa.

Diego continued working as an assistant on telenovelas and the two of us would discuss the characters with ludicrous intensity, then collapse laughing at ourselves for getting so stirred up about fictional humans. Diego insisted on pitching some of my plot ideas to his boss Fernanda. When chunks of those storylines made it onto the TV screen, I was hugely chuffed, and my friend Lupe stared at me, impressed, as if I'd revealed mysterious unseen powers.

For all Diego's talk of leaving Mexico, his friends kept persuading him to be involved in this or that project 'before he left'. He wrote the script for a short film, worked as editor on another and he often talked excitedly about a short film he wanted to direct that could only be shot in Mexico.

On the day I turned fifty, I hiked around the foot of the Quebrada mountains and prowled through hilltop cemeteries. That evening, Diego and I found a restaurant in Purmamarca where we shared a bottle of the delicious local wine and made a toast to my birthday.

'We should toast your Berlin prize as well,' I said.

The short film written by Diego had already gathered several film festival prizes and, the week before our Argentina trip, had won a major award in Berlin.

'In fact . . . so . . .' Diego spoke without lifting his gaze from the tablecloth. 'That is connected to something I want to talk to you about, Liz. Don't laugh at me when I say this.'

'I won't.'

'You might. In fact, you *should* laugh because I'm ridiculous. I am a ridiculous man. All the months, all the times, I said, "I'm going to LA very soon", "I can't stay in this stupid country." Well, you know all the things I said.'

He still hadn't met my gaze. I already knew what he was going to say.

'Now I realise I have to stay in Mexico.'

'Yes. I think you should stay.'

He didn't seem to register that I had agreed with him and launched into a rant, arguing with himself rather than me. 'It's fucking impossible to work in Mexico. There's no money, the corruption is disgusting, the politics drive me crazy but it's the crazy that belongs to me, I suppose. I have to stay and make whatever shitty things I can make and—I don't know. I can't explain.'

'I get it. I agree.'

He laughed. 'So. Happy birthday, Liz. Until now, you thought you had a temporary boyfriend—with an expiry date.'

'Well, yeah, you were supposed to be my disposable Latino toyboy.'

He reached across the table and squeezed my hand. 'I know this wasn't the contract you signed, so I understand if you . . . You must make your own decisions. But when you're thinking about it, please remember that I love you. If you stay in Mexico, if you want to stay with me, I would be very happy.'

We didn't discuss our future at all during the last few days of the trip. I think Diego was being careful, leaving me to make my own choices.

We took a taxi from the airport back to Condesa, and as I walked in the front door, the air in the house was charged with a sort of potential energy. It felt different—to think I might make the rest of my life here. The sensation was unfamiliar but not unwelcome.

15 September 1978.

I landed in Sydney the day before Rose's wedding.

It may come as a surprise to the reader that my ambitious, feminist, independent daughter had suddenly decided to get married at the age of twenty-six. I can tell you it was a monumental fucking surprise to me.

She relayed the news in a phone conversation that rapidly turned into an argument. The instant I hung up the phone, I pounded out a letter to her on Diego's typewriter. I hated the idea that she would marry in a rush, as I had foolishly done. Rose had managed so well to get through a medical degree and she'd talked about specialising in paediatrics. Why complicate her life with a marriage at this point?

And to add to the foolishness, the man she was marrying was hardly in a position to offer her security.

The January before, Rose was working at RPA casualty when Vuong Le came in with his mother Thuy, who had injured her arm working in a backyard clothing factory. While Rose stitched Thuy's arm, Vuong acted as interpreter. Rose was impressed by the tenderness and respect he showed to his mother, joking around to calm her jangled nerves.

A week later, Rose and Vuong ran into each other in a Marrickville fruit and vegie shop, went for a meal and from there the relationship developed quickly. Compared to the guys who'd gone through medical school with Rose—shiny private school boys, plump with privilege—Vuong seemed to have so much more substance and life experience, even at the age of twenty-four. As a teenager in Saigon, he'd been injured in a street explosion which left him with a scar down his neck and deafness in one ear. Having lost his father and older brother, Vuong worked as a hotel clerk and as an interpreter for the Americans. After the war, he fled the country with his mother and two little sisters, surviving a perilous boat trip to a Malaysian island. By 1978, he was working as a delivery driver in Sydney, helping support his sisters while they finished high school.

I'm not a monster. I could respect what Vuong had been through. He sounded like a responsible young man. But from my point of view, as a protective mother, he was also too young, skint, carrying huge obligations to his family, and not in any position to offer my daughter the support she would need to get through the difficult years as a medical registrar.

I slammed all my concerns into the letter to Rose, imploring her not to rush into anything, to take it slow with this man, and focus on her career. (I like to think there was no racism in my qualms about Vuong, but we can never be sure what ugly unconscious little thoughts might be simmering underneath the conscious sensible concerns.)

Rose did not respond to my letter, except to post me a formal invitation to the wedding. So, when my daughter stood waiting for me at Sydney Airport arrivals, I wasn't sure how things would be.

To begin with, it was heavenly. It was so good to embrace my gorgeous girl after two and a half years away that other thoughts were obliterated. But by the time we reached the carpark, the chill had set in. Rose drove, delivering me to Athena's Earlwood house where I would stay for the two weeks until my return to Mexico City.

I could see from the firm way Rose held the steering wheel that she planned to be defiant with me.

Eventually, I asked, 'Is there a chance I could meet Vuong before tomorrow?'

'What?' The ferocity of her tone made me flinch. 'No, you cannot meet him before—I mean, apart from anything else, I don't trust you not to be horrible.'

'Oh, come on, Rose. I'm not a monster.' (As mentioned above.)

'Anyway, you're the one who's been gone for three years—'

I jumped in to correct her. 'Two and a half.'

'Whatever. Point is, you have not been here. So you forfeit the right to say anything. If you don't trust my judgement, there's nothing I can do about that.'

'Rosie, I do trust your—I just worry—'

'No. Shut up, Mum. And do not run the feminism line with me because you have no idea what—Fuck . . . I don't even know why you came back for this. You know what? Let's just not speak.'

Being in a car with my daughter not speaking was a nostalgic experience of sorts. I stared out the car window, reacquainting myself with the way Sydney suburbs looked.

As we drew closer to Athena's place, I heard Rose inhale with an about-to-cry shudder.

'Anyway, Mum, I'm sure you'll be delighted to know the wedding is probably going to be a total disaster.'

'Don't feel you have to go through with it tomorrow just because—'

'Fuck you! No! Do you hear yourself? That's not what I—Forget it.'

Rose sniffed back tears for a moment, before she blurted out, 'Mac's not coming to the wedding. There's some drama with Gail. Last week, Auntie Pearl rang and said she can't come. Wouldn't say why. And there's the Athena and Sofia mess.'

'What mess?' I asked, but Rose refused to look at me.

She pulled the car over outside Athena's house, then yanked my suitcase out of the boot and onto the nature strip.

'You know what, Mum, there is so much going on, I'd really rather you didn't come tomorrow if you're just going to add another layer of shit to my wedding day.'

As my angry daughter drove off, I walked across the front lawn— the front lawn on which I had given birth to her. At Athena's front door, I heard footsteps behind me and spun round, hoping it would be Rose, hoping we could make some repairs. But the person behind me was Yianni, Athena's son-in-law.

'Oh. Liz. Hi.' He jerked a smile but seemed agitated and keen to escape. 'Sofia just wanted me to leave this here.'

He placed a gift, wrapped in white and silver wedding paper, on Athena's doorstep, then bolted back down the driveway.

When Athena opened the front door, she looked down at the gift with dismay, as if someone had dropped a dismembered head on her doorstep.

'Yianni left that,' I said. 'What's going on?'

Athena straightened her back, the way I'd seen her do many times as a form of armour. 'It's wonderful to see you, Betty. I'm sorry everything is so . . . Please, come in.'

I kept my feet planted on the porch. 'Tell me what's going on.'

'I will, but come inside and sit down.' Athena moved my suitcase into the front hallway.

There were no hugs, no affectionate greetings. I had landed in an emotional war zone without warning. I walked into the living room and perched my bum on the edge of the sofa. The room had been rearranged, strangely, to make space for an upright piano and an electric keyboard on a stand.

'Sofia is refusing to go to Rose's wedding if I'm there with my partner.'

'Do you mean business partner or—'

'Lover.'

I felt a twinge in my chest, wounded that I'd not been told about such a momentous thing.

'And Sofia's upset with you because . . .'

'My partner is Patty.'

'A woman?'

'Patty Reynolds.'

'My Patty?'

Athena nodded.

'Oh . . . I'm a bit—um . . . How long have the two of you been—'

'A year together. And she moved in here with me last November.'

That explained the piano. Patty was not just living in the Earlwood house, but also teaching students in Athena's front room.

'So when Patty wrote a letter telling me she'd fallen madly in love, that was you? A *year* ago?'

My best friend Athena, previously heterosexual and steadfastly single since 1963, had fallen in love and shacked up with a woman who was arguably my second-best friend. Without either saying a word to me.

'I should have told you,' Athena said. 'I worried you might disapprove.'

'What? I'm not—Of course I wouldn't disapprove of . . . Jesus H. Christ . . . You know what I do disapprove of? Friends lying to each other, keeping secrets. Friends making someone feel like a complete goose. I don't even know how to . . .'

I would not claim my next action as my most mature moment, but I just wanted to get out of there. I grabbed my suitcase and headed out the door. Athena made no attempt to chase me down the driveway or call me back. If it was impulsive and childish of me to flee, Athena's bullshit stoicism was not helpful either.

I hauled my suitcase towards the railway station and then hailed a passing cab. I needed somewhere else to stay the night.

Pearl was still living in the bijou Potts Point apartment paid for by Gerry Stankovich. I stood in its luxurious art deco entrance alcove, hitting the intercom buzzer.

'Yes?' With just one word I could hear she sounded wispy, anxious.

'It's Liz. Betty. It's me.'

'Hello! Darling Betty! Fantastic to hear your voice! But right now, I'm . . . it's not a good time.'

'Is Gerry there?'

'No. It's just . . .' Pearl was fighting tears.

'What's going on? You're scaring me, honey. Buzz me in.'

As soon as Pearl opened her apartment door, I saw the problem. And I had to control my facial muscles not to react unkindly. The previous week, she had undergone a cosmetic chemical peel, so corrosive it had burned holes in her skin, now infected with impetigo. Impetigo for God's sake—a condition I associated more with under-nourished children crammed into London slums than a kept woman living in luxury. Pearl was recovering on antibiotics but she was too embarrassed to show her raw, oozing face at Rose's wedding.

I hugged my sweet friend, made her a cup of tea and reassured her that all would be well. Once Pearl had grown used to me seeing her face, she cheered up, keen to gossip about Athena rather than talk about her own cosmetic disaster.

Athena and Patty had met through me on a couple of occasions, and then their paths had crossed again thanks to the migrant support and refuge work. Patty was smitten but cautious, not sure a 52-year-old woman like Athena was up for such a relationship. It turned out she fell hard for Patty, becoming quite giddy with this unexpected romance. 'Giddy' was not a word I would previously have associated with Athena Samios.

'Do you think she was a lesbian all along and kept it a secret?' Pearl asked me.

'She loved Nick. No question. But . . . I don't know, maybe she never had a chance to find out what she really wanted until now.'

'I don't think I'm secretly lesbotic.' Pearl closed her eyes momentarily, checking her internal gauges for lesbian tendencies. 'Are you?'

'I've never been sexually attracted to women. But who knows. I think people should do what makes them happy.'

Pearl nodded. 'And Athena seems happy. Sofia not so much.'

Athena's elder daughter was a conventional young woman, a churchgoing, rule-loving accountant who fretted about social appearances. Pearl and I agreed that Sofia would have been upset if Athena had taken up with *any* romantic partner and would have seen it as a violation if her mother had moved a new man into the house that Nick built. But for Athena to be in a relationship with a woman was mortifying for her conservative daughter. The younger daughter Thea was vehemently on her mother's side and so the sisters were now estranged.

After weeks of shrill arguments, Sofia had laid down rules: Patty would not be allowed to come to family events and she must never be present in the Earlwood house when Sofia brought her kids over to visit their grandmother.

Until recently, Athena had placated Sofia, enduring her outrage and strictures, but she had reached some threshold, tolerance exhausted. Athena announced that she and Patty would be going to Rose's wedding as a couple, no matter what. Hence Sofia's refusal to attend and the wedding gift left on the doorstep.

'Poor Rose,' said Pearl. 'She just wants the people she loves to be at her wedding.'

'And that includes you, Pearl. Rose adores you. She's keen for you to be there tomorrow no matter what. She wouldn't care about this cosmetic problem.'

Pearl swooped her hands up to cover her face, as if she suddenly remembered the infected sores were there.

'But I understand if you don't want to,' I said and kissed her goodbye on a spot on her forehead that had escaped the beautifying acid.

I caught a taxi from Potts Point and by the time it dropped me at Sofia's house, it was 8 p.m. Sofia was welcoming, hugging me with a needy intensity.

'It's a shame you missed seeing the kids, Auntie Betty. They've just gone to sleep. Have some dinner though. Yianni, go to the fridge—'

'Thanks, sweetheart,' I said, 'but I won't eat. I can't stay long. The jet lag is waiting for me, I think.'

'Of course. Mexico! So far away.'

'So. I'm not here to argue with you about your mum.'

Sofia went from hospitable to furious in a second. 'It's disgusting.'

'Well, I don't think love between consenting adults is ever disgusting. But maybe we can't agree about that right now. I think we can agree that Rose loves you, she sees you as her cousin, and she wants you at her wedding. It's an outdoor ceremony, so you wouldn't even have to breathe the same air as Patty.'

My feeble attempt at a light tone did not play well. Sofia launched into a rant about her mother and Patty, expressing the kind of ugly thoughts that we never wish to hear uttered by a person we love, as I loved Sofia. The rage morphed quickly into grief about her father, and distress that Nick's memory was being defiled. Sofia was in no state to listen to any calmer arguments from me and I'd probably already made it worse by stirring up sludge from the bottom of this murky pool. Within minutes, she was sobbing too much to speak, ran into her bedroom and shut the door.

Yianni stretched his hands out in a helpless gesture.

Before I left, I knocked gently on the bedroom door. 'I love you, Sofia. And there is not a doubt in my mind your mum loves you very much. See you soon.'

Dragging my wheeled suitcase, I walked the two kilometres from Sofia's house to Athena's. It felt right to squeeze the last bit of physical energy out of my body before the jet lag shut down my brain.

Patty opened the front door to me and waited to see if I was interested in hugging her. I wasn't.

'Come in,' Patty said, reaching for my suitcase. 'Athena went to bed with a migraine. Asleep now finally. Which is good. She left some food for you.'

It was weird to sit in Athena's kitchen and watch Patty fuss about, pulling containers out of the fridge, reheating things, knowing where stuff was kept. Patty Reynolds lived in this house now.

Patty watched me shovel Athena's delicious food into my mouth, ravenous, barely pausing to chew.

Eventually she said, 'I'm sorry. About me and Athena.'

'Eh? Don't *apologise* for—oh, that just makes me feel like a dickhead.'

'No, well, I'm sorry for—'

'Don't apologise for being in love, Patty. I mean, sure, apologise for being secretive with me, for lying to me. You should be sorry about that but—ohh, Jesus . . . I'm too tired to talk about this now.'

'Okay, but I want you to know I feel terrible about what's going on with Sofia. I think I should stay away from the wedding but Athena—she's made it a thing and . . . Oh, Lizzie, you look exhausted. I'm sorry this isn't the welcome home you were hoping for. Let's talk in the morning.'

Seeing my friend Patty disappear into the double bedroom that Athena used to share with Nick was strange. A realignment of the universe for me.

In the living room, I sat next to Patty's piano and made a reverse charge phone call. It was before dawn in Mexico City but Diego claimed to be delighted I'd woken him up. I gave him a brief but vivid synopsis of the mess I'd encountered on landing. He responded with all the sympathetic noises I needed to hear and got me laughing about how much it sounded like a telenovela episode. Diego's voice over the phone was like a balm warming my entire, aching, jet-lagged body.

'You need to sleep now, Liz,' he said. 'Sleep, sleep.'

16 September 1978.

I woke at 4 a.m. (body on Mexico time), then lay in bed until it was just light outside. I left a note on the kitchen bench saying I would make my own way to the wedding.

I spent the morning catching buses, on a Liz Rankin/Burnley Former Life Tour. Houses I'd rented, schools my kids had attended, the stretch of George Street where the Trocadero had been when I met Donald, the hospital where Mac was born, the hotel where I'd spent an afternoon with Leo Newman, and other historic sites.

It seemed the lives of everyone I knew in Australia had shifted with no place for me anymore. And there was so much painful stuff going on, which my presence here seemed only to worsen. It was a relief to know I had a return flight to Mexico City.

I'd always been wary of the expat life. Many expats I'd observed seemed to hover in a limbo in which a workable grasp of the language, love of the food, and a few local friends, acted as covers for an uncommitted life, not accountable to the country they'd left nor the country they were living in. But I'd also met individuals who had given themselves over to their new country utterly, living as if they were responsible for what happened there. And in Mexico, I had work I enjoyed and a loving relationship with a good man—not a bad foundation for me to become that substantial sort of expat.

I reached the wedding location—the park behind Bronte Beach—half an hour before the 2 p.m. start. Rose had booked one of the council picnic shelters, but when I located the spot, there was a trio of boofheads sitting there drinking beers.

I noticed a group of people walking towards the picnic shelter carrying eskies and platters of food. Rose's fiancé Vuong, his mother Thuy, sisters Giang and Tan, plus a couple of their family friends.

'Fuck off back to China!' quipped one of the boofheads, displaying a fluid approach to geography.

His companions laughed, adding their own revolting comments.

'Whatcha got in your esky? Dog sandwiches?'

'Youse eat dogs, yeah?'

'Hey—stay back. We don't wanna catch any slant-eye germs.'

Walking across the grass towards the moronic trio, I was infuriated but managed to bung on a smile and pull out my most ocker accent. 'G'day, guys. Sorry, but this area is booked for a wedding. Be great if you could move somewhere else, yeah?'

Trouble was, as a fifty-year-old woman wearing a Mexican embroidered blouse over a denim skirt, I didn't carry the macho air of authority required to handle these bozos. Things might have turned ugly if some of Rose's Anglo medical student friends had not rocked up then, prompting the racist three to scuttle away.

Vuong turned to smile at me—Rose had neglected to mention he was drop-dead handsome—and in a slightly American accent, he said, 'Excuse me. Are you Rose's mother? I've seen photos. I'm Vuong.'

'Yes! Hello! Lovely to meet you!' I spoke way too loudly.

If Rose had told her fiancé about my objections to the marriage, he was too well mannered to let on. He introduced me to his mother and sisters who were busy unpacking the bags of food. I did a lot of smiling and helped them spread a tablecloth over the bird-poo-specked table.

There were about fifty guests at the low-budget wedding—people from the Vietnamese community, young doctors Rose worked with, her old school pals and some of our family friends.

Rose arrived at the park in an orange Datsun 120Y decorated with white ribbons, driven by her pal Jen. In keeping with the low-budget event, Rose's dress was a white cheesecloth number with yellow embroidery down the wide flowy sleeves and on the bodice, from which the fabric fell loosely to her ankles. She was holding a bunch of cornflowers to match those threaded around a headband holding back her mass of dark curls.

I hurried over, keen for a moment with my daughter before the formalities.

'I met Vuong,' I said.

'Oh.'

'He seems great.'

'He is.'

'And you look so beautiful.'

'Thanks, Mum.'

Whatever sort of moment the two of us were having—a positive one, I hoped—was cut short when a bunch of her friends gathered round her, full of chatter.

A taxi pulled up behind the Datsun and, when the rear door opened, a flurry of apricot chiffon was whipped up by the wind. Pearl had decided to come.

As she tottered across the grass in spike heels, I saw she had fashioned a veil to cover her face: a square of the same apricot fabric as her dress, held in place with diamante barrettes clipped to the stiffly lacquered wings of her Farrah Fawcett-Majors hairdo, leaving just her eyes showing and concealing the majority of the impetigo sores. From her smiling eyes and fizzy hand gestures, it was clear Pearl was happy she'd found a way to come to the event. That woman always did love a party.

On the far side of the crowd of wedding guests, it was not hard to spot Patty. With her height and the swirling fluorescent colours of her op shop ensemble, she was hardly unobtrusive. Next to Patty was Athena, wearing an elegant blue pantsuit with a white silk shirt. Thea stood at her mother's side, holding her hand. I signalled hello to the three of them but planned to stay in my spot with Pearl.

The celebrant was in the process of gathering everyone in for the ceremony when we heard a voice call out. It was Sofia, running across the park, as Yianni and the two kids hurried to keep up. Patty chose to hang back, urging Athena and Thea to go ahead without her. The two of them dashed forward to meet Sofia and the Samios family formed a ball of weeping, hugging people. Patty judged (correctly I believe) that the delicate situation could not include her yet. It would take some years for Sofia to truly welcome Patty into the family. Still, the decision to be at this event together was not nothing.

Next to me, Pearl was crying with sooky delight about the reunion, using the sleeve of her dress to mop up tears without smudging her makeup. I put my arm through hers and swept her across the grass to join Patty, so she wouldn't be standing conspicuously by herself.

I nodded hello to Patty. 'Well, lady, you pulled off the ultimate friend steal.'

She laughed. 'Athena's an incredible person.'

'I'm aware.'

'I love her.'

'Good.'

The ceremony was blessedly short and secular, culminating in great whoops of joy from the guests when Rose and Vuong kissed. As people came up to congratulate them, I noticed Vuong's gracious manner and the unobtrusive way he moved himself around to offer someone his good ear. When he bent his head to listen to a well-wisher, I saw the ropey scar that ran down his neck and disappeared inside his shirt collar. Let me assure the reader—if it wasn't already obvious—that I was dead wrong to doubt my daughter's judgement. She knew what she was doing when she chose that man.

Rose was sitting at the table, signing the marriage documents, when she suddenly lifted her head and gasped, as if in pain. I followed her eyeline to see Mac, running down the street from the bus stop.

Mac was apologising over and over. 'Sorry I'm late. Sorry I missed it.' And Rose was reassuring him—'It's fine. It's fine. I'm so glad you're here'—holding her brother close.

When I ran over to embrace my children, it was my turn to be a weeping wreck. I saw Vuong's mother Thuy staring at us, bewildered by the histrionics of the family into which her son had married.

During the next couple of hours, everyone ate very well thanks to the fabulous spread of Greek and Vietnamese food. A ghetto blaster was playing music and guests started dancing on the grass.

I walked over to Athena and bowed with mock formality. 'May I have this dance, you big secret lezzo?'

My friend arched her magnificent eyebrows, then grabbed my hand and we found ourselves a spot in the dance area.

Pearl, meanwhile, was in a huddle of people, lifting her chiffon face veil to show her pitted face to the young medicos. Only Pearl Jowett could manage to transform impetigo sores into a way to connect with people.

I noticed Mac was avoiding Rose's medical school friends with all their cheerfully blokey noise. He stuck with the Le family, trying out some of the Vietnamese phrases he recalled, but mostly asking questions and listening.

When the dance number ended, Rose beckoned me over, away from the other guests.

'You okay, sweetheart?' I asked. 'It went brilliantly. And so wonderful Mac came.'

'Yeah. That makes me very happy. The thing is, Mum, I need to—look, I want you to know me and Vuong had already decided to get married. This didn't decide anything.'

Rose pulled the loose folds of the cheesecloth dress to draw it tight across her abdomen and I could see the bulge. She was five months pregnant.

I couldn't speak for a moment.

'Don't worry, Mum. I'll still work as a doctor. We've got plans.'

The following day, I rang Diego to tell him I would not be coming back to Mexico. The phone is never good for such conversations and this one was especially painful. It's an awful feeling to hurt a person you care about who doesn't deserve to be hurt.

There were many phone calls, many tears, a few angry wounded words followed quickly by apologies and then some bargaining. Whenever Diego proposed a long-distance relationship or dividing our time between Mexico and Australia, I would counter with a tougher line. That wasn't going to work. It was clear to me that his life was in Mexico and my life was in Australia. But there's no getting around the fact that Diego was a lovely man and I was hurting him.

Not every relationship has to last for years and years to be cherished by both parties. In time—quite quickly—Diego and I found our way to a wonderful friendship. Our nine months together may have been a detour, but we managed to give each other valuable things and a great deal of joy. I believe so anyway.

I wonder what would have happened if I'd stayed in Mexico and I sometimes consider that alternative life like a potential storyline. I could've had a long relationship with Diego, a good man who loved me. I might've established my own language school and used the fees from the well-off students to subsidise classes for people who couldn't afford to pay. Diego and I could've fixed up the Condesa house and shared it with struggling film-makers and artists. (Remember this is a fantasy version of my life there.) It would have been good to the extent that I can imagine.

I can offer a quick flash forward in reality: Diego Fonseca Torres made more short films and worked on telenovelas when he needed funds. He got together with lovely Valeria and had a daughter with her—Luz (the name means 'light'). We stayed in contact via letters and phone chats. Later, Diego, Valeria and Luz visited me in Sydney and I visited them in Mexico. Our connection was always immediate and energising.

Diego became a respected producer, still active by the time the Mexican film industry hit its next Golden Age.

On Rose's wedding day, once most of the guests had gone, it was almost dark and I had an urge to run down to the beach.

On the sand, I took off my boots and tights, tucked my skirt into my undies and waded into the waves. It was chilly enough to make me gasp—this was September—but the shock of the cold water settled my frazzled nerves. It felt like the right place to be.

FOURTEEN

November 1978.

I was interviewed for a job as script office coordinator by Carson Bull, Executive Producer at DBB Productions, one of the more successful companies making TV dramas and kids' shows.

'Just so you know, Liz, we've tended to go with younger women in this role in the past but that created—well, there's been some unpleasantness. It'd be tremendous to have someone with your life experience. Someone who could help the team stay grounded.'

I got the message. For this job, typing and organisational skills were advantageous, but my key attribute was the fact that I was old (fifty) and not alluring enough to inflame the sex pests. The reason I was hired at DBB may have been repugnant, but I could suck up the indignity and the low pay if it meant I secured a job in television drama.

I was comfortable with being fifty, but I still had to decide how to present myself at this new workplace without wasting precious time on appearance. Looking okay had always been a problem to be solved.

A brief history of my hair: from the 1940s to the 1960s, I battled with curlers and lacquer on the unruly frizz to create acceptable hairdos. I experimented with Brylcreem but the result was no better than smearing sump oil on my head. In 1964, I resorted to Glatt hair straightening chemicals which fried my hair into broken strands of dry spaghetti. In 1972 I tried a perm, but that created a comical shrub on my head. The hairdresser had to cut into the shrubbery, like someone pruning topiary. Then when I went long on top, short at the back and sides, I resembled a poodle. Blessedly, the day before I started work at DBB Productions, I lucked upon a hairdresser who cut my curly hair properly, advising me to let it dry naturally. Problem solved.

I'd never found shopping for fashionable clothing a fun pastime. I always created a de facto uniform for whatever job I was doing, to avoid wasting time. At the DBB job interview, I noted that people in their North Sydney office wore casual attire, so my work 'uniform' could be jeans with a series of the colourful shirts I'd brought back from Mexico.

At DBB, I had my own small desk, typewriter and filing cabinets, but many of my days were spent in the windowless plotting room, working on *The Squad*. It was an old-fashioned police drama in its fifth season, and the original writer, Brian Paley, was still in charge of the plotting and scripting of the show.

He was fifty-eight but looked older, the way drunks can. The first part of Brian Paley to enter any room was a massive belly, which seemed to have drawn its mass from the scrawny remainder of his body. He wore corduroy trousers drooping in the lee of his gut and grubby frayed jumpers inadequate to the task of covering the abdomen, so there was always a wedge of hairy belly on display. He had the largest under-eye bags I've ever seen—pouches of blue-veined skin, big enough to contain an egg—and he was bald, except for a flimsy ponytail of grey hair with a yellow tinge.

Brian was a notorious 'pussy-hound root-rat' (his term) but it was hard to imagine how he had ever persuaded a woman into his bed. By the time I met him, he'd lost his charms so utterly that his groping and 'saucy' comments with young women in the office were as sad as they were vile. (But still tolerated by the management.)

There were two other main writers on *The Squad*. Ross was my age, pale, sun-damaged and hulking like a Charolais bull, an ex-cop who'd stumbled into TV writing. Ross was a decent bloke but a limited writer—good on plot and procedural stuff but he had only a passing acquaintance with human beings and their inner lives. Murray Armfield was a former advertising copywriter in his early forties, acerbic, smart but lazy. I got along with Murray, but he did have an unfortunate eye muscle defect—his gaze would drift over the breasts and bum of any woman in his field of vision.

On plotting days, my task was to take notes on the discussion of the episode being story-lined. Brian did most of the talking while Ross stood at the whiteboard, writing up plot beats to fit inside the segments which were defined by commercial breaks.

'What's the hook for our ad break?' Brian would often bark. 'Why would any fucker stay watching this boring shit after the ads?'

Later, I would incorporate the whiteboard plot with my shorthand notes and assemble the writers' semi-coherent blather into a typed outline for the episode. My work weeks were filled with photocopying, managing the schedule and processing the script amendments. My additional duty was to type up Brian Paley's drafts, which he wrote in pencil on yellow ruled paper, having declared that 'typewriters can get fucked'. My years typing up PhD theses meant I had a knack for deciphering handwritten scrawl. This talent made Carson Bull's life easier and he was a guy who very much liked things that made his life easier. 'You're a treasure, Lizzie.'

During those early months in the job, I learned how TV scripts were constructed and Brian Paley exhibited enough of his underlying talent for me to soak up ideas about story, pace and character arcs.

One afternoon, Brian was stuck on a story beat and he sat in silence for several minutes before belching out a long, multi-faceted burp which allowed everyone in the room to share a review of his lunch.

He turned to me. 'Lizzie. You're a woman.'

'I am.'

'What the fuck would a woman do in this scene?'

And from then on, I was called upon as the consultant on Being A Woman, in much the same way a TV producer would seek technical advice from doctors or lawyers on their areas of expertise.

Another afternoon, Murray started asking questions about my two years living in Mexico and Brian twisted his neck to look at me, as if he'd noticed I was a person for the first time. He was briefly curious about my life, but pretty soon, he turned my experiences in Mexico into a series of unfunny double entendres about my supposed penchant for refried beans and my 'spiky cactus' (genitalia).

As the executive producer, Carson Bull didn't involve himself much in the scripting process, but he would occasionally pop into the room with a bonhomie as brittle as spun sugar.

'Howdy! How are our writing stars getting on? Listen, the uh, the network—'

Brian made a loud show of interrupting Carson to address Ross, Murray and me. 'Do not trust this man. Carson Bull is a gutless wonder who will bend over and take it up the arse if it makes his life easier. He would sell his own children if it meant he could avoid one mildly difficult conversation with a dickhead above him in the hierarchy.'

Carson chortled as if being insulted by Brian was a special honour. 'Ha. Yep. Well, just so you know, the network bods are very keen we don't maim any more children in this series. How you thinking re the—uh—'

'Fuck off, Carson,' said Brian.

Brian perked up after insulting Carson, so we got a cheerful hour out of him, but often his mood was unpleasant, full of sour rage about his career. Brian Paley had been the writer of Landmark Works of Theatre and Culturally Important Feature Films (I could always hear the capital letters when he spoke about them). But then he fell out with his collaborators, was fired off projects, and had now sunk to the level of series television which he considered beneath him.

Sometimes I'd smell the previous night's red wine sweating its way out of Brian's pores and on those days, he would often discharge his bitterness on some blameless young person in the office. For Brian this was cathartic, like lancing the boil of his bad temper, but it would leave his poor victims trembling, faces dripping with his caustic words still burning their skin.

I'd been in the job almost six months when Carson called me into his office.

'Lizzie, he's been AWOL for three days.'

Brian's behaviour had become increasingly erratic—missing meetings, failing to submit drafts on time.

'My assistant drove round to his house to check he was still alive. He's gone to a private psych place to dry out.'

'Wise,' I said.

'Yes, indeed. And good news! My assistant was able to prise the script for episode seventeen out of Brian before he left.' Carson handed me a wad of crumpled yellow paper held together with a bulldog clip.

It was late afternoon on a Friday, with episode seventeen due to start filming the following Wednesday, so I took the scrawled pages straight to my desk to type up the release script. Brian's drafts were usually messy, but this was something else. There were some sections of dialogue, but with many lines crumbling into incoherence, characters swapping mid-scene and moments from previous series inexplicably appearing.

Because I'd been present during the plotting, I was able to place the stray pieces of Brian's dialogue in position, with my notes filling the gaps to create the shape of the episode. But once I'd finished that restoration job, it was apparent he'd written less than a quarter of the script.

I worked all weekend to write the other three quarters from scratch. I knew the show as well as anyone by now and could mimic the style everyone was used to. I incorporated Brian's dialogue fragments, although I did take the liberty of rewriting his dialogue for female characters so they would sound like human women. On the Monday, I dropped the script for episode seventeen on Carson's desk. He flicked through it, approved it for release and by the end of the day, I sent multiple copies to the production office.

I did not do the patch-up job on episode seventeen out of kindness to Brian Paley. I did it for two reasons: I felt bad for the hardworking production team, who needed a script to do their jobs; and I felt the thrill of having a go at an interesting task. Because the writing was done with an urgent deadline, I got out of my own way and had a crack at it before self-doubt had a chance to paralyse me.

Two days later, Carson Bull called me into his office.

'I've been having another look at this.' He indicated the script in front of him. 'I can see trademark Brian lines in there. But there are other bits . . . definitely not stuff Ross would produce. Murray denies writing any of it. Am I right in thinking a lot of this script is your work?'

'It is.'

I expected to be sacked. But really the moment was about Carson Bull's vanity (pleased with himself for being so astute) and it was also about Carson Bull's desire to sidestep any strenuous confrontation.

'It's actually good work, Liz.' Then he added in his executive voice, 'But I can't give you a credit on this.'

'Oh no, I wouldn't expect that.'

'It makes the network feel secure if they see Brian Paley's name. They have no clue about—You might not realise how much I protect Brian. I don't let the network bods know he's such a handful.'

I nodded my approval of Carson's selfless protective efforts.

'But, Lizzie, I'm not sure when we'll get Brian back. We need writers who are familiar with the show to get us through to the end of this season. Ross and Murray can take up some slack, sure. But how would you feel if I gave you a go at your own episode? You'd get a full onscreen credit and I'll chuck in some extra money on top of your coordinator pay. I mean, we still need you to keep doing your regular job as well. You up for that?'

October 1979.

The night my first credited episode of *The Squad* went to air, I was at Rose and Vuong's Enmore house so we could watch it together, while their nine-month-old daughter Mai slept. Rose and Vuong cheered when my name flashed up. And I must say, that moment was gloriously, childishly thrilling.

Just as Rose had promised me at the wedding, she and Vuong were making their lives work. Rose had taken six months off when Mai was born, but she was now back on duty in the hospital and hoping to start paediatrics training in two years. Vuong was looking after Mai, working three days a week at a truck depot and studying for a science degree part-time. Vuong's mother Thuy covered childcare two of the weekdays and I covered the weekends.

I'd rented a flat in Enmore, close by, in order to be poised for last-minute babysitting duties. I'd scoot round to their house, cook dinner for gorgeous Mai, read stories and dance about with her.

I will avoid raving on about the joys of being a grandmother. It's difficult not to sound mawkish. Then again, I don't want to bung on a perversely hard-boiled attitude. Let me offer observations on some aspects that took me by surprise.

I had not predicted how it would feel to observe my daughter being a parent. Rose was a doting mother, steady or playful as needed, conjuring up energy even when exhausted, attentive to both the responsibility and the delight of it. I had not realised how much this would expand my admiration of her.

Mai's arrival accelerated my relationship with Vuong, counteracting some of the early awkwardness (my fault). The intensity of his feeling for the baby was so strong, it was a relief to have other people (for example, me and his mum Thuy) who shared that intense love, who cared about every tiny development as much as he did, to help him soak up some of the force. That created a strong, separate bond between Vuong and me.

Another surprise: I thought grandparenthood would be a less anxious experience than parenthood, but the opposite was true. As a little baby, Mai went through a phase of febrile convulsions and on two occasions was whisked to RPA to check she wasn't infected with something dire like meningitis. To see my daughter run through the hospital foyer holding her tiny baby hot with fever, jerking with a seizure—well, I discovered that it was possible to carry double the anxiety: desperate concern for Mai plus the anguish I felt for Rose having to suffer this. Double the sense of helplessness.

Becoming a grandmother induced a startling sense of time collapsing. When I held baby Mai along my forearm, listening for her breathing to shift into sleep mode, or hoisted her above my head to make her giggle, all the years since my own babies would concertina into that present moment. I'm talking about more than just memory—it was a strong physical sensation. I was simultaneously a fifty-something woman and my twenty- or twenty-four-year-old self with my own babies. The time warp was unnerving until I decided to relish it.

My friend Patty Reynolds was still playing gigs around the city and small music festivals out of town. In December '79, Patty, Athena and I shared the drive to a festival in St Albans, a village in a lush Hawkesbury River valley, taking Athena's Mazda across the river on the car ferry.

We dropped Patty off at the festival's main marquee and while she was busy with the sound check, Athena and I went for a stroll on the muddy path that ran along the bank of the Macdonald River.

I saw Athena dab her shirtsleeve at her eyes.

'Oh, honey, what's up?' I asked.

'I keep thinking . . . Nick died before he had a chance to . . . all those years, we were so busy, busy—small kids, building the business, money worries—and then he never got to see the grandkids or relax and enjoy the house he built.'

'It's impossibly sad. But you loved him very well.'

'I still feel guilty,' she said.

'Nick would never imagine you'd sail to the isle of Lesbos after he died, but there's no question he'd want you to be happy.'

'Don't think bad of me when I say this, Betty—but if Nick was alive, my life would be—how can I say this—it would be smaller. Things I can have now—my job, the migrant work, meeting all different kinds of people—all of that wouldn't be possible if Nick was still around. He never wanted to travel but I know I'll go travelling with Patty. Even for Thea—I mean, if her dad was still around, he would hate that she's living with a man without being married. There would be arguments, I know. I'm not saying it's good he's dead. I don't think that . . . He was a wonderful man. I loved him. I don't know what I'm trying to say.'

'I think I get it. The two thoughts can exist simultaneously.'

'I hate myself for these thoughts. But thank you for not thinking I'm a bad person, Betty.'

We walked on in silence. When Athena spoke again, I could hear the smile in her voice. 'So, are you thinking, "Did Athena enjoy having sex with Nick?"'

'I am, but don't feel obliged to—'

'He was always sweet to me,' she said in a measured tone. 'It felt nice to be wanted, and that was the only experience I ever had so there was no comparison. But then with Patty, it was—Oh, my God . . .'

Any attempt Athena was making to sound sedate was blasted away by the lustful chemicals flooding her brain. 'At the start, I was nervous, you can imagine. I was clumsy. But I suddenly understood the . . . Before, when I watched movies or heard songs about love and passion, I thought people were exaggerating how good they felt. But with her, I thought, "I get it now".'

We made it back in time for Patty's set, and found a spot for our fold-out chairs on the grass.

Some in the crowd gasped a little when Patty came out on stage— so tall, with wild hair, wearing white lace-up boots and a cobalt blue crushed velvet coat dress she'd found in an op shop. The day was too hot for the outfit, but Patty had decided it was worth sweating it up for the stage impact.

Patty played many of her own songs in those days, but she chose to start this set with a cover, pounding out the first chords of 'I Feel the Earth Move' on the electric piano. The reader may wish to pause here and listen to a recording of Carole King singing her irresistible song about sexual/romantic rapture. I glanced over at Athena as she watched her lover singing with such power. Singing about *her.* I was happy for Athena—my friend was being properly sexed up for the first time in her life.

I must confess there was also a pang of envy. I didn't have anyone I could look at the way Athena was looking at Patty and there was no one who looked at me like that. I tried to prop up my ego by picturing moments when Leo or Diego had looked at me. But any morale boost from those memories was quickly swamped by sadness, so I shut them down.

7 January 1980.

Gerry Stankovich was shot dead in the street by a rival crook. When I heard the news, I hurried to Pearl's apartment to find she'd already swallowed enough Valium to make her woozy but not enough to harm her.

Pearl Jowett had been with Gerry a long time. Even if she was 'with' him according to an odd, secret arrangement, my friend was grieving a relationship of nearly twenty years.

'The men all died on us, Betty,' she said. 'Your Donald, Athena's Nick and now my Gerry. They died and left us.'

I avoided analysis of those three different relationships and, instead, I made cups of tea and watched TV with her.

Like so many mistresses, Pearl had no acknowledged role at Gerry's funeral, reduced to sneaking into the church in disguise, and the Stankovich family only gave her one month's grace to vacate the Potts Point apartment. I'd bought a second-hand Corolla with my TV script money so I helped move her belongings—mostly clothes and cosmetics—to a flat she had rented in Elizabeth Bay.

I was anxious for dear Pearl. She was a beautiful woman but too old to be a floozie on anyone's payroll. She had no proper work history so I couldn't picture what employment she could find. But I should have had more faith in her winning qualities and her healthy lack of concern about status.

Pearl had been a regular customer at Adele's, a posh fashion boutique in Double Bay, and when she saw a sign in the window for a sales assistant, she applied. It would never occur to Pearl to feel ashamed that she'd gone from cashed-up client to lowly paid attendant, and she proved to be wonderful at the job. Her genuine flattery about how lovely the women looked when they stepped out of the changing cubicle helped Adele's sell more of their pricey garments. She was a valuable employee.

Even so, Pearl's retail assistant wage could not possibly cover her taste for clothes, hair salon visits, cosmetic procedures, restaurant meals and tipping taxi drivers. For a period of some years, I did not understand how Pearl financed her life.

She declared that she could never love anyone the way she'd loved Gerry, but male regard was still an essential nutrient for Pearl Jowett. Over the years, there were several boyfriends, some of them reasonable blokes, but all of them weighed down with the baggage older gentlemen bring—acrimonious divorces, debts, adult children who hated them, crumbly knees. They were all delighted by the fact that Pearl was still keen on sex and there was one beau who literally died on top of her.

Pearl was a flirt and generous with her heart to everyone. But when it came to men, she would glitter under their gaze her entire life. I saw her smile flirtatiously at the cleaner emptying the bins in her room not long before she died. But we're not up to that part of the story yet.

✴

February 1980.

Once the network decided not to order another season of *The Squad*, I doubted there would be ongoing work for me at DBB. Fortunately, I was wrong.

'Female perspective,' explained Carson Bull. 'The network tell me they're keen on a strong female skew for this new show.'

Wattle Creek had already been greenlit for a twenty-six-episode season but it turned out the cosy title was all that existed of the project. Carson had sold the network on the idea of a series set in a rural town and there was a one-page pitch document with a lot of blah-blah about the strength of community, small-town gossip, crime, romance, medical crises and the desired comedy/drama mix. Now somebody just had to develop a drama that fitted the description.

The first day in the writers' room on *Wattle Creek* seemed unreal. I was mindful of this astonishing chance to be part of the initial process, creating the characters and world of a show. I was also astonished to find myself in a team that was fifty per cent female.

In charge of the script department was Evan, a tightly wound man but with a good heart and good judgement. He hired two clever, funny young guys—one a former GP, the other a lapsed priest. Evan also somehow persuaded risk-averse Carson Bull to take a punt on Donna Silvestri. She was thirty-two, intelligent, brazenly angst-ridden, with a vulgar sense of humour I enjoyed enormously. After ten years as a playwright, Donna was fed up with being poor, and sick of the misogyny of the theatre world. (Who knew?) She found the sexism in television just as annoying as theatre but more candid and less crushing to the soul.

Our notetaker was Rivka, a 23-year-old who'd just completed a screenwriting course. She was a smart cookie who could suss out when to shut up and when to offer a thought. As I hoped, Rivka was writing her own episodes of the show by the second season.

The main female character in *Wattle Creek* was a doctor and her love interest was a cop who'd been transferred, reluctantly, to his hometown. Over the seasons of the show, we managed the URST (unresolved sexual tension) between these two, consummated their attraction, then tore them apart and all that fun stuff.

There is often snobbery towards anything that could be described as 'soapy'. I would argue that when a drama or a novel is dubbed soapy, one should listen out for the rumble of sexism, devaluing it automatically on the basis of its less important 'women's topics'.

On *Wattle Creek*, we worked hard to sneak certain kinds of story material past the network nerviness (abortion, domestic violence, racism, a teenage boy coming out as gay). I like to think the show helped generate discussions and bolstered progressive thinking in 1980s Australian homes. Good lord, I can hear my own prideful tone, bigging myself up, which is not a tolerable state of mind for me, so I'll stop. Instead, let me sing the praises of my colleagues.

Improvisational comedians talk about the 'yes and' transaction necessary for an improvised sketch to fly: performers validating, augmenting and not blocking each other. The same is true of a healthy writers' room. One of us would come up with a fragment of story and the rest would apply 'yes and' energy, adding fresh details, pinging the consequences of an event through the network of characters. And while three or four of us would gallop along, convincing ourselves it was 'story gold', there would always be one of us (unofficially we took turns in this role) who would sit back with 'hang on a minute' caution, checking the idea made sense and didn't mess with other plans. The interplay of 'yes and' and 'hang on a minute' in a room where everyone felt safe to appear stupid at times—that was the chemical process required. We were lucky on *Wattle Creek*. Even when we were under pressure, our brains addled, there was a generous spirit around the table, and I laughed with my colleagues in that windowless room for more minutes per hour than any other time in my life.

August 1984.

TV'S KILLER GRANNY

The headline of a feature article about me in *The Australian Women's Weekly.*

The journalist repeatedly mentioned my status as a grand-mother—in the tedious way a woman's professional life is often framed. Still, I was chuffed to be profiled in the magazine that had published my 'Strange But True' letters in the 1950s. I'd written the double-episode opener for season three of *Wattle Creek* in which a drug-affected truck driver slammed his semi-trailer into a school bus, killing several children—hence, 'killer granny'.

By then, I had a TV agent and almost five years of earning a living as a television writer. I'd written the miniseries adaptation of a novel set in wartime Queensland about a woman who falls in love with an Italian POW, and there were other projects being discussed. I could allow the phrase 'my writing career' to hover in my thoughts without feeling the urge to obliterate it with self-ridicule.

Around this time, I ran into Brian Paley at an awards event and felt a peculiar mix of reactions: disgust (he was still an arrogant sleazebucket) but also gratitude for things he'd taught me and the opportunity his breakdown had afforded me.

'Lizzie! How are you? Remind me—did you and I ever fuck?'

'I'm well, thanks, Brian. And no, we never had sex of any sort.'

'So I didn't impregnate you with any children?'

'You did not. Just as well for all concerned.'

Brian had stepped away from the industry, then popped up as head of the writing department at the film school. One of his colleagues told me Brian would spend much of his lecture time trying to dissuade students from pursuing their writing careers. 'Flee now! Flee while you're still young enough to find something useful to do! Become optometrists!'

November 1984.

Athena and Patty had offered their spacious Earlwood house to host a first birthday party for Rose and Vuong's son Van. Van was an extraordinarily happy kid, doted on by many and treated like a treasure by his five-year-old sister Mai.

A dozen of Rose and Vuong's friends came to the gathering, along with Pearl, Thuy, Vuong's sisters, several Le cousins and Thea Samios with her partner and baby. Relations between Sofia and Patty had eased to the point where Sofia not only brought her family to events but could chat to Patty for several consecutive minutes.

A mob of children roared through Athena's house and my eyes were following a ragged conga line of little kids when I saw a tall man walking down the side path. At thirty-five, my son Mac was arguably more handsome than ever, always tanned, strong from his physical work at the settlement, lean and healthy from eight years of that austere life. But he never looked happy, to my eyes anyway.

Since Rose's wedding, Mac and I had maintained our correspondence but I'd only laid eyes on him once or twice each year, when he travelled to Sydney or agreed to meet me in a town near his desert enclave. He would phone me sometimes late at night, out of the blue, and it was always restorative to hear his voice.

When Mac came over to hug Rose and me, there was so much we both wanted to ask. I could feel the questions fizzing in my mouth like popping candy. Why are you still living out there, Mac? Why does Gail never come to Sydney with you? What is going on in your life? But in many families, certain topics drift into the unaskable zone. The prohibited areas might seem incomprehensible to an outsider, but within the family, avoidance over time can solidify into a misshapen form.

I chose to ignore the questions in my head and just enjoy having my precious son at the party. Even though Mac was an introverted man, he managed to be comfortable at social events by being still and attentive, so people were drawn to him. He would always end up with toddlers climbing all over him and older kids recruiting him into their games.

I noticed Rose having a bit of a sob as she watched her brother with Mai, who was earnestly teaching him a dance step. Sweet but too rare a sight. Mac should have been in our lives so much more during those years. I will feel that until the day I die.

During the clean-up after the party, he came over and put his arm around me.

'Can I crash at your place for a few days, Mum?'

I'd moved to a single-storey Enmore terrace with a long narrow garden to accommodate my dog, a Jack Russell. I'd never favoured small dogs, but Chica turned out to be a jaunty companion, sitting by me when I worked at home and often coming to plotting days.

I made up the sofa bed for Mac in the small bedroom I used as an office and cooked the best last-minute supper from what happened to be in my fridge. Mac wanted to see videos of shows I'd written, since he had no access to TV at The Community. Watching episodes together, with my son making generous comments, allowed us to avoid difficult conversations for the entire evening.

I might not have woken at 5 a.m. if Chica hadn't stirred. The dog was not used to another person being in the house at night, so when Mac padded out of the spare room, she was on alert. I was on alert too. Pulling on my clothes, I heard Mac close the front door, so I shooed Chica into the backyard and hurried out to the street.

It was still pre-dawn, but I could see Mac striding towards the main road. He walked purposefully, head down, so it wasn't difficult for me to follow without being seen, but as we were approaching Newtown railway station, Mac turned and looked at me.

'You don't need to follow me. I'm not going to buy drugs. I've been sober for ten years.'

'Good to know.'

'Mum, it's—oh . . . Look, I promised Gail I wouldn't tell anyone.'

I had a sense my son was desperate to share the burden of whatever was troubling him. 'Let me say two things,' I said. 'One) not all promises deserve to be honoured. And two) if I happen to follow you, you won't have to divulge anything. You can technically keep the promise.'

Mac pulled a face but he was clearly relieved too. 'I guess I can't stop you.'

We took a train from Newtown to Town Hall station, then I let Mac lead the way on foot across Hyde Park and up Oxford Street. I didn't ask where we were going or why.

The sun was well up and it was six thirty when we reached the destination: St Vincent's Hospital in Darlinghurst. I hung back while Mac asked questions at the front desk but then he turned to me, tilted his head, giving me permission to follow him up to Ward 17 South. The dedicated AIDS ward.

The sights would clench any human heart. Gaunt young men, their skin pallid or jaundiced or marked by lesions, wheeling drip stands along the hall, steadied by a nurse or a friend or a lover who might himself be HIV positive and confronting a preview of his own eventual illness. Passing the ward rooms, I saw glimpses of the patients who were too fragile or too desolate to get out of bed.

Mac stopped at one of the doorways, glanced inside and then shrank back to flatten himself against the wall. 'It's Jacob.'

Mac's stepson Jacob had been fifteen years old when his mother caught him in a sexual clinch with another teenage boy who had spent the summer at The Community. Gail reacted about as poorly as a person could. She called Jacob a disgusting pervert, spat out those cherry-picked Bible verses about homosexuality being an 'abomination', and claimed she'd always suspected her son had a putrid soul. She wouldn't listen to any attempts by Mac to plead for Jacob. When Mac was away from the settlement one day on an errand, Gail packed a bag with Jacob's 'tainted' clothing, drove him to the main highway and dumped him there like roadside rubbish.

I don't know if Gail ever regretted her harsh position. Mac believed she was remorseful but didn't know how to walk it back. There had been trauma in her childhood—she would never tell Mac what it was—and she'd developed mechanisms for shutting off upsetting thoughts and anchoring herself to inflexible positions, a kind of obstinacy born of fear. In this case, Gail felt the need to shun her own child.

Mac went looking for Jacob, initially in Melbourne, where the other teenager lived. He searched in Sydney too, hoping Jacob might reach out to someone connected with the church, and sometimes he'd just wander past the gay bars of Oxford Street hoping to spot him. Mac had made those late-night phone calls to me when he was in Melbourne or Sydney, following up some clue he'd been given. But he never found any sign of Jacob's whereabouts and Gail refused to discuss her banished child.

Then, four years after the boy was thrown out of home, Gail received a letter from a young guy who'd been sharing a squat with Jacob. Her son was in hospital, gravely ill with AIDS. According to Mac, Gail howled with pain but then a moment later converted whatever she was feeling into fundamentalist fervour. The virus was God's punishment. She would not consider visiting Jacob and didn't want Mac to go either. When he insisted, she made him promise he would tell no one about this family shame.

In the St Vincent's corridor, Mac pressed his body against the wall outside Jacob's room. 'I can't go in there. He wants to see his mother. Telling him she won't come—it'd be like punching him in the face. I can't handle that.'

I saw the panic building inside Mac.

At first, I responded gently. 'I'm so very sorry, sweetheart. I know you love Jacob very much.'

Mac gulped in a breath to answer but because his throat had tightened up, he could only reply by nodding emphatically.

'You've been his dad for a long time. He loves you, relies on you.'

The truth I later learned was that the bond between Mac and the boy had been so strong, it had made Gail jealous. To sever the bond, she'd filled Jacob's head with lies, claiming that Mac endorsed this expulsion from the family.

In the corridor, Mac was nodding but still too panicky to move.

I pushed a firmer edge into my words. 'Telling him his mum isn't coming—that's going to be hard. But you can't avoid going in there, Mac. That's out of the question.' I pressed a tissue into my son's hand. 'You're his dad. That kid has no one else. Take a minute, then we must go in and be with him.'

I gripped Mac's arm, pretty damn firmly, and steered him into the six-bed wardroom.

Jacob Burnley was nineteen years old. I'd only met my step-grandson once, when he was eleven, but I recognised the shape of his face, the diffident smile, the eager eyes—even though he was emaciated.

'Hey, Jacob. It's Mac.'

The boy's face brightened and Mac moved to hug him, but then just held his hand. He wasn't afraid of contagion—by 1984, anyone with a brain in their skull and access to newspapers understood the ways the virus was transmitted—Mac's caution came from fear of hurting Jacob, given the cannulas in his papery skin and the frail state of his body.

A bald, barrel-chested guy who was visiting a patient in the bed opposite understood Mac's hesitation. 'You can hug him pretty tight,' the man said, with a disarming smile. 'You probably won't break anything and, even if you did, at this stage, I reckon it'd be worth it.'

Mac smiled his thanks to the guy and reached down to cradle Jacob's upper body tenderly against his own. 'I've been looking for you. I'm so glad I found you.'

The boy relished the embrace for a long time, and I heard him mumble, 'I love you, Dad,' into Mac's chest. Then he craned his neck, looking for his mother. He only saw me.

'Hi, Jacob. I'm Liz. Mac's mum. I met you a while back. You showed me your fantastic vegie garden.'

'Oh. Yes. Hello, Liz. Thanks for visiting.' His politeness almost undid me.

Mac started gabbling a bit too quickly, as if to plaster over Gail's absence. 'We didn't bring you anything, mate. Is there anything you want? Food or anything? We can scoot downstairs and bring you stuff back.'

'Is Mum coming?'

Mac inhaled, his throat constricted, and threw me a desperate look.

I took a step closer to the bed and held Jacob's hand in both of mine. 'Your mother can't be here, sweetheart.' I figured that was the most gently honest answer.

There was subtext in my head: 'Your mother can't be here because, given whatever damage was done to her, she isn't strong enough to accept you. If it were in my power, I would drag her here to be with you.' But that kid didn't need to hear my subtext. He just nodded and never asked about his mother again, as far as I know.

Mac and I spent the next days at St Vincent's. Every few hours, one of us would take a break to wander in the fresh air outside and bring back food, but otherwise the two of us were with Jacob from dawn until late in the evening.

We took in treats—whatever food we thought he'd like.

'Thank you. Yummy,' Jacob would say but he ate very little.

Mac offered to bring in a Bible to read but the boy shook his head firmly. What had those beliefs ever done for that kid but shame him? Once, I did hear Jacob ask if God was punishing him. Mac was quick to assure the boy he'd done nothing to deserve this illness.

In recent years, Jacob had developed a taste for X-Men comics. X-Men stories revolve around humans who develop mutant powers at puberty and are then subjected to prejudice and hatred. So, not surprising that a young gay man would find solace in them. I bought a stack of the comics in a Darlinghurst newsagency and Jacob and I read through them together. I sat on the edge of the bed and twisted my torso around so we could both see the pictures and I made a silly show of doing the characters' voices.

After long days at Ward 17 South, my son and I would stagger back to Enmore on the train and drink ginger tea with honey. Mac cried a great deal, shedding all the tears he didn't want to load onto Jacob. He talked about the pain inside Gail and his misguided urge to fix her, make her happy. He talked about his guilt—being too acquiescent, letting cruel words go unchallenged—and blaming himself for the predicament Jacob was in.

Mac spent time using the hospital payphones to call people in The Community, trying to send messages to Gail, hoping someone would encourage her to see her son.

I don't know if she received any messages, but Gail never came.

On the sixth day, the medical staff made it clear Jacob did not have much time left. He was as weak as a sickly infant, drifting in and out of delirium. We held him, talked to him, even if we couldn't be sure he could hear us anymore.

At one point I heard Mac say, 'Your mum loves you, Jacob.' I don't know if my son was drawing those words up from genuine belief or whether it was a comforting lie. Either way, I think it was the right call.

On the eighth day we arrived at St Vincent's to learn that Jacob had suffered a seizure during the night. We held his hands, stroked his arms, until he died a few hours later.

Mac handled the cremation and sent word to Gail.

'I've decided—and I don't want to discuss this with you, Mum,' Mac said. 'I'm not going back to Gail or the church. I'm only driving to The Community to deliver the ashes.'

After dropping off Jacob's ashes, Mac bought a kayak and made a solo trip down the Murray River from Yarrawonga to the Coorong. He then travelled to Adelaide to visit the parents of his army mate who had died beside him in the helicopter. Mac told them stories about Vietnam, and he was able to assure them their son had not been in pain in his last moments. That mission completed, my son spent eight years travelling, working in mines, on oil rigs and a stint in Papua New Guinea (he'd been curious about PNG since he was a kid listening to Leo Newman describe the place). Mac passed through Sydney a few times, always with tales to tell. He phoned Rose and me just often enough that we weren't paralysed with worry.

The day after Jacob died, Mac was busy making funeral arrangements while I went back to Ward 17 South to fetch Jacob's small pile of belongings and say thank you to the staff who'd taken such tender care of him.

The friendly bald guy we'd encountered on the first day had introduced himself to me on the second day. Rex Lightfoot was thirty-nine, tall, sturdy, his beard precisely trimmed, his magnificently shaped head waxed and shiny. I'd thought he must be a staff member but it emerged he was a kind person who devoted his time to visiting dying friends and other young men who had few visitors.

'I'm sorry about Jacob,' Rex said. 'He was a very sweet guy.'

'Thank you. He was.'

I was putting the X-Men comics into a carry bag.

'Are you going to chuck those out, Lizzie?' Rex asked. Then he called across to a twenty-something man in the corner bed, 'Denny, you into X-Men?'

'Not really,' he replied. 'But I did get off on hearing Lizzie do the silly voices.'

I'd chatted to Denny a few times when he was awake and Jacob was sleeping.

'How about I read to the end of volume eleven,' I suggested.

'Yeah. We need to know what happens, don't we?'

While I was reading the comic book with Denny, Rex did a supply run downstairs and returned with a carton of vanilla malt milk.

Denny collapsed against the pillows with an exaggerated lustful groan. 'Oh, you know how to drive me wild, Rex. Is it really cold?'

'Icy cold, mate.'

Rex handed me the milk and a straw, so I could hold the carton steady for Denny to drink.

'Oh, you'll need this.' Rex handed me a plastic bowl.

'Sorry?'

Denny started retching and I swung the bowl in place just in time to catch the milky vomit. But a second later, the scrawny young man looked up, grinning.

'Still worth it for the taste when it goes in,' Rex said in a mock-sexy tone.

I gave a salacious laugh and Rex smiled, realising I was a woman who enjoyed a vulgar joke.

I was well behind with work by this point, so on visits to Ward 17 South, I took pen and paper with me. That way I could draft scenes whenever Denny was asleep.

I would not consider my sitting there to be especially laudable behaviour. It seems to me that when any one of us is dying, we deserve someone by our bedside, even if it has to be some random middle-aged lady.

As well as hospital visiting, Rex Lightfoot had thrown himself into work with the Bobby Goldsmith Foundation, a volunteer organisation formed that year, offering meals and other home support to men and women with AIDS.

It was no big deal for me to batch cook food and take portions in foil containers round to Rex's place for him to deliver. I would park outside his apartment in Darlinghurst and he would wave down to me through the picture window of his built-in verandah. It had been converted into a bright sunroom where Rex had a drawing desk for his work as an architectural draftsman. He used to live there with Stephen, his partner of fifteen years. Stephen had been one of the first men to die of AIDS in Sydney.

'Stephen was the funny one, charismatic, the bright light everyone was drawn to,' Rex said to me once. 'I just tagged along.'

'Don't give me that bullshit,' I said, but more tenderly than those words might look on the page. 'You do okay in the charisma department, mister.'

One Saturday, Rex came to my house in Enmore to pick up a batch of meals and the poor man looked so drained, I lured him inside for dinner. That evening was the first time I saw Rex cry, describing the accumulated loss of seeing so many young people waste away, the grief stirred in with his survivor guilt.

After dinner, Rex kicked off his shoes and curled up on the sofa with Chica while I threw together a bread-and-butter pudding. I'd just put the dessert in the oven when I heard Chica snoring in a rumbling duet with Rex. I spread a quilt over him and he slept there until Sunday morning.

It's a wonderful bonus to make a good friend later in life. It's also wise to collect some younger pals—I was fifty-six when I met 39-year-old Rex. My 'young' pals have been something of a buffer against the terrible attrition in my friendship circle that would come later, as I grew proper old.

FIFTEEN

1989.

Most of us have powerful narrative software running in our minds and we like to envisage people's lives falling into a satisfying story arc. Writing television drama, I traded in certain narrative patterns—either delivering them or subverting them for dramatic effect. We yearn to see virtue rewarded and for wicked people to get their comeuppance. It's obvious things rarely work that way in real life. Uncle Gil—the vile man who abused my sister Josie and other children—won two hundred and fifty thousand pounds in the football pools in 1960, then lived in Marbella in robust health until his nineties. Bunny Shaw-Preston was awarded an Order of Australia for 'services to women's causes'.

We're always on the lookout for story reversals, 'rags to riches', 'riches to rags' and such. In a TV series, if a character is too happy for too long, the audience expects a truck or a cancer diagnosis to come screeching around the corner to wallop them. In reality, there's no reason to expect notable reversals of fortune. A person loaded up with problems, discrimination, poverty and ill health, often staggers under the weight of that into further hardship. And happy, blessed people tend to accumulate more blessings (leaving aside the inevitable final plot point of death).

One narrative trope I remember calling up in the plotting room was this: what is the worst thing that could happen to our character and how could that turn out to be the best thing in the end? Such a storyline would be turbulent, often terrifying for the character herself and for the people around her, but hopefully satisfying for an audience.

In the second half of 1989, my life was filled up, no room for air bubbles.

My work was intense and satisfying. I'd just successfully pitched an original TV project, written its pilot episode, received the series go-ahead from a network, and persuaded some wonderful colleagues to help develop scripts.

At sixty-one, eleven years single, I found myself in a new committed relationship. Eric Huxtable and I had been involved for nine months and we figured it was time to cohabit. The plan was that I would move out of my rented Enmore place into his Glebe house by Christmas. (More about Eric shortly.)

I still found enough time to prepare meals for people living with AIDS, and no matter how busy my week, time with my two grandchildren was important. On Sundays and during school breaks, the three of us would cook together, go to the beach or to whatever family gathering was on. I tried to keep special time for each one separately—so I could indulge five-year-old Van's obsession with the fish market or take ten-year-old Mai to more grown-up movies.

If my flywheel was spinning fast, I suspect I was propelled by an unhealthy urgency to make up for lost time. The world shared my sense of urgency in 1989. The Tiananmen Square massacre, a fatwa on Salman Rushdie, Yugoslavia splitting apart, first sightings of what became the internet, a Colombian passenger plane bombed by Pablo Escobar, and then in early November, the unimaginable dismantling of the Berlin Wall. The planet was surely spinning faster.

September 1989.

It was just as well Rose broke the news by phone. She'd been offered a two-year paediatric fellowship in the UK. She, Vuong, Mai and Van would be leaving for Bristol in two weeks. Hearing this over the phone, I was able to scrunch my face up tight so I wouldn't screech or sob or emit any sound that might make my daughter feel anything but excited about a wonderful opportunity.

I gathered myself enough to say what I ought to say—I was so proud of her, what a brilliant experience for the whole family, and so forth.

But then Rose said, 'The kids will really miss you, Mum. But you'll be too busy to miss us. Two years will go really fast.'

I don't know if my daughter believed that or just wished to believe it. But because I wanted her to go off on this adventure without worrying about her needy mother, I colluded with her in the fiction.

'I'll miss you all like crazy, but I'll be okay,' I said in a perform-ance worthy of an acting nomination. 'Eric and I have been talking about doing a trip early next year. We'll visit you.'

Once the call was over, I allowed myself a proper self-pitying weep. And after they'd flown away, I met up for dinner every week with Vuong's mother Thuy so we two could rabbit on endlessly about our grandchildren without boring others.

28 November 1989.

Arriving at the DBB Productions office, I was revved up. The writing team and I were pushing to have the scripts ready for the start of pre-production. I'd been experiencing a fluttery agitation in my chest. It was hard to identify if the sensation was fear or the thrill that a TV series I'd devised was about to start filming.

The reader may be puzzled that I'd chosen to develop my show with the unctuous Carson Bull. The best explanation I can offer is that the man had a knack for getting shows up with networks and I saw him as the devil I knew.

Franklin was pitched as a series about 55-year-old police detective, Vivien Franklin, a smart, earthy woman. Carson had negotiated a deal with a well-loved actor to play Vivien and that casting had helped slide the show over the line towards production.

Murder cases investigated by Detective Franklin would play out within an episode or two, but there was a long-term mystery nagging at Vivien over all thirteen episodes. The show also dug into her personal life as a divorcee with two adult daughters—one a Crown prosecutor, the other a struggling heroin addict.

An older woman being at the centre of a drama may not seem radical now, but in 1989 it was not an easy sell. I had managed to convince Carson that Vivien Franklin should occasionally date and have sex with men, even if the network execs did not consider a fifty-something woman to be, in their words, 'fuckable'.

That afternoon, Carson flinched when I walked into his office.

'Just so you know, Liz, it wasn't my decision.'

I saw him flick his greasy little eyeballs to meet the gaze of someone standing in the corridor just outside the office. I spun round to see it was Murray Armfield, my acerbic colleague from *The Squad*. The instant I clocked him, he scurried away like the rodent he was. Then the nausea hit me—knowing this was bad even if I didn't understand the nature of the badness yet.

'The network wants some changes,' said Carson.

'Significant ones?'

'I reckon you'll think they're significant. The network bods are worried the Vivien character isn't likeable enough—y'know, a failed mother with a druggie daughter. And they think the murder stories play better with a male cop.'

'Did you point out to them there are several male cops in the—'

'They want to switch the lead to a man.'

'Sorry? What?'

'It turns out a certain actor—well, this is meant to be a secret, but I'll tell you, it's Steve Yates. Audiences love Steve Yates. A show they were developing for him fell over and Steve's been talking to a writer, a mate of his, about doing something together.'

'Murray Armfield.'

Carson swayed his head and then nodded. 'Let me just say again, Liz, none of this is my decision.'

'No, no, it's never your fucking decision, is it.'

I was angry with myself for not remembering what sort of creature Carson Bull was, for not realising he might sell out my project for the sake of lubricating his passage even a tiny bit. If that last phrase sounds disgusting—good. Carson's behaviour was disgusting.

'Just so you know,' he said, 'Steve will play Detective Gary Franklin now. And Murray pitched it as a straight murder-of-the-week format and no personal life storylines. The network preferred that.'

'So, in fact the only vestige from our scripts is the surname of the main character?'

Carson had enough self-awareness to wince as he nodded at me.

'That means Murray is starting from scratch,' I said. 'We were supposed to go into pre-production in two weeks so how—'

'Well, as it happens, Murray and Steve have been working on their scripts for some time and they're ready to go.'

'Wait—what? This plan's been in the works for ages?'

Carson put his hands up as if afraid I might thump him. 'Look, Liz, nothing was definite. The network guys were hedging their bets and then they made the call. I had—'

'Let me get this straight: you manoeuvred behind my back—letting me and my writers work our guts out . . . but the whole time, you guys were sliming around secretly and now you've commandeered the budget and the crew we put together—you're hijacking the production apparatus of my series and inserting Murray and Steve's big-dick male show into it?'

'Well, I wouldn't put it—'

'Oh, you wouldn't put it that way, Carson? You snivelling piece of shit.'

If any reader happened to see Murray's show in mid-1990 before it was pulled off primetime, they would likely agree that my prediction was accurate. Steve Yates played the detective with blustery arrogance. Countless women's naked bodies were displayed either on autopsy slabs or strip club stages, with a carnival of gender and ethnic stereotypes. The main character was a 'ladies' man' and it was especially galling to see that the two actresses we had cast to play Vivien's complex adult daughter characters ended up playing Steve's sexual conquests, women with no detectable characteristics other than female bodies.

'Sorry, Liz,' said Carson. 'This probably isn't the outcome you—'

'Shut up, Carson. Shut up before all that oily bullshit in your mouth oozes out and makes a mess of your desk.'

I did an angry walk-out through the office. I was genuinely furious, but to be honest, I executed the outraged exit mostly as a ploy to avoid bursting into tears in front of the DBB staff. A 61-year-old woman weeping over a defunct script was not the dignified look I would aim for.

I made it to the fire stairs before I lost it. Some of my tears were guilty—I'd let down the writers who'd worked hard to develop the show with me. Some sprang from anger at myself for being gullible enough to be betrayed by a known betrayer, by an oleaginous worm of a man. I'd been naïve enough to feel hopeful about a process that wasn't renowned for its integrity. And some of my weeping was grief for the characters I'd conjured and loved, characters who would now never exist and whom an audience would never meet.

I'd managed the majority of my adult life as a single person. I'd nursed the image of myself as a doggedly self-reliant woman. But that day, driving back over the Harbour Bridge, I was relieved I had someone now, my person in the world.

I hadn't been looking for a partner when I met Eric Huxtable. I'd gone looking for a criminal defence barrister to research story material for a television series and Eric's name was on the list. He was generous with his time, meeting with me at his chambers on several afternoons. The two of us yabbered on together in a way that felt easy but invigorating. I liked his cleverness. I liked that his agile mind was able to find story solutions for my TV drama purposes. I liked that we shared common ground—we were about the same age, with adult kids and living alone (he was divorced), both of us focused on our work and not planning to roll downhill into retirement any time soon.

After one of our gabfests, Eric asked me out for dinner. 'I'd like it to be a date, Liz, but if you don't fancy that, I'd be happy if we just keep talking about TV plots.'

I was surprised, having observed that a lot of men in their fifties and sixties went for younger women, and it was flattering to be seen as a romantic option. There were four dinners before we had sex (which was good) and after that we fell into a relaxed and pleasing pattern: dinner or movies or weekends away when it suited our work schedules, but never any pressure from either party.

I had my own friends—Athena and Patty, Pearl, Rex, Diego, my writing pal Donna, and others—and Eric would go on weekend trips with his rugby mates to watch interstate games, leaving me free to do my own stuff.

It's hard to define the bond that holds a couple together. Eric and I both enjoyed the sex, the conversation and companionship, the many things that are tacitly understood when two people have lived on the earth for a while. At a certain age, each of us has a crust of habits and intolerances and preferences, so it's a wonderful thing to share space without giving each other the royal shits.

In September, Eric had said to me, 'I really want you to move in here, Liz.'

It made sense. I slept over at his spacious Glebe terrace many nights of the week anyway. Still, I was wary of giving up my own home, and I'd put off the move, with the excuse that the TV series would soak up my time. But there was no reason to delay anymore.

On the way back from Carson Bull's office to my house, I was driving too fast and changing gears too brutally. I kept the injection of angry fuel going as I pulled clothes out of my wardrobe, shoved them into bags and hoisted them onto the back seat of my car, the first load of my belongings to take round to Eric's house.

I would cancel the lease on the Enmore place and finally give myself fully to our relationship. I would finally have a proper life partner. As always with me, it felt good to know I'd been chosen by someone.

Eric's Glebe terrace had a dog-friendly rear garden. My lovely terrier Chica had died a year before, and Eric was up for getting a new dog together. The plan was for the two of us to do some travelling during the 1990 European summer and then find a puppy on our return.

When I saw Eric's briefcase under the hall table—he was supposed to be in court—I was relieved. I could blurt out the full ugly story about the show and rely on Eric to listen, then offer analysis that would be prudent but sympathetic.

'Eric? You upstairs or down?'

I then realised why he hadn't heard me dump my bags in the hallway—the shower was running—so I carried one load of clothing up the stairs to chuck in the wardrobe space.

On the landing, I heard the sounds of a man and a woman having sex in the bathroom, their noises muffled by the running water, but still bouncing off the tiled surfaces enough to be audible, with the woman especially vocal and enthusiastic. I was frozen outside the bathroom for several excruciating moments. Then there was a male groan that was undeniably the timbre of Eric's sexual grunting.

In those few seconds, a pile of loose details and observations assembled in my mind into the piercing realisation that he'd been cheating on me with this woman and probably others. Inklings I'd disregarded suddenly felt like certainties. Extra days added on to interstate rugby trips, hang-up phone calls, discrepancies in his stories, even the embarrassing cliché of other women's perfumes lingering on his clothes. It was astonishing how obvious it was once I shook the stray pieces into a different pattern.

I hauled my bags back downstairs and slammed the heel of my hand against the buttons on the home security unit by the front door. The whoop of the alarm tore through the house in a satisfying, frenzied way.

Eric rushed down the stairs with a towel wrapped around his waist. He was in pretty good shape for sixty-two, with just a bit of a belly. I could see the outline of his erect penis pushing against the towel. By then, the alarm was slicing through my head so I switched it off.

'I can't believe this,' I said.

'Sorry.'

'It's like someone punched me in the guts.'

'Sorry. I . . . well . . . sorry—uh—'

'Say "sorry" again and I'll shove the word right up the tiny hole in your penis. Is it someone I know in there?'

'Paola.'

She was one of the paralegals. She was twenty-five. Younger than Eric's daughter.

'Are you aiming to humiliate me?' I was surprised how controlled my voice sounded. 'Is that your plan?'

'Plan? No. Uh—no.'

'Can you speak to me like a highly evolved primate?'

'What? Uh—oh—Jesus . . .'

'Try speaking in sentences with verbs in them,' I suggested. 'Verbs are doing words like cheat and betray and destroy.'

'I don't know what to say. Shit . . .'

His mouth formed to say 'sorry' again but then he stopped himself and just stood there, fifty per cent tumescent.

I gulped a breath, rapidly losing whatever composure I'd managed. At that point Eric seemed to regain his.

'Look, Liz, actually I've been—'

'"Actually"? You're mid-fuck with some woman and you're using the word "actually" at me?'

'The fact is, this is something I've been wanting to discuss with you,' he said, strapping on his barrister voice. 'You're always so busy and you'd have to agree that a lot of your emotional space is taken up by other people, rather than me. I have emotional needs that you can't always—'

'Emotional needs you can only fill by sticking your penis in 25-year-old office staff?'

'Okay, Liz. You're upset. Maybe now isn't the time to—'

'Now is not the time for me to listen to your bullshit. Maybe the best time is—hang on, let me check my very busy calendar. It's never.'

Two seconds later I was out the door and out of Eric Huxtable's life.

I've dealt with this major relationship very briefly. Maybe that's because it's a source of embarrassment—that I was fooled by him and deluded myself I could have all the benefits of a full relationship without being fully in it. (Which is not to excuse Eric's lying and infidelity.) I don't want to be disingenuous and imply the breakup wasn't painful. But now, nearly forty years on, the experience doesn't land very high up on the list of important things in my life. Which says something about how little I'd invested in it.

I drove my carload of clothes back to Enmore. Ordinarily I would've gone straight round to Athena and Patty's place to weep and swear, but those two had flown out the week before to spend time on the tiny Greek island of Kastellorizo, Athena's childhood home.

The show falling apart, then Eric—a punch to one side of my head, then the other—left no chance to regain my balance in between. With Rose and Athena away, I lacked my usual supports. If the timing had been different, I might have blazed my way through professional betrayal and sexual infidelity using cranked-up anger. I might have been fine. But really my disintegration was a long time in the making, the chemicals already lodged in my innards ready to be activated.

I lay in bed, with spells of crying and spells of staring at the wall. From the hallway, I heard the phone ringing and the vague sound of people leaving messages. I heard Donna and the other bereft writers, but it was mostly Rex. I could picture myself getting out of bed to talk to Rex. I mentally rehearsed walking to the hallway, but my limbs would not work, as if the neurological connection had been severed.

While my body was immobile, my mind was gyrating, hypermobile, scrabbling to gather up every bit of pain and press it into myself. The killing of my television project was proof I'd been kidding myself I had any talent. My ten-year writing career had been an accident, the result of me being a certain kind of person who suited others' purposes, rather than a person of real capacity. I conjured up scenes of colleagues whispering to each other—'Jesus, look at that ridiculous woman. Does some uneducated old lady think she's a proper writer? It's laughable but also kind of sad.'

As for the Eric mess, there was a well-oiled neural pathway directly to the awareness that I was unlovable. I always had been unworthy of love, which explained why I'd never managed a long-term relationship.

I then scrolled further back in my mental files, back years and years, to find every time I'd hurt someone, every ugly thing I'd done or thought. I was diligent—careful not to miss a single loathsome logbook entry. And I worked hard to convert any good things in my story into toxic substances, as if I were suffering from one of those autoimmune disorders in which your own tissues turn hostile against your body. The volunteer work I'd done was sanctimonious and inadequate. I'd been selfish and judgemental with my friends. I wanted so much to be a good mother, but Mac was lost and unhappy, and anything positive in Rose's life had come from her own efforts and judgement, despite me. I even found a way to transform the memory of being loved by my brother Michael into a toxin, telling myself that if he had known the person I became, a woman who gave away her baby, he would've been repulsed by me. Which should have come as no surprise to anyone—even as a tiny child I'd been so vile my own mother couldn't love me. All the losses, all the shaming moments stored in my cells were reactivated in a massive surge that defeated my usual strategies of distraction and soldiering on, leaving me paralysed on the bed. Even when I had the urge to urinate, I couldn't get up, and the shame of the wet sheets was then added to the list. Offered a choice, I would rather have decomposed into a gelatinous mess on the mattress than face another moment of the pounding awareness of my disgusting self. There will be readers who know from experience what I'm trying to describe, some who can do a fair job of imagining, and others for whom it's an alien concept.

I'd been lying in bed for twenty-four hours when Rex Lightfoot gave up on ringing me and instead drove to my place and let himself in with the key hidden in the backyard.

'Oh, Lizzie. Oh, darling heart.'

I'm tearful now, all these years later, to recall the kindness in my friend's voice.

'Let's get you in the shower.'

Rex lifted me up and gently took off my clothes. I wasn't limp like a rag doll—I was able to pull my arms out of my sleeves, stand up and walk to the bathroom—but I was still feeble enough to need Rex's help. He got the water running and made sure I was steady in the shower recess before he went back to strip the sheets off the bed.

When I emerged from the bathroom with a towel wrapped around me, Rex could see that the task of choosing clothing was beyond me. He rummaged in a bag I'd brought back from Eric's and found a bra, undies, trackpants and a T-shirt. That beautiful man, Rex Lightfoot, knew how to dry a fragile person's body with a towel, then ease them into clothing, with as little awkwardness and as much dignity as possible. This was a skill he'd developed for the saddest of reasons.

Rex was well acquainted with St John of God, a small psychiatric hospital in Burwood, because back in 1983 it had been one of the few places that accepted AIDS patients. As mentioned earlier, not all religious organisations are totally destructive.

When I was first admitted at St John of God, the doctors tried me on tricyclic anti-depressants (this was in the days before SSRIs like Prozac) but I developed an allergic skin reaction within days. By then, the main shrink had decided I might manage without drugs anyway. I was an inpatient for two weeks, doing a bit of talk therapy but mostly just resting, taking a break from the bruising world.

I asked Rex not to tell anyone I was in hospital. Athena and Patty should enjoy their holiday without unnecessary worry, and it would only upset Pearl to visit me. I avoided phone calls with Rose for as long as I could before she would likely grow suspicious. I finally called her from the hospital office, explaining I'd been unwell but was on the mend. Once I was discharged and home again, I allowed Pearl to visit, if only to ease the burden on Rex. I recall it as a sweet time, with Pearl enjoying being the one doing the caring for a change.

Released back into the world, I found a psychologist—an unsentimental but soulful woman. It was as if the air in her snug consulting room was charged with different ions, because in those early weeks, when I sat on her green client chair and told stories about my life—stories I'd been telling myself and close friends for years, stories I've told here—I would suddenly be undone and weep inconsolably, no longer protected by the familiar wording and narrative shell in which I'd kept those experiences encased. I hoped the process might empty the pain out of past wounds (like draining cysts), but I don't think it works like that. Still, part of me could watch myself on the green chair speechless with grief about my distant mother or dead sister or abandoned baby or abusive husband, and I was able to pity that woman as I would a friend or a stranger.

The therapist urged me to address my younger self—that distressed, sometimes angry creature who had only a child's comprehension of events—as I would have spoken to my kids at the same age. That proved to be a startling and useful mental exercise. I'd been far from a perfect parent, but I was certainly more loving and patient with Mac and Rose, never so harsh or shaming as I had been with myself. I would never have exhorted them to strap up their injuries and get on with it.

I saw that psychologist on and off for the next decade. I won't go into more details. Hearing about someone else's therapy is as tedious as listening to a blow-by-blow account of a person's dreams. Let me say that it's my belief we should all find a good psychologist at some point in our lives, if only for the sake of loved ones who have to endure our damage.

February 1990.

Bristol was not a city I'd ever visited when I lived in the UK, but after three weeks staying there with Rose, Vuong, Mai and Van, I could've drawn a pretty accurate map of the place. During the day, while the kids were at school, Rose at the hospital, Vuong at work (as a high school science teacher), I would go walking around the city streets. Almost three months after my collapse, I was still moving gingerly in the world.

In 1990, England seemed to have sunk into one of its morose troughs—the Swinging Sixties well over and the buoyancy of Cool Britannia still several years off—many people's spirits beaten down by recession, the miners' strike, and ten years of Margaret Thatcher.

I'd never considered myself as someone who suffered depression. I would barge through low moods by making myself busy and when the kids were little, I could wait until they were asleep to have a weep about whichever misery was circulating in me. And living alone for much of the last twenty years, it was easy to withdraw from the world, curled up in bed where no one else need look at my wretched carcass. I'd just never called it depression until now. Wandering around Bristol every day for three weeks, these were the revisions of my own story I was doing.

One Saturday night after dinner, I noticed Mai throw looks to her mother, seeking permission. Rose nodded and Mai scampered across the room to the stereo.

My granddaughter had inherited my daughter's love of Elvis, but she'd also recently discovered Chaka Khan, Madonna, Blondie, Gloria Estefan and Cyndi Lauper. When 'Girls Just Wanna Have Fun' came on—loudly—there was no way I could resist Mai's invitation to join her on the loungeroom dancefloor. I realised how long it had been since I'd let my body have that simple pleasure. Mai played DJ with a series of tracks, then she fetched spoons to use as microphones so we could all lip-sync to Cher's 'If I Could Turn Back Time'.

23 February 1990.

At 3 a.m., when the phone rang, Rose and I were the only people in the sleeping household to hear it. My daughter, always on alert for an emergency at the hospital, galloped to the hall phone before I was halfway down the stairs.

I heard Rose say, 'No, no, it's okay, Auntie Pearl. Oh, here's Mum. I'll put her on. Lots of love.'

As Rose handed me the receiver, I squeezed her arm and mouthed 'sorry'. Pearl had rung in the middle of the night twice before because she'd mixed up the time difference.

'Is it late there, Betty? Have I been daft about the time again?'

'Don't worry, lovely. How are you?'

'Well, I'm good but I'm scared you're going to be mardy with me . . .'

'Ah. What have you done, Pearl?'

'Leo Newman called. Me and him chat on the phone sometimes. Anyhow, last week we were gabbing and he asked about you.'

'Right . . .'

'There's a chance I might've mentioned you had a breakdown.'

The cold wash of shame through my body was instantaneous, and my tone with Pearl was brisk. 'There's a *chance* you did, or you definitely did?'

'I did say it. I'm sorry, Betty. I knew you'd be cross. I'm sorry.'

'Bloody hell, Pearl.'

Pearl started babbling, filling the space with words so I couldn't rouse on her. 'Anyhow, today a letter arrived—well, a little card he wrote to me with an envelope addressed to you. Should I post it to you or open it and read it to you now or . . . well, I don't know what the "or" could be. Or put it in the bin, I suppose.'

'Read it to me.'

I heard Pearl tear open the envelope, alongside a stream of apologies about her big mouth.

She put on an oddly formal voice to read the letter aloud. '*Dear Liz, I do remember you asked me never to contact you, but I'm taking the liberty of writing, hoping you won't mind too much. Pearl mentioned you've been through a difficult time. I hope it's not too upsetting that she passed on this information—*'

Pearl interrupted to speak in her own voice, 'Please say you aren't horribly angry with me, Betty.'

'It's okay. Keep reading.'

'Thank you. Sorry. Yes. So, Leo says, *I wanted to write to let you know what a wonderful person I've always thought you to be, as well as to thank you for the bracing advice you gave me some years ago. Since then, following your advice, I've made valuable changes in my life.*' Pearl interjected again, 'It's true, you know, Betty. I didn't really understand it all until now.'

Pearl went on to read Leo's precis of his last fourteen years: he'd finally extricated himself from his wife and left his corporate job to take up work in immigration law, including some pro bono refugee cases. In 1984, seeing the *Women's Weekly* article about me, he'd felt tempted to make contact, but then figured I was happily busy with my life and wouldn't welcome 'botherance' from him. Soon afterwards, his daughter Ava went through one of her tough times (an eating disorder) and that became his focus.

Pearl made little surprised noises as she read the next part. '*I finally took myself for some psychotherapy—as you always suggested. I have found the process both helpful and fascinating. I've often been gripped by a strong urge to discuss it with you, more than anyone. I was tempted to write to you last year, but Pearl mentioned you were in a serious relationship, so I decided I should leave you be.*'

In recent months, Leo had been travelling, partly to visit his son David, a violinist in Berlin, and partly to conduct some research into his family.

Pearl became a little teary as she read the next bit. '*A month ago, I found a cousin living in Zurich. This discovery has had a more profound effect on me than I expected. Apart from my children, I have one living relative and possibly others. I realised you were the one person with whom I most wanted to share this news.*'

It was at this point that Pearl was so overcome, I couldn't understand the words she was trying to read between her hiccupping sobs.

'Take deep breaths, Pearl,' I said. 'How about we both go and make ourselves a cuppa and I'll ring you back in ten minutes. This call must be costing you a fortune.'

I don't know how I found the composure to handle this moment. In scriptwriting, I used to avoid having characters display too much in the way of weepy histrionics on screen so there would be space left for the audience to feel the moment in their own bodies. Maybe because Pearl was expressing so much emotion about Leo's letter, using up all the oxygen, there was no room for me to feel overcome by it. Having said that, as I made myself a cup of tea, my hands were trembling.

When I called Pearl back ten minutes later, she did her best to hold it together as she continued reading Leo's letter: '*I hate to think that you've been through a dark time, Liz, and that perhaps you haven't realised how beloved you are. That thought was unbearable to me, so I decided to break my promise and contact you. As I'm in Berlin at the moment, I must make do with writing rather than saying this in person. Perhaps that's just as well, because it leaves you free to ignore or discard this letter. The main thing I want to say is that since meeting you on the* Asturias, *I've never doubted that you are a person who deserves to be cherished so very much.*'

Leo's letter then listed what he saw as my precious qualities. The wording he used was generous but also specific enough to me that the compliments landed powerfully, as opposed to generalised fawning words that would've glanced off me.

By this stage, Pearl was weeping again, incoherent, so it took a while for her to relay the last part of the letter.

'*So there it is, Betty, Beth, Elizabeth, Liz. I have always loved you and I will never stop doing so. It's one of my greatest regrets that circumstance and my own poor decisions meant I could never offer you the love you deserve. I offer it now, for what that's worth. If this gushy letter has been unwelcome, I promise to stay out of your way from now on. I wish you all the good things in life. Yours always, Leo.*'

25 February 1990.

I was aware of the existence of family resemblance, but when David Newman opened the door to his Berlin apartment, he looked so much like Leo as a young man, I made a strangulated squeak which gave David a strange first impression of me. Despite my peculiar noise, he invited me into the small flat he shared with another orchestral musician. While he made coffee, David explained that Leo had left Berlin the week before, heading for Dresden. Since the collapse of the Wall, it was becoming easier to research family history in East Germany.

26 February 1990.

I would recommend Dresden as a surprisingly worthwhile travel destination. It's not a place that's puffed up with the smugness of longtime favourites like Rome and Paris, but it has many charming old buildings, pleasingly weird museums, and since reunification, has grown into a gracious city with the kind of hip art scene that sprouted in Germany in those decades. In 1990, Dresden was fascinating more than beautiful. There were a few splendid buildings that had survived the incendiary bombing by the British in 1945 which killed tens of thousands of civilians. In the many places where buildings had been obliterated, the spaces were filled either with stern Soviet architecture or piles of rubble left as a forty-year memorial. Other bombed patches had been converted into parks, giving the city an unintentionally modern feel.

David Newman had told me the name of the hotel in which his father was staying, and I walked straight there from the railway station.

Hotel Bilderberg Bellevue, on the bank of the Elbe River, was housed in a central baroque building which had survived the war, with modern additions clustered around it. In recent years it had served as a hotel for western visitors and as the meeting place for some of the reunification negotiations between West German Chancellor Kohl and GDR Prime Minister Modrow.

I was so chuffed with myself for finding the way from the station to the hotel that the doubts only struck once I stepped inside the grand foyer. My plan to show up unannounced suddenly felt like a silly adolescent notion, akin to an emotional ambush. I formed a new plan to find a cheap hotel, then phone Leo from there, but as I wheeled my suitcase around to go, a lift door opened and Leo Newman stepped out.

'Hello. There you are,' he said with surprisingly little surprise, as if I'd just appeared a few minutes early for an appointment.

If a reader was hoping for a passionate clinch, that did not happen.

'Are you on your way somewhere?' I asked. 'I don't want to interfere with any plans you—'

'No, no, I don't have anything more important to do—I mean, talking to you is more important than any—uh . . . Shall we go for a walk?'

I nodded and Leo left my suitcase with the hotel's front desk.

We went walking along the Elbe River and across the Augustus Bridge, chatting about anodyne topics—my train journey, the sights we were passing. On the other side of the river, we were confronted by the ruins of the Frauenkirche—the grand, domed, baroque eighteenth-century church that survived the 1945 bombing, then two days later collapsed, destroyed from the inside by the fire. In 1990, there were only a couple of broken chunks of wall standing up like burnt-out tree trunks looming over a massive pile of rubble. In recent months, Helmut Kohl had chosen these ruins as the background scenery for a speech about German reunification. In the mid-1990s, a project would begin to reconstruct the Frauenkirche, using as much of the original masonry as possible and incorporating a gold cross donated by the British who had bombed the city.

I asked Leo how it was for a bereaved Jewish man to contemplate the wartime suffering of the German people. He responded calmly about his paradoxical mixture of feelings—anger on behalf of his family, sometimes even a vengeful sense of gratification that the German population had suffered, but alongside all of that was sorrow for the anguish of any fellow humans. He was quick to point out that his more compassionate feelings did not cancel out the harsher ones—they all lived together in his head, suspended in the same cerebral fluid.

We stood for a long time staring at the blackened, jumbled stone blocks. In the face of large-scale misery and grand sweeps of history, it seemed petty to discuss the small situation facing the two of us.

But eventually I shoved my qualms aside and said, 'It doesn't feel so great for my dignity that you declared your love because I had a breakdown.'

'What? No, that's not why I declared my—'

'You must admit the timing is—'

'Okay, I understand why it might seem—but the truth of what I wrote has nothing to do with—with—oh . . .' Leo opened and closed his mouth a couple of times, anxious not to say the wrong thing and muck this, the way the two of us always seemed to do. 'Look, Liz, if I offended you, made things worse, I'm sorry and I can—well, I can—'

'You can what?' I asked. 'Disappear again and pop up in another fourteen years? You and I don't have the life expectancy for such shenanigans anymore. We're too old.'

'We are.'

'That's why I've decided not to be embarrassed about the timing,' I said.

'I'm very happy you've decided that. There's no need.'

'And I've decided not to let my dignity get in the way of us giving this a crack.'

Again, the reader should not expect a bout of pashing in front of the Frauenkirche ruins, with the damage/repair symbolism so thick, as if laid on with a trowel by a heavy-handed plasterer. In fact, Leo and I did not touch at all in that moment—there was just too much intensity to absorb right then. Instead, we wandered round the city, talking. At a busy intersection, Leo took my hand and we continued holding hands from then on. We found a place to eat lunch, during which, yes, there was a fair bit of romantic staring across the table into each other's eyes. After lunch, we went back to his hotel to consummate our new relationship.

We stayed a few more days in Dresden so Leo could finish his document searches there, then drove to Leipzig for a tour of Leopold Neumann's childhood, investigating places he remembered—some completely gone or utterly changed, but some so vividly the same as they were in 1939 that Leo would be overcome, shaking or weeping or laughing.

When he spoke German with locals we encountered, it was startling to think of his childhood language having lived in his head all these years and the strange potency of him using it again. And it was sobering to think there were memories and knowledge inside my beloved that I would never share or fully understand.

We spent time with Leo's lovely son David in Berlin and then had two indulgent weeks in Paris—a time we came to see as our honeymoon. Across the Channel, we embarked on the Tour of Elizabeth Rankin's Childhood including Deptford, Cornwall and an uproarious week in Liverpool with Brenda Goodbody. It was in Liverpool that I finally told him about the baby I'd allowed to be taken from me when I was seventeen. We even drove through Medford and past the Buckinghamshire house where I'd last laid eyes on my elder daughter. (The Georgian house had been converted into a nursing home in the years since.) It was emotionally taxing to share this with him, as the reader might imagine, but liberating too.

Leo and I finally curled our way back round to Bristol to stay with Rose, Vuong and the kids. Rose was watchful with Leo at first— checking that this man would be a good thing in my life. When I say 'at first', the truth is my daughter's protective caution lasted all of twenty-four hours. She'd loved Leo when she met him as a seven-year-old in 1959 and she loved him now.

Much like my son Mac, Leo was quiet and never pushy with children, interested, but allowing them to come to him. It did not take Van long to decide Leo was good value. Mai was standoffish until the second week when she started bringing Leo examples of her schoolwork of which she was especially proud. He gave her writing his full attention, praising her with thoughtful comments and no skerrick of condescension. As Leo was reading one of her compositions, Mai watched his face intently. It struck me that those kids had their grandmother Thuy and me, but no grandfather figure. Mai filled the position by anointing Leo as Grandpa Leo and she remained devoted to him from them on.

Wishing to make some new joint memories, Leo and I figured we should go to a place neither of us had been. During our weeks travelling in Spain, my frayed Spanish gradually came back to me in a useful way. Leo claimed that the sight of me speaking Spanish was irresistibly attractive. Seeking more opportunities for Leo to be aroused by my language skills, I suggested a flight to Mexico City. We stayed in the Condesa house with Diego, Valeria and Luz, before I dragged Leo around Mexico.

In Yucatan, at one of my favourite cenotes, the wooden steps down to the swimming pontoon were wet and a little slippery. Leo reached his hand back to hold mine so neither of us would fall. Once we slid into the pool, our bodies were held up by the sweet water and both of us were making jokey exaggerated gasps of delight. Then the cloud cover suddenly shifted and the sun shone down into the limestone cavern, sending a bright shaft of light through the water, illuminating the rock formations and fish and turtles, while our pale human legs paddled around.

'So lovely,' said Leo.

I nodded.

'You,' he said. 'I meant you're so lovely.'

'I know you meant that,' I said and wrapped my legs around his waist.

October 1990.

We had just arrived in Buenos Aires when I found the lump in my left breast. Back in Sydney a week later, tests confirmed it was malignant.

Apart from the straight-out shittiness of cancer, I had to fight my television-writer urge to see this turn of events in narrative terms—a character paying the price for being too damned happy. I'd taken the foolish risk of thinking that I was worthy of being loved by a wonderful man, so now my body had punished me with a malevolent tumour. Obviously, I knew that was superstitious nonsense. How I loathe that cruel 'law of attraction' rubbish. No, the diagnosis was not a narrative beat. It was just the crappy luck of random cell mutation which required a single mastectomy and chemotherapy.

Let me assure the reader that, even though this section has ended on a downbeat note, I can offer a period of major happiness coming up.

SIXTEEN

September 1991.

In many oncology clinics, a bell is rung when someone finishes their chemo. There was no such tradition in my time, but the other patients' graduation moments still landed loudly in my head. I had developed a chatting relationship with other women without eyebrows, as we all sat in flowery upholstered recliners having toxic chemicals pumped into our bodies. At some sessions, one of the women would stand up after her last round and wish the rest of us good luck, always kindly, sometimes blushing a little, not wanting to appear exultant in front of others still mired in it. I drew comfort from those goodbyes—to have a preview of the end. On the day my treatment finished, the finale was marked not by a ringing bell but by the arrival of Sheila.

During the chemo period, whenever I was up to it, Leo and I had gone on walks around our new Leichhardt neighbourhood and would often talk with a man about his blue heeler cattle dog. There was something about the sturdy, smart heeler that was particularly appealing.

When Leo escorted me outside after my final chemotherapy session, there was Athena waiting by the car holding a nine-week-old female blue heeler. Leo had chosen this puppy from the litter because her colouring—mottled blue with patches of caramel and a black face mask—resembled the dog I'd admired in the street. We decided to keep the name she came with: Sheila.

The value of the gift hit me when we arrived home. On our return to Australia, Leo had sold his Brisbane apartment to buy us a small house in Leichhardt. I liked our new place—it was a gracious Federation, surprisingly large for a semi, with a spare bedroom for visitors, a good kitchen that opened to a bright backyard, and it was near streets with a decent amount of life. The trouble for me was that our entire time in that house had been during my cancer treatment, so the place was suffused with a medical aftertaste. The minute we carried Sheila through the front door, I listened to her paws skitter across the floorboards, watched her sniff her way through the rooms, and my relationship to the house shifted in just the right way.

From the moment I found the breast lump, I must have said sorry to Leo Newman twenty times, thirty times, possibly more, apologising for sprouting a cancer just as we'd finally found each other. Nursing someone through a serious illness was hardly the picturesque, autumnal romance he had reason to expect. He argued that, while he hated that I was going through this, he was happier than he'd ever been in his life. Leo was persuasive enough that I eventually believed him. I was very fortunate.

October 1991.

To celebrate the end of chemo, Leo suggested we book a dog-friendly holiday house to share with Athena and Patty for a week. I was surprised when Athena suggested we go to Narrawallee—she'd not been back since Nick died on the beach track there—but she said it would feel good to reclaim that beautiful place.

The four of us spent the first part of the week going for long walks, watching Sheila lollop along the beach, taking quick cold dips in the ocean, reading, napping, watching movies. Leo and Patty made supply runs to Ulladulla based on a menu Athena and I devised together. Cooking with my dear friend, sharing the tasks, checking the flavours, gauging the timings, the two of us moving around the small kitchen space with wordless cooperation was deeply pleasurable to me.

My television writer pal Donna Silvestri had met Rex Lightfoot at my place over the years and they'd formed a separate friendship of their own. Those two decided to share the driving to Narrawallee and join us for the long weekend.

When they arrived, Rex dumped a load of groceries on the kitchen bench of the holiday house and enfolded me against his massive chest in a hug.

'Go easy, Rex,' Donna said. 'Don't break Lizzie's ribs.'

Rex released his grizzly bear embrace, and instead, knelt down to kiss my hand. Then he headed off to fetch more stuff from the car while Donna unpacked the gastronomic treats they were contributing to the weekend. She asked me a dozen questions about my health, speaking at speed, her pitch swooping up and down, riding the waves of her curiosity, affection and worry. (I believe Donna would be diagnosed as a grown-up with ADHD these days.) Then suddenly she fell silent, opened the freezer, and stood there, tipping her chin forward to bask in the icy air.

When Rex walked past carrying a box of wine, he saw Donna with her head in the freezer. 'Hot flush, darling? Let me know if I can get you anything.'

She threw me a jokey grimace as she waited for the peak of the flush to pass. 'Did you have a gruesome menopause, Liz?' she asked.

'Did you go through this shit and I didn't notice? Gawd, I hope I wasn't unsympathetic. Was I unsympathetic?'

'It wasn't too bad for me,' I said.

'Lucky you.' Donna then gripped my arm, mortified with guilt. 'Sorry! I guess a chemo-bald woman can't be accused of being lucky. I am sorry.' She shut the freezer and splashed her face with cold water from the tap. 'Oof—did not expect the hormone storms to kick off this early in my life.'

Donna was only forty-three. When I met her as a 32-year-old, she'd talked about wanting kids, but none of her convoluted relationships with men had worked out.

'So, there you have it, Lizzie—if I was holding out any laughable hope of being a late-in-life mother, my ovaries have stepped in and slapped some sense into me.'

She grunted a laugh, but a second later, she was tearful, reaching for a tissue.

'Oh shit,' she said. 'Shouldn't snivel about my own problems when conversing with a woman who just finished fucking cancer treatment!'

I gave her a squeeze. 'Honey, you bellyache and cry all you need. There's no hierarchy of suffering. One variety of misfortune doesn't invalidate another.' It was a relief to offer sympathy to someone else, having been on the receiving end of sympathy for months. That moment helped me feel like myself again.

I noticed Donna's gaze follow Rex as he walked past the kitchen, carrying bags down the spiral staircase into the bunkroom.

'It's such a shame Mr Lightfoot is a gentleman of the gay,' she said. 'That's an inconvenient habit of mine—falling for men who love men. But the thing is, heterosexual men in my age group are generally substandard. It's hard not to compare them to the gay gents and find the straight ones wanting.'

Donna had recovered her buoyant spirits by the time Rex came back upstairs from the bunkroom holding a cardboard tube.

'This is a little present for you, my darling,' he said, handing it to me. 'Congrats for getting through it.'

I took the top off the tube and unrolled the sturdy sheet of art paper inside. Most of the creamy surface was filled with a pen drawing, intricate and precise like an Escher image, but more lush, with the angular architectural elements softened by trees and tiny playful human figures. Looking more closely, I realised the drawing incorporated specific spots I recognised—Coogee Beach, Callan Park, Kings Cross, the Cooks River, the streetscapes of Newtown and Marrickville—all merging into each other to form a condensed, fanciful map of places that mattered to me.

'Oh, Rex, I love it. Who did this?' As the question came out of my mouth, I realised. 'You did this.'

He nodded, vulnerable, flushed with the rawness of having his work looked at.

'I hope you know it's wonderful,' I said.

Rex shrugged, embarrassed now. 'I've started doodling. This is one of my early efforts. I hope it's okay.'

It was more than okay. Much like the first time I heard Patty sing, I was filled with wonderment at my friend's talent. Rex's early drawing is one of my most treasured possessions, hanging on the wall next to the works by Evelyn O'Farrell and Cyrus John O'Farrell. Rex Lightfoot went on to use the combination of his architectural drafting skills and his inventiveness to create many splendid works on paper, conjuring up imaginary buildings, towns and cities. His 'doodles' ended up fetching several thousand dollars apiece.

That evening after dinner, the six of us took camping chairs onto the lawn outside. Leo had lit a brazier hours before, so by 8 p.m. there was a pile of glowing coals. The brazier kept the fronts of our bodies warm while our backs were chilled by the night air, like bread toasted on one side and frozen on the other. I wore a beanie on my bald head and Leo held Sheila on his lap, bundled up in a towel against the cold.

So far, my close friends had not pushed me to express a vision for the future. The truth was, after a breakdown, my new relationship, and a bout with cancer, I was wary of making a plan, other than being with Leo and spending time with people dear to me. Then again, I was only sixty-three and, even at this point, knocked around by chemo, I didn't feel ready to retire.

Everyone had been restraining themselves from asking questions, but that evening, Donna—bless her undiagnosed ADHD impulsiveness—jumped in.

'So, Lizzie, when are you going to come and work on my new show? We're gonna get the green light on it soon. It'd be brilliant to have you in the team.' She turned to the others to explain, 'I keep asking her to work with us. She's been fobbing me off. Using cancer as some kind of excuse.' Donna did a goofy laugh to clarify the last bit was a joke. 'But come on, Liz—fuck Murray Armfield and Carson Bull, fuck cancer—you're too good to give it away.'

'I might just mull things for a bit,' I said, hoping my wan, just-finished-chemo smile would signal I didn't want to discuss it now.

But Donna was too fired up to follow such a signal. 'Okay, okay, what about if you don't want to work on someone else's show, what about you use this time to develop some of your own projects? I always loved that idea you had about the secretly working-class woman in the fifties who fakes being posh and marries the rich guy who turns out to be a charlatan.'

'Ooh, I'd watch that show,' said Patty.

'Well, it was just a scrap of an idea,' I said. 'Would've borrowed things from my life—being married to Donald, chucked into the universe of Bunny Shaw-Preston—but in my fictional version, the Donald character wouldn't die and the main character stays with him, struggles to raise her children, handle the husband's dodgy business dealings, and stop her low-class origins being revealed, blah blah.'

'Yeah, yeah, I love it. What was the title you had?' Donna asked.

'*The Swimmer.* I fancied the idea the character swims in the ocean every day. Maybe fakes her own death off a cliff or maybe it's the husband who does. But I never got the story worked out.'

'I'd definitely watch that,' said Patty.

'You should pitch it as a TV project,' added Donna.

Like a trailer on fast-forward, I envisaged trying to make that story for television, pouring my soul into it, pitching it, facing the rejections and the compromises. It was suddenly clear to me that I no longer had the stamina to deal with the machinery of TV drama, the muscle spasms of hope and dejection, the delicate calculations of conciliation and obstinacy required of you. I admired the way Donna handled all of that. I possibly could've handled it too if I had been ten years younger. But sitting there on the lawn with my face burning from the brazier and my bum cold from the night air, I accepted that I could no longer cope with the scramble of writing television.

Later that night in bed, Leo said, 'The TV drama you talked about, could you write the story as a novel? I didn't say anything in front of the others in case you hate the idea. Anyway, just leaving the thought here before we go to sleep.'

Leo promptly fell asleep, but I was awake for some hours after that. The characters from that old half-developed story kept floating into my thoughts like restless, disoriented houseguests wandering into our bedroom. When the characters began talking to each other, it was clear there'd be no sleep unless I climbed out of bed and scribbled down their dialogue on a scrap of paper.

I would never have had the self-belief to start writing a novel in a regular way. But because there were already stray bits of story in folders for the television drama I might once have written, I could start by using techniques from my scriptwriting years—putting story beats on file cards to lay out on a table, talking about the plot with Donna or with Leo. I could sneak up on the project without the who-do-you-think-you-are doubt that might easily have paralysed me.

19 February 1994.

My first novel, *The Year-Round Swimmer*, was officially published on the second of February and I'd already done a few bookshop events before the Saturday afternoon book launch. Donna had banged on about the importance of having a proper celebration to mark the occasion. The publishers kicked in some money to help pay for the drinks, adding book industry and press folks to the guest list, while I paid for extra booze and finger food for the party.

I've skipped over the two and a half years leading up to this point, so as not to bore the reader with descriptions of a woman sitting at a computer for many hours every day, periodically standing up to wail to her long-suffering partner that the book she was writing was rubbish. I've jumped over the months of redrafting, hanging out for publishers to read the manuscript, absorbing rejections, latching on to an offer, rewriting the manuscript again. That stuff is not very photogenic. But I agreed with Donna that the effort warranted some kind of celebration.

I picked the party venue—the Dawn Fraser Baths—because I liked the idea that people could have a swim if the mood took them. The tidal pool, named after the Olympic swimmer, lunged out into Sydney Harbour from the shore at Balmain. Repairs had been done to the original 1880s pavilions and bleachers, but it still had a pleasingly daggy quality. Which is not to say it wasn't a spectacular location. From the decking on the far edge, swimmers could look out over the boats moored in the harbour, and the fabulous defunct cranes and dry docks of the island called Wareamah by the Aboriginal people and Cockatoo Island by the British. Beyond that were sandstone coves with houses tucked in bushland, and finally the CBD skyline.

The sight of stacks of my novel on the folding table was still unreal and magnificent to my eyes. There had been much churning about what author name I should go by. 'Burnley' was a name I'd used pragmatically because it matched my children's, but I didn't fancy having the association with Donald's family on a book cover. And my first name had always been a shifting matter. In the end, I went with the gender-neutral B. L. Rankin: my childhood surname plus initials to represent Betty, Beth and Liz. The cover image was a luscious Cyrus John O'Farrell painting of a woman lying on a beach. Leo was the only person who knew I'd been the model for it.

My publisher Annie—one of the many magnificent women I've been fortunate to know in my life—did a short speech to officially launch the novel, then I spluttered out a reply, rattling off thankyous. While speaking, I had to force my eyes out of focus so the faces in front of me were blurred. I would have started blubbering if I'd been able to clearly see the people assembled by the pool—Leo, Rose, Athena, Patty, Pearl, Rex, Thuy, Nola from Save Our Sons, dear friends from different pockets of life including a dozen colleagues from my TV-writing days, as well as my grandkids and numerous other children.

Once the speechy bit was done, I sat at the book-seller table and signed copies for people. I was delighted when eleven-year-old Van persuaded Thea's son and some of the other kids to jump into the pool, their whooping voices bouncing off the surface of the water.

Donna Silvestri fronted up to the signing table to introduce the plus-one she'd brought to the event.

'This is Walton,' she said.

Walton Reid was thirty-nine, tall, with glossy black curls, and so astonishingly handsome it usually took people a moment to collect themselves the first time they saw him up close. Not that he carried himself as if he believed he was a major spunk. The man was just walking around with the face he lived in, and I suppose he had come to accept the discombobulated responses of people he encountered. Walton was from Western Australia, a Yamatji man, even if I didn't know enough to appreciate such terms at the time. He'd befriended Donna years before, during a theatre production in Perth, where he'd built a strong stage career, playing Hamlet, Tartuffe, John Proctor, a string of Indigenous roles in new works, as well as directing several contemporary plays.

'Thanks for coming, Walton,' I said. 'My apologies if Donna's bullied you into a purchase.'

'All good. Thanks for having me at this do. And big congratulations on your book.' Walton offered me a smile that was modest, almost diffident, but at the same time he made eye contact with that seductive intensity which actors often wield.

While I signed his copy of *The Year-Round Swimmer* and wrote a message on the flyleaf, Donna was babbling.

'I'm stoked I finally lured Walton across from WA,' she said. 'He's going to be one of our leads—did I already tell you this, Lizzie?—he's playing the legal aid lawyer in the new series.'

'Oh, fantastic.'

'Yeah well, Donna's script is fantastic,' said Walton.

'They always cast him in those predictable fucking roles,' Donna groaned, 'drunk derro, gaol inmate, or the mystical otherworldly Black guy. That shit.'

Walton did a jokey grimace and threw me a smile before Donna dragged him off to be introduced to every person she'd ever met in her life.

Rex had been watching this interaction from a safe distance and I beckoned him over. 'Is he Donna's new boyfriend?'

'Oh, lord no,' Rex replied. 'Walton Reid is gay.'

Rex appeared agitated, even pained, and when I followed his eyeline, I realised that he was unable to wrench his gaze away from Walton.

'He seems like a lovely guy,' I said.

'Very. I met him briefly at Donna's place last week.'

'He's drop-dead gorgeous too.'

'Well, *der*. There is no impairment in my vision, Lizzie.'

'So . . .'

'What? What sentence was your "so" going to become?'

Before I could answer, Rex launched into a fervent rebuttal of a case I had not actually made. 'No, Liz. That man is out of my league. And don't go on about how wonderful I am, what a good catch I am. No. No. Do not run that argument. There are generally acknowledged levels of attractiveness—there just are. Not only am I ten years older than him, but I was never good-looking enough to be in the same category as Walton Reid.'

'Who says it has to work like that?' I argued. 'I mean, not only are you selling yourself short—because you are wonderful and attractive and you cannot legally stop me saying so—but you're selling Walton short as being so superficial a person that he wouldn't even consider—'

'The words coming out of your mouth may sound reasonable, but you are living in a dream world if you think—'

'Oh look, poor Walton is stranded over there on his own,' I pointed out.

Donna, in her over-excited way, had darted away to greet friends she'd spotted, leaving Walton awkwardly alone.

'Go over there.' I shoved Rex on the shoulder. Quite hard. 'He doesn't know anyone here. At least he's met you before. And you have excellent social skills to offer. Go.'

Rex shook his head emphatically. 'I wouldn't be able to hide how attractive I think he is and then he'd feel sorry for me and I would not be able to bear that.'

'So, you're going to avoid talking to him for the rest of the event? And at the many other social occasions Donna is likely to drag him to? Is that your strategy?'

'Yes,' said Rex firmly. 'That's my strategy.'

Since the death of his partner Stephen more than ten years before, Rex had stayed single and resisted throwing himself back into the fray. Which was a terrible waste. I was about to remonstrate with him again, but my attention was taken by Patty.

She was in the corner of the main pavilion, where she'd stowed her small amplifier and other music gear, ready to perform a few songs later in the afternoon. Even from a distance, I could see she was upset, flicking her sleeves across her eyes to wipe away tears.

As I made my way across to her, I realised she was caught in a fraught exchange with Athena. When Patty fled, ducking into the ladies, Athena stalked out of the pavilion with a scowl accentuated by her darkest Eyebrows of Displeasure.

My policy is to stay out of friends' relationship tumult (except in the case of abuse when there is obligation to speak up). But by the February of 1994, Athena had been snapping and chipping at Patty for many months. Behaving like a right cow.

I had theories about the problems stewing inside my dear friend. Patty's music career had recently moved up a gear: recording a new solo album, and doing national tours as a backup singer for big-time artists. Athena was dead proud of Patty. Trouble was, just at the point Patty was in demand, Athena had retired from her job, ambushed by the sense of uselessness that can hit a person who has always been a worker, always purposeful, always needed.

When Athena saw I was walking towards her, she glared at me from under those ferocious eyebrows and I was hit full in the face with a blast of Athena Koutsis pride—a powerful force that could achieve great things, but if thwarted, could fly off and slice into a bystander.

'Athena, are you okay? Is Patty upset?'

'Don't say it, Betty. I know what you're going to say.'

'Ah, so you're psychic then.'

'Just because you write a novel, doesn't mean you know everything about everything.'

'I would never think that and you bloody well know it.'

She hissed a stream of Greek curse words at me.

I tried to respond in a steady tone. 'Lady, you've been snarling at everyone for months. But mostly at Patty. You don't want to sabotage what you two have, so I reckon—'

She snapped back with a phrase I'd heard her use years before, 'The tongue has no bones but it crushes bones.'

'I'm not trying to crush you, my friend. I just don't want you to hurt Patty and end up making both of you unhappy.'

She spun around to walk away with another volley of ugly-sounding words. Greek is a terrific language for expletives. I would have chased after her, tried to ease things, if I hadn't seen Mac appear at the entrance to the baths. My son had promised to travel down from Darwin for the launch and he was here, late but—wonderfully—here.

I was flustered from my encounter with Athena, but Mac didn't notice because he was flustered himself.

'Hi, Mum.' He hugged me. 'Sorry I'm late. And sorry that I can't stay very long. Things are a bit . . . Anyway, the main thing to say is how fantastic this is, how proud I am of you.'

Seconds later, Mac was scooped out of my arms by a gang consisting of Rose, Thea and Mai, who dragged him off, bombarding him with affection and questions.

Pearl Jowett waved to me from the other side of the pool. She was wearing a lovely blue dress she'd bought especially because it matched the colour of the beach towel on the cover of the novel and because the fifties-style full-circle skirt fitted the period of the book. As she tottered in high-heeled sandals along the edge of the water, I could see how tipsy she was. The idea of holding an event with alcohol next to a body of water suddenly seemed foolish. I was heading over, planning to coax Pearl to sit away from the pool, when I noticed a woman poke her head through the entry gate to the baths, searching for someone. Mac ran towards her, trying to persuade the woman to come in, but she resolutely stayed outside. She was in her late thirties, wearing an orange and green Hawaiian shirt over loose cotton pants, with a messy ponytail pulling the blonde hair back from her tanned face.

Mac then hurried across to me. 'Mum, I need to head off. Sorry about this.'

'Who's that woman?' I asked. 'Did you invite her to join us?'

'Yeah, but she won't come in. I thought when we got here, she'd— well, then she wouldn't get out of the car.'

'You left her sitting in the car like a dog? Oh, Mac. I'll go and make it clear she's very welcome. Is she your girlfriend? What's her name?'

'Tanya. And yes, she's my girlfriend.' He grabbed my arm to stop me moving towards the gate. 'But please don't you try to . . . Mum, *you* are the problem.'

'Me? How am I a—'

'Tanya's intimidated by this family. I mean, you're a published author, Rose is a doctor, Vuong's a school principal, Leo's a lawyer, Patty plays gigs with Jimmy Barnes.'

'Eh? We're not up ourselves about stuff like that. I'd like to meet her. She'll see there's no reason to feel—'

'I know that, Mum. But it's better if you don't go over there right now.'

I'm ashamed to tell the reader that the strongest thing I felt in that moment was dismay that someone would not want to meet me. I was personally stung, too caught up with my own wish to be liked that I didn't consider why that young woman might feel the way she did.

Leo came a step closer and gently took my elbow. 'A few more people want their books signed.'

Sitting at the book-signing table, I watched Leo walk across with Mac, persuading Tanya to perch on one of the benches just inside the gate. Leo chatted calmly to her, pointing out various individuals, explaining who belonged to whom.

Mac came back to sit by me and offer some details. He'd met Tanya Quinn in Darwin where she worked as a pastry chef. (His love of baked goods seemed to drive his romantic life.) By then, Mac had finished the psychology degree he'd been doing part-time for some years, unbeknownst to me. My son was a person who liked to acquire skills discreetly, as a means to keep expectations and anxiety at bay. He'd never outright lied to me about his life—instead, he kept the details elusive, radiating an aura that discouraged interrogation. It turned out that, for the last three years, Mac had been working as an addiction counsellor in Darwin and living with Tanya.

'Tanya's a reserved person, Mum. She's not confident the way you can *seem* to people. But she's wonderful.' When Mac described how smart and tough and loving his girlfriend was, I could hear that he adored her.

Over at the bench, I noticed Tanya relax a little, even laugh a few times, as Leo offered up juicily humiliating stories about me. She would soon realise our lot weren't high-class types or stuck-up.

And it must be said that, over the next half-hour, my friends at the party helped the process along by behaving like a pack of undignified buffoons.

First, Athena and Patty's simmering conflict flared up into a screaming row, their voices loud enough to cut through the music and halt the burble of conversation.

'What did you say to Betty?' Athena bellowed at Patty. 'Are you wrecking my friend's book launch blabbing about our private business?'

This time, for a change, Patty fired back, fierce rather than conciliatory. '*You* are the one making a scene and wrecking the book launch.'

When Athena started swearing at Patty in Greek, Thea and Sofia rushed over to intervene. If the Samios daughters were hoping to de-escalate the situation, their tactic of yelling at their mother in a spicy mixture of Greek and English did not serve that purpose.

Pearl Jowett was so busy gawping at the ruckus that she tripped and fell into the pool, fully clothed. For three long seconds, she sank deep under the water, too shocked from the fall to save herself. Even when she floundered her way to the surface, she was so tipsy, as well as hampered by the blue folds of her voluminous skirt, heavy with sea water, that she could only thrash about and yelp.

Immediately, Rex yanked off his shoes and dived in. He swam over to Pearl, cradled her head above water, murmuring reassuring words as he carried her over to one of the poolside ladders. When Thuy and Vuong reached down to lift Pearl out, she was so disoriented, limbs flailing, that she unwittingly kicked Rex as he was paddling underneath. Copping a high heel in the face, Rex fell back in the water, grabbing hold of part of the wooden structure of the pool to steady himself.

As Rex pulled himself up the ladder, I could see that his legs, bare below his linen shorts, had been cut about by the oyster shells on the pool supports, and blood was trickling down his shins. I was on my way across to him when I felt someone brush past me. It was Walton Reid, rushing towards Rex.

'Hi, Rex. Walton. We met at Donna's place the other day when—'

'Yes. Hello.'

'I played an ambulance officer in a kids' show once, so even though I have no medical qualifications, I can look the part when I carry the gear.' Walton smiled and brandished the pool's first aid kit.

'Oh, thanks,' said Rex, plonking himself onto a bench. 'Be careful you don't get blood on your clothes. I can handle this, I think.'

Walton sat just along the bench from him. 'Let me fish out the stuff you might need.'

Walton rummaged in the first aid kit and handed over saline, cotton swabs, iodine and Band-Aids, so Rex could set about dressing his oyster shell cuts. I backed away, leaving them to it.

Meanwhile the Athena and Patty floorshow had progressed beyond shouting mode. On the far side of the pool, Patty was slumped, sobbing, being comforted by Sofia Samios, while Thea barked at her mother to walk away.

Athena ran towards me with her face contorted in pain. Out of her mouth came a mixture of English and Greek words, all in a breathless staccato rhythm. I clasped her hands between mine, held her steady, while she uttered enough pieces of sentences for me to follow.

'I know Patty will leave me, Betty . . . I've become an old woman now—I'm boring, I'm—ugghh—and Patty is so wonderful and for her now everything is—Why would she stay with me? There's no good reason! I don't want her to stay because of duty or because she thinks—ohh . . . I don't know what to do, Betty. I love her so much but now, now, everything is . . . How can she love me the way I am now?'

I ducked my head down, forcing her to make eye contact and truly listen. 'The woman loves you. Even though you've been giving her shit for months. If you were trying to drive Patty away, it hasn't worked. It will all be fine. Maybe don't be so shitty with her, yes?'

Athena turned to face Patty who was sprawled on the concrete on the opposite side of the pool.

'Patty! I'm sorry for my tongue! I don't want my tongue to crush your beautiful bones!' She started smacking herself in the mouth. 'I will stop my stupid tongue saying horrible things to you!'

I lunged over to hold Athena's wrists, to stop her whacking herself but she wrenched clear of me and yelled across the water to Patty, 'I am an idiot!' She then hurled her body into the pool with an ungainly belly flop—the most undignified thing I'd ever seen my very dignified friend do.

'See what a big idiot I am!' she shouted, spluttering water, then she laughed.

As Athena swam across the pool towards her, Patty started laughing too. She reached down to help Athena climb onto the walkway and they kissed passionately in a way I would never have expected Athena to do in public. Water dripped off Athena's sopping wet silk shirt and trousers, making Patty's sixties red corduroy jumpsuit sodden too. The two women switched between weeping, declarations of love, apologies and more kissing.

By this point Leo had coaxed Tanya into the party zone, although she still avoided coming anywhere near me. The idea that Mac's partner would feel comfortable with Leo but not with me—well, that thought stabbed me in some deeply lodged childhood location in my body. My stomach muscles tensed to shield myself against the desire to be liked and the wounded pang of not being liked. Ridiculous that, at the age of sixty-five, I could still be so self-absorbed and needy.

The photographer who'd been taking various shots of the event tapped me on the shoulder. 'Liz, could we get a family photo? Maybe with you holding a copy of your book and with the pool in the background?'

After some faffing about, my immediate family formed a line beside the pool with Rose, Vuong and Van on my left, Leo, Mac and Mai on my right, while I stood holding a copy of *The Year-Round Swimmer* at chest height. Just as the photographer was setting up the shot, I noticed a Hawaiian shirt at the edge of my peripheral vision. Mac's girlfriend Tanya stood on her own. This young woman—whatever she might think of me—had been my son's partner for three years. She counted as family.

'Tanya? Hello. Please come and be in the family shot,' I said.

To demonstrate my eagerness for her to join the family tableau, I lurched sideways, flinging my arm out to indicate the space thus opened up next to me. It was not an elegant manoeuvre, but I hoped it would come across as welcoming. I was so intent on conveying that message I failed to notice how far I'd shifted back and how much the arm-flinging would throw off my balance. A second later, I tumbled backwards into the pool.

'I'm okay! I'm okay!' I waved from the water, floating on my back like a perky otter. I made it across the pool to the nearest ladder, where Leo hoisted me out. I towelled my hair into a fuzzball, pulled off my wet sandals and squeezed some of the water out of the bottom of my green linen dress. Rose dashed off to find my swimming costume and a sarong.

While I scrubbed at my wet clothes with an extra towel, the photographer took snaps of the novel which had also landed in the water. It was already swelling up in that florid way paperbacks can do when dropped in the bathtub.

I realised Tanya was hovering nearby. I took a step towards her, offering my hand. 'We haven't properly met. I'm Liz. Please excuse my sogginess.'

Tanya shook my hand. 'Hi, Liz. Um, I should tell you . . .'

I tensed up, anxious she was about to say something that would create more awkwardness between us, but then I realised she was discreetly pointing at my chest. 'I think your prosthesis has moved out of place.'

During my vigorous self-towelling, the fake bosom had escaped from my bra and migrated towards my collarbone like a fugitive lump.

'Whoops—my wandering boob!' I shoved the prosthesis back inside the bra cup. 'Thank you very much, Tanya.'

The rest of the event went splendidly. Patty sang half-a-dozen songs. Many people swam or danced or both. Pearl, now donning a glamorous swimsuit and matching robe, only needed another sip of champagne to fizz up into her vivacious party self. And Walton and Rex remained deep in conversation together.

Towards the end of the function, Mac and his girlfriend came over, holding hands, bashfully formal, to tell me that Tanya was six months pregnant.

There have been a number of happy, or at least satisfying, periods in my life, but the next run of years was especially so. Apart from cohabiting with my beloved Leo, I had two of my children living within five kilometres. Rose and Vuong bought a house in Annandale, close enough that Mai and Van could wander round to our place to cadge meals. Not long after Mac and Tanya's daughter Nicola was born, they moved to Sydney, wanting some family support.

Something I came to understand, and respect, about Tanya Quinn was that she was a person who revealed herself in layers as she felt more comfortable with someone. She didn't *present* herself as a display package the way many of us do, desperate to be liked or admired. And when she did give her affection, it was a solid and enduring thing.

My daughter-in-law would often bring baby Nicola to our house while Mac was at work. Later, when she started her own small business making cakes and pastries for cafes, Leo and I minded Nicola two days a week. For me, the best two days of any week.

I believe Mac had been as good a stepfather to poor Jacob as he could have been under the circumstances, but he was unquestionably a wonderful father to Nicola. A number of people told me Mac Burnley was a compassionate drug and alcohol counsellor, which I can well imagine.

I have sometimes felt I was born too early, missing out on the era that would have suited me better. I wonder if the same is true for my son. Mac landed in the world before there was awareness of what life was like for a person with anxiety, before a young man with his strengths—gentleness, empathy, skill with language—was properly valued in Australia. There are examples of individuals who forged their own paths as unblokey men, but my boy was too damaged by early traumas, too misunderstood by me. Then again, he did find his own way eventually and I was impressed by the man he became.

Those years in the late nineties proved to be a joyful time for other people dear to me. Rex Lightfoot and Walton Reid attempted to take their relationship slowly, before they accepted that they were madly in love and shacked up together. One of the great pleasures of my later life has been watching Rex's face as he watches Walton being electrifying on stage or on screen.

Athena resolved to find somewhere purposeful to direct her energy and settled on two projects. She helped Thea win the election for a state Labor seat, plus she decided to rebuild her grandmother's ruined house on Kastellorizo, flying to the island to wrangle the bureaucracy and tradesmen.

My pal Donna Silvestri enjoyed a great deal of success in television drama. I would sometimes jump into brainstorming sessions on her projects which was enormous fun. But I didn't have enough of the sinewy self-belief necessary to survive in that world.

During those years, Leo took on immigration jobs, some paid, others pro bono refugee cases. The two of us were intensely happy to be together, but I don't want to imply there were no problems. Like all couples, we could fall into clunky emotional dance routines, stubbing toes, tipping off balance. For example, I have a habit of going quiet sometimes, withdrawing into myself. Such spells of emotional distance could plunge Leo into an anxious state, fearing my silence was an accusation of wrongdoing on his part. If he said anything to that effect, I would be snappy, which would exacerbate his discomfort. I came to understand that his reaction was a legacy of his punitive marriage and that my years of living alone meant I could be insensitive, unthinking about how my moods might affect a partner. So, like most people, we had to navigate around such debris.

Leo's son David travelled the planet as a musician, along the way marrying a Japanese flautist and having two daughters with her. He was a devoted brother to his older sister Ava, ringing and visiting her regularly. There can be a special bond between siblings who have grown up together in an unhappy home, and since David was the stronger of the two, he felt responsibility for his sister.

As for Ava, she ended up living with us in Leichhardt during periods when her life was wobbly. I was happy to have her around. She was a loving woman and could be good company. She would sometimes sulk, tell her father lies that were insultingly obvious and blame him for every squall and gust in her moods. Leo would make allowances for Ava that did her no favours. Leo did not appreciate me making any kind of comment and I learned to keep my mouth shut.

I won't blather on too much about being a novelist, conscious of the risk of disappearing up my own bum.

At the beginning, I worried it would be a problem that I was elderly and not notable in another field (famous actor, stand-up comedian, colourful criminal), but it turned out that the book club and literary festival crowd enjoyed the idea that an old dame had started writing her first novel at sixty-three and then found a small amount of success. The book world is hungry for some sort of narrative surrounding the author, so that was mine.

I can see in retrospect that many of the stories in my novels were sparked by curiosity about what might have happened if there had been some bend in the narrative line of my life, like switching tracks on a railway system. If I'd kept my first baby and come to Australia as a young single mother, if I'd travelled to Italy with Cyrus John O'Farrell, if I'd stayed in Mexico or stuck with Eric Huxtable. It was driven by curiosity but also greediness—a greed to live many more lives than just the one.

I'm aware that I only found my way as an author—producing six novels and various short pieces—after I found a level of happiness and security with Leo Newman. I don't mean to downplay my own efforts—I was the person who wrote the books—but it's no coincidence that I did so while I was being cherished by a partner who loved me.

September 1999.

Pearl had given up her retail job in 1997, at the age of sixty-nine, claiming she couldn't manage the new electronic till in the shop. I assumed she then received the aged pension, but mystery remained about the source of funds for her considerable spending on clothes, beauty, gifts and outings. A few times, I gently asked about her financial situation.

'Don't worry,' she responded. 'Leo's the executor of my will, Betty, and you're the ben—oh—what's the word?'

'Beneficiary?'

'That's it. You get everything when I die.' She waved her hands around her small flat.

I wasn't sure what I would do with a rented apartment full of childlike knick-knacks and tizzy costume jewellery, but I was touched by her generous impulse.

I was Pearl's emergency contact, so the day she was admitted to St Vincent's in the September of '99, seriously ill with a kidney infection, the hospital rang me. She recovered quickly but once her febrile delirium cleared, it was as if a camouflaging fog had lifted, revealing the reality of her dementia.

I berated myself for not having noticed the cognitive deterioration sooner. Mind you, the daily routine Pearl had adopted over the last year had muddied the picture. She would snooze until nine in the morning, then drink a wine spritzer in bed. Occasionally she would catch a taxi to a beauty appointment, but she mostly stayed home, pouring herself a Cointreau as a pre-lunch aperitif, then a tumbler of moselle with lunch, which consisted of a small mound of salad leaves. After a nap, there would be more wine with her evening meal (cheese and crackers), then Bailey's Irish Cream while she watched TV. She had been smudging the sharp contours of the dementia by maintaining a tipsy state. In recent months Pearl Jowett, the most gregarious human I've ever known, had made excuses to avoid social gatherings, stopped meeting her colourful pals in the cafes of Kings Cross, and would only schedule visits from friends around midday—that is, after she'd put her face on, and gathered whatever neurones she could muster. The clues were so obvious in retrospect, I felt like a goose.

The doctors were firm that Pearl could no longer live independently. Leo and I applied for an enduring guardianship and a financial management order to look after Pearl's affairs. With her customary sweetness, she refused the invitation to move in with us.

'Thank you, darling Betty. But I'd prefer to live in my own suite in a retirement establishment,' she said. 'Is there a place in the eastern suburbs with a lovely garden where I can entertain visitors?'

Pearl had never been a fake-posh person, but her tone of voice made me think of a dowager queen choosing to live in private apartments within a royal palace. I was doubtful her finances would stretch to a royal apartment, so there was relief as well as surprise when Leo and I discovered that, back in the 1960s, Gerry Stankovich had put three properties in Summer Hill in Pearl's name. Gerry had probably been trying to conceal the real estate temporarily, as part of a development scam he didn't have the chance to carry out. After Gerry died, Pearl had discovered she was the owner of those three properties. She'd quickly sold one and the rent from the other two had been providing her mysterious spending money.

Leo and I sold one of the remaining houses to pay the hefty bond on an eastern suburbs nursing home with a lovely garden and fancy communal lounge areas. The rent from the other house covered the purchase of whatever treats it was possible to have in the home. I arranged visits from a hairdresser and a manicurist to do her nails because it gave Pearl joy to have someone fuss over her.

Even as Pearl's cognition crumbled, her buoyant spirit survived, and once she felt safely held within the care home, she regained her social confidence. She invited friends to afternoon tea in the grand main lounge. If the staff of the high-tone eastern suburbs joint were horrified by her visitors, including drag queens and sex workers, Pearl did not notice.

I regularly joined her for lunch and it was clear Pearl had become the social queen of the dining room, chattering irrepressibly to her fellow residents, many of whom were away with the pixies. Occasionally I would detect a momentary wretchedness on my dear friend's face. For all its chandeliers and French-polished furniture, the place still had the aroma of cooking oil, disinfectant and urine. But a moment later a sweet dessert concoction could buoy her spirits. She grew plump as she tucked into the starchy institutional food.

Looking across the table at Pearl, it was difficult to ignore how peculiar her face looked after decades of cosmetic assault. There were tidemarks along her jawline and neck from chemical peels. Her tattooed eyebrows looked like two clumsy crayon lines on a child's drawing. Her skin was puckered where various surgeries were no longer compatible with the underlying musculature, and her lips were creased and saggy now that years of fillers had dissolved, leaving bags of skin like deflated balloons. Despite all of that, my friend was still beautiful to me, with her cornflower eyes and her sweet self shining out from the cosmetic wreckage.

For me, the loss of youthful looks was not as painful as it is for some, given I'd never been in a position to trade on beauty. During my fifties and sixties, it was possible to see remnants of my young face on the front of my skull, enough to notice it crumbling and to feel the urge to slow the decay with whatever creams might help. But sometime in my early seventies, I found I'd tipped into wrinkly oldness and it was a relief. That chance to happily sink into one's old face is probably messed up for people who've filled their faces with Botox and injectable packing beads. It also helped that I was being loved up by a man who managed to make me believe he found me beautiful.

One aspect of ageing that did bother me was the experience of being regarded as a silly old duffer—spoken to in a patronising singsong, ignored at shop counters, shoved aside on public transport, presumed to be an idiot. The first few times I was on the receiving end of this, I went off at the perpetrators. Undeniably gratifying in the moment, sure, but I was wary of curdling into a rancid grump. I pursued a different strategy. I pictured myself as that kid in the Clyde Road classroom—humiliated by the health visitors, walloped by Miss Greene and stared at by classmates. Seven-year-old me had silently soaked in those blows and belittling glances, then converted them into a power source, with the added satisfaction that no one knew I was secretly fuelling myself. That was what I attempted to do as an increasingly old lady: soak up the insults of the world and use them as fuel.

I noticed that many women in the old-dame stage of life became more fired up about politics, impatient that so much appalling bullshit remained unfixed—violence against woman, racist behaviour, poor families anxious about money and expected to send their kids to ragged underfunded public schools while rich kids swanned through the gates of private schools with plush grounds and elite sport facilities (hyperbaric chambers!), government-subsidised for Christ's sake and—well, I'll settle myself down. The point is, there were still so many infuriating inequalities and ugly spectacles in the world.

In 1997, the Australian government released the Bringing Them Home report about the forcible removal of Aboriginal and Torres Strait Islander children from their families. Many people already knew about the history of the Stolen Generations, but even so, the report was an excoriating reminder.

On 28 May 2000, a walk across the Sydney Harbour Bridge—the People's Walk for Reconciliation—saw First Nations people alongside other Australians walking from the northern side of the harbour towards the city, as a way to demonstrate solidarity with Aboriginal people, support for an apology, land rights, and the urgent process of reconciliation. Walton Reid, by that point famous for his television roles, was asked to march up the front with other well-known Aboriginal people. Meanwhile, Rex Lightfoot was with me, Leo, Donna, Athena, Patty, all our children and grandchildren.

The atmosphere had been upbeat as we'd travelled with other prospective marchers on the train to Milsons Point. Once we were heading down the wide roadway of the bridge, I was surrounded by earnestly cheerful people with children, flags, banners.

It was a bright day, so the harbour looked as ravishing as the first day I laid eyes on it in 1947 from the deck of the *Asturias*. I was keyed-up, joyful to be walking anywhere with an assemblage of my dear ones, but also anxious about the turnout and the symbolic success or failure of the event.

Halfway across the bridge, Rex tapped me on the arm. 'Lizzie, look.'

I twisted round and took in the wide river of bodies behind us. In the end, two hundred and fifty thousand people showed up that day and it took six hours for the crowd to cross the bridge. Huge marches happened in other cities too, including three hundred thousand people in Melbourne.

Seeing all those people, my lungs expanded. I could fit in more air. But if I felt a surge of sugary optimism that day, it was cut by a lemon squeeze of awareness—changes never happen as rapidly or take root as solidly as we hope. Then I glanced sideways and saw the hopefulness on 21-year-old Mai's beautiful face. I didn't want any such thoughts in my head to sour her positive spirit.

On that May 2000 walk, there was euphoria and indeed some self-congratulation for what was really a tiny personal effort (catching the train across the bridge, going for a stroll on a pretty day alongside a bunch of smiling, like-minded individuals). There was naïvete too—most of us deluding ourselves about how quickly things would improve. Contemplating the reconciliation progress from where I sit today—well, it's woefully, shamefully poor. But for all the self-delusion and petty vanities of that walk, I do believe such events are better than nothing. Imagine a world in which we had found out about all those moral crimes and said nothing. Of course that walk was an inadequate thing. But doing nothing was not acceptable.

A dollop of wild optimism is necessary fuel for progressive causes—alongside dollops of anger. Sometimes it seems as if things are sliding backwards, but I would rather be a woman, a gay person, a person of colour, in 2028 than 1928.

There was no logical reason to expect the ticking over of the dial into the 2000s would be marked by meaningful change, but the mind likes to form thoughts around such scaffolds.

A new century—surely things would be better.

SEVENTEEN

2008, The Year of Three Deaths.

I've become a connoisseur of funerals, much like younger people are connoisseurs of weddings. I'm not a fan of churchy funerals in which some priest exploits a person's death by hectoring mourners about the spiritual jeopardy they face if they don't urgently convert to the religion on offer. Funerals are way better in the twenty-first century—idiosyncratic options, relevant music, and an appropriate mixture of solemnity and joy.

Leo and I had expected Pearl's funeral on 9 January 2008 to be a small event, but word spread through the networks of people she had delighted during her life, including beauticians, customers from the dress shop, a variety of Kings Cross folk, waiters from Beppi's. The crowd ended up spilling out the crematorium chapel doors.

During Pearl's last months, I had sometimes taken my laptop into the nursing home, so I could sit in her room writing while she dozed, ready to chat whenever she perked awake.

Towards the end, Pearl reverted to a thick Yorkshire accent and often believed herself to be in scenes from her childhood. If I could decipher who she was talking to in the moment she was reliving—usually her mother—I would do my best to respond in character. Once, she laughed girlishly and said, 'Ma! Look at my dress! It's black bright!'—Yorkshire slang for 'grubby'. That was a standard expression where she came from, but it seemed special and fitting that our radiant Pearl could describe a dirty garment so joyfully as 'black bright'.

After she died, I packed up her knick-knacks, costume jewellery, tiny porcelain dogs and framed photographs. I had been putting a selection of them on the shelves in her nursing home room, cycling through the collection with a new batch every month. It had pleased her to see familiar favourite items and to discover them freshly when I switched them round.

At Pearl's wake—a simple affair with sandwiches on the lawn at the crematorium—I laid out the collection of her treasures on a trestle table and suggested people take one each as a memento. For myself, I kept aside some spoons and crockery with 'SS *Asturias*' on them—items Pearl had half-inched during the voyage we'd shared.

With the deaths I've been close to, my project was to make it as good a death as it could be—alleviating physical pain, indulging whims where possible, talking as baldly or cryptically as the dying person wished. However sharp the grief, it is a privilege to aid a person's process through this stage.

The death of your own child is not like that.

In February 2008, just after Pearl died, Mac was troubled by vague symptoms—back pain, nausea. He had always been on alert for liver problems, thanks to the intravenous drug use in his twenties, but the diagnosis of late-stage pancreatic cancer was a disorienting blow for him.

The few rounds of chemo hammered him, and those efforts were never going to make much difference anyway. With the support of the oncologist, Mac chose to suspend treatment, apart from palliative stuff, so he could hang on to as many weeks of decent health to spend with his daughter Nicola, then only fourteen. Mac and Tanya were a great team—loving and honest with their child, letting her be part of the process but also free to go off and be a teenager.

Mind you, Mac, Tanya and Nicola were all so busy sparing each other pain that they left little room for their own necessary moments of personal collapse. I ended up being the person with whom each could temporarily disintegrate.

Once, driving Nicola to the hospital to visit her dad, I heard her voice come out strangulated, throat constricted.

'Can we hang on for a sec, Nana?'

I found a quiet spot to pull over while Nicola had the weep she needed to have. She then checked her face in the sun-visor mirror to ensure her eyes didn't look puffy from crying before she decided she was fit to go inside the hospital.

Later that afternoon, I was with Tanya in a supermarket buying fruit to take to Mac. Even if he wasn't really eating solid food by this stage, she wanted there to be a bowl of his favourite fruit in his room. But in the produce section, faced with the array of apple varieties, the poor woman was poleaxed.

'I can't remember if Mac likes Fujis best or if he'd rather have the Galas.'

Tanya started heaving with sobs in front of the apples. I slipped my arm around her, holding her upright, while she cried. A few shoppers flicked looks at her, but one bloke stared in a way that seemed uncharitable.

I shot him a spiky look. 'Galas or Fujis—it's a tough choice for all of us. Any advice?'

The man scurried away, terrified that some mad old witch had accosted him. And a bonus: the sight of his nervous scuttle made Tanya laugh.

My son could speak candidly with his wife about all sorts of arrangements, but he saved the talk about his fear of dying for times he was alone with me. To meet the eyes of a person as they talk about their imminent death, to hold their gaze without glancing away and without letting your own feelings flood in to saturate the connection—well, it's one of the few meaningful things you can give someone at that time.

I offered Mac the support I would offer any dying dear one, but when it is your child, there is an undigestible lump of pain underneath all your sensible efforts. What is happening is outrageously wrong at a primitive level that cannot be processed by the brain. My Leo, as always, was there to hold me close and offer soothing words, but without ever trying to dismiss the pain.

During the final weeks, Mac was in a hospice, with Tanya sleeping on a foldout bed beside him, and Nicola, me, Leo and others in there much of the time.

The day he died in late June, Rose was the one who was in bits. Since Mac's diagnosis, my robust daughter had felt obliged to be the medical liaison for the family. That was helpful certainly, but it did interfere with her own response, and the loss of her brother hit her in an unguarded state.

Mac Burnley was fifty-nine years old when he died.

December 2008.

I carried the baby monitor with me whenever I left the room to have a shower or prepare food. The little speaker would crackle to life on the kitchen bench or bathroom ledge and I would hear the tinny sound of Leo asking for something or shifting around in the bed in a way which suggested he might be in physical discomfort. It turns out those baby monitors can be handy at the other end of life too.

During his years in Brisbane, Leo had undergone surgery on his calf to remove a melanoma. When another melanoma was discovered in mid-2008, Leo said nothing during the early phases of his testing because I was immersed in grief over Mac. In August, he shared the news that the melanoma had already metastasised to various organs including his brain.

'I keep thinking, Betty . . . I was supposed to die during the war. But here I am: eighty-three dying of an ordinary thing. So really this is a triumph over the Nazis.'

'Yes,' I said. 'Your cancer is a magnificent fuck-you to Hitler.'

With support from the palliative team, it was possible to care for Leo at home for the last months. His son David cancelled an overseas tour to stay close by and Ava visited as often as her friable state of mind could handle. One of my duties during those months was to manage the schedule of visitors—our kids and grandkids, Athena, Patty, Rex, Walton, Donna, Leo's legal colleagues and many others—so he could have the joy of them without feeling overwhelmed. Tanya and Nicola had always had a special connection with Leo and, despite their own fresh grief, the two of them would visit, perching on Leo's bed to watch DVDs with him—Eddie Izzard stand-up, Mitchell and Webb sketch shows and such, Leo having expressed a preference for comedy and other short-form stuff.

'I don't want to start a story where I won't find out how it ends,' he joked.

When a dear one is dying, the grammar changes, the future tense carefully deactivated. But there are still unseen landmines in conversation.

'Rose reckons Mai and her boyfriend are trying for a baby,' I said to Leo one day.

'Wonderful,' he replied. 'How would that fit with her work?' (Mai had just qualified as a doctor.)

'Well, even if they fell pregnant already, the timing could—let's see . . .' I started counting the nine months on my fingers. But then it struck me that I was counting months of a year that would not have Leo in it, so I just wiggled my fingers and shrugged. 'Anyway, Mai will manage.'

'You don't have to do that,' said Leo.

'What?'

'Avoid mentioning the future. You don't have to censor yourself. It can still bring me happiness to imagine Mai having a baby even though I won't see it. Which reminds me, Betty,' Leo said with a sly smile, 'should we eat that expensive goat's cheese Donna brought round? Have you checked the best before date?'

He laughed so gleefully that it set me laughing too. I made a show of rushing to the kitchen to stand by the open fridge door and yell out the expiry dates on items inside. Over the next few days, we sampled cheeses, fancy biscuits and other delicacies people had given us.

'I feel like I'm beating the system,' Leo said when he nibbled a piece of nougat which would not expire until long after he would. Mind you, he was only eating tiny symbolic morsels of food by then.

Leo Newman stared back at his own death as directly as anyone I've known, but for all his sturdy candour, he could be caught by surprise. He had always loved the fuss and food and family gathering of Christmas, despite his Jewish upbringing. One day in late November, he was speculating on how to manage a Christmas Day feast so he could take part from his bed. As he calculated how many chairs could fit round our table with a card table added at the end, I tried to keep my expression neutral. But he read my face.

'Ah. Of course,' he said. 'I won't be here at Christmas.' He already understood the medical reality of it, but the idea could still hit him as a shock. It is impossible to comprehend that our own existence will cease, and life will go on without us. At a logical level this is obvious, but at some animal level it is beyond the psyche to truly grasp.

In those last weeks, Leo made a point of expressing extravagantly loving things to his children, grandchildren and friends, saying the kind of overt things—'I love you so very much. You've always brought me great joy'—that often make people uncomfortable, even excruciated, in the moment the words are said out loud. But Leo believed, and I do too, that such words would sink into their skulls gradually afterwards like time-release medication and bring much comfort.

Leo Newman taught me how a person can die well, and when it's my turn—soon, surely—I will attempt to draw wisdom from his example.

In the last weeks, he was on prednisone, a steroid to reduce the swelling in his brain and buy him more conscious days, and I had been taught how to administer the pain medication that kept him more or less comfortable.

'I'm sorry you have to nurse me,' he said while I was giving him a sponge bath. 'I wanted to be the one nursing you.'

'You already nursed me through the breast cancer,' I pointed out. 'Are you saying you wish I now copped some other cancer on top?'

He grinned, tipping his head to acknowledge I had won that point. Then, his voice thicker with emotion, he said, 'I'm very sorry to be leaving you on your own.'

I made a jokey 'psh' noise. 'I've got plenty of friends.'

He laughed, more boisterously than I thought his frail body could have managed. He beckoned me closer and I curled myself around his body, which was still damp and gardenia-scented from the sponge bath.

In between visitors, I spent most of the days and nights lying in the bed with him, feeding him slivers of mango and German marzipan. He was too mentally fuzzy to read or even watch TV, so I would read aloud to him—sometimes messages from friends, including the relatives in Europe he had only found in the 1990s, and sometimes the Stegner novel *Crossing to Safety*, the ending of which he already knew.

The week came when the doctor suggested we cease the prednisone, and my darling sank into unconsciousness over the next couple of days. He wanted me to keep reading to him, saying it felt good to hear the sound of my voice. For me, having the page of the book to focus on was like an anchor for my eyeballs that kept weeping at bay and held me where I needed to be. The morning Leo died, I lay beside him for an hour, soaking in the warmth of his body, before I called David, Ava, Rose, and the doctor.

This is one of those moments in my story when I won't go on and on. If a reader has stuck with me this far, they will most likely understand the mixture of feelings—grief that I had lost my Leo, frustration that we had squandered our earlier chances, gratitude that we had eventually grabbed many glorious years together. In my most expansive mood, I can feel grateful to the universe that I have been the beloved of the person who was my beloved.

EIGHTEEN

July 2011.

Once I'd walked into the park beside the harbour in Kirribilli, I could let easy-going Heidegger scamper off but kept Nietzsche close. Despite his hefty dose of Prozac, Nietzsche couldn't be trusted around small children. Even so, when he looked at me from under the stiff grey awnings of his clipped eyebrows, there was something about his crazy eyes that I found endearing.

The two schnauzers were not my dogs. I hope by now a reader would assume I'd never give my pets such insufferably pretentious names. I was just minding this pair. For the last two years, I had been living the itinerant life of a house-sitter and dog-minder.

After Leo died, I signed over the Leichhardt house to his daughter Ava. A few weeks later, I flew out on what I considered my 'Farewell World Tour', spending some of the time with friends in Mexico, the UK, Vietnam and Greece, but also relishing the anonymity of solo travel in Chile and Turkey. My travel expenses were funded in part by the rental income from the Summer Hill house Pearl had bequeathed me.

Landing back in Sydney, I lacked the emotional fuel to make a new home for myself anywhere, so I pounced on the idea of house-sitting.

I'd been in the Kirribilli place for two months so far with one further week before the owners returned from an African safari and a high-end cruise. Like the other houses I'd perched in temporarily, it was plusher and more glamorously located than anything I could afford—a substantial two-storey thirties residence with well-proportioned rooms, marble bathrooms, valuable artworks, and a garden with sandstone-edged lawns down to a harbour frontage. Cleaners and gardeners showed up every week, so all I had to do was look after the dogs and make the joint look inhabited.

In the six different places I'd lived as a minder (this one, Double Bay, Avalon, Balgowlah, two in Bellevue Hill), I was playing at other possible lives, picturing myself as someone who might own a certain kind of house, pretending I lived the same kind of life as the people I mingled with in the local parks, cafes and shops. It reminded me of my married years in The Gables, Donald's grand, gloomy mansion, when I always felt as if I were play-acting.

The big bonus of this way of living—apart from the reprieve from decision-making—was the chance to borrow other people's dogs. Sheila, our clever, soulful blue heeler, had died in 2006, having given Leo and me many years of delight. It didn't seem fair to take on another dog in my eighties, given I might cark it any day, and I couldn't bear to have another dog die on me. During the house-sitting gigs, I had the joy of companion animals without the commitment.

Back from the park, Heidegger and Nietzsche skidded along the floorboards in the hallway, knowing that dinner would be served shortly. As I hung up the dog leads in the vestibule, I was startled by my reflection in the oak-framed mirror opposite. A shockingly old woman, her white hair frizzed up by the dry wind in the park.

That was one thing I didn't like about the Kirribilli house: too many mirrors. Why would people want bathrooms and wardrobes lined with mirrors? Was it about maximising interior light, simple narcissism, a sex thing?

I wanted to pull against ageism and sexism about physical appearance, so I made rigorous efforts to love my 83-year-old body. One of my techniques was to focus on an elderly stranger in the street (discreetly). I found I was able to generate warm, appreciative feelings towards the bodies of other old people. I could see the undoubted beauty of their wrinkly faces and I would then try to transfer those positive feelings to myself, like carrying a fragile glass bowl across a room—no, that's not quite right. Here's a more accurate metaphor: it was like carrying positive thoughts in a bowl punctured with tiny holes, so by the time the goodwill reached my old carcass most of it had leaked out. Better just to avoid the mirrors in the Kirribilli house.

I gave the schnauzers their evening meal of cooked chicken and rice, with Nietzsche's psychoactive medications secreted inside the goo. While preparing my own dinner I had an exuberant Skype catch-up with Diego, chatted on the phone to Rose, swapped some silly, smutty texts with Rex, then watched a selection of episodes of *Gavin and Stacey*, *30 Rock* and *Friday Night Lights*, my viewing these days being a self-curated selection of tear-jerkers and comedies.

While the two dogs snored at my feet, I wrapped up a present for Mai's two-year-old daughter Stella (my great-granddaughter!). I was very much looking forward to Stella's birthday party on the weekend. So indeed there were many blessings in my life at that time. The blessings sat alongside the miseries, like scoops of food on the plate of a child who cannot abide different foodstuffs touching each other.

I loathe when people say, 'You lost your partner and your son but at least you have your daughter/grandchildren/friends/career.' As if a person can tip a bucket of good feeling from one channel into another one to dilute its pain. It doesn't work that way. Even now,

I am aware of several channels flowing through me simultaneously—grief, joy, anger, gratitude. At any one time, circumstance might draw me into the strong current of one of them, or I might deliberately allow myself to sink into one channel and wallow there for a while.

September 2011.

By the start of the northern hemisphere autumn, the tourists have mostly gone from Kastellorizo but the sea still holds its warmth from the summer months. I loved being back on that island, having three weeks to mooch around with Athena. Just the two of us.

My friend had recently sold the Earlwood house that Nick Samios built in 1947 and had shared with her for sixteen years. She had then shared the house with Patty for thirty-two years. When Patty died from ovarian cancer in 2010, Athena had no interest in staying there alone. Now the plan was to divide her time between a granny flat at the back of Thea's Sydney place and the Kastellorizo house.

The Koutsis residence had always had a pretty courtyard garden, its own olive grove and laughably picturesque location, with a pathway to a spot where it was easy to get into the sea. But Athena had extended the original house to a much more comfortable home than it ever was during her childhood.

While Athena slept late every morning, I would go for a swim. Don't worry—I manoeuvred myself into the water with the care of an old duck aiming to avoid bone breakage, and I didn't venture out far. By the time I was back at the house, dried off, Athena would be up and ready for our daily excursion.

The Koutsis house was a fair distance from the port area where the shops and tavernas were clustered, but the path was on the flat, so we two ancient dames could walk there with rest stops as required, with no need to worry about holding up younger folk.

We would have lunch in one of the tavernas Athena favoured, sitting on the very edge of the water, while a couple of caretta caretta turtles swam a metre away from our table, popping their lovely pale heads above the surface hoping the fishermen would throw them scraps.

The port was lined with brightly painted houses which were always pleasing to my eye. (I wish some of the 'tasteful' countries in the world would paint their houses such cheering colours.) Not far behind the strip with the houses, small hotels, shops, churches, a former mosque, vegie gardens and olive trees, the craggy escarpment swooped up abruptly to loom over everything and gaze out over the vibrant fishing boats and the ardent blue of the Mediterranean. It really is a gorgeous place.

Stuffed with lunch, our mouths still holding the flavours, our clothes dotted with spots of olive oil (we were both enthusiastic eaters but our hand-eye coordination had been diminished by age), Athena and I would stroll back to the house to nap, read, chat to our offspring on Skype, prepare something light for supper, drink wine, then talk or not talk as the mood would take us.

There's a precious kind of ease when spending time with someone who's been around for most of the events of your life. On top of the sturdiness of the friendship, Athena and I had both lost our darlings in recent times, so many things were understood without the need for too much verbiage.

I was also lucky to have the chance to suspend my aged limbs in the clear Mediterranean Sea, still a warm twenty-five degrees in late September. The water is a gracious and lenient environment for the body. I recalled the relief of lowering my young heavily pregnant body into the harbour at Nielsen Park back in 1949. And then my mind would roam to other aquatic memories—happily pummelled by the surf at Narrawallee, thighs congealed with the cold on a Cornish beach at the age of eleven, swimming with Leo in a Mexican cenote, wrapping my legs around his waist.

Let me offer a qualification to the 'you must live in the present' advice which is bandied about, often in a prescriptive way. I can see the value of it up to a point. I've done meditation practice and felt the calming effect of focusing on the breath going in and out. All that vagus nerve goodness. But let me put the case for positioning the mind at different points on the timeline, as needed. Savouring a past joy is a risk-free way to circulate some lovely mood-enhancing chemicals. And I believe 'living in the future' has value too—to imagine, plausibly, a future moment when one's present suffering will have ended and good feelings will likely return. The trick is knowing when to live in the past, present or future. Anyway, don't let some moist-lipped smug know-it-all shame you for not 'living in the present'.

By October, Kastellorizo empties out, leaving five hundred or so permanent residents. That created the ideal window for Athena to book up accommodation for her family and friends before the hotels closed for the winter.

Athena wanted to gather her daughters, grandkids, great-grandkids, cousins, and other beloved people in one place for a belated eighty-fifth birthday celebration, and with some gentle emotional blackmail, my friend managed it. Over the next few days, Kastellorizo filled up with Athena's guests and she arranged boat trips to lovely spots like the Blue Grotto, hikes for the younger folk and long lunches in the sun for everyone.

For that week, I moved into a villa with Rex, Walton and Donna. Rex joined me on morning swims. He was trying to maintain fitness, but a recent diagnosis of diabetes had knocked him around.

'Type one is the kind children get. But it hit me at sixty-six! The diabetes, like my career as an artist, is very late-onset.' He did a jokey grimace. 'Weird to think I made it through the worst AIDS years, like surviving the battle of Stalingrad. I mean, there weren't enough days in the week to bury all those fallen comrades. And now I've tripped over my own pancreas.'

'But it can be managed,' I said. 'I mean, with the insulin and—'

'Hopefully. Although there's the prospect my extremities will fall off, my genitals will fail to tumesce and my eyeball arteries will shrivel up. Do you reckon Walton will still fancy me if I'm footless, blind and impotent?'

I thwacked him around the head with my beach towel and he laughed as he fended me off.

'Let's change the subject,' Rex said. We maintained strict time limits on medical talk. 'Ooh, look at the gorgeous water!'

Rose and Vuong arrived the next day, sharing one of the big houses at the port with their kids, the kids' partners, plus Mai's delightful toddler Stella. I'd booked an apartment nearby for Tanya and Nicola, who was about to do her last year of high school. At the last minute, Tanya decided to bring her new boyfriend, Jimmy, a genial, hairy fellow (in the sense of a voluminous beard and shoulder-length hair). Nicola seemed to approve of her mother's choice of partner and I trusted my granddaughter's judgement.

I felt sorry for gentle-mannered Jimmy—being dragged to this event full of noisy people who've known each other a very long time. But I need not have worried. He hit it off with my grandson Van, launching into enthusiastic talk about sourdough, craft beer, pickling, cheese-making and similar fermentation topics that captivated young men at the time. Van had won a couple of young chef awards and there was talk of him opening his own seafood restaurant.

The birthday party started at 1 p.m. and went on into the evening when the courtyard filled with the tangerine glow from a dozen paper lanterns. There was an absurd amount of food, some prepared by Athena and her cousins, plus catering from her favourite taverna.

Athena didn't want any speeches but Thea and Sofia insisted. I love speeches at parties, weddings, funerals. The stickybeak in me loves hearing people talk about someone they cherish, with anecdotes, impenetrable private jokes, all of it. Even bad speeches are good. I hope my speech about Athena was adequate at least. I'd written it with only a day's warning, and emotion did interfere with my delivery as I spoke about my magnificent friend.

After the speeches, assorted Koutsis cousins led the dancing and I couldn't resist. Luckily, Greek dancing is a forgiving style which can welcome little kids, the elderly and any other kind of wobbly individual.

My plan had been to do more house-sitting back in Sydney after the party but seeing how Athena had gathered her dear ones together, fed them and got them dancing, I was inspired to rethink. Time for me to stop being a cuckoo in the nests of rich dog-owners. I should make a home again where I could welcome guests who needed a place to stay, a home in which I could cook and people could bring over food they'd cooked. I decided I should remodel the Summer Hill house to make it that sort of place.

When I took a break from dancing, I mentioned the idea to Rex. The two of us perched on one of the garden ledges, doing rough sketches. By knocking out some walls, I could create a huge kitchen and dining area for gatherings, with bedrooms upstairs for visitors or lodgers, and a self-contained, easy-access flat on the ground floor for me. By the end of the night I had a new floorplan for Summer Hill, drawn by Rex, an architectural draftsman, on a paper napkin.

After Athena's party, all the guests flew away again. I had a Sydney flight booked the following week which left me a few days with Athena, just the two of us.

She was exhausted from the effort and excitement of the party, so needed to take it easy. I did the cooking while she dozed in sunny patches in the courtyard.

One afternoon, when I took some tea outside for her, she tugged at my sleeve for me to sit by her. 'I need to ask a favour, Betty.'

In 2003, Athena had been diagnosed with multiple myeloma. She had responded to treatment, felt pretty well, the disease kept at bay for years. After the shocking speed of Patty's cancer, caring for her, losing her, Athena then discovered that her own illness had progressed.

'I saw the doctors in Sydney,' she said. 'I had more tests in Athens last month. My kidneys are failing. And my bones hurt. More every day.'

I now understood Athena's slow, stiff walking had been a result of pain. And the draining effect of constant pain was the reason she'd stayed in bed late and napped often. For the week of visitors and the party, she had dosed herself with analgesics and hauled up the last of her strength with formidable determination.

'I want to drink some stuff to go finally to sleep. I can't tell the girls about this. Sofia would disapprove and try to stop me. And even if Thea understood—anyway, it would be too upsetting for them.'

It was upsetting to me too, but I attempted to keep that in check and listen.

'But I want to go now,' Athena said calmly. 'It's time.'

'Ah. The party was . . . It was like you went to your own funeral and wake. You got to hear everyone say nice things about you.'

Athena shrugged and smiled. 'I did. So, Betty, will you help me?'

'Oh my darling friend, I wouldn't know what to—'

'I have it all worked out,' she assured me. Of course she did. 'First I take an anti-emetic so I don't throw up. A doctor in Athens gave me some for nausea. Then I drink this.'

Athena reached into a padded bag and pulled out three bottles of cologne.

'Are you hoping to kill yourself with perfume?' I asked.

'In here is Dilaudid. Hydromorphone.'

The opioid had been prescribed for Patty during her last weeks at home, but in the end other painkillers had suited her better. Athena had hidden the large, unused Dilaudid bottle in a high cupboard, then later she decanted the liquid into the three perfume bottles to get through customs.

'Tomorrow, we could have a late lunch, watch the sunset,' she suggested. 'You don't have to do anything with the drugs. I would drink the stuff myself. But I would rather have someone with me. Then you would report that you found me in the morning. I've timed it so the next day, there is a doctor on the roster at the medical clinic who has good English. A nice man. There would be no problem. So, Betty, think it over and we can talk again in the morning. Either way, let's have a good lunch tomorrow.'

That night in bed, I wept as if Athena had already died. But I believe that weeping was helpful: it squeezed out my immediate selfish grief, so the next day I was able to offer my friend the support she'd requested.

We had a good lunch and watched the sunset together. I could see the pain in Athena's face as she shifted in her chair, but I could also see the peacefulness the decision had brought her. We said the loving things to each other that any of us would want to say and hear. She sat up at the kitchen table to drink the anti-emetic and the opioid, saying it felt more dignified that way, then I helped her to lie down on her bed as the drowsiness overtook her. I lay beside her, holding her hand.

'Thank you, Betty.'

She fell into a deep sleep quickly and over the next couple of hours, I heard her breathing slow and eventually cease. As Athena had planned, the doctor on duty at the clinic the next morning was kind and helpful. It was the dignified end I would wish for my friend.

I apologise for the sheer number of deaths in these chapters, but all the dying goes along with living as long as I have. Rest assured there is still some fun to be had in this story (hint: includes psychedelic mushrooms).

NINETEEN

September 2017.

Mud on the bush track was waffled with recent tyre marks. The bloke in town who was leasing me the cabin had drawn a rough map of the path to the creek, but I'd been walking for twenty minutes without finding it. Tyre marks were a surprise because I hadn't seen a vehicle in the valley for the two days I'd been there.

Then I spotted a hand-painted sign hanging from a tree:

PRIVATE ROAD. TURN AROUND. LOCKED VEHICLE GATE
AHEAD.

When the track curled around a bend, there were more menacing signs.

GOOD AT REVERSING? YOU BETTER BE! THE GATE IS
REALLY LOCKED!
STILL ON THIS ROAD?? YOU MUST BE TOO MORONIC
TO READ OR YOU HAVE A DEATH WISH!!!

All my bravado about this off-the-grid plan was suddenly flushed out of my body. Possibly everyone was right: an 89-year-old woman staying alone in a remote valley was a stupid idea.

I heard a rustle in the undergrowth and glanced sideways to see a child astride a quad bike. The bike, its engine switched off, rolled forward out of the forest and onto the track. I then realised the rider was an adult, twenty-something, jockey-sized, with close-set eyes in a raw pink face, tufts of coppery hair on his scalp and protruding from his blue singlet. He looked like a rhesus monkey.

'You sniffing round for something?' he asked.

'I was trying to find the creek. I'm Liz. Or Betty. Whichever you rather.'

The man tapped his chest. 'Nutsack.'

I opened my mouth, about to laugh, but then realised the name was not a joke.

Nutsack peered at me. 'Creek's down that way.'

'Ah, right. I went the wrong direction. Thanks.'

He tipped his small bony head, satisfied with our transaction, and started up the quad bike. I was retreating along the track when I heard the bike engine switch off again.

'Hey!' Nutsack called out.

I turned back to face him, hoping I looked more friendly than terrified.

'Do you want a tattoo?' he asked. 'Twenty bucks for a small one.'

'Oh . . . uh . . .'

'Got my own tatt gun.' Nutsack pulled up the leg of his pants to show off an indecipherable blue blob on his ankle. 'No, wait—I got better at it after that one.' He swivelled round to show his other ankle which sported a lop-sided anchor tattoo.

I nodded and smiled.

'So do you want a tatt or not?' he asked.

'Not. I mean, no. Thanks anyway.'

Nutsack flapped his arm back towards my cabin. 'The creek is near your place but the other side.' Then he revved the quad bike and disappeared into the forest.

Let me explain how I came to be in this valley off the grid.

In 2012, I'd remodelled the Summer Hill house according to the blueprint Rex Lightfoot had helped me draw on the paper napkin in Kastellorizo. In the renovated house, I hosted regular Sunday lunches around the huge dining table and spilling out onto the back terrace—family members, friends and random folk I thought might get on together, with people bringing platters of food, eating, drinking and yabbering for hours, sometimes dancing. Over the years, the upstairs bedrooms were occupied by a series of lodgers and visitors. My little flat on the ground floor had its own entrance but internal access to the big kitchen of the house. I could stay in my own burrow, writing, reading, watching telly, then wander into the main house whenever I had a hankering for company. It was a sweet set-up.

Things started to sour in that gradual way a once-sweet arrangement can. I was proper old by then, needing to manage my energy, and there were periods when I should not have had so many people in the house. My romantic vision of the Sunday lunches was sometimes spoiled by the crackle of disagreements between guests. Meanwhile, Rex and my daughter Rose urged me not to be too trusting when it came to inviting individuals I barely knew to live in the house. I dismissed their warnings, stubbornly backing my own judgement. In the end there were several cases of people betraying my trust, thieving from other residents, and even one violent incident. My confidence was shaken.

Still, I had a mightily privileged life, and if there was a bad taste fermenting in my mouth, it was really a result of two factors: the state of the world and the unwise way I chose to engage with the world.

The period between 2012 and 2017 was no more infuriating than any other run of years. But things happening in the world at that time got to me and I failed to respond with wisdom-of-the-elders equanimity. I kept stuffing my face with news reports, documentaries, comment pieces, sticking my mouth under the tap of online information. I picture the video I saw once of the awful practice of gavage, the force-feeding of geese, pushing grain down their poor throats to fatten their livers to produce foie gras. Except that metaphor doesn't hold in my case because no one was forcing this foolish old goose to guzzle media content about the climate crisis, terrorism, gun violence, genocide, and other varieties of human cruelty. I chose to open my throat and shove it all in.

I was supposed to be working on a new novel, but I kept interrupting myself to write opinion articles for newspapers and websites. I wrote an op-ed for the *Sydney Morning Herald* about male violence against women, laying out the statistics, calling for action, demanding men face up to the misogyny that underpinned those brutal crimes. It was an angry piece, but reasonable. I have no regrets about writing it. What I regret is choosing to pay attention to the trolls afterwards. There was a spray of revolting comments on the newspaper's website which I should not have read. I was also a passionate contributor to Twitter. (I accept that was foolish, but this was 2015/2016 and I fancied myself as a social-media-savvy woman.) I engaged with the trolls, answering back, copping threats of death and lurid sexual violence. Logically I could discount those vile comments, but some of the poison still soaked in. I let toxic online individuals colonise more of my mental capacity than all the lovely people in my life added together.

As 2016 ground on into 2017, I allowed world events and the cacophony of opinions to spin me up into an exhausted, infuriated wreck. There is simply too much opinion in the world, including my own. (I realise I'm being opinionated as I write that.) Too much opinion and not enough curiosity.

US airstrikes in Afghanistan killed hundreds of civilians. Brexit. A gunman opened fire with semi-automatic weapons in a Latino gay nightclub in Orlando. In Australia, the tally of Aboriginal deaths in custody was ticking over, relentless and shameful. An Islamic State terrorist drove a truck into a crowd in Nice, killed eighty-six people and sparked a racist backlash. Then came the stupefying election of Donald Trump. And constantly, constantly, constantly, across the planet, men brutalised women. In Iraq, ISIS were subjecting women and girls to slavery, rape, violence, but in any year of any decade, there was some version of the story. Sometimes, I would be consumed, burning up, with the thought: 'Men hate us. They hate us.'

It's hard to identify the line between my own emotional baggage and what was a reasonable response to world events. What I am sure about is that by early 2017 any protective coating I had was worn away. I was skinless. Any piece of news about injustice or the suffering of a friend or a distant stranger seemed to land on my raw flesh in an unbearable way.

But I had no self-control. I checked my phone relentlessly, plugged into the awfulness of the world in a way that did the world no good and did me no good. I scrutinised strangers in the street, wondering what ugly thoughts were brewing in their skulls, and all the while my phone dinged in my pocket with another horrifying news story or another notification letting me know a troll wanted to rape my grandchildren. I needed to unplug myself from the world for a while.

When I announced my plan to live off the grid in a bushland cabin, Rose was disbelieving at first, then annoyed.

'This is insane, Mum. You can't do this.'

I arced up, loathing the idea that my autonomy would be constrained. 'This is my business. And I need to get away.'

'Do you, though? Why do you have to lurch from one extreme to another? An obsessively connected woman one minute and now you're a fucking forest nymph? Why does it have to be all or nothing?'

'Maybe sometimes it does have to be, because these damn things . . .' I pulled my mobile phone out of my jacket pocket and held it as if it were a live hand grenade.

'No. Do not demonise a piece of equipment. Most people manage to use digital communications without being total nutcases. Switch off your phone now and then, meditate, sit under a tree. How long do you plan to hide away in the wilderness?'

'I don't know. Maybe I'll only last a week. Maybe a few months.'

'You're eighty-nine. You cannot live on your own in a remote place. Even if you are absurdly healthy for your age. Oh, wait . . . shit . . . is this a suicide plan?'

'No. It's an experiment. I'm not expecting you to take responsibility for it.'

'But you must realise I'll be in a constant state of anxiety about you. Is that fair?'

I conceded it wasn't entirely fair. We reached a compromise position. I would choose a spot within three hours' drive of Sydney and submit to a medical check at regular intervals.

It took a couple of months to find a suitable rental. My grandson Van was the one driving me around on the day I found the right spot. The real estate agent had done a hand-drawn map because the satnav would cut out before we reached the destination. Looking at my phone, seeing the bars disappear from three to two to one, my breathing slowed with each drop. When the farmland gave way to more scruffy country, my phone read 'SOS calls only'. A little further on, it was 'No service'. A few roadside mailboxes indicated there must be houses somewhere in the bushland, but eventually even those petered out.

We turned off the decent dirt surface onto a corrugated branch road—more of a track really—which swooped up and dropped again, as if depositing the car down between the hills. The rough road then ran along a narrow valley floor, with thickly forested hillsides rising steeply on both sides. Those hillsides seemed to tuck in behind us, folding over the mouth of the valley—a topographical illusion—making this place feel enclosed and hidden. A few kilometres in, the track hit a steep rockface, a dead-end.

There were two properties visible from the valley floor, both owned by city people. One had a small mudbrick house which was rarely occupied. On the other block, an old construction-worker's hut had been towed onto a flat patch of land. There was a stack of building materials, but I never saw the owner and weeds were growing through the piles of unused stuff.

My rented cabin, a hundred metres up the slope from the valley track, hidden among the trees, was the remnant of someone's forsaken vision for a self-sufficient life. There were abandoned vegetable beds on the wedge of flat ground, with a derelict chicken coop built against the side wall of the house—a two-room kit home with a front porch and tiny bathroom tacked on the back. A large tank provided water and solar panels provided power, with a backup diesel generator and LP gas cylinders for the stove.

The day I moved in, Rose and Van unloaded supplies into the storage space under the floor. Van was enthusiastic about the place and he spent a couple of hours turning over the rich soil in the galvanised steel vegetable beds. Meanwhile my daughter did a lot of performative sighing.

'Mum, you don't have to go through with this just because you said you'd do it. No shame in admitting this isn't a good idea. I can drive you home again now. We could come up here for weekend getaways.'

But I was not to be dissuaded.

Once Rose and Van drove away, I was alone, disconnected from the world. (Full disclosure: I had one possible communication thread. My daughter had contacted the city folk who owned the mudbrick house on the valley floor and she'd negotiated that I could use their satellite phone in an emergency.)

At dusk on the first evening, preparing my dinner, I heard furtive crunching noises just outside and a flush of panic went through my rib cage. I peered out the side window and saw four chickens making their way inside the dilapidated coop to settle for the night. The chooks must've been descendants of the original flock, the lucky ones who had evaded feral cats and foxes.

That night, I lay in bed listening to the susurrance of the wind in the trees. I wasn't sure whether the fluttering in my belly was fear to be alone here, cut off, or elation to be alone here, cut off. I chose to believe it was the latter.

The next day, it rained nonstop, so I stayed inside indulging in the childlike pleasure of arranging my new cubby. I filled a shelf with the books I planned to read and notebooks I planned to fill with profound writings about my off-grid life.

The day after that, I ventured outside in gumboots, looking for the creek, which was when I first encountered Nutsack and declined his offer of a tattoo.

Nutsack was a member of the Pope family, the only permanent inhabitants of the valley, who lived in various slab huts and caravans deep in the forest. Arthur Pope had named his son 'Nutsack' because that was what he looked like at birth. Born in a shed in the valley, the boy never went to school and, even as an adult, hardly ever left the forest. His older brother, Lunch Pope, made occasional trips to town in a battered truck, but mostly stayed put, tending the family's marijuana crop. There was no mention of the Pope boys' mother, but their sister, Girl, had apparently left the valley on account of being 'clever'. I could only hope Girl Pope was making a good life for herself somewhere. I rarely saw any Popes other than Nutsack and odd sightings of Uncle Roy Pope walking his foul-tempered Shetland pony on a leash like a dog.

During my first week, it became clear that the chickens were voluntary tenants in the old coop and still used the laying boxes. I scored a few fresh eggs. In return I gave the chooks my vegetable scraps and had a go at repairing the door to the henhouse.

'This way you ladies can be safe at night from foxes,' I said out loud to the chickens.

Having no one else to talk to, I chatted to the chickens whenever they were around the cabin. They were very beautiful, with luscious dark caramel feathers and creamy underlayers, happily focused on pecking for worms in the leaf litter.

I'd once heard a radio segment claiming chickens were calmer if humans wore one colour consistently. That fact had made me lose respect for poultry—for being so easy to manipulate. As an experiment, I wore blue trackpants and a blue sweater every day for that first week and the chickens did indeed seem more relaxed. And I discovered I was more relaxed too. The release from making choices, even about something as simple as clothing, helped reduce my stress.

By the end of the second week, I was definitely feeling the benefits of disconnection. My thoughts could still loop back to horrible happenings in the world, but without fresh data there was no fuel to keep things burning as hotly. I made a conscious effort to fill my brain with healthier activities—reading fiction, meditating, listening to Nat King Cole, Dolly Parton, Aretha Franklin, mariachi bands, all on vinyl, thanks to the turntable Mai had found for me. I made sure to take myself outside several times a day to sit still in the forest long enough that the birds would forget I was there and resume their activities. I deliberately envisaged my pituitary gland pumping out less cortisol and the tissues through my body gradually dialling down the inflammation. I did miss my family, my pals—no question. But so many people precious to me had died by this point, I already had well-developed emotional pathways for missing dear ones in a bearable way.

Despite being only a few hours from the city, the place was surprisingly isolated. Occasionally, people would lose their way and drive along the valley floor until they hit the dead-end, then wander around their cars holding phones up to the sky, appealing to the gods of connection to save them. But apart from the odd sighting of a Pope, I saw no one for three months.

Given my enormous age in this isolated spot, I tried to be sensible—for example, I would step out of the shower carefully and steady myself before reaching for a towel. One of the cautionary scenarios my daughter had emphasised was me slipping on a wet floor, immobilised by a broken hip, with no way to call for help. I suggested Rose issue me with a cyanide capsule to wear in a locket around my neck, but my flippancy did not go down well.

During my fourth week, I was walking to the creek when Nutsack popped up on his quad bike. I cleared my throat, conscious that I hadn't used my voice for many days, aside from muttering to chooks.

'Good morning, Nutsack,' I said. Neighbourly.

He nodded. 'Wanna buy a bag of weed?'

'No, thanks.' The two times in my life I'd tried marijuana, it made me morose. 'What I would like to buy is a bag of chicken feed.'

He tipped his bony head in an unreadable gesture and buzzed away on the bike.

That afternoon, Nutsack parked out the front of my cabin and rolled a sack of poultry feed off the back of the bike and onto the porch. After a brief chat about canned goods, he asked me to pay for the bag with tinned tuna.

For the next two months, I spent my days making omelettes, tending to a few salad greens I'd planted, reading, paddling in the creek, my mind gradually circling down to a calmer state.

In early December, Rose showed up to check on me. She and Vuong drove out to the valley, leading a convoy with Van's station wagon, then Mai in another car with her two daughters, eight-year-old Stella and five-year-old Ruby. It was only when I watched them drive up that I was aware of the aching absence that must have formed in my body during the last three months. Seeing them filled me up.

They had carloads of gear, with the intention of camping overnight and exploring my hideaway. I took them to the best swimming spot in the gully and we picnicked there, splashing about in the stony part of the creek bed or swimming in the deeper colder water where a sheer sandstone wall created a natural reservoir.

Back at the cabin, Vuong and Mai got busy setting up tents and Van recruited his nieces to help unload seedlings and horticultural supplies. My grandson had researched what crops would grow well in the valley and require limited physical exertion by an elderly vegetable gardener.

Meanwhile, Rose conducted a medical check on me, taking my blood pressure, listening to my heart.

'You look well, Mum.' She sounded slightly disappointed.

'I feel well. Apart from my hip and my bunion. Oh, and my eyeballs get gritty. I hope you brought me some more of the drops.'

'Mum, are you really going to stay here? Haven't you got whatever it is you wanted out of this little escapade?'

Rose was (and still is, at the time of writing) a wonderful woman—smart, compassionate, strong—but not the most poetic soul. I think Mac may have understood why I wanted to stay in the valley for a longer stretch. And now that I've written that thought down, I feel terrible—guilty for comparing my children in a way that's unflattering to either one or in a way that hits one over the head with the strengths of the other. But I will fight the urge to delete the above comments. I wish to be as honest here as I can bear.

'Come back with us now,' Rose argued. 'Or stay a few more weeks then come home for Christmas.'

But I was afraid that I would be sucked back into toxic patterns. I didn't trust myself.

'Thanks, my darling,' I said. 'Thanks for everything you're doing to make this possible for me. But I might stay on a bit longer.'

When I handed Rose a bunch of letters to post for me, she sighed but accepted it.

That night, Van made a campfire and cooked delicious prawns and whole fish for the seven of us. Stella and Ruby, their bellies full of the chocolate mousse I'd made for dessert, were excited about the chance to sleep in a tent. Around the campfire, it was understood that there was to be no discussion of ugly world events. Instead, there was lively conversation about Mai's experiences as a GP, Vuong's work on a new high school science syllabus, Van's food truck business. I loved hearing every detail of their activities and it was the loveliest of weekends. But when the three vehicles headed off on Sunday afternoon, back to the world, I didn't feel as bereft as I'd feared.

Rose had brought the medications and food supplies I needed to last the three months until the next visit. My stores included rice, pasta, cooking oil, spices, long-life milk, tea, coffee, chickpeas, lentils, nuts, tahini, salamis, dried peas, tins of tuna, sardines, tomatoes, corn, tomatillos, jars of olives, minced garlic, pickled onions and morello cherries, packets of biscuits and blocks of dark chocolate. Tubes of condensed milk were saved for moments I needed a special boost. The non-perishables were supplemented by plenty of eggs, plus the fresh stuff Van had planted for me (spinach, salad greens, cauliflowers, herbs). It turned out Nutsack was crazy for tuna, so I could barter tins for fresh peaches, cheese and other items he seemed able to source. I'd brought boxes of achiote paste and dried chillis that Diego had sent from Mexico, so my diet was far from bland.

Rose had also brought a stack of mail for me—letters from friends and a few notes from readers of my novels forwarded by the publisher. I set myself the task of replying to all of them. Knowing a letter wouldn't land in the hands of the recipient for many weeks, it prompted me to write more thoughtfully. In regular life, I used to message or chat to Rex and Donna every day, but that meant communication had sometimes skipped across the surface of quotidian detail and immediate laughs (mind you, all kinds of laughs are precious). In the letters I wrote to my pals from the valley cabin, there was space and the weight of time that allowed me to be more considered or expansive, as well as playful. Very satisfying.

I was sitting on the porch one afternoon, writing a rough draft of a letter in my notebook, when Nutsack puttered up on his quad bike.

'G'day, Liz.' He'd opted to call me 'Liz' instead of 'Betty'. There had been an Auntie Betty whom he described as 'only quite nice', which translated as 'an absolute monster'.

'D'you like goat's cheese?' he asked. 'Uncle Roy makes it.'

He pulled a parcel out of his backpack—a roll of fresh white cheese in plastic wrap. Should I have trusted a cheese made in a caravan by Uncle Roy? Perhaps not, but I was choosing to live dangerously.

'I'd love some goat's cheese. Thank you.'

I fetched some tins from the kitchen so Nutsack could decide what was a reasonable swap for the cheese. As he considered his selection, his gaze wandered to the half-written page in my notebook.

'What do you write in there?'

'Letters to people. Notes about stuff I see.'

'Do you write about me in there?'

I couldn't tell from his expression if he felt threatened or flattered by that idea.

'There's one bit about you bringing me the chook feed. I'd be happy for you to read it,' I said.

I flicked through the pages to find the relevant passage to show him, but Nutsack waggled his hands and took a step back, as if the notebook were hazardous.

'Oh no . . .'

It struck me that this young man might not know how to read. I didn't want to embarrass him by saying anything to that effect, so I offered, 'My handwriting might be too messy. Would you like me to read out—'

But Nutsack interrupted abruptly. 'I can't read.'

He scrutinised my face to see my reaction. I nodded, careful not to make him feel ashamed in any way.

'I could have a go at teaching you to read if you'd like that.'

I expected him to shake off the idea, but he shot back immediately with, 'Yes. Yes, please.'

On random occasions from January 2018 onwards, Nutsack Pope would appear on his quad bike outside the cabin and I would suspend whatever I was doing to dive into a reading and writing lesson. Most of the books I had with me were small print and inappropriate for a beginner, so I ended up composing basic readers for my neighbour, creating short stories about the creek, chickens and quad bikes, and then expanding out to scenes from city life, folk tales, funny stories. It turned out Nutsack was a perfectly bright person and learned quickly. After a month of lessons, he started bringing old publications—novels with yellowed pages, 1960s school textbooks, magazines from fifty years ago—which must have belonged to Popes of previous generations. He also brought a chainsaw maintenance manual, which became his special focus. I reckon I could check the throttle trigger, change the fuel filter and sharpen the blade on a chainsaw with reasonable proficiency. It reminded me of days learning about random topics as I typed up PhD theses, over forty years back, and it also reminded me how much I'd loved my time teaching in Mexico.

Nutsack tried to pay me for the lessons, but it was only an hour or two per week and I enjoyed the company of this unusual young man who knew a lot about the animals and plants in the area, marijuana cultivation, and could tell tales, real or apocryphal, about things that had happened in this valley.

I would not wish to give the reader the impression of Nutsack Pope as a blessedly innocent, noble forest dweller. The reality was, he was a sad figure, lonely, neglected and malnourished as a child, allowed to languish uneducated, unskilled to handle the world beyond a small radius, a young man who had clearly been physically abused by Uncle Roy and possibly others. I don't want to romanticise his situation. But for the time I was there, Nutsack and I found value in each other's company, and we were kind to one another.

March 2018.

With the *Top Hat* soundtrack on the turntable, I danced with a chair cushion. I had prescribed the Astaire–Rogers dance sequence for myself to buoy my spirits.

The day before, Rose had arrived for my March check-up. My sparky great-granddaughter Stella came with her and Rose's other passenger was Rex Lightfoot. A splendid surprise.

As my friend eased himself out of the car, he emitted a flamboyant groan of pain about his aching back. Rex was seventy-three by this point. Even my young friends were old now. But then he roared out 'Lizzie!' with youthful gusto and scooped me into one of his rib-crushing hugs.

'Walton sends his love. He wanted to come but he's still filming in Queensland,' Rex explained.

'So. Mum.' My daughter's stern tone indicated I was in for a scolding. 'Before we go to all the hassle of unloading three months' worth of chickpeas, can you please consider calling an end to this? Isn't six months offline enough for you? Just come home with us now.'

I could feel Rex's eyes on me, waiting for my response.

'I'm sorry to disappoint you, sweetheart, but I'm—'

She jumped in briskly. 'Right. Okay. You do what you like. As fucking always.'

'The thing is, Rosie—'

'No. No. I'm not going to discuss it with you. Let's just do what needs doing.'

Rose made a noisy, cranky show of grabbing her medical bag and flinging it open on the porch. She conducted my medical check without saying a word or making eye contact (which is a tricky feat).

The four of us ate lunch on foldout chairs on the porch. We let Stella's bright chatter fill the air so there was no space for lecturing from Rose or defensiveness from me. As soon as lunch was over, Stella was ants-in-her-pants keen to plant the seedlings Uncle Van had given her and Rose took the chance to further avoid me by helping her granddaughter.

Rex and I took a stroll along one of the forest paths.

'Rose is just worried about you,' said Rex. 'All the way here in the car, she was saying she hoped you'd be ready to leave this time. She reeled off a list of the things you haven't been around for.'

Van had announced to the family that he'd fallen in love with a woman called Anusha and they were expecting a baby in October. Ruby had started big school. Mac and Tanya's daughter Nicola had completed her psychology master's and started the extra training to be a school counsellor. I'd missed all those moments and many others over the six months.

'But I've gotta say, Lizzie, you seem better. This has done you good.'

'Meaning I was a pain in the bum before I came here.'

'You know you were. And you were making yourself miserable. But you seem happier here. I don't know if I should feel *wounded* that you seem happier when you're far away from friends and—well, far away from *me*.'

'Rex my darling, I miss you so much I have a little cry quite often.'

'Well, that's okay then. As long as being apart from me can occasionally make you wretched to the point of tears, I'm happy. How much longer do you reckon you'll stay?'

'Not sure. But I can always toddle down to the satellite phone and call for a pickup.'

Rex stopped and gripped my hand. 'Promise me you will call if you get sad. I know I said you look happy, but being on your own all the time, it can be risky and . . . well, I worry.'

I circled my arms around his vast torso and hugged him tight. I had to remember that he was the person who'd found me at my lowest point, lying in urine-soaked sheets. It was unkind of me to ask this man to worry about me now.

'I promise,' I said.

June 2018.

Rose didn't even come for the next quarterly supply run, sending Mai to do the medical check in her place.

'Is your mother very pissed off with me?' I asked.

She grimaced. 'Very.'

Mai did bring two passengers: her daughter Stella and my friend Donna. Both of them burst out of the car with childlike eagerness. Stella was busting to plant a new load of seedlings Van had given her, and Donna was excited about everything she laid her eyes on, in the scattergun enthusiasm that woman still possessed at the age of almost seventy.

'Oh my God, Lizzie! This place is incredible! Show me everything! Oh, I can see why you love it! The battery thing is so clever! You have chooks! I could live here! I could so live here!'

Stella galloped over. 'You have to see the creek, Auntie Donna!'

'Yes, please!'

We all walked down to the creek after lunch and Donna's gushing about the place continued. 'I think I have nature-deficiency. That's a thing. Nature-deficit disorder. I need to get more nature into me!'

On the way back to the house, Donna described, at motor-mouth speed, the professional problems she was wrestling with. I admired her stamina to still be writing and producing TV projects all these years on.

'The junior exec wanted to cast—I am not kidding—he wanted to cast a twenty-year-old as the doctor. Fuck me dead! Am I too old to be putting up with shit from the smooth-cheeked marketing graduates who run streaming platforms? Why do I feel the need to keep doing it? I should just stop. But I don't know how I'd—'

Donna suddenly planted her feet on the path. 'Oh! I should come and stay here for a while! A week or something. To reboot my brain. I'd bring my own tent and food and everything. Would you hate that, Lizzie? Say if you'd hate it.'

'I wouldn't hate it,' I said. 'It'd be fun. I mean, you might find things here a bit—'

Then just as suddenly, Donna gasped. 'I know who we should cast as the doctor! Of course we should cast Freya! Yes, I could sell the distributors on her! Ooh—I need to tell Nathan so he can check Freya's availability . . .'

She pulled her phone out of her pocket and then a second later, barked a laugh at herself. 'Der. No reception here.' Donna started striding up through the trees, holding her phone ahead of her, hoping for connection. 'If I walked to higher ground, could I get a couple of bars?'

At the end of the visit, Donna hugged me tight. 'I miss you to death, Lizzie, but I love the idea of you being here.'

September 2018.

A hundred metres along the track from my cabin, the way was blocked by a huge, steroidal ute with a spotlight rig and four dogs in a cage.

Pig-hunters had started coming to the valley, thanks to websites in which hunters exchanged information about good spots to kill animals. Even in a pocket of the planet that was off the grid, the internet could send its tentacles in to destroy things. I had no argument with the piggers as such—it was beneficial to rid the bush of destructive feral animals—but I hated the way most of them treated their dogs.

The mastiff crosses on this truck had chunks torn off their ears and chests scarred from being ripped by wild boars. Standing by the vehicle were two rough-headed blokes with more dogs than teeth.

'Shut up! Stupid fucking animals! What ya barking at anyway?' the taller man bellowed at the unfortunate creatures.

The dogs were barking at me. Trouble was, I needed to move around the ute to return to my place. When one of the mastiffs threw itself at the side of the cage and snarled at me, I took a step back, flinching.

The shouty guy glared at me. 'What's up your arse? Scared of dogs or just being a shithead about mine?'

I kept my head down, hoping to avoid a confrontation. But then the shorter pigger started barking and growling at me like a dog, spluttering into laughter at his own performance.

'That's pathetic, mate,' said the tall pigger. 'She's only scared of real mongrels.'

He poked a crowbar into the cage to make the dogs bark, tormenting them, jabbing one of them in the ribs until it howled in pain.

That was when I lost control of my mouth. 'Leave that poor fucking animal alone!'

An old lady swearing can be a handy surprise, but unfortunately, it only shut the guy up for a second.

'Excuse me, bitch? I thought you hated my dogs.'

'No, I love dogs. What I hate is monumental dickheads who bully their dogs.'

I regretted the words the instant they were out of my mouth. I didn't want to die on this track, an impulsive fool, with a crowbar denting my stupid skull.

Just as I was picturing such a death, Nutsack appeared on his quad bike in front of the ute. I was scared for him—he was so much smaller than the two hunters—but he didn't seem scared at all.

The piggers noticed that Nutsack had a chainsaw sitting across his lap.

'Is that chainsaw meant to scare me, mate?' asked the short guy.

'He's one of the Popes,' the tall one hissed to his mate, suddenly nervous. He'd obviously heard stories about the family.

'The chainsaw's meant for cutting firewood,' Nutsack replied. 'Need to be careful with it but.'

I imagined the testicles of the piggers shrivelling up into their groins with fear and I found myself smiling. The two of them looked at me and they figured the sweary lady with a shrub of frizzy white hair, wearing grubby blue clothes, must be a Pope matriarch. They shouldn't risk inciting the anger of that family by disrespecting me. The tall pig-hunter did a bit of macho cursing under his breath then ordered his mate into the ute and they drove off. I hadn't realised how much sharing the valley with the Pope family could be a form of protection.

When I made it back to my cabin, it was a surprise to find Rose waiting there, three days early for my September check-in. There was shock on her face when she clocked me walking around the chicken coop and I saw myself through my daughter's eyes—a feral old lady unfit for the wider world.

'Hello, darling,' I said. 'It's wonderful to see you.'

'Is it? It's been a whole year now, Mum. Will you come back with me today?'

When I hesitated for two seconds, Rose grunted, stalked back to her car and started unloading boxes of supplies.

'Rosie, can we just talk about—'

'No. No chat. No lovely picnics or campfire catch-ups. Let's just get this over with.'

As I helped her carry the food into the cabin, she avoided my gaze.

'Is anyone else coming this time?' I asked.

'I told everyone not to come. It only encourages you to keep going with this bullshit.'

When the unpacking was done—a painful, non-speaking hour— she handed me a stack of mail.

'I don't care how healthy you are for your age, Mum, the chance of you dying out here is . . . You're being selfish and it's—I've had enough of this shit.'

'If I just fell down a hole in the gully, it might save you a lot of angst.'

Rose was in such a state that my frivolous comment landed like a lit match on a kerosene-soaked mattress.

'Excuse me?' She was loud, shrill. 'Are you suggesting it'd be good if you fell down a hole and I was left not knowing what happened?'

'No, sorry, darling. That was just an example—'

'An example of what? An example of you not thinking about—
Fuck you, Mum. You do not care what's happening to anyone else.
Why don't you want to live near us? Don't you love us anymore?'

'Oh, Rosie. Oh, my darling. I love you all so much.'

But my daughter refused to listen to any more of my bleating.

As she drove away, I realised what I should have said.

It wasn't that I didn't love people anymore. I was bursting with
love for my dear ones. But I couldn't let myself *need* any other human
being who might die on me. My system couldn't take it. That's what
I should have explained to Rose. But I hadn't understood it myself
until the moment after she left.

Inside the cabin, I looked through the new stack of mail.

A brisk typed note from Rose filled me in on Vuong's recent
cardiac problems. Apparently there had been a scary period, but
then a pacemaker was put in and he was doing well now. I had not
been around to support my family through any of that.

On notepaper bordered with whale illustrations was a letter from
Stella, addressed to 'Dear GG' (the name my great-grandkids called
me), appealing for my help. Inspired by Greta Thunberg, Stella was
determined to go on strike over the climate crisis, and like Greta,
her plan was to sit outside her school with placards. Her parents
had forbidden this, but Stella hoped that I could intercede and argue
the case for activism. Inside the whale envelope, she had included
printouts of articles about climate change, with alarming statistics
marked with her primary school green highlighter. The idea that my
great-granddaughter, who'd only just turned nine, was carrying the
burden of those heavy worries—well, it was profoundly sad.

I flicked through the rest of the letters, wary of opening another.
When I recognised Rex's beautiful hand-lettering on an envelope,
I grabbed it. Inside, there was only one page. It began with an apology
for the brevity—understandable once I read the note. Rex was writing
to inform me that our friend Donna Silvestri had died at the end of

August (two weeks back). Her death had been very sudden: she'd collapsed in the production office with a searing headache and by the time she was taken to hospital, it was clear the sub-arachnoid haemorrhage was fatal. The note ended with another apology: Rex had not driven to the valley to share the news because he'd been busy organising Donna's funeral, and given my series of bereavements, he didn't want to add to my emotional burden.

I clutched his letter hard against my belly as if applying pressure to a bleeding wound. I now understood that at least some of Rose's anger was because she knew I had colossally let Rex down. She had reason to be angry. I started breathing hard, head clanging with grief about vibrant, brilliant, loving Donna, and guilt that I had abandoned Rex when he must have been distraught beyond measure. The pounding of the pulse in my head muffled the sounds from outside the cabin until the noises were unmissable.

'Get back here! Get over here, you brainless fucking dog!'

Through the window, I saw one of the mastiffs bound down the slope and jump up into the cage on the back of the piggers' ute. As the truck drove off, I saw white feathers caught by the wind then flutter down onto a chicken lying on the ground. I used to leave the coop open in the daytime so the chooks could come and go, only shutting it at night to keep out foxes. The dog must have pounced on the chicken as she wandered in the area around the porch.

She was dead, throat torn open, feathers smeared with blood. I carried her inside, holding her beautiful toffee and cream body against my chest as if I could protect her somehow, and put her gently on the table.

Suddenly feeble, feeling the weight of every one of my ninety years, I stumbled through to sprawl on the bed. I'd let so many people down. I was no use to anyone. Worse than no use—even if I went back, I'd always be a source of worry and effort for Rose, Mai, Van, Rex. Every loss I'd endured, every world event that distressed me, every single bad thing I'd come to this place to avoid, all of them rushed along the valley floor and up the slope like a twister, filling the air in the cabin, pressing down on my body.

An hour later I still hadn't moved from the bed. And then I found I couldn't move. It wasn't a stroke. Just the incapacitating effect of shame and grief.

I lay there all night and into the next morning. When Nutsack showed up, he saw the chicken guts and feathers on the ground outside, and through the side window, he saw my feet on the bed. He came inside, brought me a glass of water but couldn't persuade me to eat anything. I muttered a few things about me being a loathsome person—I'm not entirely sure—but whatever I said, it prompted him to return an hour later with an offering.

'If you're sad, Liz, these might make you feel a bit better.' Nutsack was holding a plastic yoghurt tub half-filled with wild mushrooms.

'What are those? Are they—'

'Special mushrooms.'

Nutsack used my mortar and pestle to pound the mushrooms, then squeezed the juice from two lemons. He stirred mulched-up mushrooms into the juice for ten minutes or so and put a small glass of the mixture on the bedside shelf.

'It's there if you fancy it. Bit of a pick-me-up.'

I'm a curious person. I sat up and sniffed at the citrus and fungus cocktail. Through the window, I could see Nutsack sitting on his quad bike outside, leaving me in peace but keeping watch. I trusted that gentle young man enough to know he wouldn't try to poison me and I'd read enough about psilocybin to know it was unlikely to kill me. On impulse I downed the mushroom drink like a double shot of tequila. I put a Nat King Cole LP on the turntable, thinking a mellow sound would be beneficial.

A brief note: I've never been a fan of people going on about their drug experiences, which can seem phony or inaccessible to a reader

who is sober at the time of reading. But for the sake of its importance in my story, I will offer some description of my six-hour trip.

On my empty stomach, the effect came on quickly, within twenty
minutes. My body felt heavy in the armchair but in a pleasurable
way. I started staring at the cross-hatched pattern on the kitchen
cupboard and it was enthralling. Soon after that, the whole room
was shimmering with colours. As Nat sang 'The Very Thought of
You', the melody sent magenta and green ribbons into the air. The
walls of the cabin and the trees outside the window were pulsating
in time with my breath, as if the whole world was breathing through
my lungs. Impossibly lovely.

But then painful things started to ooze up unbidden. I had the
sensation that all the people I loved who had died were pressed against
me—my mother, Michael, Pauline, Leo, Mac, Pearl, Athena, Patty,
Donna and others. For a terrible moment I thought the coldness of
their lifeless bodies pushing against mine would kill me, but then
suddenly it seemed I could warm them all up with my own body
heat. I found myself smiling. I could sit with the sorrow of losing
them and it was okay.

Next, I felt the urge to go outside. I was aware of the need to be
careful, ensuring I had handholds as I stepped down from the porch.
There was Nutsack sitting on his bike, nodding his bony head—his
beautiful little head—but asking nothing of me, so I was free to lie
down on a soft patch of grass and stare up into the foliage, intensely
green against the sky.

That was when the most wonderful hallucinations came—colours
dancing through the trees, my body floating in sweet water, all three
of my children as unborn babies inside my belly in turn. Then my
relinquished daughter Frances as an adult woman, smiling, soaking
up my love for her. Mac laughing. Leo gazing at me. I could let go of
stories I told myself about how I'd failed people and how they'd failed
me. For a glorious slice of time, I loved and cherished every person

I'd ever known, including myself. And after that, the very notion of my self dissolved (an experience often reported by psilocybin users). There was one moment when my spiky little ego arced up and wrestled with that, fighting to survive as a special singular entity. But a moment later, I gave in and let myself evaporate into the air pulsing through the trees around me. Everything in the universe was okay. It was all okay.

I would not suggest that a psilocybin trip is the answer to everything, and that potent sense of everything being okay does not stick as a permanent mindset. But those mushrooms were a blessing to me on that day. And almost ten years on, even when I am at my most testy or wretched, I can call up that memory—or some of the juice of it anyway—the memory of how it felt to let my petty, suffering ego dissolve into the air for a moment.

When the hallucinogen started to wear off, I yanked the top off a jar of olives Rose had brought and scarfed down the salty contents. The bloodied body of the chicken was still sitting on the table, so my next project was to bury her. I was hoping Nutsack could help me dig a grave, but he'd disappeared. I took a trowel from the vegetable garden and walked to a spot where the soil was loose enough that I could dig a serviceable grave for the dear chook. I lay down for an hour to recover from the exertion of that and to finish sobering up, then made my way slowly down to the mudbrick house on the valley floor, found the hidden key, and used the satellite phone to ring my daughter.

The summer after I left the valley, Van used the cabin as a weekender, which gave me considerable pleasure. During those visits, he got to know Nutsack Pope a little and that made me happy too.

The following summer, in the last days of 2019, bushfires went through the valley, destroying every dwelling and many square kilometres of forest. To ease my worry, Van drove out there as soon as the road reopened. He found Nutsack safe in an evacuation centre, in surprisingly good spirits, talking about moving down the coast where there was another branch of the Pope family.

My grandson described driving into the valley and seeing endless stands of blackened trees. Because all vegetation had been burned away in the firestorm, the shape of the hillsides was defined against the sky, like a body stripped of its flesh to reveal the skeleton. When Van stepped out of his car, he felt the crunch of the ash under his boots. The fire had burned so hot there, some people said it may have destroyed the seed bed forever.

Those first days after leaving the valley, in September 2018, the jolt of re-entry was almost too much. The world was as full of ugliness as it had been when I'd sought to escape. Noises—the grating gears of a truck, strident music from a passing car, booming male voices— seemed amplified in my head. The signage in the street, ads in shop windows, on screens, were garish, eyeball-scrambling. Everything was too bright, too loud, too insistent. The only way to stop myself hyperventilating was to close my eyes and imagine myself lying in the forest, away with the pixies on psilocybin.

But I had to come back. I had obligations. I should make things up to Rose. I must look after Rex. I had to help my great-granddaughter Stella solve the climate crisis. I needed to come back to my life, however much of it was left.

TWENTY

8 April 2028.

Today is a Saturday, several days before my actual birthday on the twelfth.

From where I'm sitting, I can see, through the wall of glass along the front of the party venue, a glorious stretch of Sydney Harbour framed by gum trees, with a string of sandstone headlands covered in bushland on the opposite shore.

Choosing a venue with a harbour view was the first of many thoughtful choices for this celebration. My daughter Rose and I were consulted about the event, but the grandkids have made all the arrangements. It's a daytime do, to accommodate extremely old guests and the very young. The catering, organised by my chef grandson Van Le Burnley, has a nod to English, Greek, Vietnamese and Mexican dishes. I'm confident it will be spectacularly good food. Mai has selected a playlist that sweeps through many decades, starting with Astaire–Rogers dance tunes. Nicola arranged for a young woman to come to the house this morning to apply my makeup and do her best with the white frizz which passes as my hair. With such cosmetic help, plus a spectacular Mexican embroidered top Diego sent as a gift, I look as presentable as an almost hundred-year-old person can.

Rose has extracted a promise that during the party I'll stay seated in the motorised chair I use to travel to the shops. I can still walk reasonably well, but with a crowd of people including children darting about, and hopefully some exuberant dancing, she's worried I might get knocked off my feet. A fair call. Wiser to sit, cruising the room on wheels.

Celebrations of birthdays that end in zeros can stir people up to feel expansive and sentimental in the best way. Right now, I'm looking at Rex Lightfoot and Walton Reid across the room. The two of them are standing with their hands on each other's shoulders—both still so damned handsome—engaged in some kind of mutual romantic declaration. It makes me happy to think those two men continue to delight each other, continue to shield and sustain each other through the barrages of crap the universe hurls at them.

I'm still living in the Summer Hill house bequeathed to me by Pearl Jowett, mostly hanging out in my ground floor flat. Currently, the main part of the house is occupied by my granddaughter Nicola, her lovely partner, their twin toddlers and effervescent Cairn terrier Matthew. It's invigorating to hear life going on under our shared roof and to know I can totter through the connecting door to the big kitchen whenever I fancy conversation with adults or chatter with small children.

I still cook a little but I'm wary of fumbling with knives or hot pans, so I have most of my meals brought in, either by family or a commercial enterprise. For now, I manage my own ablutions—very slowly—but once I no longer can, I'm determined to have a carer come in for that. I never want family or friends wiping my bum.

A little over a year after my return to the city, the Covid lockdowns began, a time of suffering for many people—so much anxiety, financial strain, isolation. I felt unsettled by the constant discussion of my frailty and the danger I faced from every other human being. But once I accepted the reality of the situation, I found the lockdowns offered a chance to establish new connective tissue with the world. There were many video calls from within my quarantine bunker, including regular videochats with Diego. I would meet Rose or Rex in a park, and we would stroll along in parallel, three metres apart, pausing to face each other to gesture or smile—like a modern version of an Elizabethan galliard. There were weekly family gatherings online which involved performances from small children, raucous parlour games and quizzes. Most nourishing of all, I found a way to be useful while locked down: teaching English as a second language online through the Asylum Seeker Resource Centre. Two of the language students, Nour and Hibaaq, became pals of mine, and they're both here at this party.

Rex Lightfoot's response to the grimness of the virus months was to text one poem and one painting to a list of friends every morning, so we could fill our eyeballs and our minds with something beautiful or thoughtful or enduring, something that hovered in a dimension beyond daily infection numbers and footage of people expiring across the globe. Rex has kept that practice going ever since, and during distressing times it's helped me to keep balance.

I try to do a walk in the neighbourhood every day. I enjoy meeting the dogs and the babies, including Baby Hazel, from the house two doors down, with her luminous smile and spectacular eyebrows that remind me of Athena. Depending on the season, I soak up the intense purple of tibouchinas in flower, the scent of gardenias or whatever is on offer in the street. But the reader should not imagine I've become sentimental, sinking into 'oh it's all about babies and flowers and living in the present'. I still churn myself up about old injustices and current outrages. I'm still thrilled by breakthroughs that were inconceivable when I was a young woman. But I limit my ingestion of news to a defined period per day, then try to put all media aside.

I swim whenever health and circumstances allow. Ashfield Aquatic Centre caters for crumbly older patrons and I can also totter down to the ocean at certain beaches if one of my grandkids will take me.

I do feel lonely sometimes. It's ungrateful to complain about that when I have my daughter, grand-offspring and younger friends. But now that everybody of my generation has gone, there is a special kind of lonesomeness. I sometimes yearn for the ease of being with individuals who've lived through the same decades as me. I might make eye contact with some other wrinkly duck at the hydrotherapy pool and there is a great deal that's understood between us. Then again, I prefer to avoid fatuous talk of the good old days. So, I lurch between a desire to be with the elderly and a drive to seek out the company of younger folk. I regard myself as a geriatric vampire, sucking up the life force of young people.

In the months before this party, my great-granddaughter Stella assembled a slide show of images, and my task was to rummage through boxes for photos she could include. I was ready for the photographs to have a powerful effect on me, but what took me by surprise were the artefacts with handwriting on them. Leo's letter which Pearl had read aloud over the phone to me. One of Mac's chirpy letters from Vietnam. A sheaf of newspaper clippings with Patty's handwritten commentary around the margins. A postcard from Kastellorizo with Athena's neat book-keeper's printing.

A week ago, Rose rang to say there would be some surprise guests. I assumed she meant Diego's daughter Luz and her family who were flying in from Mexico. Sadly, Diego and Valeria are both too ill to travel.

'No, I'm not talking about Luz.' Rose was using her slightly patronising doctor voice, as if she needed to land the words softly. 'It'd be best if you meet these guests ahead of the party. We'll drop by this afternoon.'

Rose has a key to my flat in case I'm sprawled on the floor after a stroke/cardiac arrest/some other ancient person catastrophe. Last Sunday, she knocked at my door to alert me to her arrival, but then just came in.

'So. Mum.' Rose's voice was thick with emotion and what sounded, intriguingly, like excitement. 'You need to meet your granddaughter Audrey.'

She signalled to someone by the door and in walked a 54-year-old woman who looked so much like my Rose, it momentarily sucked the air out of my lungs. Following Audrey into the room, tentatively, was her twenty-year-old daughter Nell, who had also copped a fair swag of my genetic traits (the hair, the eyes, the nose). I was so overcome, both Rose and Audrey worried that they'd managed to kill me. They had not.

This late in the game, it's structurally inelegant to launch into a backstory but that's how things go sometimes. Here's a brief version of the story I was told over the next several days.

Frances, the baby I relinquished in 1945, was unofficially adopted by Catherine, the pearl-wearing woman I'd seen in Buckinghamshire. That much I already knew. Catherine's parents were horrified by the adoption and cut her out of their lives. Catherine's husband left soon after, so from early days, Frances and her adoptive mother were isolated, shunned by everyone in Catherine's previous social world.

Frances was never told she was adopted but there was always an insinuation that Catherine had paid a high price to have her, and this mysterious price was presented as an emotional debt she owed her mother.

After the incident in 1971 when I showed up in their driveway, Catherine claimed I was a nutter and destroyed the first letter I sent. But Frances found one of the later ones and kept it.

She married and had one child, Audrey, but Catherine resented the little girl, seeing her as a rival for attention. When Catherine finally died, after years as a dependent invalid, Frances felt released, grasping the chance to live unburdened.

After Frances's death in late 2027, Audrey discovered a small suitcase in her mother's belongings. Inside was a letter I'd written to the Buckinghamshire address in 1975. The adoption revealed in my letter was a surprise to Audrey, but it made sense of many things and she was determined to find me. She emailed my publisher and then conferred with Rose to arrange our meeting.

Audrey generously gave me the suitcase and all its contents. There were newspaper articles about B. L. Rankin, and copies of all my novels, which had the creased spines and scuffed edges of paperbacks that had been read many times. The reader might appreciate how intensely sad it is that Frances collected this material, but we'd never had a chance to know each other. There is some consolation in the thought that she had known me, a little at least, through stories I'd written.

The other items in the suitcase were drafts of letters, most abandoned mid-page, addressed to me but never posted. In one letter, Frances wrote about giving birth to Audrey and how the experience had conjured up conflicting emotions: compassion towards me as a teenager forced to relinquish a newborn, but also disbelief that I could ever have given up my baby, and resentment I'd abandoned her, a woundedness. In a later letter, Frances explained that she felt so liberated by the death of her adoptive mother, she decided against contacting me, not wishing to feel obliged to another sort of mother. In some of the later draft letters—all of which have been sitting on my bedside table since Sunday—Frances wrote about her regret that she never made contact. 'I'm ashamed I've left it too long and you must hate me.'

I hate that she worried I could ever hate her. I hate that the tendency to feel shame may be a genetic trait I passed on to my first daughter. I hate that she had an unhappy childhood. I hate that I didn't push harder to find her. I know there is nothing I can do about all of this now, but it's still there as a burning pain in my belly.

Let's cut back to the joyful reunion in my living room last Sunday.

I was weeping but also grinning like a keyed-up toddler, clutching a photograph of Frances against my sternum as if I could absorb her image into my body.

Rose and Audrey kept embracing, then springing apart to marvel at their resemblance, laughing, both of them exclaiming, 'Aren't we lucky! Aren't we lucky!'

Meanwhile, young Nell was hanging back, the poor kid not quite knowing what to do with herself in the face of so much emotion.

'Nell,' I asked, 'can I see the rest of the photos?'

Nell darted forward, shy but glad of a practical task. She perched on the arm of my chair and showed me the family album Audrey had assembled.

Right now, sitting here dolled up for this party, I can see Rose ushering Audrey and Nell around the room, introducing them to other guests. And on the four large screens around the walls, I can see a photo of my first daughter—a strong 35-year-old woman staring directly at the camera. Stella managed to insert several photos of Frances, Audrey and Nell into the slide show in time for today's event.

There's no guarantee I'll make it to Wednesday when I officially hit three figures. I know a few older people who declare they are eager to go, sick of the whole palaver of living, and I have shared those feelings in my bleaker, pain-filled, lonely moments. But even though I'm at peace with dying, I'm happy to stay a bit longer. I'm curious. Keen to see how things turn out for my offspring, for the world.

I will stop writing this story without any final flurry of wise statements about life. I'm the same bewildered fool I've always been—maybe marginally less bewildered, having had certain realities hammered into my bony skull often enough. But there will be no big conclusion. Life stories don't work that way. That's why I've never been a fan of biopics. They either excise one juicy slice of a life in a potentially misleading way or they squish the events of a life into a narrative-shaped mould in a spurious process. (I've probably been guilty of that, even in this doggedly chronological account.) I do hope there is a certain kind of illumination in the sweep of one individual's existence over a long period. Anyway, I've laid out the events as honestly as I can, offered some thoughts en route, and will leave others free to draw conclusions, adjusting for their own biases and experiences.

I'm grateful to anyone gracious enough to stick with my story this long. The reader may like to picture me—a hundred years old, one-breasted, white hair still a wilful frizz, buzzing around a party in my motorised chair, surrounded by most of my dear ones who are still alive, and surrounded by rolling images of my younger self at various points, along with photos of my parents, my siblings, Leo, Mac, Frances, Athena, Nick, Pearl, Patty, Brenda, Thuy, Donna, and other people who've gone now. I invite the reader to lose sight of me in the party crowd, like one of those sequences at the end of a movie when the camera pulls back and then further back until the character blurs into an indistinct detail in a vast wide shot.

ACKNOWLEDGEMENTS

Many people helped me write this book, offering expertise, story ideas, and encouragement. My thanks to Annabelle Sheehan, Sarah Stein, Kerrie Laurence, Michael Lucas, Matthew Kalitowski, Jane Martin, Rebecca Huntley, Shane Henning, Garry Scale, Karen Oswald, Elizabeth Elliott, Jude Herskovits, Patricia O'Brien, Dale Druhan and Shelley Eves.

I'm grateful to Jane Palfreyman for her crucial support for the book at the start of its life.

My thanks to my dear friend Jacques Bonnavent for help with the Mexico chapter, and to Michael Wynne as Liverpool consultant and for being my staunch, funny, big-hearted writing pal over many years.

I owe huge thanks to Cate Paterson and everyone at Allen & Unwin for getting behind 'Betty'. Alex Craig generously took on the project and she's been great to work with. I'm grateful to Deonie Fiford for copy editing the manuscript so thoughtfully. Thanks to Christa Munns for steering everything deftly, Christa Moffitt for the gorgeous cover design and Peri Wilson for being a publicity goddess.

Thanks to my wonderful agent Anthony Blair who has always been supportive, listening, reading and giving wise notes.

And as always, I'm enormously grateful to my partner Richard Glover. For forty-four years, he's been ready to listen to my story ramblings, read drafts and offer astute feedback, maintaining the faith even when I can't, buoying my spirits to keep me going.